SISTERS AND STRANGERS

By Helen Van Slyke

SISTERS AND STRANGERS

ALWAYS IS NOT FOREVER

THE BEST PLACE TO BE

THE MIXED BLESSING

THE HEART LISTENS

ALL VISITORS MUST BE ANNOUNCED

THE RICH AND THE RIGHTEOUS

HELEN VAN SLYKE

Sisters and Strangers

Doubleday & Company, Inc., Garden City, New York, 1978

ISBN: 0-385-12776-6
Library of Congress Catalog Card Number 77–27720

Printed in the United States of America
First Edition

For my friend Jean, who generously shared
her time and her "mile-high knowledge"

SISTERS AND STRANGERS

Chapter 1

Laura's first thought when she awakened in the darkness of that pre-dawn October morning was that in two days she'd celebrate fifty years of marriage to Sam Dalton.

Fifty years. Half a century. Five decades with the same man. Perhaps she'd make a little speech about that at the party.

"Two score and ten years ago we brought forth upon this community a marriage created by convention, conceived in monotony and dedicated to the proposition that all wedlock is enchained and unequal."

She smiled, imagining how they'd all look at her if she said such a thing. Sam would think she'd taken leave of her senses. Her daughters would be shocked. No. Barbara and Alice would be shocked. Frances probably would think it was funny. The relatives would not understand. And the friends would feel embarrassed, as though she'd taken off her clothes in public.

Of them all, Sam would be closest to the truth. Sometimes she thought she was going crazy. Proper Laura Dalton, perfect wife and home-maker, pillar of the church, past-matron of The Eastern Star, mother of three, survivor of domestic disasters, keeper of the peace, tender of the flame of fidelity for fifty years. I have everything in the world to be grateful for, she told herself sternly. A paid-for house. Good health. A dependable, provident husband snoring beside me. I'm seventy years old, but in this day and age that's not "old," as it was when I was growing up.

Why, then, am I ticking off my blessings as though each one was a superstitious knock on wood? Why do I feel so unsatisfied, so trapped? My children are women. Not even young women. And for the first time in nearly thirty years they're all sleeping safely under one roof. My worrying days should be over. All the things that hurt so much when they happened are far behind me. Sam and I got through them together. No, not really together. We suffered them independently, though we pretended otherwise. All that trouble with Alice and Frances. Even Barbara's departure was a reproach, though she didn't intend it to be. But that's all in the past. The scars have healed. Or have they? Has each of us come to terms with what had to be? I don't know. I don't know my children any more. Or my husband. Or myself. Perhaps I never did. Never will.

All I know is that, all things considered, I've had a good life. A good marriage.

Day after tomorrow I'll prove that by accepting congratulations for having lived through eighteen thousand two hundred and fifty days of being Mrs. Samuel Dalton of Denver.

Sam stirred. "What time is it?"

"Six-thirty."

He grunted, sat up in the double bed and scratched his head in that irritating way she'd hated for fifty years. Why did he start every morning by scratching his head? To make sure the thick mane of hair, now so handsomely white, had not disappeared while he slept? Laura smiled, thinking what a ridiculous little thing it was to object to. But that's what marriage was about: loving so many important things about a man and hating so many trivial ones.

"Why do you always scratch your head when you wake up?" She wondered why she'd blurted that out after all these mornings.

"What?"

"For fifty years you've awakened, asked me what time it is and then scratched your head."

He looked at her as though she'd lost her mind. "What are you talking about? You're not making any sense."

"I know, dear. It just occurred to me that we all have funny little habits that never vary from year to year." She smiled at him.

"What do I do that irritates you, Sam? I'd like to know."

He climbed out of bed, hitching up his pajamas at the waist.

"That, too," Laura said. "You always hitch up your pajamas that way. What do *I* do that's exactly the same every morning?"

He glanced at her over his shoulder as he headed for the bedroom door. "I never thought about it. I don't know what's gotten into you this morning, Laura. You don't sound like yourself."

She sat propped up in bed, the pink nylon nightgown with the fake lace discreetly covering her shoulders. The shoulders that, like her arms, were better hidden these days. She used to be so proud of her arms and shoulders and her long, unlined neck. No more. I may not feel my years, Laura thought, but once in a while the mirror reminds me. No, she didn't sound like herself this morning. Sam was right about that. She didn't feel like herself, either. She supposed it was the awareness of the oncoming golden anniversary. Or the fact that the girls were home and there'd be such a fuss going on in the next few days. Sam thought she was crazy with all this talk about sameness. He probably was right about that, too. He hadn't answered her question. Surely she must have habits that drove him mad. Or maybe not. Maybe he never noticed any more.

"I'm sorry," she said. "I'm just spouting nonsense. You'd better get into the bathroom if you want it first."

Sam shook his head as he left the room. Another time-worn gesture, that half-annoyed, half-indifferent motion he made when things puzzled him. The little shake of his head that clearly said, "I'll never understand women." Or, for that matter, present-day politics, sexual mores, taxes, the tactics of the Denver Broncos, the "young squirt" who replaced him in his old job at the telephone company. A long list of non-understandables. There was so much he refused to understand. He was a kind man at heart. A good man. But uncompromising and becoming more rigid every day, more narrow in his interests, less tolerant of a changing world. In the eight years since his retirement he'd become old. At seventy-three he was a being with no purpose, no aspirations, no particular interest in anything. It's no good for a man like Sam to retire, Laura thought for the hundredth time. On Sam's pension we're too poor to travel, too inflexible to move out of this dreary old house to some nice "Sun Belt Community" where we could make new friends, too bored with each other after fifty years to even try to communicate.

But we've never communicated. The realization was like a new thought. We've talked and argued and made love, but we've never spoken as one voice. Not when the children were growing up. Not when they needed the solid support and comfort we should have given them. If only Sam hadn't been such a biblical patriarch when Alice got into trouble. If I'd been more aware of Frances' restlessness. If both of us had discouraged Barbara's interest in politics. If only we'd broadened our horizons early on, been adventurous enough to see the world or even widen our circle of friends here, or if we'd taken up hobbies to occupy us in these declining years.

If. What a useless word. And what ridiculous thoughts plagued her these days. If only I had someone to talk to. There I go with my "ifs." There was no one. Not even the children. I don't understand my girls. I know so very little about the way they think, even the way they live. Don't even know whether they're happy or miserable, whether they love us or hate us, whether they're here out of desire or duty.

What on earth is happening to me?

She watched the light slowly sneaking through the window. Another day. More exciting than most because of the preparations for the party. But it was only a brief respite from sameness. It would soon be over, and within a week her daughters would be gone and the predictable way of life would return.

She sighed heavily.

It all seemed so pointless.

Frances opened her eyes and felt the old, familiar wave of apprehension waiting. The nonspecific, ugly one that greeted her every morning. It was always the same. Her first conscious moments were filled with unfocused fear, a suffocating depression she privately called her "insecurity blanket." She dreaded each new day and at the same time feared it might be her last. She'd tried everything—from tranquilizers to TM. Nothing helped. Not even geography. Denver or Deauville, anxiety claimed no nationality. She was as frightened coming back to life in her old room in her parents' house as she was in any apartment or hotel suite or chateau or manor house in the world. Why did she think it might be different here? *I'm* no different, she thought. I'm still Frances Dalton Mills Stanton de St. Déspres. Madame Dalton-Déspres. Social figure. Thrice divorced. Pointed, reluctantly, toward my fiftieth birthday. Sophisticate and super-failure. The prodigal returned for the celebration of Sam and Laura Dalton's golden wedding anniversary. She was back in the bed she'd left nearly thirty years before. Back in body, but not in spirit. The spirit, if she had one, was someplace else.

The house was very quiet. Alice glanced over at the other twin bed, half-expecting in this first waking moment to see Spencer and momentarily surprised to see, instead, the peacefully sleeping figure of her younger sister. Barbara still looks like a young girl, Alice thought, though she's forty. And Fran, in her own room next door, was a cleverly face-lifted forty-nine. And I'm a year younger and look old enough to be their mother. Especially in this unflattering half-light.

It wasn't true, of course. Alice Dalton Winters, like most middle-aged women in 1976, could have lied by ten years about her age and gotten away with it. Provided one didn't know she had a twenty-three-year-old son and a twenty-one-year-old daughter. But everyone did know, back in Boston where she lived and here in Denver where she'd come for the celebration. What most of them didn't know was about the other one. The one born in 1946. Johnny, she'd called him. The baby she'd given away.

She didn't want to think about him now. Didn't want to wonder where he was and what his life was like. And whether he was as curious about her as she was about him. She didn't want to think about any of her children, legitimate or otherwise. Or her husband or her home or her life back East. She wanted to be a girl again, a seventeen-year-old girl with everything to live for and nothing to hide.

It was strange to wake up in her old room. Stranger still to realize there was someone else there. Most mornings Barbara was alone, except when Charles could stay the night. And those sweet awakenings were rare and special occasions, moments when she could pretend that she, not Andrea, was Mrs. Charles Tallent.

She lay very still in the narrow twin bed, trying not to disturb Alice. Her big sister. She could still remember sharing this room in the little Denver house with a young, popular, pretty Alice Dalton. How she'd envied her, back in the mid-forties. How she'd envied both Alice and Frances, her "grown-up" sisters. It had made her angry to have arrived so late in her parents' life. At least it had seemed late. Eight and nine years, respectively, after Allie and Fran. She was still a "baby" when they were dating, and they treated her as a little pest, ignoring her adoration, blind to her desire to be not only a sister but a peer. Time had narrowed the distance. The three of them seemed of an age, now that they'd all crossed forty. But their worlds were as far apart as ever. Farther, really. Incredible they'd had no "reunion" in thirty years. Astonishing how little she knew of their lives, or they of hers. Sisters and strangers. We might as well be three uneasy house guests visiting two people we barely know.

Chapter 2

"I wish you and Daddy had agreed to let us give you a party in some snappy place."

Laura looked at her eldest daughter who was smoking her fourth cigarette over her second cup of coffee at the big old oak table in the dining room. Frances looked, well, dissipated, her mother thought. For all the creaminess of her silk robe, the sleek cut of her hair, the carefully applied make-up (imagine doing one's face at eight in the morning!) she seemed like some world-weary visitor from a debauched realm beyond Laura's imagination. What kind of life must she lead? All those marriages and divorces, all that flitting around the world since she was nineteen. What has it done to my firstborn? Terrible things I'd guess, from the look of her.

"Your father and I thought it would be much nicer to have a little party at home. You girls were sweet to offer, but all our friends do it this way. It may not be grand, but it's suitable for us."

Fran shrugged. If that was meant as a reprimand for her own extravagant way of life, she chose to ignore it. She could afford to give parties, big, lavish ones with orchestras and French champagne and clever, expensive florists' creations on small, chic tables set for ten. Not that one probably could produce such splendor in a Denver hotel, but surely the Brown Palace could turn out a smarter background than this shabby old house where nothing had changed in nearly thirty years. The party will be a middle-class horror, Fran thought, but that's the way they want it: dull, stolid and boring. She wished she hadn't come home. Memory was kinder to the scene of her youth than reality. She wondered how Alice and Barbara felt. Of course, they'd been back to visit and she never had. Probably the whole dreary little house wasn't such a total shock to them. And certainly their basis of comparison was less drastic. They'd "kept in touch." She hadn't. She wrote rarely, sent birthday gifts from Cartier in Paris and Christmas presents from Gucci in Rome. But she'd not come back since the night she eloped (what an extraordinarily old-fashioned word!) with that stupid young actor, Stuart Mills. She regretted many things about that first marriage, but she was grateful for one: It had gotten her out of this house and this town and this stultifying atmosphere of respectability.

"It's nice, the four of us sitting around the table like this." Alice smiled at them. "Can you believe how long it's been since we all had breakfast together?"

"If you can call it breakfast," Laura said. "You girls don't eat a thing! I'm glad your father was fed and out in the yard before you all came down. He'd have a fit, seeing you have nothing but coffee and juice. You know how he is."

Barbara laughed. "I can still hear him. The voice from our childhood. 'You girls eat your breakfast! Most important meal of the day. Got to stoke up after fasting all night.' Does he still feel that way, Mother? Does he still have his fruit and cereal and eggs and bacon and all those things?"

"You know he does. You saw him last year when you came out at Christmas. And he's right. The body can't go from dinner to lunch on nothing but caffein and nicotine."

"This one can," Fran said. "The only eggs I've been able to face in years are *oeufs en gelée* at lunch."

"Fran, you really are a pain in the behind," Barbara said suddenly.

"Beg pardon?"

"Oh, come on! You're home, remember? You're just Frances Dalton around here. Not Madame Dalton-Déspres! Get off our backs with that 'snappy party' stuff and your damned '*oeufs en gelée.*' For God's sake, look at you! The rest of us are in bathrobes and curlers, and you look like you're about to be photographed for *Town and Country!*"

"My, my!" Fran's voice was coldly amused. "Will you listen to the baby! The little kitten has grown up into a snarling pussycat. What's the matter, darling? You sound like a frustrated old maid. And I'm sure you're not *frustrated*."

"Not nearly as much as you, I'll bet!"

"Hey, cut it out, you two!" Alice spoke sharply. "What's the matter with you idiots? You're picking up right where you left off." She tried to make a joke of it. "Listen to them, Mother. The same as ever. They were always fighting, remember?"

"Only because Fran was always so full of phony airs and graces," Barbara said.

"And you were such a damned goody-goody!"

"I was only ten years old when you left, for God's sake!"

"Sure," Fran snapped, "and even then I could tell you'd be the prissy spinster in the family! You're just jealous because three men have married me and nobody has legalized your situation, whatever it is."

"Frances! Barbara! Stop this!" Laura's face was white with distress.

"Mother's right," Alice said. "You're both behaving like children! Can't you see how you're upsetting her? For heaven's sake, we're here for a happy time! What on earth is the matter with you?"

"I'm sorry," Barbara said. "It's just that . . ."

Alice nudged her under the table, as if to say, "Don't bring up a lot of things Mother doesn't know."

"I'm sorry, too, Barb," Fran said unexpectedly. "I don't know how we got into this silly ruckus. Probably it's my jet lag. And the altitude. I keep forgetting we're in the 'mile-high city.' When I got here yesterday I was so tired I was walking into walls. Air travel at best is like being cooped up in a Greyhound bus. I'll be in a better humor when I recover."

What would you know about Greyhound buses? Barbara was tempted to ask. But she said nothing. Maybe I do envy Fran, she thought. Maybe I envy her money and her freedom. Even her notoriety. Maybe I envy her those three rotten marriages—one for escape, one for money and one in sheer desperation. Do I somehow feel inadequate, being the only "single sister"? How crazy! In this day and age, there's no stigma to being single. No sign of "failure." It's a woman's option. I wouldn't marry Charles even if he were free to ask me. I love my job. I love Washington. I love my lover. I'm more my own person than either of my sisters. And, what's more, I suspect I'm happier than either of them.

Bolstered by her own thoughts, Barbara stretched and smiled. "Well, what's the program for today? Duty-calls on the relatives? Preparations for the party? Catch-up time with childhood chums? What do *you* want to do, Mother?"

The momentary crisis passed, Laura relaxed. "You needn't do any of those things unless you want to. You'll see your aunts and uncles and cousins at the party tomorrow. Uncle Fred and Aunt Mamie are flying in from Chicago. Uncle Earl's here, of course. I'm sorry Aunt Charlotte couldn't come from Boston, Alice. It would have been nice if she could have traveled with you."

"She's really too frail, Mother."

"I know. She's eighty. Imagine. My sister Charlotte eighty! Well, so much for my relatives. Fortunately your father's live in Denver."

"Aunt Mildred and Aunt Martha still sharing that gloomy old house on Race Street?" Barbara asked.

"Yes, dear. And very nice for them it is, since they're both widows."

"How are they?"

"Quite well for their age. They're both older than your father. Of course, Mildred has trouble with her eyes and Martha doesn't hear too well, but they manage. This family really is blessed to have so many left on both sides. Most of our friends have lost their brothers and sisters, but we're fortunate."

Fortunate, Fran thought. What's fortunate about a bunch of creaky old brothers and sisters who probably do nothing but talk about their ailments, complain about neglect by their children and spend most of their waking hours watching soap operas and game shows on television? She didn't know that was the way it was, but she'd have gambled she was right. She hadn't kept track of her aunts and uncles. She'd almost forgotten their names. Sometimes when she got one of those stilted letters from Laura she wasn't sure whether Aunt Mildred was Daddy's sister or Mother's. Or whether Uncle Fred had two boys and a girl or the other way around. What difference did it make? She hadn't seen any of them in years and she wouldn't again until it was time to come home for her parents' funerals. God! Just let me get through this week so I can hop on that big, shiny "Greyhound bus" and get the hell out of here! But where then, Frances Dalton Mills Stanton Déspres? Back to Europe, she supposed. There wasn't anything there for her except an endless round of trips and parties, occasional brief affairs and too many unadmitted nights with only a book for company. But there was less here. She'd long since cut her ties with everything. With her family. Her old friends. With America itself. She realized Laura was still going on in answer to Barbara's question.

"As for party preparations," her mother was saying, "all I have to do is set the table and get out the dishes and glasses, and it's almost easier to do it myself than tell you girls where everything is."

"What about food?" Alice asked.

"Oh, everybody who's coming has her assignment. Some are bringing appetizers, some the main course. Others will contribute salad and dessert."

Fran's eyes widened. "You mean the guests bring the meal?"

"Of course, dear. That's the way we've always done it for big affairs. Don't you remember? I take whatever's requested when I go to somebody else's party. It makes it all very easy and inexpensive when you divide it up that way."

"What can we contribute?" Alice persisted. "Liquor?"

Laura looked uncomfortable. "We're not much for hard liquor, Alice. You know your father disapproves of it entirely. We'll have a little punch and soft drinks. And tea and coffee, of course."

Barbara chimed in. "I know what we'll get: the wedding cake." She looked at her sisters. "How about that? We'll get the most gorgeous five-tiered, rose-decorated, goo-ey cake in town."

"Well, that would be nice," Laura said. "I admit I thought of having one, but with Bernard Paige's wife offering to bring brownies, I gave up the idea."

Fran snapped to attention. "Bernard Paige? Buzz Paige? Don't tell me he's still around!"

"Of course he's still around," Laura said tartly. "What did you think, Frances? That all your old beaux committed suicide when you ran off? Bernard is a fine man and very successful. He has a lovely wife and three handsome sons. We don't see them much, of course. They're another generation. But I thought it would be nice to invite some of your old friends and your sisters'. They're all dying to see you again."

Good God! Buzz Paige! She'd thought herself in love with him when she was seventeen or eighteen. She'd even thought they'd get married. But that was before she met Stuart Mills. What would my life have been like if I'd stayed in Denver and married Buzz? Awful. He's, let's see, fifty-one or -two by now. Probably paunchy and balding and given to loud ties and a Kiwanis button in his lapel. Fran shuddered. She could picture his wife. A plain little woman, very housewifey. He probably had grandchildren. Damn. The whole thing made her feel old. She couldn't stand feeling old. She couldn't stand the idea of trying to make conversation with an overweight bore who'd once been a young and beautiful captain of the high school football team. She remembered they'd gone in for some very heavy necking in the back seat of his 1942 Chevrolet. But it had never gone beyond that. Maybe if it had, I'd have stayed, she thought wryly.

"You dragging up anybody else from our misbegotten pasts?" There was a slight edge to Alice's voice.

Laura pretended not to notice her middle-daughter's tone. "Just a few of the young men and women all of you used to be so close to. The ones who are still around, that is. So many of them moved away years ago." As all of *you* did, the sentence continued silently, accusingly. The youngest and the oldest couldn't wait to leave the nest. Only Alice was forced out. But Laura didn't want to think about that. It was the closest they'd ever come to disgrace. Still, it had worked out. Thank heaven for Charlotte in Boston.

An awkward silence came over the four women. Then Laura said briskly, "Why don't you girls go out for lunch today? Barbara still knows the town pretty well. I'll do my chores around the house and see you later this afternoon."

"Okay," Barbara said. "If you're sure you don't need us."

"No. Everything's under control. Go enjoy yourselves." She

sounded suddenly wistful. "You're sisters. Maybe you can get to be friends."

Later, as she went to find her father and borrow the car keys, Barbara couldn't get those last words of her mother's out of her mind. It was sad, but Laura was right. We should be friends, the three of us. In our way, we're all nice people. Even Fran, much as she tried to be brittle and cynical, had a romantic streak she couldn't shake. Maybe I've been wrong, thinking she married for practical reasons. Maybe each time she fancied herself in love, thought she'd found the answer and ended up so hurt and disillusioned that she's wrapped herself in this hard shell of pseudo sophistication.

Of course, it wasn't easy to maintain a closeness with anyone who lived thousands of miles away and never came back even for visits. It was different with Allie. We could be closer, Barbara thought. Boston and Washington aren't that far apart. Less than two hours by plane. Yet we never visit each other, rarely even phone. There's no excuse for us. I haven't seen Allie's children since they were babies, and she doesn't have any idea that I'm somebody's mistress. I don't know what her life is like, any more than I know how Fran exists, except for what I read in the gossip columns. Is Allie happy with Spencer? After almost twenty-five years, is she content? To be so ignorant of your sisters' day-to-day lives was weird. More than weird. It was obscene. As though we're all ashamed of the paths we've chosen and don't want those we really love to know what stupid roads we've stumbled down in our search for happiness.

The morning sun was warm, but Barbara shivered. There was something ominous about all of them being together again. Why did she feel it was a trick of fate that brought them back for this presumably joyous occasion? Why did she feel this was a visit that would make a difference in the future? Jackass! she scolded herself. You and your bloody imagination! It wouldn't be like that at all. They'd spend this week in reasonably harmonious play-acting with their parents and relatives and friends from the past. They'd put on their "dutiful-daughter faces" even among themselves. And then they'd go away again, as they had before. Back to whatever separate, secret worlds they occupied. And that's the way it should be, Barbara thought firmly. It's too late for us to find each other again. Why should we even want to?

She forced herself to smile as she had at the breakfast table, pretending to be relaxed and untroubled as she came near her father. Sam, in old shirt and pants and a light pullover sweater with a hole in the elbow, was bending over a bed of yellow chrysanthemums, gently pulling weeds away from their roots.

"Good morning, Daddy."

He looked up. How much he's aged in these past eight years, Barbara thought. What a damned shame he had to leave the job he'd had long before she was born. He was withering away with boredom, rusting with disuse like an old car in a junkyard. She remembered how he used to go off to work each morning, full of confidence. The provider. The hunter out to kill for his family. Now, though he and Mother lived comfortably on his Social Security and his six hundred dollars a month retirement pay, in a house whose mortgage had long since been "burned," Sam Dalton must feel useless, displaced, missing the "business jungle" with the small challenges that, to him, had been so stimulating. Head of an accounting section for the phone company. What a dreary little job it seemed to Barbara, so used to the powerful men of Washington. Yet Sam had been proud of it. Proud to have worked his way up from clerk to "middle management" and eighteen thousand a year. Proud he'd gone to night school to study accounting and that for more than forty years he'd been "a boss." Now he was just another "old-timer," moved out to make room for younger men with more modern ideas and training. These men had to have their chance too. Had to know vacancies would come up as the long-ensconced managers took mandatory retirement at sixty-five. The policy probably was right for the company, right for business. But it was painfully wrong for the men who'd lived only through their jobs and who now had nothing better to do than weed chrysanthemum beds.

"Morning, Barbara. Sleep all right?"

"Just fine. I'm sure we all did. We were a tired bunch straggling in here yesterday."

"I know. You all came from so far away."

It was a simple statement and yet Barbara felt a pang of guilt, as she had when Laura had silently accused them of "running away." Why do they make me feel I've deserted them? Is it all right for the married ones to leave home but not "suitable" for me? I won't feel guilty. There's no need to. For all I know, the accusation may be in *my* head, not theirs. What accusation? I have a right to my own life too. She pretended not to notice Sam's subtle reprimand, if, indeed, it was one.

"Mother says she doesn't need us around here today, so Fran and Allie and I thought we'd go out to lunch. May I use your car?"

"Sure. The keys are on the dresser. Be careful. I take good care of that car, you know. I'm in no position to replace it if anything happens to it."

"What about us?" Barbara's voice was teasing. "Aren't you worried about replacing your daughters if there was an accident?"

"Don't talk crazy, Barbara." Sam got to his feet. His knee bones creaked in protest. "I don't know what's gotten into you women this morning. First your mother wants to know what she does to irritate me, and now you're talking foolishness about how I wouldn't care if something happened to you. I feel like I'm in the middle of a conspiracy."

Barbara laughed. "You're not used to having so many women around at one time any more, Daddy. We're just needling you. I know you'd care if we got hurt. You always cared. I remember how it was when we were kids." She paused. "You were always my hero. The best father in the world."

Sam turned away, embarrassed. She'd always been his favorite. He supposed he resented the fact that she preferred to live away from home. That's why he was gruff, not wanting her to know how much he wished she wouldn't go away again. Laura fretted that Barbara had never married. But he was only sorry she couldn't find her happiness at home.

"The keys are on the chain with the rabbit's foot," he said tersely.

"Right-o. We'll see you later." She kissed his cheek swiftly. "Your mums are gorgeous. This is such a pretty time of year. Everything's golden. Like your anniversary."

He didn't answer but watched her as she walked swiftly back to the house. Golden, he thought. It's all turned to tarnished brass. As Laura had early that morning, he determinedly counted his blessings. Health. Reasonable security. A good wife. Three handsome daughters. He'd long since stopped being unhappy that they'd not had a son. Or had he? Deep down, didn't it sadden him that there'd be no future Daltons? His sister's children were girls, too. Not that it would have mattered. They weren't named Dalton. Only he and Laura could have perpetuated the name, and they hadn't been able to. What difference did it make? There was nothing distinguished about the lineage. Let it die out. Who cared?

He pushed from his mind the thought that there was a male Dalton somewhere. Alice's illegitimate son. He had no idea where the boy was or what his adopted name was. If we'd let her keep the baby, there'd be a Dalton to carry on, Sam thought, but there'd been no way. No way at all.

He knelt again and viciously pushed a trowel into the soil, cutting too deeply into a root. Drat! He'd killed another one of Barbara's "golden things." No matter. He still had plenty left. More than enough of this "fool's gold" to leave behind.

love, babies that they were? But they were "unofficially engaged" and talked confidently of the day they'd marry, in three years, when Jack finished college. Allie was happy for most of those two years. Happy and yet miserable, made miserable by Jack's pleading, by her own desire. She could still hear the conversations they used to have, months of them before she agreed.

"Please, Allie." Jack's voice would be low and earnest. "Please do it. We love each other. We're going to be married."

She'd push him away, reluctantly, removing the fingers she allowed to reach inside her sweater and fondle her breasts. She'd be so excited herself at those times as he held her close in the front seat of his little car, gently easing his hand up under her skirt and inside the little panties to touch her. But she always moved away, straightening her clothes, trying to control the breathing that was as heavy as his own.

"We can't, Jack. Not till we're married."

"Why not? We're *going to be* married. Don't be scared, Allie. Nothing will happen. I'll take care of it."

"Something might. I might get pregnant."

"You won't. I promise. I have those things right in my pocket." He'd reach for her again. "You're afraid I won't respect you. You're wrong, sweetheart. I'll respect you all the more."

She'd shaken her head, knowing he'd now turn angry.

"Dammit, Allie, you're nothing but a tease! You don't have any idea what it does to me to get this close and not be able to go all the way!"

"Yes, I do," she's said, almost in tears. "I know how *I* feel. I want to, Jack. I really do."

"Then, for God's sake prove it!"

"I can't. I just can't."

He'd turn away in disgust then, starting the engine and driving her home, dropping her off on South Carona Street, leaving her standing forlornly on the curb in front of her house at number 1016. She'd always say something placating through the car window before he left, half-promising that next time it would be different, begging him not to be mad, terrified that this time he'd go away and never come back. He seldom answered but he always came back, always accepted her frightened refusal. Until that night early in January.

Chapter 3

Squashed in the back seat of Sam Dalton's little 1974 Toyota, Alice felt more than physically uncomfortable. Whenever she came back to Denver it was as though she lived through 1946 all over again, the terror of it, the helplessness and rejection she'd felt on all sides. Those few awful weeks almost blotted out the seventeen happy years that preceded them. It was why she so seldom returned. Not more than ten times in thirty years, she realized. And then only out of a sense of duty, as though, even after what they'd done to her in their well-meaning way, she couldn't put her parents out of her life as Fran had been able to do.

I'm more like Barb, she thought. Neither of us can sever the emotional umbilical cord, much as we'd like to. What holds children to parents with whom they have nothing in common except the accident of birth? Maybe my Johnny is lucky, wherever he is. Or maybe his adopted parents are as unfathomable to him as mine are to me.

As Barbara expertly pushed the little car toward Larimer Square, Alice closed her eyes and reluctantly retraced the unhappy early days of her life.

She'd been so frightened when she found out. So ashamed. She and Jack Richards had known each other since they were children, had been "going steady" since she was fifteen and he seventeen. They were in love, they thought. Love. What did they know of

It was a Saturday. She recalled it vividly. Every detail. He called for her after dinner as usual and she told her mother they were going to a movie. She really thought they were. But instead, Jack headed in a different direction.

"Where are we going?"

"My house."

"Your house? Why?"

"Because the family's away for the weekend and I have the whole place to myself."

Something in his voice told her he'd come to a decision. He sounded rougher, colder than she'd ever heard him. Allie was silent during the short drive. This was the long-avoided showdown. She'd either give him what he wanted—what they both wanted—or she'd lose him. She was as certain of it as she was of her name. She didn't need his words to confirm her thoughts.

"Make up your mind right now, Allie," he'd said. "Either we're really in love or I'm calling the whole thing off."

She'd pretended not to understand. "You know we're in love."

"Don't play cute. You know what I mean. I can't stand any more of these nights. We're not babies." He stopped the car in front of his house. "Decide now," he said more gently. "Either you're a woman or a child. I'll take you home, if that's what you want. But if you come inside with me, I'm going to take you to bed. Your choice, Allie."

She'd hesitated for a long moment, recalling all the things she'd heard about high school girls getting pregnant, all the disgraced families, the dangerous, ugly abortions, the "shotgun weddings."

"If . . . if something went wrong . . . That is, would you . . . I mean, what if . . ."

He'd put his arms around her. "I've told you a hundred times. Nothing will go wrong. But if you're still afraid it might, I promise we'd get married right away, Allie darling. I swear it."

She'd believed him. And that night, in Jack's bed, in his room with the college pennants and the pictures of his high school hockey team and the delicious smell of him all around her, she'd tremblingly discovered that sex was even more wonderful than she'd imagined. She had no way of knowing how inexpert they were. Not until much later did she learn there were nuances unknown to a nineteen-year-old boy and a seventeen-year-old girl.

When he took her home at midnight, she crept into the room she shared with nine-year-old Barbara and lay wide-awake, reflecting on the gloriousness of it all. This, she thought, stroking her thighs under the covers, was what love was all about. This was what it was to be a woman. She supposed she should feel ashamed. It was wrong. Sinful. But she didn't feel shame at that time, and certainly no sense of sin. She was not one of those "easy" girls. She'd done what was natural and right with the man she would marry.

In the weeks that followed, they made love often in Jack's car, forgetting the cold, ignoring the discomfort of their cramped quarters. Alice hated the precautions, but was grateful. Though she knew he would have married her, she didn't want them to "have to marry." They'd have a family later on. For now they had passion.

And then, in April, she realized that what she feared had happened. When she told him, he looked horrified.

"Are you sure?"

"Pretty sure." She blushed. "I haven't . . . that is, I've missed."

"Have you seen a doctor?"

"No. Of course not. I don't even know one except our family physician."

"Well, you can't go to *him*. That's for sure. I'll get the name of somebody. Maybe it's a false alarm."

"And if it isn't?"

"Now, don't start worrying. Bet you a hundred dollars you aren't even that way."

She'd felt cold. Even now she could remember the awful, sick feeling in the pit of her stomach. She was pregnant. She knew it.

"You said we'd get married if this happened."

"Well, we will. Except I'm sure you're wrong. It couldn't be. I haven't taken any chances. You know that."

"But those things aren't always reliable, are they?"

"Allie, for God's sake! Wait until you see the doctor!"

A few days later she sneaked off to some out-of-the-way office and shortly after that the test came back. Positive. She was "about six weeks along."

"I don't see any problems, Mrs. Smith," the doctor said. He underlined the name as if to say he knew the story. "You're very young, but you're healthy. You should have a nice baby. Check with my nurse on the way out. She'll give you a date for your next appointment and some suggestions about diet and things."

She'd made the appointment, knowing she'd never keep it. She and Jack would get married right away and tell their families later. Lots of women had "premature" babies. It wasn't as they'd planned it. Jack still had three years of college. But they'd manage. They loved each other. She refused to think it would be any other way.

But it was. Jack, looking sheepish, said it just wasn't possible for them to get married. How could he support a family? He had to finish school and God knows they couldn't count on their parents to help out.

"Then, what shall we do?" She knew what he'd say and hated him even before he said it.

"Look. There's a guy at college who knows somebody. I'll get the name. It's perfectly safe. It's a real doctor who just does this kind of thing on the side. We'll figure out how to get you away for a weekend and have it taken care of."

Even then she was more mature than he. "Why can't you say the word? Abortion. You want me to go to some dirty place and have an abortion! I won't do it, Jack. I've heard about those places. Women die on kitchen tables. Or later, of blood poisoning. Or they bleed to death."

"Don't be silly. It's done a thousand times every day."

She began to cry. "No. No, I can't."

"You have to, Allie. You know we can't get married. I'm not ready for that responsibility."

Her tears stopped. "You lied," she said coldly. "You lied all the way. I wouldn't marry you now, Jack Richards, even if you begged me to. How could I have loved you? You're . . . you're nothing but an infant yourself!"

"Be practical. What choice do we have? I *do* love you. I just didn't think this would happen. We'll still get married. Later. Like we planned. This won't make any difference."

"Maybe not to you. It's not your body. Or your life you're so willing to risk. You can't love me if you'd let me take such a terrible chance." She turned away from him. "I think I'd like to go home now," Alice said.

"Are you going to tell your folks?"

"Of course. I'll have to if I'm going to have a baby."

"They'll raise hell! So will mine! Allie, you're being stupid!"

Maybe I was, an older, wiser Alice thought now, driving with her sisters to their "get-acquainted" lunch. Maybe I was stupid not to have had the abortion. But I couldn't. It wasn't just a moral thing. I was too frightened. Too hurt. But maybe I'd have been less hurt if Johnny had never been born, if I hadn't had to part with a real, live child.

It had been terrible, telling her parents. Laura's stunned disbelief was worse than Sam's towering, patriarchal rage. I feel as though I've betrayed her, Allie had thought. As though I've canceled out all the things she tried to teach us, all the faith she had in us.

"I'm sorry, Mother."

"Oh, darling, I'm sorry for *you!* My poor baby!" Laura's initial shock turned to instinctive maternal protectiveness. "Alice, dear, we'll arrange things immediately. You and Jack must get married at once."

She assumed Jack was the father. Why not? They knew Allie went out only with him. It also would never occur to Laura that there was any acceptable alternative to this situation. Sam Dalton's thoughts were the same as his wife's, though his reaction was not one of compassion but of anger. Anger initially directed at Jack.

"I'd like to kill him!" her father said. "Damned little seducer! Wait till I get my hands on him! Young punk! I'll break his neck!"

"Daddy, it wasn't rape." Allie's voice was miserable. "He didn't force me. I'm as much to blame as he."

Sam glared at her. "I know that too. Don't think I'm not just as furious with you, Alice. How could you do this to your mother and me? Haven't we taught you any sense of decency? Did we raise you to bring us this kind of shame? Look what you've done! Given away your most precious possession, your virtue! And look where it will take you: into a shotgun wedding at seventeen! How could you be so wanton?"

"Sam, please!" Laura tried to stop him. "Don't blame the children. What they did was wrong. But they're human. We mustn't hold this mistake against them. We must stand by them. We and the Richardses. The families will have to stick together, get these two married immediately."

"No," Allie said. "I'm sorry, Mother, but Jack and I aren't going to get married."

"What!" Sam exploded. "You mean he won't marry you? Well, he will! By God, I'll see to that!"

"He doesn't want to." Allie's chin went up. "And I don't want to marry him."

Laura looked bewildered. "I don't understand . . ."

"He wants me to have an abortion. I'm afraid to. I won't. And even if he changed his mind, I wouldn't marry a man who'd suggest such a thing."

They'd stared at her, open-mouthed, speechless. Sam recovered first.

"This is no time to be so high and mighty, young lady! Of course you won't have an abortion. But you'll get married. Never mind what either of you think you want. The fact is you're going to have a baby and he's the father and he'll do the right thing by you! I'll talk to his father. George Richards will agree with me. That boy won't get away with this. As for you, Alice, there's no other solution. You've sinned and maybe you'll pay for it, but you won't disgrace us with an illegitimate child!"

"I won't marry him, Daddy. No matter what you want. I don't love him."

Sam snorted. "Fine time to think of that! Why didn't you reach that conclusion while you were behaving like a little tramp?"

"Sam! Stop it!" Laura broke in again. She turned to Alice. "We don't understand, dear. You're not thinking of having this baby with no husband, are you? What would people say? We'd be the talk of Denver! Allie, darling, be sensible. You and Jack must get married." Her voice was soothing. "It will work out. You'll see. Right now you're just hurt and frightened. You love each other. And certainly you want to give your baby a name, don't you? You wouldn't be that unfair to a helpless child."

She hadn't thought of the child. She forced herself to say it. The bastard. Maybe they were right. Maybe she and Jack had to marry for the sake of the unborn baby.

"All right," she'd finally said, wearily, "I'll marry him. But I hate it. I hate the idea of someone having to marry me. I hate the idea of being married to someone who doesn't want me. But I'll do it."

She didn't do it. Not because she wouldn't have, but because Jack Richards' parents did not agree with her own. There'd been an ugly scene in the Daltons' living room, with Alice and Jack sitting mutely by while their parents wrangled and shouted over their future, each blaming the other's child for this catastrophe. Terrible things had been said. The Richardses had painted Allie as an immoral girl who deserved no better than she got. The Daltons had responded that their spoiled, heedless son had taken advantage of an innocent child. It was unbearable. And it went on and on until, humiliated beyond endurance, Alice jumped up and screamed.

"Shut up! All of you shut up! It's our decision. Jack's and mine. You're acting like we're . . . objects! Like things you can push around to suit yourselves! Well, you can't! We've already made up our minds. A marriage we don't want is worse than any disgrace. It's obscene and I won't do it!"

She'd run sobbing to her room. Sometime later her mother had come in to find Barbara trying to calm her hysterical sister. Barbara, who had no idea what was going on. Who simply knew Alice was unhappy and who was trying to help. Laura had sat on the edge of Allie's bed and tenderly pushed the long black hair out of her daughter's eyes.

"It's all right, darling," she'd said. "Stop crying, Allie. We'll work something out."

Barbara hadn't said a word then nor later when the Daltons made hasty arrangements for Alice to go to her mother's sister, Aunt Charlotte, in Boston. It was years before Barbara and Alice discussed the episode. And in the meantime, Allie's baby boy was born and given away, to God knows whom.

"Where shall we go for lunch?" Barbara asked as they approached Larimer Square. "The two places I like best are The Promenade Cafe and LaFitte's."

"Since I've never been in this area," Fran said, "I wouldn't have a clue. What's the difference between them?"

"The Promenade is an outdoor place, and LaFitte's is dark and New Orleansy-looking."

"LaFitte's, without question," Fran pronounced. "To hell with the food. Give me that nice subdued lighting. Who needs to sit over lunch with your face hanging out in the sunlight? My God, I haven't been able to cope with that since I was twelve!"

The others laughed. "LaFitte's it is," Barbara said. "But I presume you could afford to explore The Square a few minutes before we duck into the darkness? It's interesting down here. A great restoration project, with lots of good little shops."

"Like Ghirardelli Square in San Francisco?" Alice asked.

"Kind of. On a smaller scale."

"They're doing the same thing in Boston with the Quincy Market development near Faneuil Hall. Fascinating, with all the old stalls and the brick and cobblestone walks. I'm glad it's happening all over."

"I wish I knew what language you two were speaking," Frances said.

"Serves you right for being an expatriate," Barbara answered. "But it seems to me I read they're doing something of the same in Paris, putting back an old section on the Left Bank of the Seine the way it was before it went entirely to pot. It's good to preserve old things."

Fran shrugged. "Okay if they're buildings, I suppose. A terrible idea if applied to people."

"I take it you don't approve of old age." Alice's voice was amused.

"I loathe it. I won't have it."

"Then you're obviously planning to die young." Barbara was teasing, but Fran took her seriously.

"I certainly am. I won't get old and wrinkled and ugly. Never. I'll take advantage of every kind of lift there is, face, bosom, buttocks—you name it. And when they don't work any more I'll use my saved-up sleeping pills."

Barbara was shocked. "You're kidding! Life is precious at any age."

They were walking slowly through the narrow little streets and arcades, passing the old black iron benches on the sidewalks, the carved sandstone Bear and Bull from Denver's original Stock Exchange transplanted over a doorway. Fran glanced with disdain at the restored façades and the ornate drinking fountain with its Victorian cherub on top.

"I can't bear things that are decrepit and quaint," she said. "Things and people should be young and vital. Your Larimer Square is like an old lady trying to be coy. Look at the names of some of these places. 'The Sobriety Sarsaparilla and Sandwich Shop,' for God's sake! And that plant store called 'Foliage Bergère'! The whole place proves how ludicruous it is to try to turn back the clock."

"I don't find it ludicrous," Alice said quietly. "I think the Square is charming and genteel and meaningful. As though a big busy city is determined not to forget its past. I like that. In cities and in people. Remembering is important."

"It's infantile," Fran snapped. "I'd think *you* of all people would agree with that."

There was a long moment of silence before Fran went on. "I'm sorry, Allie. Hell, all I've done this morning is put my foot into it and apologize!"

"It's okay. Neither you nor I have such pretty pasts, Fran. But that doesn't mean we should forget them."

"No, I suppose not. There's something to be learned from every experience, isn't there? At least, that's what people keep telling me. I hate that, too. Why does one have to suffer to mature? It's ridiculous. As though understanding is impossible without bad experiences. Who decided that good experiences don't teach anybody anything?"

"They do," Allie said. "It's just that we don't notice the good ones as much."

"Like headlines, you mean. Bad news sells newspapers. That kind of thing?"

"Precisely. A disaster is much more interesting and memorable than something dull and pleasant."

"Then your life and mine would make juicy copy," Fran said. "We seem to specialize in disasters. Not so our baby sister, however. She's revoltingly serene."

Alice smiled at Barb. "Maybe she just doesn't broadcast her mistakes the way we do."

Fran turned to Barbara. "Is that true, Barb? Do you have a secret life none of us knows about? What are the skeletons, past and present, in your closet?"

Barbara brushed aside the probing question. "My current secret is that I'm going to faint if you don't have lunch. Come on, philosophers, let's eat."

I wonder if I could tell them about Charles, Barbara thought. Would they understand my utter devotion to a married man? They wouldn't condemn me for it. Allie would probably feel sorry and sensibly try to talk me out of it. But Fran would tell me I'm nothing but a damned fool, wasting my life.

Maybe before this week is over I will tell them. I want so much to tell someone. That's the worst part of it: being in love and not able to let anyone know. Even if they think I'm crazy, it would be good to share the happiness I feel inside.

Chapter 4

"How are you going to feel when you see your old girlfriend?" Dottie Paige managed to make the question sound almost clinical.

Buzz lowered the pages of the *Rocky Mountain News* and looked innocently at his wife.

"What old girlfriend?"

"Really, Buzz! You know who I mean. Frances Dalton whatever-whatever. She's home for her parents' anniversary. We're invited there for the party. You know that."

"Oh, *that*."

"Well?"

"Well, what?"

Dottie was annoyed. Sometimes Buzz was so transparent. "How are you going to feel, seeing Frances again after all these years? You were crazy about her when we were kids. I used to be insanely jealous."

"That's nice. Are you still?"

"Should I be?"

"Honey, don't be ridiculous. I haven't seen Frannie for thirty years. Do you think I'm still lusting after her?"

"Could be. She's terribly glamorous. All those marriages and divorces and living in Europe. It really doesn't seem possible she's the same girl."

"I'm sure she isn't. Any more than I'm the same boy." He patted his slight paunch. "I'm a settled, contented, middle-aged grandfather. Not that jock she used to date. We probably won't even recognize each other. And I'll bore hell out of her, unless she happens to be interested in Ford dealerships."

"Some women are. I'm sure you haven't forgotten that!" She wished she hadn't said that. She'd promised never to again. She didn't add that from what she gleaned from the gossip columns, any presentable man was of interest to Fran, whether he sold Fords or owned Lincoln Continentals. She told herself Frances wouldn't try anything with Buzz. She wasn't like that other woman. It was just that Dottie knew, by comparison, she'd look like the little brown wren. The hometown girl Buzz married after he lost what turned into an international peacock. Peahen. Oh, blast, what difference did it make? She was nervous, thinking of seeing Frannie again. She wished she had something smarter to wear, wished she hadn't accepted Laura Dalton's invitation, wished, most of all, she hadn't volunteered to make those damned home-spun brownies. Why hadn't they offered to bring champagne instead? Because, idiot, the Daltons don't drink. Because nobody brings champagne to these local gatherings. Because you're behaving like a teen-ager instead of a woman who's been married to the same man for twenty-nine years. And that, at least, she thought, is more than one can say for Frances.

When he brought the second bloody mary, Fran eyed the waiter speculatively. Not bad. A kid, of course. Somewhere in his late twenties, which, to her, was a baby. But he'd looked at her in a way she recognized when he put her drink in front of her. The old "international invitation," she thought. She'd had it from bartenders in Madrid and croupiers in Nice. And usually, out of desperation, she accepted it. One-night stands. A few hours of pretended enchantment with some young, virile stranger. The fleeting satisfaction of feeling desirable. Sometimes they wanted money. Or the excitement of going to bed with a rich, social "older woman" whom they assumed, incorrectly, to be a nymphomaniac. She wasn't. She didn't care that much about sex for its own sake. It was admiration and reassurance she craved. Maybe even danger. One of those pick-ups could rob and kill her in whatever bed they occupied. Perhaps that made it all the more exciting. God knows it was a relief from loneliness or the sterile company of the unattached "gays" who were only too happy to squire her around.

She watched the waiter as he retreated to a corner of the restaurant near the ladies' room. He's done this before, too, Fran thought cynically. He's giving me a chance to excuse myself and make a date with him. Maybe I will. Anything to get through this week.

That's how I met Jacques, she remembered. I picked him up in the Carlton bar in Cannes. Of course, he wasn't a waiter. Just an opportunist with a phony title. Jacques de St. Déspres. He'd been thirty and she forty-two. They'd flirted openly, he from his table alone and she from her seat among her boring party of six: three rich divorcees and a trio of faggots. She'd been ready to cut out and go up to her room when she saw him. Dark, handsome, smiling his invitation. She'd gone to the ladies' room, discreetly dropping her calling card beside his chair, knowing he'd pick it up, sure he'd check with the desk clerk and find her room number, positive he'd keep calling the suite until she answered and invited him up.

They married a month later. She still wondered why. At the time it had seemed amusing to become a marquise. The Marquise de St. Déspres. For a little while, she'd thought the title was real, just as she thought Jacques' passionate protestations of love were real. But she supposed she knew, even at the start, that neither was genuine. Jacques' father was a Paris butcher, and the closest the family had ever come to a title was supplying racks of lamb to people with real family crests. She'd laughed when she found out. Laughed when Jacques blurted out the truth in the middle of one of their monumental fights. He'd thought it would humiliate her. It had only struck her funny.

They stayed together a year. She'd have gone on with it, out of inertia, if Jacques had not become so flagrantly unfaithful. Her pride couldn't take that. In that way, she remained "American." Even after all the years in Europe, she couldn't handle the upper-class European woman's relaxed attitude toward a husband's affairs; could never become sufficiently sophisticated to accept and ignore the fact that her husband had a mistress. Or perhaps it was because the mistress was twenty-eight years old.

Whatever, she divorced him and settled handsomely, giving

him a sizable chunk of her second husband's money. "Share the wealth," she'd thought at the time. Arthur Stanton paid to get rid of me, and now I'm passing some of it along to get rid of Jacques. It seemed equitable, somehow, even though she'd gotten short-changed. She never used the title, aware that the really elegant people knew it was a fake. So she hadn't even gotten that out of her third marriage. At least Stuart Mills had provided a way out of Denver. And Arthur had made her financially secure. But Jacques had given her nothing except some unusually expert French lovemaking in the beginning and a short-lived feeling that she still had the allure of a young woman.

Barb and Allie were chattering on. She paid no attention. She stared steadily at the LaFitte waiter, accepting his challenge.

"Back in a minute," Fran finally said. She sauntered toward the ladies' room, aware that heads turned as she passed. They didn't know the pants suit was custom-made St. Laurent, right out of the couture. Or that Boucheron made her jewels in Paris. But they knew she was Somebody. There was always satisfaction in that.

She passed close to the waiter. "Give me your name and number when I come out," she said, barely moving her lips. "I'll be in touch."

Her sisters watched her progress, unaware of the exchange with the waiter.

"She's really something, isn't she?" Barbara shook her head. "Do you think she's as blasé as she tries to appear? Something tells me it's an act."

"I don't know," Allie said. "I do know she's an unhappy woman."

"I remember when she ran off with that actor, Stuart Mills. I was a kid, but I'll never forget it. It was the year after you left, Allie. Mother and Daddy were still so broken up over you. And then Fran got that job in summer stock at the theater in Elitch Gardens. We didn't even know what was going on. Everybody thought she was going to marry Buzz Paige until we woke up one morning and there was that note saying she'd left for New York and was going to marry Stuart Mills. And one telephone call, a week later, saying she had. Did you ever meet him, Allie?"

"Once. They came to Boston with a road company, and Fran called me at Aunt Charlotte's. She wouldn't come to the house. I met them at the Copley Plaza for a drink." Allie smiled. "At least they had a drink. I had tea. I was still such a kid, even though I'd had a baby." The smile faded and she was silent for a moment. "Anyway, Stu Mills was terribly good-looking, but Fran told me privately that the marriage wasn't working out. I didn't know she'd already met Arthur Stanton. He was much older, you know. A widower and one of the 'angels' of a show Stu had been in the season before. Fran married him six months later, but she never bothered to tell me. I read it in the papers."

"She called Mother and Daddy," Barbara said. "She just said she'd married a wonderful, wealthy man and was very happy. But she never brought him home. She never brought any of them home. In fairness, she did invite the three of us to New York when she was married to Stanton, but Daddy wouldn't go. So she never asked again. Not in that marriage or later. Daddy's so stubborn. He never forgave her for running off with Mills. And she's just like him. So she just disappeared. Except for occasional cards and gifts, none of us has seen her until last night. I'm surprised she came home for the anniversary."

"So am I. Maybe there comes a time when you'd like to recapture something. Maybe it's part of getting older."

Barbara looked worried. "Do you think she meant what she said when we were walking around? All that business about sleeping pills."

Allie shook her head. "I don't know, Barb. I don't know her well enough. I can't imagine anybody not wanting to live, no matter what." She gave a little laugh. "Funny. Last night I picked up a magazine Mother left in our room. Something called the *Colorado Woman's Digest*. There was an ad on the back. Some radio station, I think. It said something like 'Do not resent growing old. Remember, many are denied that privilege.' Maybe I should put it in Fran's room."

"I saw that. What a strange magazine for Mother to have. It's very 'liberated woman' stuff, I gather."

"Not entirely. It covers the spectrum, from jobs to politics, but it also has things like 'Community Care for the Elderly' and an amusing article on what to do with a husband who's retired. Anyway, you never know about Mother, do you? I often think there's much more to her than meets the eye."

"Much more to whom?" Fran slid back into her place on the banquette.

"To Mother," Barbara said. "We were just saying that she's not as uncomplicated as she seems."

"She's female," Fran said matter-of-factly. "When have you ever known an uncomplicated female? Let's order. I'm getting bored with this place."

They returned to the house on South Carona Street about four o'clock that afternoon. She'd been back once a year since she'd moved to Washington fourteen years before, but Barbara had never looked at her parents' home quite as appraisingly as she did this day. It really was a dreary place. Dreary but respectable. A two-story brick dwelling with three bedrooms, a front porch and those hideous stone urns on either side of the steps leading to it. Inside, nothing had changed in Barb's memory. It was all scrupulously clean and depressingly ordinary. The living-room furniture, including the cut-velvet "divan" and Daddy's big easy chair, stood exactly where they'd been placed fifty years before. Even the lamps and the few ornaments were the same as they'd been in her childhood. So was the dining-room "suite" with its big oak sideboard and its Tiffany lamp hanging precisely over the center of the table. It was as though time stood still. As though it was the late nineteen-thirties when Barbara Dalton was growing up in a middle-class house in a middle-class neighborhood in a middle-class family.

On her trips home these past years, she'd just taken it for granted. Now she supposed she saw it through her sisters' eyes as well as her own. How different Sam and Laura's surroundings were from her own sleek little apartment in Washington with its good modern furnishings. As different as they were from Allie's big house on Beacon Hill, which she'd visited once, years ago. Certainly different from Fran's Paris flat, which she'd never seen.

She felt suddenly homesick for her own place in Georgetown. That's where her life was. In that unobtrusive little converted brownstone with the landlady-owner on the premises, but no inquisitive doorman to note that Charles let himself in with his own key. She wouldn't let Charles pay the rent. He thought she was silly, but she'd been adamant about that from the start.

"I'll take your gifts and your flowers and as much of you as you can spare," she'd said early on in their relationship, "but my home is my castle and I can maintain the moat."

He'd laughed. "I know you're a high-paid government official," he'd teased, "but this chic tenement is expensive. It's nineteen sixty-three, love. The age of Camelot. Everybody wants to live in Georgetown and the landlords know it. You are not a Kennedy, after all."

"But I am an able-bodied, twenty-seven-year-old woman working for a highly respected Colorado congressman," she'd said. "and I bloody well can afford to entertain one of his colleagues in my own paid-for apartment. So you just be quiet, Congressman Tallent, and don't trouble yourself about the cost of my turret."

"Okay. As long as you promise not to pull up the drawbridge one day."

"You could always set up a siege."

"Nut!" He'd taken her in his arms that night as he had so many nights in the thirteen years that followed. Thirteen years! Barbara thought. Where have they gone? I'm forty years old and Charles is fifty and we're as much in love as ever. She didn't want to think what would happen if her own boss did not get re-elected. Or if the voters in Charles's state turned him out of office one day. Would he leave Washington? Could she follow him back to that midwestern country he came from? She lived with that fear at every election and so far they'd been lucky. The age of Camelot disappeared. Administrations changed. But Charles and her boss kept being returned to their seats in the House. Thank God. That's the way it would be. Anything else was unthinkable. I'd go crazy if I lost him, Barb thought. I'd be far more grief-stricken than his widow would be if he died.

But Charles wasn't going to die. Any more than he was going to leave her. Or any more than he was going to marry her. Why did that thought keep popping up here in Denver? In Washington, where the reminders were much more prevalent, she was almost able to forget Charles's wife and his grown-up children and the house in Chevy Chase he shared with Andrea. She was content with her situation. Busy all day on Capitol Hill, occupied with theater at Kennedy Center or movies or restaurant dining with "girlfriends" on the nights Charles was fulfilling the social obligations of which she had no part. She shopped in Georgetown for food for the delicious little dinners she prepared on the nights he could get away: croissants and special cheeses from the French Market; Smithfield hams from Nimes; delicate veal from the Boucherie Bernard. My life is full and happy, Barbara thought again. God knows there are no marriages in my family to envy. Not Fran's three. Not even, she suspected, Allie's. There was something mysterious about Allie's marriage. Spencer was arriving tomorrow, but the children weren't coming. Allie had just announced that, giving no explanation. She'd also announced that she and Spencer would stay at the Hilton. Laura had been disappointed.

"Why? There's room here, dear. Barbara and Frances can bunk in Frances' room and you and Spencer can have the other."

"It's better if we go to the hotel, Mother. Spencer is a crank about his comfort. Not that we wouldn't love to sleep here, but, honestly, he'd go crazy without his own bathroom."

No word about her children, Christopher and Janice. No reason given for their failure to come for their grandparents' fiftieth wedding anniversary. Laura and Sam hadn't seen them since they were teen-agers and Alice brought them for a visit on the way to Vail for a skiing holiday. Now they were twenty-three and twenty-one respectively. And obviously disinterested in family reunions.

I'm curious about that marriage, Barbara admitted to herself. Allie had stayed on in Boston after the baby was born. She'd worked at Filene's and lived with Aunt Charlotte until she was twenty-three. Then she'd met and married Spencer Winters in 1951. He'd given her two babies and, apparently, a comfortable, nearly rich life, thanks to his successful law practice. But had he given her happiness? Barbara sensed not. In fact, she suspected quite the contrary. Allie seemed quiet, almost fearful somehow. It was nothing one could define. There was simply an air of resignation and sadness about her.

I wonder if Spencer Winters knows about the other child? Not necessarily. Jack Richards' baby was adopted long before Alice met her husband. And she'd been in virtual seclusion in Boston during her pregnancy. That much Laura had later confided. But there was something not good about the marriage. Maybe, even thirty years later, Allie had never gotten over her first love.

If Jack Richards still lived in Denver, it was damned certain he wouldn't be invited tomorrow night. The Daltons and the Richardses had never spoken since their last confrontation. And Allie obviously had no desire to see the man who'd fathered her baby. She'd been home often enough over the years to have looked him up if she'd wanted to. Barb was sure she never had. No one ever mentioned his name, for that matter. It was as though he were dead. Or as lost as the son he'd never seen.

It wasn't Jack Richards who haunted Alice, but it might be a longing to know about their child. Or maybe Allie's tentative attitude had nothing to do with any of that. Maybe it was something entirely different.

Good lord, how her mind wandered, starting with her thoughts about this house! She was being snobbish about it. It was a nice house. A good house. The proper setting for the only happily married people she knew. Or were they? At seventy, something seemed to have come over her mother, something Barb had never sensed before. Restlessness. Or regret. She'd always thought of her parents as perfectly mated. But now she wasn't so sure. If it was difficult for her father to be idle, it must be equally difficult for her mother to have him underfoot twenty-four hours a day. It could be as simple as that. Or the normal anxiety that usually came with age, an anxiety underlined by the reminder of a golden wedding anniversary. So many years together. So much sameness in the way they lived, the people they saw, the things they did. The same unchanging, unchallenging life represented by the static state of this very house.

Were they bored? Could people at their age possibly begin to chafe at the pattern of a lifetime, suddenly realizing how limited it was, how much they'd missed? It seemed unlikely. Almost inconceivable. And yet Sam and Laura could have many more years to look forward to. Perhaps, Barbara thought, they don't really like what they see.

Or maybe they feel they failed all of us. If so, they're wrong. They shared all the things they believed in, tried to instill the values they were brought up to respect. It's not their fault they produced a trio of disappointing daughters who never fell into the safe little well-married roles they envisioned. If anyone's failed in this family, Fran and Allie and I have. We've never given Mother and Daddy what they really wanted: a part in our lives.

And it's too late now.

Chapter 5

Alice met the United Flight when it arrived in Denver the next day bearing a predictably surly Spencer Winters. He didn't kiss her. It crossed her mind that at least he didn't hit her. Not that he would, in public. He only did that in the privacy of their home. And quite often. Spencer Winters was a wife-beater. Proper, prominent, conservative Spencer Winters regularly doled out his share of bruises and blackened eyes, and once even a broken arm.

He was not rare. There were thousands like him. Sadists who enjoyed physically punishing their wives. And all of them married to women like Alice, women who endured the cruelty out of fear or helplessness or, no doubt, masochism. She read about this phenomenon often, more often these days than ever, it seemed. She also read that many wives finally found the courage to "come out of the closet" and reveal what had been going on in their lives for years. There were organizations now to help such victims. Groups of other women willing to offer emotional counseling and practical assistance to those who wanted to escape this demeaning, brutal existence.

My good sense tells me I should be one of those, Alice thought. I should leave Spencer. I have no reason to stay. My children are grown and no longer in need of me, and I'd always find a way to support myself. I could come back here, to Denver. Or stay on after this "festive week" ends. But I won't. I'll go back to Boston.

To the mental and physical cruelty I've known most of my married life. Why do I go on with it? Because I love Spencer? No. I haven't loved him for years. I never loved him. He was a way out of Aunt Charlotte's house: an escape from those self-righteous eyes that never stopped accusing me of my sin and reminding me of my lost child.

Johnny is why I stay. Even after all these years I must want to be punished for abandoning him. I suffer Spencer's beatings as I would a spanking from my father, knowing I've been a bad girl and compulsively determined to pay for it forever. I am a masochist. "Sick," the children would say. Sick in the head. There was no need for me to confess to Spencer about that schoolgirl mistake or the baby born of it. No reason he ever had to know. I wanted him to know. Wanted him to chastise me. And he's done so. He's used the knowledge like a whip, almost literally, every time I do something to annoy him. And I take it, feeling I deserve it. Feeling I'm not worthy of anything better.

If only I knew where Johnny was. If I could be sure he's well and happy, perhaps I'd get over this terrible guilt. But I never will. They wouldn't tell me who adopted him. I'm sure Aunt Charlotte knows, but she won't tell me either. She thinks I deserve to suffer. As Spencer does. As I do, myself.

In the taxi, she forced herself to smile at her husband.

"How was the trip, dear?"

"Boring."

"Are the children all right?"

"How should I know? Chris is dead, as far as I'm concerned. And Janice might as well be living with that man instead of just sleeping with him and coming home to change her clothes. Things haven't changed in two days, Alice," he said sarcastically. "Or did you think your absence might encourage your children to become paragons of virtue?"

She didn't answer that. "I've checked us in at the Hilton," she said instead. "We have a very nice room."

"I'll bet. Seen one Hilton you've seen 'em all. Couldn't you, for Christ's sake get us into some more civilized place? What's wrong with the old wing of the Brown Palace?"

"It was full. We're lucky to have gotten any accommodations." She hesitated. "Of course, we could still change our minds and stay with the family. There's room."

"Not on your life! My God, isn't it enough that I've made this idiotic trip? Do you expect me to stay in that stuffy little house as well? You really ask too much of me! You know I can't stand those people. Damned hymn-singing teetotalers! As for those sisters of yours! An international whore and a Washington swinger!"

"Spencer, you're not being fair! You hardly know any of them. You've met my parents three times and Barbara only once. And you've never met Fran at all!"

"Their reputations precede them. As yours did. No wonder your own children are so immoral. They take after their mother and their aunts."

"I don't understand you," Alice said slowly. "If you hate me so, why do you stay married to me? We have nothing, Spencer. No love. No sex. No companionship. And God knows we have no friendship. What *do* we have?"

"My reputation. My standing in the community. Not to mention my religion, which frowns on divorce."

"It's not *my* religion, though your children were raised in it. But with your influence, Spencer, you probably could get this twenty-five-year farce annuled."

"We were married in the Church."

"Yes, and I respect your church. I respect all religions. But I never converted. I'm sure you could find a way out."

"Forget it. My law firm is stuffier than any priest. You know how J.B. feels about divorce."

Yes, she did indeed know. J.B. The Senior Partner was a "veddy, veddy proper Bostonian" of the old school. Despite Spencer's more than twenty-five years with the firm, and a junior partnership, he was still an "outsider," a "newcomer from Chicago." Every move in the past and present was made with J.B. in mind. The choice of their friends, the right address, the correct club, the subscription to the symphony, the brilliant parties for which she was famous. All to enhance Spencer's future and raise him in the estimation of J. B. Thompson. I wonder how the old man would like it if he knew his "young associate" regularly punched his wife around? Alice thought. He'd not approve of the ungentlemanly violence, but he'd probably secretly be in favor of a man showing who's boss in his own home. Spencer was terrified J.B. would find out about Alice's "lurid past" or discover how defiant and uncontrollable his own children were: Chris, considered "dead" since he brazenly told Spencer he was a homosexual; Janice, barely spoken to by her father since she took up with that art director from an advertising agency. Spencer was outraged, disgusted by both discoveries. Alice was saddened, heartsick about her son, but admiring of his honesty. As for Janice, the girl was only following her convictions. And, thank God, with more courage than her mother had shown.

My guilt is endlessly compounded, Allie thought. The children had been all too aware, most of their lives, of the anger in their house. They heard the screams and the angry shouting, saw the bruises she tried hard to hide. Chris had reacted with a violent hatred of his father and a fanatic devotion to his mother that even three years of psychoanalysis had not been able to change. She still saw him, outside of the house. He was a gentle young man and at least he had found happiness in his own way, revolting though it was to Spencer. Chris worried about her, begged her to leave, even suggested she move in with him and Peter. She'd sadly refused.

"I'm not going to spoil your life," she'd said. "Look, Chris, I won't pretend I don't wish you'd taken another path. But this is the one you want, the one that brings you contentment. Peter's a nice boy. I like him. But I'm not sophisticated enough to handle that household, even if I were selfish enough to intrude."

"You disapprove," Chris had said.

"Disapprove? No. That's too strong a word. I'm of another generation. It's hard for me to understand why you can't fall in love with some nice young woman. Hard for me to accept something no parent really wants to accept. But I love you. And who am I to set standards for others?"

"So you'll stay on in that house with that brute."

"I suppose so."

"Why, Mother?"

She couldn't tell him. Couldn't confess this thirty-year-old guilt that seemed to become more of an obsession as she grew older. He didn't know he had a half-brother somewhere. He'd never know. She supposed she kept quiet out of shame. She'd not be able to bear reproach in the eyes of one whose adoration was dearer than life itself.

She'd never told Janice either, though her daughter's attitude would have been much more casual. Janice still maintained a token residence at home, but she'd been "independent" for two years. When she spoke of her father it was as though she talked of some clinically disturbed case history she'd read about.

"He's weird. Talk about your male chauvinist pigs! Of course he's worse than most. The physical stuff, I mean. My God, I'd never stand for that! Why do you?"

Alice hadn't known how to answer but she flinched under Jan's obvious scorn for both of them. In Jan's eyes I'm no better than Spencer, she thought. She despises him for the way he treats me, but I think perhaps she has even less respect for me for putting up with it. She's right, of course. But I've never had her kind of strength. Not even when I was twenty-one. How I envy girls of today who don't even want to be referred to as girls. Women, they call themselves. Young women. Sisters. Persons. However they refer to themselves, the meaning is the same. They're individuals, free and honest, unburdened by the taboos I grew up with, untroubled by what other people think. Jan made no secret of her affair with her young art director, Clint Darby. They worked at the same advertising agency, ate their meals together, slept together. Spencer was right. She might just as well have moved in with him instead of keeping up the pretense of living at home. But Alice couldn't come out and ask her why she didn't. Jan might think she wanted her to leave. She didn't want that. Neither did Spencer, despite what he said. She supposed it was more selfishness than propriety that kept Janice theoretically at home. Home was a place where your underwear was done by the laundress, where Mother took care of your dry cleaning and had new heels put on your shoes, where the housekeeper tidied up your room and where Father paid your phone bills. Home was where you sulkily spent Christmas while Clint went back to Ohio to see his own parents. Home was a stopover, convenient and impersonal, where you checked in and out, counting on your mother's loving anxiety and your father's reluctant affection masked by the disapproval he felt compelled to register in his self-righteous way.

She saw Spencer frown as they pushed into the crowded elevator in the Denver Hilton, jostled by fat women in stretch pants and men with convention badges on the lapels of their ill-fitting brown suits. "Cowboy attire," complete with string ties and wide-brimmed hats, also abounded. She could feel his scorn. He was so intolerant. So damned superior and *Eastern*. He'd brought only an overnight bag, and when they entered their room she looked at it inquiringly.

"Traveling light, aren't you?"

"A couple of clean shirts. Some underwear. The usual. What did you think I'd bring for this great social event—white tie?"

I won't rise to the bait, Alice thought. "No. But for a week, I thought . . ."

"A week! You're not serious! You don't really think I could spend seven days here!"

"But we planned it. A week . . ."

"*You* planned a week. I said I'd come for this damned anniversary, and that's tomorrow night. After that, forget it."

"Spencer, that's so mean of you! We've almost never been here together. I thought just this once you could sacrifice a little of your precious time to be with me."

She saw the redness begin to creep up from his collar, the recognizable sign of rage. Don't let him, she prayed. Don't let him fly into one of those fits of uncontrollable anger. Not here. Not now.

"Goddamn you, Alice, you never appreciate anything! I've come all this way just so you could show your bloody relatives and friends that you have a real, live, legitimate husband. Well, they'll see me. Isn't that enough to prove your children have a father?" His voice was mounting. Surely the people in the next room could hear him. "You drive me insane! Never make an ounce of sense! You are the most infuriating, ridiculous . . ." He moved toward her, his fist raised. She backed away.

"No! Spencer, don't! My God, don't humiliate me this way! Not here. Please, Spencer!"

He lowered his hand. "Then stop nagging me! You can stay a week. Hell, you can stay a year! But not me. You should know better than to suggest it!"

"All right. I'm sorry. I realize it would bore you."

"Damned right it would. It bores me already." He opened his bag and threw a few things in the dresser drawer. "Call room service and order me a double scotch."

"There's an ice machine down the hall."

He turned and looked at her witheringly. "How nice. But I am not a traveling salesman, my dear. I do not go about with a bottle in my bag. Now will you kindly get on that telephone and tell them if they're not here in ten minutes there will be a scene the like of which they have not witnessed since they erected this convention hall they laughingly call a first-class hotel?"

"Drive me downtown, will you, Barb?"

"Sure. Something you want to buy?"

Frances smiled. "In a way. But first I want to rent a car."

"Rent a car? What on earth for? Don't tell me you're a sightseer."

"Hardly. I've been in Rome fifty times and I've never set foot inside the Vatican."

"Then what in the world do you want with a car? You planning to look up old friends? You can use Dad's car, if you are. Or I'll be glad to take you anywhere you want to go."

"For heaven's sake, Barbara, will you just shut up and do what I ask you? I want a car while I'm here. I get claustrophobic in this hellhole. I want to be able to move wherever and whenever the mood strikes me. Don't make a big deal out of it."

"Sorry."

"And don't look so damned injured." Fran smiled. "Listen, pussycat, your old sister never goes anywhere without looking for excitement. And excitement is synonymous with mobility. Get it? I'm not going to be stuck in this house for a week, or have to explain where I'm going and when I'll be back, which I'd have to do if I used the family car. No problem, right?"

"No problem. I'll drive you to a rental agency."

"Now, there's my dear little baby sister. Thanks."

Barbara didn't pursue it, but her mind was full of questions. Where was Fran planning to find "excitement" in a town she no longer knew? Surely, she wouldn't go out haunting the local bars alone at night. Or would she? Doubtful. She'd find them much too "provincial." And she didn't know anybody here any more. Except Buzz Paige. She'd perked up when Laura had mentioned him. It wasn't possible that Fran was planning to get in touch with her old beau! Maybe she already had. Maybe she'd arranged to meet him. But she'd had no opportunity unless she'd managed to call him at his office this morning. Certainly he must be listed in the phone book at a business address as well as a home one. But Fran wouldn't be so rotten as to start trouble with a happily married man. No? How about you, Barbara? That's different, she defended herself. Charles isn't happily married. Besides, with us it's a long-term arrangement, quite different from breezing into town for one week and disrupting a contented household just for kicks. Even Fran wouldn't do that. She half-smiled as she realized she'd thought "even Fran." As though Frances was so immoral she'd do anything. Well, maybe she was. Maybe she'd do anything outrageous and "amusing" to relieve a dull, dutiful stay in a place she obviously didn't want to be.

Driving downtown, she couldn't restrain herself.

"I don't mean to stick my nose into your business, Fran, but are you by any chance thinking of seeing Buzz Paige?"

Her sister's laugh was genuine. "Is that why you think I want the car? To set up an assignation with poor old Buzz Paige? Oh, Barbara, you really are ridiculous!"

"You still haven't answered my question."

"Only because it's too silly to answer. Look up a tired middle-aged man who had the hots for me thirty years ago? What on earth for? No, darling, if I get into mischief I'll pick a stranger. So set your mind at ease. I'm not here to wreck homes, if that's what you're afraid of."

Barbara felt relieved. That would be all Laura and Sam needed: Fran coming back and creating another scandal in the community. So what did she have in mind?

Fran seemed to pick up her thoughts. "You're dying of curiosity, aren't you?"

"Frankly, yes."

"Okay, but keep your mouth shut. I have found someone here who may be momentarily diverting. He's young and sexy and available. I think he'll be good for a few laughs for a few days. Now are you satisfied?"

Barbara glanced quickly at her and looked back at the road. "Who is he? And where in the name of God did you find him? You haven't been out of my sight since you arrived."

"You're just not very observant. You or Allie. He's a waiter at LaFitte's. Name's Cary Venzetti. I picked him yesterday when we had lunch there. I'm meeting him tonight."

"Fran, you can't!"

"Why not? There's nothing special planned for tonight, is there? The party's tomorrow night. As far as I know, we have nothing more divine to look forward to this evening than meeting Allie's highly respectable husband. And my hunch is that I can do nicely without that."

"Mother will be upset if you're not with us for dinner. Allie and Spencer are taking us out."

"All right. If it's so vital, I'll arrange to meet the baby stud later."

Barbara felt a twinge of disgust. It was not only Fran's vulgar phrasing, it was her wild pursuit of someone to go to bed with. Anyone, it seemed. Picking up a waiter! My God, it was obscene, especially at her age. Never mind that it was dangerous. It was sickening. The revulsion turned to pity. Poor Fran. She had to keep denying the truth. She was so fearful of growing old, so desperately in need of reassurance that she'd accept it from anyone. Even from some calculating young man who probably expected to be well paid for his services this week. It was pathetic. Barbara wished she knew how to stop her.

"Hey," she said, "what do you need with that scene? Good lord, Fran, you'll only be here a week. Why not relax?"

"There's no such thing as 'only a week.' It's seven days and seven nights out of my life. Hours not to be wasted sitting around the living room listening to Daddy talk about his Masonic Lodge and watching Mother patiently resigning herself to old age. It's Allie, all matronly and settled. It's even you, my love, with your damned young face and your apparent secret happiness. What about you, anyway, Barb? What do you do with your life? Do you have a lot of lovers? Is there as much action in Washington as people say?"

"Very little. Not as much as you hear. It's really a small town grown big. You'd find it stultifying."

"*You* don't."

"I'm not you, Madame Dalton-Déspres."

"And you're still not talking, are you?"

Barbara didn't answer. Then she finally said, "There's not much to talk about."

Fran looked at her appraisingly. "You know, I somehow doubt that. Why don't you open up to your big sister?"

Barb laughed. "You've been reading too many sexy Washington novels."

"Lots of spicy stories in the papers about congressmen these days. They even make the Paris papers."

Barbara glanced at her sharply. Fran seemed to be looking idly out the window, but she was watching her sister in the glass. A shot in the dark. But dangerously close. Silly to be suspicious. Fran had never heard the name Charles Tallent. A few people did know about Barbara and him. It was nearly impossible to keep such a secret in Washington after so many years, no matter how careful they were. But the press mercifully had kept quiet about the liaison. It was local gossip exclusively.

Andrea Tallent knew, of course. That was inevitable. But Charles's wife seemed to accept the situation with equanimity, even nodding cordially to Barbara when they happened to run into each other at some cocktail party or charity event. Barb marveled at the way Andrea handled the whole thing. I couldn't be that unperturbed if it were my husband, Barbara often thought. I'd be wounded and furious. I'd demand he make a choice. But, according to Charles, Andrea had more "common sense" than that. When she first heard about Barbara—Lord! It was ten years ago!—she'd simply shrugged and said, "I don't really care what you do, Charles, as long as you don't publicly embarrass me or upset the children. If you must have someone else, and apparently you must, then I much prefer it be one intelligent woman rather than a series of vulgar little encounters."

Barbara had been open-mouthed when Charles repeated the conversation to her. When he told her Andrea knew about them, she'd been glad, thinking they'd surely divorce and she'd become the second Mrs. Tallent. She'd wanted to marry then. But he'd made it clear that this never was to be.

"You know there'll be no divorce," he'd said softly. "I've been that honest with you from the start. There are the children to think of. Even though I don't love Andrea, I adore those kids. I couldn't walk away from them, Barb."

She'd been terribly hurt. Resentful. "You love them more than you do me."

"No, darling. I love them differently. I come from a broken home, Barbara. It's a sad and terrible thing to lose a parent. I'd never do that to my own. They're only eight and ten. They need the security of a mother and father."

"But they must know you and Andrea aren't happy together! It's wrong to bring children up in a house filled with tension. Worse than letting them live with one peaceful parent. People who stay together 'for the sake of the children' aren't doing them any favor, Charles. You're probably warping their lives."

He'd been very gentle with her. He knew she was not pleading their case but her own. Though she might believe what she was saying, her motivation was not concern for his children's psyches but hope for her own happiness.

"There isn't any tension in our house, dear," he'd said. "Andrea and I never quarrel. We don't care enough to fight. The kids think they have perfect parents and Andrea and I never give them reason to suppose otherwise. They're very contented and secure. I won't destroy that. Neither will she."

"You even sleep together." She sounded like a petulant child herself.

He'd looked grave. "We share the same room. That's all. We don't sleep in the same bed. We haven't since the year after I met you. When I realized how deeply in love I was, I stopped having sex with Andrea. She soon knew something else was going on, of course. She's not a stupid woman. So she finally came out and asked me. And I told her about you. We agreed to stay married. I won't break that promise, darling. Not even for you. Andrea's given me a lot. She was with me through the hard years and she deserves the rewards."

"And what about me? What do I deserve?"

"Something better than what you have," Charles had said. "I know this situation is terribly unfair to you. I know how selfish it is of me. Monopolizing your time. Cutting you off from seeing other men. I think they call it 'taking the best years of your life.' Much as I love you, Barbara, I think you're foolish to go on with me. I wouldn't blame you if you didn't. It's a lousy life, sneaking around corners, spending all our time here in your apartment. God knows I'd be miserable if you stopped seeing me, but I'd understand. I'll understand whenever and if ever you decide that the little I can give you isn't worth all the sacrifices you make."

She'd held him close. "I don't want anyone but you," she'd

said. "I never will. I don't need a gold band to feel married to you. I don't need anything but your love. I love my life. Our life. I love you because you're good and loyal and unselfish and more wonderful than anyone I could ever find."

Ten years ago, Barbara thought again. And nothing has changed, except Charles and Andrea and I are that much older and so are his children. They're eighteen and twenty now, old enough not to be "traumatized" by their parents' divorce, but in Charles's eyes they'll never be old enough for that. Not even when they're parents themselves. And with each year it probably seems more unfair to Charles to even consider leaving Andrea. She's his age: fifty. What happens to a lone woman of fifty used to the security and privileges of marriage?

No, it will never be different for us. We don't even discuss the possibility of his divorce any more. We haven't for years. I wonder if Andrea has found her own "outside consolation" in all this time? She must have. She's a healthy, attractive woman. Surely she couldn't go on year after year without physical satisfaction. But if she finds it, she's even more discreet than Charles and I. I've never heard an iota of gossip about Mrs. Tallent. And if Charles has, he's never mentioned it.

What would he do if the tables were turned and Andrea fell in love with someone the way her husband has with me? Unwillingly, Barbara didn't want to think about it. It was an unworthy suspicion, but she was afraid he'd not have his wife's cool attitude. She didn't want to believe it, but she couldn't dismiss the idea that if it came to that, Charles might trade his own affair for the cessation of his wife's. How terrible of me to think that way! He's a bigger man than that. He'd be glad if Andrea found the same kind of happiness he has. His male ego is not as great as his passion for me. I must believe that. I do believe it. But could he possibly believe Andrea has remained faithful to him, knowing what she knows? Perhaps. Men, even those as intelligent and understanding as Charles, usually are outraged when their wives do exactly what they're doing. By the standards of his generation, extracurricular sex, even freely admitted, is acceptable for the husband but an affront when practiced by the wife.

My God, how cynical I sound! It must be Fran's influence. She's been disenchanted since she was ten.

Chapter 6

Laura carefully descended the stairs to the basement where Sam was puttering around his woodworking bench. She often wondered why he'd taken up this particular pastime since his retirement. He'd never been handy around the house. In forty-two years she'd hardly been able to coax him into hanging a nail on the wall for a picture. He had no interest in anything manual. He freely admitted he was "all thumbs," giving the deprecating phrase a strange little ring of pride when he said it in company, implying that the men in their circle were laborers at heart while he was the cerebral type with his mathematical skills and his staff of underling accountants.

But in the past eight years it was as though he considered his mind useless and all he had left were his hands. He was either in the garden during the day or down here with all these saws and hammers and chisels. And as far as Laura could see, it produced nothing, all this cutting and nailing and measuring. Not so much as a picture frame or a cabinet door. It was simply a pastime. A way to pass the hours that hung so heavily on Sam's inexpert hands.

A little wave of sympathy swept over her. He'd taken so quickly, so hopelessly, to the idea that he was old and good for nothing. She wished she could convince him otherwise. He could use his knowledge in so many ways. Probably become a volunteer teacher at one of the vocational schools, giving youngsters or adults the benefit of his accounting knowledge. There were interesting opportunities for a man with Sam's background, but he wouldn't even investigate them. In the beginning she'd tried to encourage him to see whether he could be useful at the Emily Griffith Opportunity School, which offered all kinds of classes for adults, but he'd dismissed the idea without even looking into it. Just as he'd brushed off all her other suggestions. He'd finally gotten angry one day, about two years before.

"Blast it, Laura, can't you leave me alone? I'm too old and tired to start trotting around looking for ways to be useful! I've been working since I was fifteen! Fifty-eight years! I'm retired. Think about the word. Retired. Slipped into the background. Disappeared into the shadows. Gone to bed. That's what retired means. It also means peace. No demands. For Lord's sake, woman, stop nagging me!"

So she had. She left him to his garden and his "workshop" and his television and his retreat from the world. But she hated seeing him this way. There was no need for it. She could hardly get him out of the house any more and she knew he was even dreading the party at home tomorrow night. She'd liked to have taken the girls up on their offer to have it at a hotel. It would have been something different. And secretly she supposed, though it was prideful of her, it would have been satisfying to have her daughters show the world how loving they were, how generous and thoughtful of their parents. But Sam wouldn't hear of it when Barbara wrote and said she and her sisters had corresponded and wanted to arrange a big celebration for the fiftieth year.

"Waste of money," he'd said.

"They can afford it, dear. They'd like to do it for us."

"They can come home for a change. That's what they can do for us."

She'd sighed and written to Barbara, thanking them but saying that she and Sam really would prefer a quiet little gathering at the house.

"It's enough of a 'party' for us," Laura said in her letter, "to think of having the three of you home again. Please plan—all of you—to stay at least a week. And of course I hope and expect that Spencer and Christopher and Janice will come with Alice. We won't be able to house everybody, but I've already spoken to Aunt

Mildred and Aunt Martha and they have plenty of room in their house. They can put up Uncle Fred and Aunt Mamie and Charlotte if she comes. You're a dear to take over the 'organizing' for yourself and your sisters, Barbara darling. It saves me writing three separate letters. Anyway, it will be a happy time for us and, I hope, for all of you."

Maybe it will be a happy time, Laura thought, but certainly not quite as I pictured it. Frances is so changed. If I met her on the street I wouldn't know my oldest child. And it's disappointing that Alice's children won't be here. I suppose they don't want to spend a week with us "old fogies." Can't blame them, I guess. It wouldn't be very exciting. Still, a golden anniversary is special. I'm afraid I feel Alice should have insisted. She hasn't really explained. I imagine she's a little embarrassed. Well, at least Spencer is arriving. We hardly know him, either. What a queer family this is!

She reached the bottom of the stairs and called out to her husband.

"Sam, dear, it's past four o'clock. Don't you think you should stop what you're doing and rest awhile before we get dressed? Alice called from the hotel. They've made a dinner reservation for six o'clock at the Continental Broker on Fillmore Street. They'll meet us there."

He grunted. "Darned foolishness, traipsing out to a restaurant. Why can't we have dinner here?"

She scolded him playfully. "Don't be such an old grouch! It will do us good to go out. Besides, don't you think I'd like a night off from cooking? I still have a lot of last-minute things to do for the party tomorrow. It'll be nice to be waited on for a change. And Allie was sweet about the time. I told her you liked to eat early."

"What time do she and her snooty husband usually eat? Ten o'clock?" He was determined not to enjoy this. "Where are Barbara and Frances?"

"They should be back any minute. They went on some kind of errand."

"In the car?"

"Yes, of course."

"They didn't ask permission to use it."

Laura couldn't contain her exasperation. "Really, Sam, you're just going out of your way to be difficult about everything! They're not children who have to ask for the keys to the car!"

"It's still my car. Only polite to ask."

There was no use arguing with him when he was in this mood. "I've put your blue suit out," Laura said. "It will be ready when you decide to come upstairs."

"My blue suit? Why do I have to wear my blue suit? I thought you wanted me to save that for tomorrow. Why do we have to get all fancied-up to go out to dinner?"

She was suddenly angry. "What do you want to wear? Your dirty old gardening clothes? Is this the way you're going to act the whole time the girls are here? If it is, I'm not surprised they come home so seldom. They'll probably never come back if you go on behaving so badly! What on earth is the matter with you?" She stopped. "I know. It's Spencer Winters, isn't it? You never have liked him."

"I don't trust him. Something shifty about him."

"Sam! He's your son-in-law! Allie's husband! Your grandchildren's father! You've seen him three times in your whole life and one of those was at their wedding twenty-five years ago. How can you continue to dislike a man you hardly know?"

His mood changed suddenly from near-belligerence to anxiety. "Laura, have you taken a good look at Allie? She looks like she's suffering inside. It's that man. I know it. All that business about 'Spencer's comfort' and staying at a hotel! He's cruel to that girl. I just feel it. And why didn't their children come? Has Alice ever explained that? I think he doesn't even like his own kids. I think he's a terrible man and I wish he wasn't here."

She was amazed at his perception. She had no idea he was aware of many of the same things that troubled her. They were both going on nothing more than instinct, but they had the same intuitive feeling that Allie's life was hell. Laura slowly nodded. "I feel as you do," she said, "but perhaps we're wrong, Sam. Maybe we're being unfair to him. It may just be his way."

"I wish I could think so. I wish I could believe he's nothing worse than a stuffed shirt." He was silent for a moment. "I wish I felt all our girls were happy, but I don't think one of them really is."

That, too! Her heart went out to him. Why did she think he

was just a self-pitying, oblivious man? His senses were as keen as ever. His concern perhaps even greater. Above all else, he was a good husband and a loving father. Why did she think only mothers worried about their children, were attuned to them? In the brief time he'd spent with his daughters, Sam was as aware as she of the nuances, the undercurrent of unrest that seemed to be under the surface of all three.

Impulsively, she went over and kissed him. "I love you, Sam Dalton. After half a century you still surprise me."

He patted her lightly on the rear. "After more than half a century I still surprise myself. But it's true, Laurie. Those girls are in trouble. What are we going to do about it?"

"I'm not sure. It's probably too late to do anything now. Maybe we should have started long ago."

He shook his head in regret. "Yes. Maybe we should have, at that."

"Of all the ungodly hours to dine!" Spencer paid the cab driver as they arrived at the restaurant. "And I suppose I won't even be able to have a drink for fear of shocking your mother and father's sensibilities."

"Of course you can have a drink. I'm sure Fran will want one. Barbara, too, probably. Mother and Daddy don't expect other people not to drink. They don't serve liquor in their own house, but they don't impose their personal beliefs on others." Allie was distressed. "Please, Spence, be nice tonight. I know it's tiresome, but Mother's so excited about going out to dinner."

"You don't have to tell me how to behave. And for God's sake, stop calling me 'Spence.' You know I detest it."

"I'm sorry."

I *am* sorry, Alice thought. I'm sorry for so many things. For marrying this cold, cruel man. For staying with him. I'm sorry I let the family send me away "in disgrace" all those years ago. If they hadn't, I wouldn't have met Spencer. But if I hadn't, I wouldn't have Chris and Jan. And for all the heartaches they've brought, they're worth everything.

As they went down the steps to the restaurant, Alice saw Sam and Laura, Barbara and Frances already waiting. She rushed to them, apologizing for being late.

"Darlings, I'm sorry! Have you been here long?"

"No, dear, just a few minutes," Laura said.

"Sixteen, to be exact," Sam said.

"Forgive us. We had a little problem with cabs at the hotel."

"We should have come down and gotten you," Barbara said.

Alice shook her head. "I have a mental picture of the six of us packed into Daddy's Toyota!"

Frances spoke for the first time. "We're a two-car family as of this afternoon. I rented one for the duration." Her eyes were on Spencer, standing silently behind Alice. "By the way, love, aren't you going to introduce us?"

"Fran, forgive me! This is my husband, Spencer. My sister, Frances Dalton-Déspres, dear. And of course you know Mother and Daddy and Barbara."

"Delighted to see you again," Spencer said formally. He turned to Fran. "And nice to meet the famous expatriate at last. I've heard a great deal about you, Mme. Dalton-Déspres."

Fran smiled icily. "I'll bet you have."

"Darling, you're being so formal!" Alice took his arm affectionately. "'Madame Dalton-Déspres' indeed! She's Fran!"

Laura held out her hand. "It's good to see you, Spencer. It's been a long time."

"Yes, it has. You're looking well, Mrs. Dalton." He shook hands with Sam. "You, too, Mr. Dalton. Retirement obviously agrees with you." His gaze went to Barbara. "How are things in Washington?"

"Hectic, as usual. Everybody's edgy before an election."

"No, no politics tonight!" Alice said. "I hear enough of that at home! Let's go in to dinner, shall we?"

The dining room was already crowded, but Spencer's table for six was waiting. Sam immediately picked up the menu.

"Daddy, you don't mind if we don't order for a few minutes, do you?" Alice was obviously nervous. "I'm sure Barb and Fran would like a drink."

Laura answered for him. "Of course, dear. We're in no rush." She looked around. "Such an attractive place, Alice. It's sweet of you, Spencer, to ask us to dinner. It's a real treat."

"My pleasure, Mrs. Dalton."

Liar, Barbara thought. You hate the whole thing, you pompous ass. But instead she said, "You and Daddy have a harem tonight, Spencer. The Dalton women outnumber you."

"I'm sure we can handle it, don't you agree, Mr. Dalton?"

Sam grunted. "Always have before."

A pert little waitress approached the table for their drink orders. Spencer turned to Laura on his right.

"What will you have, Mrs. Dalton?"

Laura looked flustered. "Oh, I don't know. Ginger ale, I suppose."

"Why don't you try a virgin mary, Mother?" Alice asked.

"What's that?"

"It's the nonalcoholic version of a bloody mary. Tomato juice with spices and the vodka left out." Alice laughed. "Spencer, remember the time we had dinner with that priest who's a friend of yours? Father McLaughlin. I was dieting and wanted to order a virgin mary but I was afraid Father McLaughlin would be offended, so I asked for it by its other name, a 'bloody shame.' And when it got around to the priest, guess what he ordered."

"A virgin mary," Barbara said.

"Exactly. We broke up!"

"Alice, you're delaying everyone's order." Spencer's voice was cold.

"Oh, I'm sorry. Anyway, try one, Mother. You'll like it."

"All right, dear."

"One virgin mary," Spencer said to the waitress. "Same for you, Mr. Dalton?"

"No. I'll take a cup of coffee. Cream and sugar."

Spencer's face was impassive. "One coffee," he repeated. "Frances?"

"Double vodka on the rocks with a twist."

"Barbara?"

"Scotch and water, please."

"Mrs. Winters and I will have scotch and water, too," Spencer said. "White Label. Be sure. None of that bar scotch. You have all that?"

"Yes, sir. Three White Labels and water, one double vodka, one virgin mary and a cup of coffee."

There was an awkward pause as the girl departed. Laura turned her attention to her son-in-law. "How are the children, Spencer? I'm so sorry they couldn't come."

Alice held her breath, but Spencer, thank God, was going to play out the game.

"They're fine," he said. "They were sorry not to be here, but you know how young people are. Always a million 'unbreakable engagements.' Alice and I barely see them ourselves any more, even though we all live in the same city."

"They must be handsome," Fran said. "I've never seen them, but they must be beautiful. Do you have pictures of them?"

Barb glanced with amusement at her sister. Fran was being bitchy. She knew damned well a man like Spencer Winters would die before he'd walk around with pictures of his children in his wallet.

"No," Spencer said. "Sorry. No pictures." He turned abruptly to Sam. "I'm sure you must be enjoying your retirement, Mr. Dalton. Great to get out of the old rat race, isn't it? You're playing a lot of golf, I suppose."

"Don't play the game."

"Oh? You should take it up. Marvelous exercise."

"And where do you think I'd play?" Sam asked.

"Well, I don't know, I'm sure. I'm not that familiar with Denver, but there must be a country club."

"There's a country club all right. There are also a lot of big mansions above it in a place called Strawberry Hill. But we're not in that league. We're very simple folk, as you know. We get our fresh air in our back yard. Or once in a while we take a walk through Washington Park. It's city-owned and just a block from our house."

Alice leapt in nervously. "Washington Park! My lord, what memories that brings! Remember, Fran? We used to swim in the lake there. And we always cut through it on our way to South High. Good grief, South High School! It seems a thousand years since we went there!"

"It was," Fran said. "At least a thousand."

"I was so jealous of you two," Barbara said. "You were always going to the park with your friends and I was just an ugly little kid who wasn't allowed to tag along."

"Well, you have the last laugh," Fran said. "That eight or nine years' difference was on our side then, but it's on yours now."

Allie looked wistful. She was remembering those walks in the park with Jack Richards. Those precious young moments that led up to a nightmare. Those forever-lost days of happy innocence. "What's the park like now, Daddy? Has it changed much?"

"Yes, it's changed," Sam said. "Everything changes. It's very crowded now. Mostly full of ugly men in their underwear."

Laura explained. "Your father means it's a favorite place for runners and joggers. They also have tennis and volleyball and all kinds of things that weren't popular when you children were growing up. But it's still a pretty place, Alice. Dad and I go there sometimes when the weather's nice." She looked fondly at Sam. "We should go more often than we do, but it's hard to get your father away from his precious garden and his workshop in the basement."

"At least I know I won't get mugged there."

"Oh, Sam! The park's perfectly safe!"

"Denver's no different than other cities, Laura. Crime. Dope-users. Perverts. They're in every park in America." He shook his head. "Can we order now?"

They were halfway through their drinks and Fran desperately wanted another, but she could see that her father was anxious to eat his dinner and get away. Get home where he felt safe and at ease. God knows he wasn't at ease here. None of them was. You could cut the tension with a butter knife, she thought. What a motley crew. We have nothing in common. No more than I have with that crude little waiter I'm going to meet in an hour. But at least with him I won't have to make conversation.

Spencer looked as though he'd blundered into an episode of "All in the Family." Alice was nervous, sensing his disdain. Laura was trying too hard to be cheerful and chatty. Even Barbara seemed put off by this dreary conversation about parks and fear of crime.

"Good idea," Fran said. "Let's order. Sorry to be a party-poop, but I'm meeting a friend in an hour."

Her mother, surprised, opened her mouth to ask whom she was meeting, then closed it again. It's none of my business, Laura thought. She's a grown woman. But as Barbara had, she wondered where Frances could be going. Sam was less tactful.

"What friend?" he asked. "Who are you meeting at this time of night?"

Fran finished off the last drop of her drink. "Daddy, it's exactly seven o'clock. Hardly the witching hour! I ran into some old friends today and said I'd join them later. Any objections?"

Again, Laura answered. "Of course not, dear. Your father didn't mean to pry."

Like hell he didn't, Fran thought. He's always felt it was his privilege to know every place we went and everyone we saw. He never trusted us, the way Mother did. Maybe he was right at that. We weren't to be trusted, at least not Allie and I.

They ordered and ate quickly, forcing conversation, all as eager as Sam to be done with it. Once again, Laura felt sad. Her dreams of the "happy family gathering" were absurd. They weren't going to come together like a picture on a Christmas card. They were too far out of touch.

She worried about Frances. What on earth was she up to, this desperate-seeming, driven woman? And Alice, agitated and jumpy whenever that dreadful, condescending man spoke. Even Barbara was so private. Sweet and dear, but giving out nothing, hiding something. Sam's right, Laura thought. They're in trouble. All three of them. Each in her own way. And probably there's nothing we can do to help.

Chapter 7

Barbara sat silently in the back seat while Sam drove her and Laura home from the restaurant. She'd offered to be the "chauffeur" but her father had almost brusquely rejected her suggestion that he might not want to drive at night. She instantly realized she'd make a mistake.

"Nothing wrong with my eyesight," he'd snapped.

"I know, Daddy. I didn't mean there was. I just thought maybe you were tired."

"From what?"

"Now, Sam," Laura said, "Barbara didn't mean to hurt your feelings. She was just trying to be considerate. It has been an exhausting day."

"There wasn't anything wrong with the day. It was the dinner that was so terrible."

Laura protested. "Mine was delicious. Didn't you like your roast beef?" She looked over her shoulder. "How was yours, Barbara?"

"Just fine. It's a nice restaurant."

Sam snorted. "You know I wasn't talking about the food."

They lapsed into silence. Laura knew very well what he meant. Spencer Winters with his patronizing attitude toward Sam, his talk of country clubs and golf, his cutting remarks to Alice. And then there was Frances, who could hardly wait to escape to wherever it was she was going. Heaven help us tomorrow night,

Laura thought, when everyone gathers for the party. She could imagine how supercilious Spencer Winters would seem, how nervous Alice would act, how unpredictable Frances would be.

Nothing more was said until they entered the house. Then Laura put her hand on her husband's arm and said, "I'm sorry you didn't enjoy the evening, dear. Tomorrow will be better."

"I'm going up to bed," he said. "You coming?"

She hesitated. She couldn't go to bed just yet. Couldn't lie there unhappily contemplating the anniversary, fearful it would seem "tacky" to her own children.

"I'm really not sleepy," she said. "It's only nine o'clock. I think I'll stay down awhile."

"I'll keep you company if you like," Barbara offered. "I'm not sleepy either."

Sam started for the stairs. "Don't sit up too late, Laura. You'll be worn out tomorrow."

"I won't, darling. Goodnight."

They stood for a moment, watching him laboriously make his way upstairs. Then, simultaneously, mother and daughter looked into each other's eyes, reading each other's thoughts.

"Poor Daddy. He's so upset."

"Yes. So am I, Barbara."

"About Spencer? Don't be, Mother. That's just the way he is, I'm sure. Allie must understand him after all these years."

"It's just not Alice and Spencer. It's Frances too. Where has she gone this evening? Do you know?"

Barbara hesitated. What would Laura say if she knew her eldest daughter had raced off to go to bed with a young stranger she'd picked up the day before? She'd be out of her mind with worry if she realized what Fran had turned into. To lie now wasn't wrong; it was merciful.

"She ran into somebody she knows when we were at lunch yesterday. She's going to meet him for a drink."

"Somebody she knows? Who?"

"I'm not sure of the name. Venzetti, I think. Something like that."

Laura wrinkled her brow. "Venzetti? We don't know anybody named Venzetti. I never heard of him."

"It might be somebody she met in Italy, Mother. Now stop worrying! She's a grown woman. She knows what she's doing."

"I hope so."

"Count on it," Barbara said cheerfully. "How about a cup of tea? We used to have some of our best conversations over a cup of tea at the kitchen table. Come on. This is the first chance we've had to talk. You haven't filled me in on the local gossip. It's been almost a year. What's going on in Denver these days? You still going to Eastern Star meetings?" Barbara laughed as she steered Laura to the kitchen. "My Lord, remember when the three of us were all members of Job's Daughters? I can still see those white robes and purple sashes! Fran got to be a Princess once. It killed her she never made Queen!"

"It was a fine organization for young girls. Job is a character one can relate to, poor man, with all his suffering. The Lord tested him. Like He tests all of us, every day."

Barbara glanced at her as she put the water on to boil. "You believe in the Bible, don't you, Mother?"

Laura looked shocked. "Of course! Don't you?"

"I don't know. I don't go to church, but I guess I still believe in something. The way I figure it, Mother, if there's a God, He'll judge us by the way we live and receive us accordingly. I mean, if we do the best we can, every day, that's about all there is, don't you think? If we try not to hurt other people. If we try to be decent human beings, that's religion to me. It doesn't require going into a building one day a week. I think God—if He's there—understands. And if He isn't there, it doesn't really matter, does it?"

"Is that what you do, Barbara? Try to be decent, try not to hurt?"

"Yes. I know what I am inside, so I figure He does too."

Laura slowly stirred the tea in front of her. "Something's troubling you, isn't it? Do you want to talk about it?"

No, Barbara thought. I don't want to talk about it. Not with you. You'd never understand the kind of life I lead. You'd be disappointed in me. Your "baby" stealing another woman's husband. Your youngest "living in sin" all these years. You'd never comprehend how pure and beautiful it is. You'd still like me to be a little "Job's Daughter" believing the things I learned in that all-girl junior offshoot of the Eastern Star. You can't believe I've outgrown all that.

"Tell me about your life," Laura suddenly said with surprising passion. "Please, Barbara, let me in. I feel so shut out. So alienated from all of you. Help me. Sometimes I think I'm going out of my mind, worrying about you and your sisters. You've never been a mother. You don't know what it's like to realize that your children think you're too stupid or too provincial or too strait-laced to understand and accept and, if need be, forgive. I can endure anything except this total ignorance you've all conspired to keep me in. I sense things, Barbara, but I can't put my finger on anything. It's becoming an obsession with me. As though everything I've done is meaningless. As though I were just a bitch who produced a litter of puppies and had no idea where they went." She wiped her eyes. "I know you love me. All of you. I know you want me to be happy and protected. But this isn't the way to do it. I'm a woman. Let me share the lives of the women who are my daughters. At least, darling, let me share yours."

Barbara stared at her. Laura was right. They all thought of her as limited in understanding, in intelligence. But she wasn't. She had deep needs too. She'd been so undemanding all these years, letting them all go their own ways. What other woman would have asked so little? She's lonely, Barbara thought. Funny, I never thought of Mother as lonely, or introspective, or even unhappy.

"All right," Barbara said. "I won't speak for the others. I can't. I don't know that much about them myself. But I can tell you about me, Mother."

She told her about meeting Charles Tallent a year after she went to Washington. She described their attraction for each other, explained truthfully that at first she'd run away, refused to see him, knowing he was married. It had seemed silly and pointless. He'd said from the start that he wouldn't get a divorce, couldn't leave his own children as his own father had left him.

"I couldn't picture myself in one of those 'Back Street' situations," Barbara said. "I was twenty-six years old and worried about finding a husband. In those days I still thought it was important to be married. And the way I grew up—the way you brought me up—I felt there was something shameful about being in love with a married man. Even an unhappily married one." She gave a rueful little smile. "Of course, I knew all along I was trying to talk myself out of what I wanted to do. I loved Charles as I'd never loved any other man. I still do. I'm happy, Mother. Much happier than most of the married women I know."

Laura looked pensive. "Aren't you lonely?"

"Sometimes. Mostly on holidays when Charles has to be with his children. But by and large, no. I'm not lonely. I see him nearly every day, no matter how briefly. And the knowledge of him, of his love for me, warms me when he's away. He is my lover and my friend, my comfort and support. In every way, except legally, he is my husband." She paused. "Are you shocked, darling? Have I made you unhappy?"

Laura shook her head. "Neither. Of course I wish you were married, because to me that has always meant a woman is safe and secure. And I can't pretend to be enlightened enough to condone adultery. I'm the product of another time, as well as another world. But, Barbara, I have sense enough to know that each of us has to find his own way. If this is yours, then I pray it never brings you pain. My only hope is that you won't regret not having a husband and children of your own. My only fear is that circumstances might take your Charles from you."

"Circumstances could, in any case," Barbara said, "even if I were married. Husbands die. Or leave home. Or they're hell to live with. I wonder how many married women could say, after thirteen years, that they are blindly, ecstatically in love? I can say that, Mother. So can he. He's a wonderful man. I wish you two could meet. He gives me everything."

"Except public recognition. Isn't that important?"

"Yes. I won't lie. I'd like that. I'd like to be seen with him. To show I'm loved. Keeping this kind of precious secret is hardest of all. I so want the world to know that I am the center of Charles Tallent's life and he of mine. But that's a small price to pay for the other things, the tender things, the kind of meeting of soul and spirit that most couples never have."

Laura nodded. "I can understand that. But what of the practical side, Barbara? What happens when you're old? What if something happens to him?"

"When I'm old I'll probably be alone, like ten million widows. Marriage is no guarantee against that kind of loneliness. We mostly outlive men in any case and end up alone. And if you mean money, Charles has taken care of that. He's already set up a trust fund in my name that will take care of me. Not even Andrea can touch that."

"Andrea? That's his wife? Does she know about you?"

"Yes."

"Poor woman. What she must feel, knowing her husband cares for someone else."

"I suppose. I try not to think about that. Charles is very good to her. Neither of us would ever publicly embarrass her or their children. She seems to handle it very well. She's civilized about leading her own life."

For the first time, Laura looked disapproving. "You don't believe that. You couldn't. I don't condemn your love, Barbara, but I won't accept your hypocrisy. In your heart you know you're hurting another person. That can't be a very comfortable feeling, knowing you're depriving a woman and her children of a man's total devotion."

"I'm not depriving them! If it weren't me, it would be someone else! Charles doesn't love Andrea. I didn't destroy their marriage. That happened long before we met."

"Oh? Then this passion Charles feels for you might have gone to anyone. Is it possible you're really saying he hates his marriage more than he loves you?"

"No! That's not what I'm saying! You're twisting things, Mother. I never should have told you. You don't understand. You couldn't, living happily with one man for fifty years."

"What makes you think I've been so happy? There've been bad times for your father and me too, but we're not such romantics that either of us went flying off to find someone else to build up our egos!"

Barbara was horrified. "Is that what you think Charles is doing? Using me to build up his ego? That's ridiculous! If that's all it was, we wouldn't have lasted all these years."

"Please, darling, don't misunderstand. I'm not accusing Charles of anything. Or you. I know you must love each other or this couldn't go on. Unless," Laura said carefully, "it's a very easy, self-protective thing for both of you."

"What do you mean? Mother, you're not going to say that old stuff about a man 'having his cake and eating it, too'!"

"*You* said it, Barbara. Not I. But no, I was thinking more of you. Perhaps you're really afraid of marriage. Some women are, you know. Afraid of the responsibility, afraid of the hurt. Afraid to make a life-long commitment. Are you, my dear?"

Barbara stared at her. Was this the naïve little seventy-year-old lady who thought about nothing but her husband and home and her "good works"? Was this the unsophisticated matron she'd always assumed Laura to be? If she doesn't know us, Barb thought, we know her less. Instinctively, Laura had reached in and pulled out the very core of her daughter's fears. One she hadn't admitted to herself for many, many years.

"Isn't there anyone you ever wanted to marry?" Laura went on. "Never a man at any time in your life whose name you wanted to carry? Whose children you wanted to bear?"

Barbara gave an embarrassed little laugh. "If I told you, you'd think I was stark raving mad."

"Tell me."

"The only man I ever idolized was Jack Richards. Are you ready for that, Mother? I was nine years old when he got Allie in trouble. I worshiped him. A kid, I was. But I've never forgotten him." She paused. "Now you know that's crazy! What does a little girl know about such things? She has a crush on her big sister's beau. A crush she remembers for thirty years! I remember being so jealous of Allie when she was dating Jack, and deciding even then that if I couldn't find someone like him, I'd never get married at all. I'll never forget the night all of you had the pow-wow about their future. I didn't understand everything that was going on, but I knew enough to see that one way or another everybody was miserable because the two of them weren't going to get married." She stopped. And then she said slowly, "Maybe I turned off marriage at that very moment. Maybe I saw it as some kind of necessity, rather than joy. Something a person was *expected* to do. I've always resented everything that was expected of me. Do you suppose it was because I was so sorry for two people I loved that I made up my mind never to be hurt as they were?" She tried to smile. "I probably should be with a shrink. Listen to me! Acting as though something that happened when I was a kid could have changed my outlook on life!"

"Perhaps it did," Laura said. "I don't understand such things. But, Barbara, there must be some reason you haven't married. Lord knows you've had chances. Instead, you've gotten mixed up with someone you can't possibly marry. Is that why you're satisfied with your present arrangement? Because you know Charles can't possibly make you his wife?"

Barbara grew stubborn. "Marriage is not impossible for us. Something could happen."

Laura gently touched her daughter's hand. "What are you saying? Are you wishing Mrs. Tallent dead?"

"No! What a horrible thing to say! Of course I don't wish her dead! I don't wish anyone dead! My God, Mother, what do you think I am?"

The older woman remained silent. Do I really wish that? Barbara wondered, appalled by the idea. No. I couldn't. But if Charles will never get a divorce, that is the only answer, isn't it? Wrong. Not the only answer. The answer is that I don't really want to marry him. I adore him, but I don't want to be his wife. I don't want to be anybody's wife. Why did I suddenly spout all that nonsense about Jack Richards and a schoolgirl crush? I barely remember him. I do remember thinking he and Allie would get married and they didn't. Just as I thought Buzz Paige and Fran would get married. But *they* didn't. At least not to each other. Did all that make me stop believing in anything? Did it make me feel that nothing is to be counted on? That vows are a joke? Have I always felt that faithfulness is a myth, whether it's to an ideal or another person? Did my sisters' lives going so wrong somehow affect me even in those early years?

Her head began to ache. It was all so unexpectedly distressing, this probing into influences that may or may not have made her choose the life she had. She hated remembering how she'd felt as a child. How she'd despised her parents for sending Allie away. How she'd been angry with Fran for abandoning a shocked and grief-stricken Buzz Paige. Yet, young as she'd been, she'd also sensed the weakness in both Jack Richards and Buzz. Why hadn't they fought for what they said they wanted? Why hadn't one shouldered his responsibilities and the other been man enough to stop a headstrong young woman from running out on him?

The minutes ticked by. I've no respect for any of them, Barbara realized. Not for my sisters or the "nice boys" I thought they'd marry. Not even for Mother and Daddy. Probably I have no respect for myself. Maybe I'm as shallow as they. Too shallow to pledge myself. "An easy, self-protective thing," Laura had called her long affair with Charles Tallent. Perhaps she was right. I don't want to think about it any more. I wish I'd never had this conversation. She pretended to yawn.

"I'm tired. I think I'll turn in. How about you?"

"Barbara, stop running away." Laura's voice was gentle.

Anger flared. "Running away! How can you say that to me? I'm the only one who stayed! Stayed until I was twenty-five years old, right in this house with you and Daddy! I was the 'dutiful daughter,' trying to be the child you wanted. Trying not to disappoint you. Trying to make up for the hurt that Fran and Allie caused. I stayed and watched my friends get married, watched you being apologetic that I hadn't, watched my life slipping slowly into a dull, dreary spinsterhood that was all this place had to offer me! I stayed until a new career and a new life opened up for me. My God, Mother, I'm the only one who's even bothered to come home regularly!"

"I know all that," Laura said. "I know how hard it was for you, how duty-bound you felt to make up to us for what your sisters never gave. I didn't begrudge you your freedom when you found a way to have it. I still don't. I didn't mean running away in the literal sense, darling. Like upstairs or back to Washington. I mean running away from your fears, whatever they are. Stop avoiding your duty to yourself. You're very special, Barbara. Too special to go on living the make-believe life you've described to me."

"What do you suggest?" Barbara asked sarcastically. "That I demand Charles get a divorce and marry me? Or should I dump him and go out looking for somebody who'll make me 'respectable'? I'm forty years old, Mother. Isn't it a little late for the vine-covered cottage and the patter of tiny feet?"

"It's never too late."

"Oh, come on!"

"Don't pretend to be cynical, dearest. You're a romantic at heart. The dream world you're into proves that. It's unreal, unnatural for a woman like you to settle for second place. Unless you're afraid of first place."

"You don't understand. You don't have to *be* married to *feel* married."

"Perhaps not. I'm sorry, Barb. I shouldn't interfere in your life.

You don't trust anyone to do that." Laura rose. "You're right. It's time to turn in." She paused at the kitchen door. "But I'm glad we talked. Even if we don't see things the same way, I'm glad we talked."

In the middle of Cary's passionate lovemaking, Fran suddenly thought, "Godammit, I don't have a house key! I'll have to wake up the whole damned family when I go home."

It amused her to think that at the height of the sex act her mind would turn to something so routine. Amused and saddened her. She felt nothing for this young animal who was just another body on hers. What am I doing here in this shabby little room with a child I know nothing about? What am I hoping to find? Why do I pretend ecstasy and feel no satisfaction? It's sordid and stupid and terribly, terribly routine. All of them are. All these faceless, expert young men who think they're doing me a favor by going to bed with me. But they're not as stupid and sordid as I, who thinks one day the magic will return. The magic hasn't existed since I was a girl. It won't come again. All I can do is pretend and get it over with.

She moaned and gasped and cried out, play-acting as she'd done so often. And then she and Cary lay still.

"You're wonderful," he said. "Fantastic."

"So are you. I've never known anyone so exciting."

"Really?"

Ah, the infallible ego. Fran smiled. "*Really.*"

"When will I see you again?"

Never, she said silently. You'll never see or hear of me again. I'm never coming back to this dingy one-room apartment with the rumpled, drip-dry bedsheets and cheap Picasso prints on the wall. You're not the answer, dear Mr. Venzetti. But don't be upset. There is no answer.

"Very soon," Fran lied in answer to his question. "I'll call you."

"Stay in Denver awhile. Please." She'd told him she was here only for a week. "Don't go away. I've never known anyone like you."

She slipped out of bed and began to dress. "Stay right there in bed," she said. "You look beautiful."

"How can I reach you?"

"You can't, my darling. But don't worry. I'll reach you."

"Promise?"

She came to the bed and kissed him lightly. "You have my word of honor."

She drove hesitatingly through the dark streets, not absolutely certain of her way back, annoyed that she'd forgotten to get a key. Careless. She hoped her parents wouldn't hear the doorbell and that Barb would let her in. That way there'd be no questions.

Funny, but she did remember the way home. She made only one wrong turn, and as she parked the car in front of the house it seemed only yesterday when she'd been sneaking in, hoping Mother and Daddy didn't hear. She could see the darkened windows of her own room, but next to it Barbara's light was on. Two in the morning. What was she doing still awake? Good. She'd be most likely to hear a discreet buzz at the door.

And then she remembered something else. She and Allie had often used Barb as an accomplice when they wanted to get in unnoticed. The Daltons didn't believe in latchkeys for fifteen- and sixteen-year-old girls. They wanted to know the time of their comings and goings. So sometimes she or Allie would throw pebbles at Barbara's window late at night and the kid would tiptoe down and let them in. She always was scolded for it, as they were, but it made Barb feel "grown-up," being part of the conspiracy. Maybe it would still work.

She picked up three or four little pebbles and aimed them at the lighted window. I feel like a jackass, she thought. Damned near fifty years old and standing in the yard pegging rocks at my sister's window! But she was relieved when Barb stuck her head out and waved. In a few seconds the front door quietly opened. Fran started to giggle.

"My God, it still works!"

"Hush! You want to wake everybody up?"

"Barb, you remembered." They spoke in whispers. "Thanks, baby."

"You're welcome, you bloody fool. Have a good time?"

"I got what I went for."

Barbara wanted to put her arms around her and comfort her. What a lost soul she was. If Mother thinks I'm running from reality, what would she think of Fran? She probably has a good idea without actually knowing.

"Go on up to bed, Fran. It's late."

"Right. Tomorrow's the big day. Whoopee." The voice was tired, disenchanted. "Tomorrow's the golden day." She stared listlessly at her sister. "It's all working out just swell, isn't it? We're all so thrilled to be here."

Barb pushed her toward the stairs. "Shut up," she said affectionately, "and get some rest. You look as though you need it."

Spencer slammed the door of their room.

"Christ! What a tacky two hours that was!"

Allie unfastened her pearls. "They enjoyed it, Spencer. You were nice to do it."

"Enjoyed it! Like hell they did! No more than I did. Not that I give a damn about them. What a family! Is your father always so defensive about his impoverished state?"

"He isn't impoverished. He's . . . he's middle America. He doesn't belong to country clubs and play golf and you know it. Why did you have to act so hoity-toity?"

Spencer laughed mirthlessly. "Hoity-toity? My God, Alice, you've even reverted to talking like them. That sounds like something your saintly mother would say! And your dear, 'social' sister Frances! A slut if I've ever seen one!"

"Spencer, stop it! I won't have you speak of them that way!" She was angry and knew she shouldn't be. It was fatal to cross Spencer, who retaliated with physical force. I mustn't let him get into a rage, she thought. He'd love to hit me. He'd like to take out his fury about this evening on me. I can't have that. I can't show up at the party tomorrow with a black eye or a bruised throat. She deliberately calmed down, hoping he would. "It's once in a lifetime, dear," Alice said. "You were very patient and I could tell they were impressed. As they should be. You're the kind of successful, sophisticated man my parents only read about."

He seemed slightly mollified. How easy it was if she could only be such an actress all the time. Sometimes the injustice welled up so strongly inside her that she fought back, knowing she couldn't win, preferring the black-and-blue marks to the demeaning acceptance of his hatred. But not tonight. Tonight, no matter what he said, she'd not be goaded into what he wanted: a battering whose evidence might be hard to conceal and impossible to explain.

She undressed and climbed into the king-sized bed. Why

hadn't she insisted on a room with twin beds? She'd been so glad to get any hotel accommodations at all that she hadn't dared make special requests. It was years since they'd slept in the same bed. She lay as far as she could on one side, hoping to give him plenty of room, praying he wouldn't start in on her again for this "inconvenience."

Fortunately, he didn't. He looked at the bed but said nothing, simply climbing into his side and turning his back to her. Allie almost literally held her breath as she said, "Goodnight."

There was no reply.

Chapter 8

He couldn't let himself believe it. He shouldn't. It probably was just another false lead, a slim clue going nowhere, like the dozens of others he'd tracked down to no avail in the years he'd been searching for his mother. But something told him at long last this was it. He didn't know why he felt so sure it was she—this "prominent hostess" described in the gossip column of the Boston *Globe*.

John Peck read it for the third time.

"That perennially inventive hostess, Mrs. Spencer Victor (Alice) Winters, did it again when she arranged one of the most imaginative dinner parties of the year to honor J. B. Thompson's fiftieth year as head of Thompson, Wallingford and McClean. (Insiders say it soon will be Thompson, Wallingford, McClean and Winters, but the expected announcement was not made at the 'purely social' gathering.) When they went in to dine on caviar and quail, Mrs. Winters' eighteen hand-picked guests found her Beacon Hill dining room transformed into a posh 'courtroom' complete with a 'judge's bench' for J.B. and Mrs. Thompson and 'defense table' for the Wallingfords and McCleans. Other guests occupied the 'jury box,' where they dined on special tables set with Waterford and Vermeil. Waiters were dressed as bailiffs and a 'court stenographer' recorded the tributes to one of Boston's most distinguished attorneys. Guests carried away small silver gavels as souvenirs and Mr. Thompson was presented with a gold humidor, suitably engraved.

"Mr. and Mrs. Winters leave this week for Denver to attend still another fiftieth anniversary, that of her parents, Mr. and Mrs. Samuel Dalton, who're marking half a century of marriage. Also, coming to the Colorado celebration will be Alice's sisters, Madame Frances Dalton-Déspres of Paris and Miss Barbara Dalton of Washington, D.C."

It was the last paragraph that intensely interested John. He'd known since he was ten that Wilbur and Sarah Peck had adopted him. Loving people, much older than his friends' parents, they'd carefully explained he was "special," that they'd chosen him to be their little boy, that he was more "wanted" than many children. He'd accepted this as the compliment it was meant to be, and even when unwittingly cruel playmates tried to torment him about not having "real parents," Johnny just smiled and said, "Your folks got you by accident. Mine went looking for me." He hadn't been sure exactly what that meant, but he knew it was good. Mother and Dad said so. He never thought of them as anything but his parents until he reached his late teens and full awareness and insatiable curiosity set in. Then he asked, time and again, who his real parents were, but Sarah and Wilbur stubbornly refused to give him that information.

Sarah had, in fact, seemed wounded that John even thought about the people who'd conceived him. She pretended not to know anything about them. All she'd say was that John had come to them soon after he'd been born, in Boston where the Pecks also lived.

"Was I born in a hospital?"

Yes, Sarah reluctantly admitted. Massachusetts General on November 10, 1946. But she insisted that was *all* they knew.

"Johnny, why do you care? Haven't your father and I been good parents to you? Haven't we loved you? Why do you want to find people who cared so little that they gave you away?"

He picked up quickly on that. "You *do* know who my real parents are. At least, you know they voluntarily put me up for adoption. I mean, I wasn't orphaned, or something like that."

Sarah bit her lip. She hadn't meant to reveal even that. She was hurt and angry. "All right, son. Your mother didn't want you. Isn't that reason enough for you not to think about her? We've been your family for eighteen years. Your mother is a stranger.

How could you feel anything but resentment for a woman who could part with her own flesh and blood?"

He'd fallen silent. He didn't want to hurt Sarah. He loved her and Wilbur. But there was this passion to know about himself. What kind of people did he come from? Good stock or bad? What if there were some awful hereditary problem, physical or mental, he might pass on to his own children when he married and had a family? But most of all, what could they be like, these people who were his natural parents? Didn't they ever wonder what happened to him?

He longed to know, yet to pursue it seemed disloyal to the pair he thought of as Mother and Father. Forget it, he told himself bitterly. You weren't wanted. You probably still wouldn't be, even if you found them. Yet he couldn't shake this feeling of rootlessness, this desire to know. But without anything to go on, without even a name, there was nowhere to start. Sarah had spoken only of his mother. *She* didn't want him. *She*'d given him away. I'm probably illegitimate, Johnny reasoned. I probably was born out of wedlock and disposed of out of shame. It made him sick to think about it. Sarah was right. His loyalty was to those who took him in and loved him and gave him everything within their moderate means. At great sacrifice, they'd sent him to college, bought him a car, done everything for his happiness. And he wanted to repay them by looking for the mother who'd turned him away.

He now thought only in terms of his mother. Not his father. Probably because he was convinced that the woman who bore him had no husband. Otherwise, why would Sarah always say "she" and not "they"?

He tried once to talk to Wilbur about his curiosity, hoping to appeal to him, man to man. But the conversation produced no more concrete evidence than Sarah had given. Wilbur did not seem to share his wife's strong feeling of reproach, but he respected her wishes and said so.

"Johnny, your mother is deeply hurt by the way you feel. She thinks of you as her own. We both do. We tried for twenty years to have a family before we got you. Leave it alone, boy. What good would it do to stir up trouble after so many happy years?"

"But you know who my real mother is."

Wilbur's lips had tightened. "I didn't say that." He'd suddenly turned angry. "Dammit, why are you so selfish? Do you want to break your mother's heart? Can't you understand how emotional she is about all this? Don't bring it up again! We have nothing to tell you."

"All right, Dad," he'd said. And he'd done nothing more about it, though the wondering was always in his mind. He'd read that adoption records were sealed by law; that they could be opened only after a long, humiliating and expensive court hearing, and maybe not even then. Hospital records were impounded and birth certificates sealed to "protect" all the parties involved. He had no information, even if he were determined to instigate a search for his beginnings. Not even his mother's first name, much less her last.

And then on a Saturday morning when Johnny was twenty-one, the elderly Pecks climbed routinely into their car to go to the supermarket and do the weekend shopping. They never got there. A reckless young man in a souped-up hot rod sped through a stop sign and plowed into their old sedan. The boy came out with barely a scratch, but Wilbur and Sarah were dead on arrival at the hospital. They left everything to Johnny. The house, the insurance, a few stocks and bonds in the safe deposit box. And in the same box they left him his first clue to his past: their copy of his adoption decree.

For the first time he knew his mother's name was Alice Dalton. And his father was "unknown."

In the weeks of grief mixed with disbelief that followed, he barely realized the significance of what he now held. And when he did, he didn't know what to do with his information. Alice probably had another name by now. She could well live somewhere other than Boston, if, indeed, she were still alive. He looked up "Daltons" in the Boston telephone directory and called every one. None had ever heard of an Alice. The hospital informed him that everything he wanted to know was on microfilm which, because he was adopted, he was not allowed to see. He attended a meeting of the Adoptees' Liberty Movement Association, an organization dedicated to helping adoptees find their parents, and though he was strangely comforted to learn that there were about five million adoptees in this country, and probably anywhere from two to five thousand children looking for their parents, he came up empty in terms of his own problem.

In the next six years he did everything he could think of to find his mother. He ran "blind ads" in the "personal columns" of newspapers in major cities asking for information as to the whereabouts of Alice Dalton. Several "Alice Daltons" responded, but they were never the right ones. He became even more obsessed with his search when, at twenty-five, he met Carol and fell in love with her. For two years they "dated," but Johnny was reluctant to marry, fearful of the unknown, for himself and her and the children they wanted. At last, Carol put her foot down.

"I've had enough of this, John Peck! You're not the only person in the world who doesn't know who his parents are! Good Lord, if there were some terrible reason you shouldn't marry, don't you think the Pecks would have told you? They might not have wanted you to find your own people, but they'd have warned you about something awful! They loved you too much *not* to! I think you just don't want to marry *me*. Okay. Why don't we call it off?"

It shook him. She probably was right. Mother and Dad would have said something to him if there'd been anything to say. And he wouldn't lose the third woman he cared so much about. In his mind, Carol was the third. His real mother was the first; Sarah was the second. And he'd lost both of them.

They were married in 1973 and Johnny reluctantly stopped his search. For the next three years, his life with Carol was happy. A commercial artist, she continued to work at free-lance advertising while he progressed in his career in banking. He was a branch manager now and slated for better things. When he got his next promotion, they agreed, it would be time to start a family. He was thirty and Carol twenty-eight. They didn't want to wait much longer.

"You've gotten over being afraid of our having children, haven't you, darling?"

"Yes. I know you're right about my background. There can't be anything terrible. And I love kids. Maybe more than most men, because I know how important it is to want them and make them feel secure. Not that I was an unhappy child. Don't misunderstand me. I had the best parents in the world. But I guess I always felt separate. Different. Like some part of me was incomplete." He'd tipped the pretty young face up to look into his. "You're a beautiful lady, Carol Peck. You'll have sensational kids."

"And you won't worry about anything?"

"Only the normal things. Will they kill themselves on their roller skates or break their necks on the playground swings. Just the everyday, parental fears."

He believed it true. He thought he had gotten over this hopeless, infantile yearning. And then he read her name in the Boston paper. Alice Winters, *nee* Alice Dalton. He showed the item to Carol.

"Do you think it could possibly be my mother?"

Carol was wide-eyed. "Mrs. Spencer Winters? You must be kidding! They're high society, darling."

"What does that prove?"

"Well, I mean, a woman like that . . . with her background and all . . . that is, I doubt that she'd . . ."

"Have a baby and give it up for adoption? Why not? We don't know whether she was born into society or married into it, and what difference does that make anyway? 'Nice girls' got into trouble thirty years ago, just as they do today. Of course, I don't know how old this Alice Dalton is, but she's bound to be about right. She's going to her parents' fiftieth wedding anniversary. So she could be in her late forties. Which means she could have had me when she was a teen-ager."

She tried to calm him. "Darling, don't get your hopes up. It says she's from Denver. You were born here."

"So what? Maybe she grew up here."

"Well, I don't know. What would she be doing in Boston if she was just a teen-ager?"

"I don't know, sweetheart. Something in my bones tells me she's the one." He stopped. "But now that I think I know, what do I do about it? Can I just call Mrs. Spencer Winters and announce that I think I'm her son? Hardly. It might not be so. Or Spencer Winters might not know about me. Or," Johnny said slowly, "even if it's true, she might not want to see me. All these years. She's never tried to find me."

Carol was troubled. Much as she knew Johnny wanted answers, she wished this had not happened. He'd just seemed to be settling down, putting the search out of his mind, and now he had his hopes up again. It was a long shot that this very social Alice Winters was his mother. And if it turned out to be true and she didn't want to see him, that would be a rejection too terrible for him to bear.

"Hey," she said lightly, "take it easy. Don't go jumping to all kinds of conclusions until we know more. You've heard of other Alice Daltons and they never matched the vital statistics. Let's go slowly, sweetheart, before we make any moves." She wrinkled her brow. "Spencer Winters. I know that name from the papers, but there's something else." She clapped her hand to her forehead. "Of course! My God! I know. Janice Winters!"

"Who's Janice Winters?"

"She's the daughter! And she's a copywriter at one of the agencies I do work for. Her boyfriend's the art director. I remember hearing that her father's a big-shot lawyer, but I didn't realize he was *the* Spencer Winters. Sure. He has to be. She couldn't dress so well unless she was loaded."

"Do you know her?"

"No. Not really. I've just been introduced to her. But I can double-check with Clint Darby. That's her fella. If Alice Dalton Winters is her mother, maybe we can find out something about you before we get into this with both feet."

Johnny shook his head. "Honey, I know you're persuasive, but I really doubt that Clint Darby would tell you about this, even if he knows anything. In fact, I'd be surprised if Janice Winters has any information. It's not the kind of thing women tell their children."

"Well, at least it's a lead." Carol was defensive. "It's a helluva lot better than going up to Beacon Hill and ringing the doorbell and identifying yourself as the baby she gave away. If she *did*. If you *are*. Oh, damn, Johnny, do you really think this could be it?"

"Yes, I do. I just feel it. And you know something else? I'm scared to death. I've wanted this so long, and now I'm almost sorry the search might be over. God, Carol, I couldn't stand it if my mother didn't want to see me!"

"I know. But you have to find out, don't you?"

Johnny nodded.

"All right. Don't do anything rash for a few days. There's nothing you can do anyhow. She's going to Denver. Let me nose around a little, okay?"

"Sure."

"Listen, are you positive you want to belong to a woman who turns her dining room into a courtroom? Sounds pretty contrived to me." She was laughing at him now, trying to tease him out of his fears. "I can't imagine any mother of yours going in for such obvious apple-polishing with the boss!"

He smiled. "You're one step ahead of me. I can't imagine any mother of mine *period!* I've tried for years. I have no mental picture of her." Johnny looked troubled. "The only face I can see is Sarah's. That lady was a good mother to me, and if she didn't want me to know about the real one, she must have had a good reason. Maybe I'm not meant to know. Maybe I'm wrong to tempt fate."

Carol yearned to encourage this thinking, to tell him he should forget it all, in deference to Sarah's wishes. But she couldn't. A child had a right to know about his parents. No matter what he found out.

In a way, she was glad this had come up right now. There was something else Johnny didn't know, something she'd been waiting for the right moment to tell him. She was pregnant. It was an accident, ahead of their "schedule," but she'd been happy when she found out last week. There was no need for them to wait for Johnny's next raise. They could manage nicely. She could work right up to the last minute. She'd planned to tell him the good news the very day he read about Alice Winters. Now she decided to wait a little. If he had a happy reunion with his mother, her announcement would only add to his joy. But if it was a false alarm or turned out badly, at least he'd have the compensation of discovering he was going to be a father.

Everything was timing, Carol thought. There must be a reason for Johnny to be "reborn" just at the time he was going to learn about his own child.

She felt hopeful, optimistic, realizing that she, too, believed her husband had accidentally found his mother. She had to help him get at the truth. Maybe he was right that Janice Winters wouldn't know anything useful, but she was the only key. When she saw Clint Darby tomorrow she'd ask him to come to dinner and bring

Janice. He wouldn't find that unusual. He'd heard Carol speak of her husband, and said they "must all get together sometime." Well, this was the time, unless Janice had gone to her grandparents' anniversary party too. But that seemed unlikely. If the Winters' daughter had been part of the Denver trip, the paper probably would have said so.

Now all she had to do was make Johnny hold still until they knew a little more.

Chapter 9

Laura's silence next morning was more telling than any questions she might have asked. She'd been awake when Fran came in at two in the morning, heard Barbara go down and let her in. She was angry with both of them.

Barbara appeared while her parents were still at the kitchen table. She was full of cheer.

"Happy Anniversary! Well, it's finally here! The big day." She kissed both of them. "Congratulations, darlings!"

Laura managed to smile. There was no reason for her to be annoyed with her youngest. It was Fran who was so worrisome. Remembering last evening's conversation with Barbara, her mother still felt unhappy about what she'd learned. But she shouldn't feel angry because Barbara had conspired with her sister to keep things from their parents. That's the way it always had been. Barb would do anything to please the two older girls.

"Thank you, dear," Laura said, "though I don't know why people should be congratulated simply for living together so long."

Sam's eyes twinkled. "You don't? I think they should get the Croix de Guerre with orange blossom clusters. And maybe a purple heart for surviving the battle." He was in a good mood. Barbara always put him in a good mood.

"Some battle!" Barbara teased. "A few skirmishes maybe, but no big conflicts that I know of. You're a lucky pair."

"I know that," her father said. "I chose well."

Laura looked at him affectionately. "*We* chose well," she corrected.

Sam patted her hand. He was not one for public displays of affection. Never had been. The few quiet words were as close as Barbara had ever heard him come to expressing love for his wife. What do they say to each other in private? It was hard to think of Sam as a passionate man or Laura as an ecstatic woman. She supposed one always felt that way about one's parents; as though they had no private lives, no secret comings-together, no moments of abandon when they were simply a man and a woman filled with desire. What had they been like when they were young and lusty? Children never thought of that. They must have been happy and unhappy too. They must have had moments of anger and disappointment about things that did not involve the daughters. How selfish children are! We think our parents exist only for us. We rarely think of them as individuals. I hate their getting old, Barbara thought fiercely. I can't bear to think of losing them.

"Where's your sister?" Sam asked.

"Still sleeping, I guess. You know Fran always hated getting up early, Daddy."

Laura flashed a look at her. Yes, the loyalty persisted. Barbara didn't know her mother had heard the whisperings in the night. Where had Frances been until all hours? I wonder if I dare ask. She wished Frances would confide in her as Barbara finally had. She wished Alice would too. Small chance in either case. Frances had been gone too long and too far. And despite her gentle ways, Laura felt that Alice still harbored a terrible resentment toward her and Sam for what they'd done so long ago. We were wrong, Laura thought again. We were wrong to have handled it as we did. We were wrong the way we handled all of them.

Enough of this. There was too much to be done before the party tonight. Spilled milk, Laura thought. No use weeping over it now.

"Barbara, would you mind going out and getting Aunt Mamie and Uncle Fred at the airport? They arrive at noon."

"Glad to. Shall I wear a sign so they'll recognize me? I'm not sure I'll know them. I don't think I've seen them in twenty years."

"They'll recognize you," Sam said. "You haven't changed."

"Why, Daddy, what a compliment! It's a terrible lie, of course, but I love you for it."

"It's no lie. You're still my little girl."

She blew him a kiss. "Maybe Fran will go with me. What else can we do for you, Mother? The cake should arrive from Child's early this afternoon. Wait till you see it! It's a Weight-Watcher's nightmare! About four million calories, give or take a million or two."

"Poor Dorothy Paige," Laura said. "Her brownies won't stand a chance."

"What's she like? I've never met her."

"Very nice."

"Oh, help! Deliver me from that dubious compliment! You mean she's dull. Is Buzz dull too? I remember him as such a hero."

Sam rose from the table. "You ladies will excuse me, please, but I have more important things to do than discuss the Paiges. You go on with your woman talk. I hear my garden calling. Dratted leaves are falling all over the place. Got to get them raked up before company comes."

They looked after him with amusement as he left the kitchen.

"Your father never could stand gossip," Laura said.

"Gossip? You mean what he calls 'woman talk'?"

Laura's eyes twinkled. It was un-Christian of her, she supposed, but she did enjoy a good tidbit now and then. "He's sure I'm going to tell you about the Paiges. They separated a couple of years back. The talk was that Bernard had taken up with some woman over on Bonnie Brae Boulevard. A rich widow who bought a car from him. Personally, I never put much stock in the whole story, but apparently Dorothy Paige was convinced he was having an affair with her. Anyway, Bernard moved out for a few months and Dorothy went into seclusion. They say she had a nervous breakdown and still sees a psychiatrist. She's always been a very high-strung girl. On the outside she seems calm as a millpond, but people who know her well say she's never been too stable. And she's insanely jealous." Laura hesitated. "I'm not sure I should have invited them tonight. She once told me she knew Buzz had married her on the rebound from Frances. Of course, I assured her that was nonsense."

"Is it?"

"Well, nobody would know that but Buzz, would they? But I doubt it. Dorothy was always a pretty little thing. She's given him three nice children, and personally I've never known her to be irrational. Anyway, I couldn't leave them out of the party. We see them often, mostly at church, and they'd have been hurt if they weren't asked. My Lord, Barbara, that high school romance of his with Frances is ancient history! It would be ridiculous to think Dorothy would be upset by her husband seeing one of his old girlfriends."

"How did they get back together? After the widow, I mean."

"I'm not sure. I guess Dorothy came to her senses. Like I said, I never felt we knew the whole story. They certainly seem happy enough now." Laura laughed. "I don't know what makes me go off on these flights of fancy! Imagine worrying that Buzz would still care about a girl he hasn't seen in thirty years. The last few days I've really been acting crazy." She lowered her voice. "You know, I even thought of asking the Richardses. Jack and his parents. It seemed like the moment to make things up, to let bygones be bygones. Of course I didn't. Your father would never hear of it."

Barbara stared at her. "Mother, you didn't! You didn't even *think* of asking Jack Richards! I don't believe it! Allie would die!"

"I know. It was a foolish notion. But it seemed kind of like Buzz and Frances. It was all so long ago. Oh, I quickly discarded the idea, of course. The thing with Jack was much more serious. But isn't it terrible, Barbara? Think of it. We live only a few blocks from the Richardses and we haven't spoken in thirty years. We didn't even acknowledge the death of Jack's wife when we heard about it. That was wrong, I think. I told Sam so. In times of sorrow, old feuds don't matter any more. Poor Jack. He was no more to blame than Alice for what happened. They were so young, Barbara. Do you remember?"

"Yes, I remember."

"It was a heartbreaking time, but people weren't so broadminded in those days. We did the only thing we could. It was the only decent thing. For everybody involved." She sounded as though she was begging for reassurance, and Barbara's sympathy went out to her.

"I'm sure it was, Mother. And Alice has long since forgiven you for it."

"Has she? I wonder. I wonder if I could forgive anybody who made me give up my baby."

"What about Jack? You said his wife died. Whom did he marry and what happened?"

"She passed on seven or eight months ago. The beginning of this year, right after you went home from your last visit. She had cancer, poor woman. I never knew her, of course, but I heard she was lovely. And so young. Only forty-five."

"Did they have children?"

"No. I heard she couldn't. But they say Jack adored her. He's done very well, by the way. Has a big insurance agency here. They say he was grief-stricken about his wife. Sold their house and took an apartment out in Stoneybrook. One of those new condominiums."

Barbara smiled. "For somebody who doesn't keep in touch, you sure keep in touch."

"Everybody who grew up in Denver knows everybody else. I hear lots of things indirectly. Of course I never mention anything about Jack to your father. He's never spoken the name Richards since the day Allie went to Boston. Barbara, do you think Alice is all right? Has she ever talked to you about . . . about anything?"

"We don't keep in touch as we should, Mother. I'm not sure why."

"Your father and I have a feeling she's not happy with Spencer."

Barbara tried to speak lightly. "Well, he's not exactly Mr. Warmth, I'll admit, but I'm sure she's content. Which reminds me, have you heard from her this morning?"

"No. I expect she'll call soon."

There was a pause before Laura said, "I wish you girls *would* stay more in touch. Particularly you and Alice. You live so close. Why don't you?"

"I don't know, Mother. It's just that our lives have taken such different paths."

"Does she know about your Mr. Tallent?"

Barbara smiled at the quaint phrasing. "No. Not that I'm aware of. Not many people know."

"Is that why you've cut yourself off from her? Are you ashamed, Barbara?"

"Of course not! Really, Mother! How did this whole conversation get back to me? Allie hasn't made any more effort to bring me into her life than I have to include her in mine! Why do you blame our lack of contact on me?"

"Don't get angry. I'm sorry. It's just unnatural that sisters don't see each other."

"There's nothing unnatural about it," Barb said more calmly. "We're three separate people who happen to be related. We're grown-ups with lives of our own. We have very little in common these days. If you're really sensible about it, there's no more reason for us to stay in touch than for me to try to sustain a friendship with some friend I grew up with here. We're an accident of birth, Mother, that's all. It doesn't mean we have to be buddies."

"I suppose not. I suppose your generation takes a different view of things. More realistic, probably, but still hard for me to understand." Laura began to clear the table. "My heavens, we've wasted half the morning again, just sitting around talking!"

Barbara felt a sudden surge of compassion. "It hasn't been wasted as far as I'm concerned. I think I've come to know you better in the past two days than I have in forty years. I hope you understand me a little more too."

Laura turned from the sink. Her eyes were full of tears. "I don't have to understand you, darling. Not any of you. I love you. That's enough."

The trouble was, Buzz thought as he drove to his office, that Dorothy had a peculiar way of building things up in her own mind and managing to put them into his. The prospect of tonight's party was a perfect example. He'd really meant what he said a few days ago about feeling nothing for Frances. It was ancient history and he'd almost forgotten that reckless, tantalizing girl he'd been in love with. But now he was apprehensive about seeing her in a few hours. Not that it would mean anything to either of them, but thanks to his wife's jealousy, he'd be ill at ease, conscious of every thing he did and said, knowing Dorothy's eyes would be on him every minute. Damn it, why was she so suspicious? It had been the same with that Stacy Donovan episode.

There'd been nothing to it. Nothing at all. He'd simply sold the woman a car and gone to her house a couple of times when she called with minor complaints. But Dot had built it into a full-fledged affair in her mind. She'd carried on so that he'd finally moved out for a while, but not in order to see Mrs. Donovan. He'd never seen her again. No, that time he'd simply walked away from the last straw in a series of ridiculous accusations created out of his wife's own insecurity. He'd known he'd be back. He'd simply hoped to teach her a lesson. But in spite of psychiatrists and tranquilizers she hadn't really changed. She had no self-confidence and consequently no trust in him. It was like living with a volcano that could be dormant for months, years, and then suddenly erupt for no reason except that it couldn't contain itself.

Okay. He'd been wrong to marry her. He'd done it out of a feeling of injury when Fran ran off with that actor. As though he had to prove to the world that he hadn't been "jilted," as they said in those days. As though he had to prove he could get any woman he wanted. As though he believed Fran would hear and be sorry she'd let him go. What a bunch of bull! He'd regretted the marriage almost immediately, but his damned pride wouldn't let him admit his mistake. And then Dot got pregnant and suddenly he had a family and responsibilities and there was no way he could walk out on the whole thing.

Not that it had been all bad. If only Dorothy weren't so neurotic. If only she could believe in herself. He'd tried to make her happy and he supposed he'd done as much as any man could. He hadn't been all that unhappy himself, most of the time.

But it would have been so different with Fran. Stormy too, probably, but always exciting. He was sure of that. She'd also have driven him crazy. But it would have been because of her independence, her unpredictability, her greedy zest for living. She'd been that way as a girl. From what he'd heard, she'd stayed that way ever since.

He was suddenly excited about seeing her. Why? They were middle-aged people, not wild kids. I was right when I told Dot I'll probably bore her, Buzz thought. Maybe I'm going to hate that most of all.

Frances sulked in the front seat of Sam's car as Barb drove to the airport.

"I don't know why the hell we have to play shuttle-bus. Why couldn't they have gotten themselves into a taxi and over to the aunts by themselves?"

"Don't be such a grouch just because I rousted you out of bed at eleven o'clock. I didn't need you to come with me, but I thought if Mother asked me one more time why you weren't up, I was going to scream."

"So scream. Might be good for you. I do it a lot. It shakes up the liver."

Barbara ignored that. "You think we'll recognize Aunt Mamie and Uncle Fred?"

"Sure. They'll be the ones with the plastic clothes-hanger bags over their arms."

"Snob."

"Right. And getting worse every day." Fran stretched and yawned.

Barbara couldn't resist. "But not too snobbish for waiters. You're really done in this morning."

"Waiters don't count. Or truck drivers. Or masseurs. They're at least useful. Middle-class aunts and uncles bring out the worst in me, my love. In fact, this whole damn week brings out the worst in me."

"You could make an effort. For Mother and Dad."

"I will, I will! My God, I'm here, am I not? I'll be Saint Frances tonight, I promise you! I'll even be nice to dear Aunt Mamie and Uncle Fred and to those old relics Mildred and Martha when we drop the Chicago contingent off at their house. I'll be on my good behavior. Hell, I wasn't even rude to that uptight idiot Spencer Winters last night, was I?"

"Only moderately. Asking him if he carried pictures of his children! You know that was a put-down, Fran. He knew it, too."

Her sister pretended innocence. "Is that the way it seemed? I thought all proud fathers carried snapshots in their wallets."

Barbara couldn't help laughing. "You're impossible! Allie's children are in their twenties. Besides, you know damned well Spencer would consider himself far too chic to go in for anything like that, even if they were babies."

"He's not chic. Under that veneer of pompous ass beats the heart of a pompous ass. He may have made a lot of money and established himself in Boston society—whatever *that* is—but he's still from nowhere. I'd bet on it."

"Like *we* are."

"Yes. Like we are. Except you have style, Barb. I don't know where you got it, but you do. And I think I've learned what real sophistication is all about, from rubbing elbows with so much of it."

"And Allie?"

Fran lit a cigarette and exhaled before she answered. "Allie hasn't changed a bit. She's the only one of us who's produced babies, but she's the only true virgin in the lot. If they made a movie, Doris Day would play Allie. She's always been naïve. She still is. Anybody who stayed married to that pretentious boob would have to be."

"I want to stop at the desk and see if I have any mail," Spencer said.

"Are you really expecting any? For such a short stay, I mean."

"The office may have sent something."

Allie waited in the lobby while he went over to check. He was right about the hotel. It really was a convention hall. People were signing in at booths set up for registration; groups of cigar-smoking men were exchanging boisterous greetings while their wives twittered in clumps nearby. But the hotel itself was pleasant enough. In spite of the things Spence complained about. He'd called twice about the air-conditioning, which couldn't be shut off even though it was too cool at night to sleep in it. He'd given the waiter hell because it took thirty minutes to bring their breakfast, and then the man forgot a knife and Spencer had to spread jelly on his toast with a coffee spoon. He's scared the maid half to death with his yelling about the lack of towels and facecloths and the fact that there were only three sheets of writing paper in the desk drawer. They were inconveniences, of course, but Allie wouldn't have complained. Spencer didn't seem to realize that this was a giant operation. He allowed for no unavoidable errors among such a big staff. For that matter, he allowed for no errors in anything, including his business or his personal life.

He returned and they took the escalator down to the street level. They were on their way to the Brown Palace for lunch.

Spencer, needless to say, had wangled guest privileges at the hotel's private club. It seemed odd to be going to lunch with him. They never did that, unless they were away and there was nowhere more interesting for Spencer to go. Today he'd have gone anywhere to avoid the family. Bad enough, he said, that he'd have to face them tonight.

In the cab he handed her a letter. "Something for you."

Surprised, she opened it. There was a note in Aunt Charlotte's spidery handwriting.

> My dear Alice,
>
> I do hope you and Spencer have a pleasant visit. I feel quite sad about missing my sister's anniversary and hope you will give her and your father my fond regards. I am enclosing a little clipping from the paper about the dinner party you gave before you left. It sounds most original. I've not been feeling very well the past few days and I've heard nothing from Janice or Christopher since you left. Not surprising. Still, you would think they might call, if only to see if I'm alive. I daresay I'll hear from none of you until you return, but I trust you enjoy your visit.
>
> Devotedly,
> Aunt Charlotte

Allie sighed. She'd asked Chris to check on his great-aunt, knowing Janice couldn't be depended upon. Apparently Chris hadn't bothered either. It wasn't surprising, this cold yet self-pitying complaint from Charlotte. I'll call her tomorrow evening after the party, Alice thought, and she and Mother can talk.

She read the clipping, shuddering. It was so vulgar. It had been Spencer's idea, this fatuous fawning over the senior member of his firm. Her protests that a simple, elegant dinner would be in better taste had provoked nothing but anger and a terrible black-and-blue mark on her upper arm where he'd grabbed her to make his point.

"Damn it, don't tell me about taste! J.B. will be impressed that we've gone to special trouble to lay on a party that isn't just run-of-the-mill, and it will give the papers something to write about, since they think you're such an 'imaginative' hostess! If it weren't for me, they'd never know you were alive! I have to think up all the ideas. You don't know how to give a party you can't copy out of an etiquette book!"

So she'd done all that terrible, corny stuff with the courtroom atmosphere. And of course he'd been vindicated. As usual.

Alice handed over the clipping. "You were right. J.B.'s party got quite a write-up."

He read it, pleased.

"Who sent it? J.B.'s secretary?"

"No. Aunt Charlotte. Along with a note complaining that the children haven't called her."

He gave a derisive laugh. "What in hell made you think they would?"

Chapter 10

He'd had kind of a "funny feeling," as Laura would describe it, all day. Several times while he was raking the leaves, he'd had to stop to catch his breath. And his stomach felt queasy. I hope I'm not coming down with flu, Sam thought. Can't afford to get sick this week, not with the party tonight and all the out-of-town visitors here. He realized he lumped his daughters in with the "visitors," along with Laura's brother and sister-in-law. Well, why not? That's what his children were: Visitors. And rare ones at that.

It was wrong of him to reproach them for not coming home more often. There's nothing here for them, he reflected. They find it dull. The city. The house. Laura and me and our daily routine that becomes more proscribed with each passing year. Like now. He glanced at his watch. Twelve twenty-five. In exactly five minutes Laura would come to the door and summon him to lunch. Just as at five fifty-five she summoned him for dinner. At six-thirty we watch the news followed by our regular programs. And at ten o'clock we're in bed. You could set the clock by us, day in, day out.

He hadn't realized how monotonous life was nor how much he resented certain things. Other people of his and Laura's age had their children nearby, had grandchildren and even great-grandchildren to enjoy. But his daughters hadn't given him that. Quite the contrary. They'd gotten as far away as possible. And only one of them had produced children of her own, kids the Daltons never saw growing up, young people too remote and disinterested to even come to their grandparents' golden wedding anniversary.

"Sam! Lunch!"

He put down the rake and slowly went into the house. She'd made ham and cheese sandwiches. The sight of food made him nauseous. He knew he couldn't swallow a bite. He stood at the kitchen table looking at his plate.

"I think I'll skip lunch if you don't mind, my dear. I'm not really hungry."

If he'd said he was running off with another woman, Laura couldn't have looked more shocked.

"Skip lunch? Sam, what's the matter? Are you sick?"

"No, no. Just a little off my feed. In fact, I think I'll go up and rest a bit."

Second shock. "Rest? At this time of day?" Her face clouded with concern. "You *are* sick!" She felt his forehead. "I think you're running a temperature. Sam, you're not coming down with something, are you? I'd better call Dr. Jacoby. You must have picked up a bug. Oh, dear, what an awful time, with the girls here and the party . . ." She stopped abruptly. "I didn't mean that the way it sounded. None of that's important. It's you I'm concerned about. You never get sick! If you want to go to bed in the middle of the day, you must feel terrible!"

"Now, Laura, stop making such a fuss! I'm probably catching cold, that's all. Good Lord, I don't have a terminal illness! You know Jacoby gave me a thorough physical two months ago and said I was sound as a dollar." He managed to smile. "I'll just go up and lie down for an hour or so. I'll feel fine by this evening."

"You're sure?"

"Positive."

"I still think. . . ."

"I think you have enough on your hands getting ready for tonight. I told you: Stop worrying about nothing. I'll take a couple of aspirin and be okay."

"Can I fix you something? A cup of soup? Maybe some toast and tea?"

"Not a thing, dear. You just go about your business."

Reluctantly, she nodded. She supposed she was silly, making

such a to-do over nothing. Except it was unheard of for Sam to admit he didn't feel well. In all the years at the phone company he'd never taken one "sick day." Maybe I should call the doctor, she thought. No. Sam would be furious. And he's probably just tired, as I am, from the strain of all this. It was more emotional than physical, this fatigue she felt. She didn't know why, but she'd been having a bad case of nerves ever since the girls arrived. As though she had to be on her good behavior, make them happy, try to keep them from being restless. How silly that was. They were her daughters, not acquaintances for whom one had to put on "party manners." Yet the tension was real and communicable. Perhaps Sam felt it, too. She never thought of him or, for that matter, any man, being nervous, but it could be he felt the same inexplicable anxiety.

A thought she did not wish to entertain came into her head: It's really much more peaceful without them. What an awful thing to think! To find one's own children upsetting, when she and Sam had been looking forward for months to their return! What had gotten into her these past couple of days? She was feeling the stress of these disparate personalities, making too much of an effort to recapture the "old days" when they really were a family. Yes, that was all that was wrong. And, yes, she faced the fact, she'd be relieved when everybody went home. You're a terrible mother, Laura Dalton, she scolded herself. No, I'm not, she answered the silent voice. I'm just realizing that we're too old to put up with "house guests" and even the minimum of entertaining. We're not parents any more, except in the legal sense. We're simply two quiet people unused to adjusting to our children's needs. We've not had to for so many years.

And yet they were good daughters in their way, she thought, smiling at the wedding cake Child's had delivered earlier. Barbara was right. It really was a "production." Three tiers of it, with pink icing—roses and the years 1926–1976 in gold letters at the base. There was even the inevitable, vapid bride and groom on top. It was a hideous cake and exactly right for the occasion. We never had anything this elaborate at our wedding. Only fitting we should have it now. She willed herself to be cheerful. It would be a nice party. It would be good to see Fred and Mamie again, and celebrate with all the friends and relatives. Childishly, she looked forward to the gifts too. Not that she expected anything grand. She simply loved presents. She hoped Sam would like his gold tie-clip. She'd saved for it out of the household money he gave her. I wonder if he bought something for me? Laura wondered. We agreed we wouldn't give each other anything, but I hope he broke his promise, as I did. I'd like him to be a little more sentimental than usual on this day. There's so little romance in my life.

The idea of still craving romance almost made her laugh aloud. She'd never grow up. She'd never stop anticipating the kind of euphoria enjoyed by the leading ladies of soap operas and the heroines of Gothic novels. You fool! In your heart, you're still young and vain. Well, why not? No matter what the mirror said, she could still fantasize. She did a little waltz step around the kitchen, pretending she was a nineteen-year-old Laura Burrows, engaged to be married to a man who would smother her with love and shower her with gifts. And he had. Not the kind of dashing love she'd hoped for or the extravagant gestures she'd have liked. But Sam had been devoted. She lacked for none of the modest creature comforts.

And tonight would be the highlight of her life.

They began arriving a little after six.

Barbara, looking lovely in a blue chiffon tunic and wide-legged silk pants, went over to pick up Fred and Mamie and Mildred and Martha from the house where she'd dropped off the Chicago pair a few hours earlier. Alice, in black velvet, came by cab with Spencer, a big, interesting-looking, gift-wrapped box in her hands. Fran drifted down in a shockingly low-cut white crepe dress, slit up one side. Laura saw Sam look disapprovingly at his eldest daughter's décolletage. Thank goodness he seemed much better after his rest. He'd gotten up feeling perfectly okay, he'd said, much to Laura's relief. She hoped he wouldn't chide Frances for her revealing neckline or the expanse of leg. It was quite unsuitable, of course, but so like her. She was used to being the center of attention, and the arresting gown, not to mention the diamonds and emeralds at her ears and on her fingers, were designed to assure that.

Laura had bought a new, long, pale-pink dress for the party and knew she looked well in it. The color contrasted with her white hair and emphasized her still youthful complexion, and she was pleased when everyone complimented Sam on his "young and beautiful bride," and told her how lovely she was this evening.

They came in a steady stream. The neighbors deposited the "assigned" food where Laura directed—the clam dip and potato chips, the tuna casseroles and green salad, the rolls and biscuits. She'd baked a ham and filled the big cut-crystal bowl with fruit punch. Her table looked pretty, with the old lace cloth used only on special occasions, the china that had been her mother's, the silver she and Sam had received as their wedding gift from his family, and the wedding cake occupying a place of honor in the center.

There was a babble of greetings, of introductions and reunions, of kissing and hugging and exclamations of delight, particularly over seeing "the girls," most especially Fran, whom some had never met and others had not seen in thirty years. It was an atmosphere of warmth and affection. Even Spencer unbent enough to be polite to his wife's relatives and her parents' friends. Unlike Sam, however, who had enough control not to mention it, Spencer couldn't resist commenting on Fran's spectacular outfit.

"You're certainly stealing the show." It was a quiet aside, but his eyes went to her half-exposed bosom. "Is that the outfit *Vogue* recommends for black sheep?"

Frances looked at him with open dislike. "Naturally. Black and white. Isn't that the way everything is to you, Spencer?"

"What is that supposed to mean?"

She glanced at Alice in her conservative black velvet dress with the almost prim neckline and the strand of good pearls. "I'd think it was obvious. 'Nice' women wear careful clothes. 'Loose' ones wear flamboyant ones. That way everybody knows where they stand. It's all black and white. No gray areas. I'm sure there are none in your life, Spencer."

"Gray's an indecisive color."

"Exactly. And you're a decisive man, aren't you?"

"I hope so. A man should be decisive. And disciplined."

"And a woman? What should she be? Obedient and subservient? Above reproach?"

Spencer flushed. He suspected she was testing him to find out whether he knew about Alice's "past." He hadn't known when he married her. She'd deceived him. She and that damned old woman she lived with. If he'd had any idea that quiet little twenty-three-year-old girl had borne a baby out of wedlock he'd never even have taken her out, much less made her his wife. It had all come out during an angry quarrel. He remembered that night well. She'd been defiant, brazen about it. And he'd given her a beating she'd never forgotten. But Fran, he was sure, didn't know that. She knew about the baby, of course, but probably not that Alice had confessed. She didn't know about his violence either, he guessed. Alice would be too proud to tell anyone in her family about that. Too stubborn to admit she deserved it. He smiled coolly at Fran.

"Alice is all those things. I've taught her how to be a lady."

"Really? I thought she already knew." She saw Allie watching them even while she was making polite conversation with Aunt Mamie. She's wondering what Spencer and I have to talk about, Fran thought. She knows we despise each other.

At that moment she saw him come in. She recognized him immediately, even after all these years. Buzz Paige. Older, heavier, but surprisingly unchanged. Still handsome, still possessed of the smile that could melt icebergs, the smile he bestowed on Laura as he leaned down to kiss her gently on the cheek. Gentle. Buzz had always been gentle with women. Too gentle. That's why I didn't marry him, Fran thought. He wasn't tough enough to handle me. I knew I could always get my way, and that's always been the last thing I wanted. I need a man to dominate me. I've never found one. They've all turned out to be such miserable excuses for men.

She looked back at Spencer, so sure of himself, so egomaniacal. The cruelty showed in his eyes. You bastard, Fran thought. I should have married you. You wouldn't scare me the way you obviously do Allie. I would have served you right. And you're just about what I deserve.

"Excuse me," Fran said. "I just saw an old friend come in."

She approached Buzz and the attractive but rather faded-looking woman who stood with him. So that's his wife. Just about what one would expect. A dim bulb. A washed-out watercolor. Yes, that's what Buzz would have gone to after me: someone peaceful and placid and safe.

He hadn't seen her yet. She was at his elbow before he noticed her. Then he turned and looked into her eyes with an expression she couldn't read.

"Hello, Buzz. Long time."

He took both her hands. "Fran! You look wonderful!"

"Thanks. So do you. What's your secret?"

He laughed. "Clean living and tender loving care. Fran, you remember Dottie. She was Dottie Kravett when you knew her." He put his arm around his wife.

"Hello, Frances," Dorothy said.

"Dottie! My God, Dottie Kravett! Of course!" Fran kissed her, French-style, on both cheeks. "How marvelous! And you're married to Buzz! Imagine! All these years!"

"Twenty-nine, to be exact."

Fran pretended to shudder. "Don't say that. I can't bear to think how long ago it was when we were a gang of young lunatics tearing up this town!"

"I was never one of your crowd. We just knew each other from school." The voice was strained, taut.

"Fran means we all grew up together, honey," Buzz said. "And by God we did, though I'll never know how we didn't kill ourselves in the process. Remember that crazy old Ford convertible I had, Fran? It's a miracle it didn't turn us all into statistics!"

"Only because you drove it like you were Barney Oldfield!" Fran clapped a jeweled hand over her mouth. "I mustn't say things like that. Barney Oldfield! My God, that gives away my age!"

"It's no secret," Dottie said. "What are you now, Fran? Fifty? Fifty-one?"

The other two looked at her in surprise. The hostility was undisguised. Buzz reddened, embarrassed by his wife's rudeness.

"Darling," he said, "you know a lady never tells her age."

Dorothy smirked. "No. A *lady* doesn't."

Jesus! Fran thought. She's crazy. Crazy with jealousy, I suppose. That's crazy in itself. How could she be jealous of somebody from so far in the past? Poor Buzz. He really picked a loser. She decided to make light of the petty barb.

"That was no lady I saw you with," she said. "That was my high school girlfriend." Fran smiled. "We have no secrets, Dottie, have we? Fifty my next birthday. How *about* that?"

"You must tell us all about yourself," Buzz said quickly. "Are you still living in Paris?"

"Yes. I travel a lot, but that's officially home. I think Mother's looking for me. See you later."

"What's the matter with you?" Buzz turned angrily on his wife after Fran drifted off. "My God, Dottie, you were an absolute boor! Fran was merely trying to be pleasant. She was only showing us courtesy."

"Courtesy and everything else she has. You're such a fool, Buzz! Didn't you see the way she looked at you?"

"No, dammit, I didn't see anything but a woman who was trying to be gracious while you were downright insulting. Please, Dottie, don't behave this way. You're going to spoil the whole evening."

"Why should't I? She's spoiled my whole life. You've never gotten over her, Buzz Paige, and you know it!" Her voice had risen. A couple of people nearby turned to stare. Don't let her make a scene, Buzz prayed. Not here. Not now. I was wrong to antagonize her. I know how volatile she is.

"Okay, honey. Forget it. Let's go talk to Mr. Dalton. We haven't had a chance to congratulate him."

Dottie didn't move, but she lowered her voice. "You're still in love with her, aren't you?"

He tried to soothe her. "Of course not! That was years ago, honey. We were kids. I had a crush on her, that's all."

The anger turned to resignation. "She was your first love. Nobody forgets his first love."

Buzz laughed. "Only in novels, sweetheart. What I felt for Fran wasn't love. It was schoolboy stuff. I fell in love when I found you. You're my first and only one."

She seemed mollified. "You won't let her take you away from me, will you?"

"What kind of silly talk is that? Come on. Let's circulate."

As they moved about, chatting with other guests, getting reacquainted with Barbara and Alice, meeting Spencer, being polite to the aunts and uncles, Buzz seemed to be relaxed and thoroughly at ease. But inside there was the old excitement. There'd never been anybody like Fran. Dottie was right. He'd never gotten over her. But what he still felt couldn't be called love. It was physical desire, tinged, he supposed, with the remnants of wounded pride and the memory of how sensual she'd been, even as a girl. She was even more provocative now with that cool assurance that made Dottie seem gauche.

He saw her glance at him as he and his wife went from group to group. He wondered what she was thinking. What she was remembering. Was the attraction still there for her, too? Helplessly, he wondered how to find out.

"Tell me about Washington. It must be a very exciting place."

Barbara started as her aunt spoke to her. Mamie stood in front of her, smiling. Barb realized she'd been daydreaming in the middle of the party, thinking about Charles, wishing he was here. She came back to the moment and smiled at the "Chicago aunt."

"I enjoy it. It's changed a great deal since I've been there. I hear Chicago has too."

"Oh my, yes. So much going on. The city is very progressive with all the new buildings and shopping areas. Michigan Avenue quite outdoes Fifth Avenue in New York, I hear. You should come and visit sometime, Barbara. It's been so many years since we've seen any of you girls."

"I'd like that, Aunt Mamie, but I don't get a lot of time off from my job. It's all I can do to get here once a year to see the family. It's a nice party, isn't it? Doesn't Mother look pretty?"

"Yes. She was always the best-looking of the three of us." Mamie made a little face. "And of course, being the baby, she was also spoiled rotten. She's six years younger than I am, you know. And ten years younger than Charlotte. Almost like you, Barbara, now that I think of it. The youngest of three girls, with quite a gap between the second and third. Sam and Laura spoiled you the same as our parents spoiled her. Frankly, I was surprised when she married your father. Not that he isn't a fine man. But Laura was always daydreaming about the 'Prince Charming' who was going to come into her life and take her off into some wonderful, glamorous life. Listening to her, I thought she'd never marry, because that kind of idealism can sometimes stand in the way of reality. It makes some women go through life seeking and yearning for the kind of relationship they never find. I never knew a spinster who hadn't had a chance to marry. I've only known those who never found the 'man of their dreams.' Pity. While they languish with their visions of a 'great love,' time slips by and they wake up to find themselves alone. I'm glad that didn't happen to Laura. Thank goodness she realized she wasn't a princess. She's had a good life. Fulfilling. It's wonderful to be here celebrating with her and Sam. Fred and I had our fiftieth two years ago. Laura and I are lucky. We still have our husbands. Poor Charlotte lost hers early, you know." Mamie's voice sank almost to a whisper. "He died the year before she took Alice. Sometimes I think all that business with your sister was God's will, terrible as it was. It gave Charlotte something to think about besides her loss. And it was salvation for poor little Alice. Just think, Barbara, if she hadn't gone to Boston she'd never have met that lovely, successful man and had two real children."

"Real children?" Barbara echoed. "What a strange thing to say, Aunt Mamie. Jack Richards' child was real."

The plump little woman looked flustered. "Well, of course it was. That is . . . I mean it was real but it wasn't . . . you know what I mean. Anyway, I'm glad Alice is safely married. I wish Frances' husbands had turned out better."

Barbara felt an anger that was difficult to control. How dare this smug, elderly matron stand here and patronize all of them? She and her talk about "safe marriages" and "yearning spinsters." And the omission of my situation is obvious. She's sniping at me. She thinks she's so subtle, reminding me that I'm forty and unmarried, as though it were something idiotic or shameful. All that prattle about never finding one's "great love." She doesn't know I've found mine.

"Forgive me, Aunt Mamie," Barbara said, "but I think your standards are a little outdated. Marriage isn't the answer to everything any more. Some of us are single by preference."

Mamie was unruffled. "Oh, dear, you liberated young women are missing so much. The Lord intended us to go two by two, Barbara." She patted her niece's cheek. "Never mind. At least you have a career. Poor Frances has nothing but money."

Barbara clenched her teeth. Damned old biddy! I wish I'd left her at the airport.

Spencer, smiling like a loving husband, took Allie's arm and walked her into the deserted kitchen.

"How soon can we get the hell out of here? I can't stand much more of this. My God, what people! Can't we leave now?"

Allie was appalled. "Spencer, you know we can't! We have to stay until the very end. Mother and Daddy would be humiliated if we walked out in the middle of the party!"

"I've never been so bloody bored in my life. Damn it, I knew it was a mistake to come. I wish I'd stayed in Boston."

Alice looked at him with hatred. "I wish so too," she said and walked out of the kitchen. I'll pay dearly for that, she thought. I don't care. I wish he'd go away now. I wish he'd go forever.

"Nice shindig, Sam," Earl Dalton said to his brother. "Almost makes me regret never having taken the plunge myself."

Sam smiled. "Now, that's the biggest whopper you've told in years. You never had any use for marriage and you know it."

"No, I guess not. You got the only girl I ever wanted. Laura's quite a woman."

"Yes, she is. A good wife. A good mother."

"And you have three beautiful daughters. You're a lucky man."

Mildred and Martha sat together on the sofa, surveying the scene. Sam's widowed sisters detested each other, as they detested a world that virtually ignored them.

"Get a look at the bookends on the couch," Fran said quietly to her mother. "They haven't missed a thing. My lord, what sour expressions! What are they waiting for—people to come and kiss the hem of their garments? Or are they merely constipated?"

Laura tried not to laugh. "Frances, you must be more respectful! They're very old and not very happy. It isn't easy to be alone in the world. After all, they both lost their husbands years ago and they're still quite disappointed that they don't get much attention from friends they had when they were married. I must say, I feel guilty about them myself. I try to visit now and then, but they're not much pleasure to be with. Your father's even less tolerant. He can't stand being around them. I have to bully him into it."

"Families," Fran said. "Don't you sometimes think they're more trouble than they're worth?"

"No," Laura said. "I never think that."

The party broke up soon after Sam and Laura opened their gifts. Or, more correctly, after Laura opened them. Sam stood back, letting her have the fun of untying the ribbons and gasp with pleasure as she took each present out of its box. She was like a child at Christmas, excited and flushed with pleasure, giving every donor the same grateful kiss of appreciation, whether the offering was extravagant or modest.

Our presents tell a lot about us, Barbara thought as she helped her mother with the wrapping and boxes. Fran's is costly and useless—two solid gold bars from Cartier, miniature pendants to be hung from chains around the necks of people who "have everything." Sam and Laura would never dream of wearing such things. The very idea of a necklace on a man would stun her father, and Laura would not understand that she'd received one of the year's status symbols. Alice and Spencer's gift was also expensive, as befitted their "station," but at least it had some possible use. It was a handsome Vermeil flower vase, far too elegant for the house on South Carona Street, much too ostentatious for the objects it would live among. Still, Laura could put her precious garden flowers in it.

At the very end, after all the gifts were opened and admired, after Sam had shown pleasure over his tie-clip and Laura had cried a little over the heart-shaped pin he'd bought for her, while the friends and relatives were being thanked for their gold-plated letter openers and gold-colored bookends and gilt picture frames and all the other well-meant, absurd mementos, Barbara sneaked out to the garage and returned with a wicker basket with a big gold bow on top.

"I saved mine for last," she said to her parents. "I hope you don't hate me for it."

Laura took the little basket and looked inside. Her expression turned from surprise to rapture as she lifted out a tiny creature. "It's a puppy!" Laura said. "Look, Sam! It's a darling little dog!"

"A dog!" Sam was startled.

"If you don't want him, we can take him back," Barbara said hastily. "I know he'll be a lot of trouble. He's only three months old and not housebroken, but I thought maybe he'd . . . he'd be company." She gave an embarrassed little laugh. "I fell in love with him when I passed the pet shop window this afternoon. And when I found he was a golden retriever, I couldn't resist." She looked anxiously at her parents. "I guess it was a silly idea. We've never had a dog in the house."

Laura held the puppy close to her face and its little pink tongue reached out to kiss her cheek. She snuggled it like a baby.

"Oh, Barbara darling, he's wonderful! He's beautiful! Isn't he, Sam?"

Anything his "baby" did was all right with Sam Dalton. Even something crazy like giving them a damned troublesome dog. "He sure is. And he'll grow up to be a beauty. Thank you, honey."

Most of the guests crowded around, enchanted by the tiny animal, petting and scratching him under his little jaws. Only Mildred and Martha stayed in their places, their eyebrows arched in identical disapproval at such foolishness. And Spencer Winters muttered to his wife that it was the dumbest present he'd ever seen. "What the hell do they need with a dog? For God's sake, is your sister out of her mind?"

"Maybe she wants to give them something faithful and loving and totally uncritical," Alice said softly. "Maybe she wants to bring new life into this old house."

"Oh, for Christ's sake, Alice! What nonsense is that?"

She didn't answer, but she watched her parents' faces. Barbara instinctively knew the moment was right to give them something to protect and care for and be completely loved by. Alice felt sad. A puppy was the grandchild they never were able to play with, a helpless thing that needed them as no other living creature did. How perceptive of Barb to sense that they needed some new purpose, some sense of responsibility for a life—even if it was only a dog's. Alice had cheated them of the only grandchildren they had. Chris would never give them a great-grandchild to love. And Janice had already announced she never planned to have babies, probably would never marry, for that matter.

Someday I'll be reaching out like that for something to love, Alice thought. Spencer would never understand that kind of emptiness late in life. Barb did. Even Fran seemed to grasp the deeper meaning of the gift. There was a suspicious moisture in her eyes.

A tear rolled slowly down Alice's face and she didn't wipe it away. She heard Spencer's exasperated sigh.

"Can we go back to the hotel now, or are you going to stand there blubbering all night?"

"You go," Alice said. "I'm going to stay here, Spencer." She surprised herself by the sudden decision. "I'll come by the hotel tomorrow and get my things before you check out."

He stared at her. "Have you gone crazy too? What are you talking about? Why are you spending the night here?"

"You told me to stay in Denver as long as I wanted. I'm taking you up on it. Starting now."

"Come outside. Away from all these people. I want to talk to you."

"No. I'm not coming back to the hotel with you tonight."

"How will you explain that?"

"Maybe with the truth," Alice said. "Maybe after all these years I'll explain everything with the truth." She looked straight at him. "I'm not afraid of you any more, Spencer. I'm not afraid of your punishment. I don't need it. Maybe I never did."

He was too outraged to argue with her. Silly bitch! If she wanted to stay on with her family awhile, well, let her. Who cared?

"When will you be coming back to Boston?"

"I have no idea."

"For God's sake, Alice, what will I tell Janice? What shall I say to J.B.?"

"Tell Janice I love her and Chris. And tell J.B. to go to hell."

Chapter 11

By eleven o'clock, they'd all gone, the friends and relatives, leaving only Sam and Laura and their daughters to survey the aftermath of the party. Laura sank into a corner of the sofa, the puppy in her arms.

"Would you believe twenty-five people could create such a mess?" She looked at the litter of tissue and ribbon and boxes, the plates and punch glasses on every surface, the overflowing ashtrays, the remnants of food on platters and the demolished wedding cake reduced now to one small slice on which the bride and groom were precariously perched.

"You go to bed, Mother," Alice said. "We'll clean up. You must be exhausted."

The others looked at her, the same unspoken question in their minds. Why had Spencer stormed off in a taxi, barely saying a civil goodnight to anyone? What was Alice doing here instead of returning to the hotel? Only Fran was bold enough to come right to the point.

"Is that why you decided to stay here tonight? To help us clean up?"

Alice hesitated. "I'll explain with the truth," she'd said to Spencer only moments before. But how could she? How could she tell her family she'd lived twenty-five years with a sadist? Could she say she wasn't willing to go back to Boston and the horrors and sadness it held for her? That maybe she'd never go back?

They were waiting, looking at her, curious about this strange turn of events. She knew she could count on her mother's sympathy, her sisters' understanding. But what of Daddy? Would he remind her of her "duty" to her husband and children? He didn't like Spencer, that was obvious, but Sam Dalton had a curious code of ethics. You made your bed and you lay in it. You did the "decent thing," no matter what it cost you. That was Sam's attitude. He'd proved it to her many years ago.

"What is it, darling?" Laura's voice was kind. "Have you and Spencer had a fight? You can tell us, Alice."

I'm a coward, Allie thought. I haven't the guts to tell Mother and Daddy the truth. Not yet. Not tonight.

"Yes, we had an argument. That's all. I just decided I didn't want to go back to the hotel tonight. It's nothing," she lied. "Just your everyday domestic spat. But I didn't want to continue it. So I thought I'd stay here."

Laura seemed to accept that. Perhaps there'd been nights in her own life that she wished there were somewhere to go to get away from a quarrel for a while. But Sam was not so gullible. Husbands and wives did not sleep apart. Not unless there was something seriously wrong. He'd felt that ever since Alice had been at home. The man was no good. Allie's unexpected decision only verified his feeling that this was a bad situation.

"You going back to the hotel tomorrow?" he asked.

"To get the clothes and things I left there, Daddy. Spencer's returning to Boston tomorrow. He's too busy to stay the week. I'd like to, though, if it's all right with you."

"Of course it's all right," Laura said. "We expected you to stay. I'm sorry Spencer can't. You just tuck into your old room with Barbara tonight, dear. I'm sure tomorrow you and Spencer will iron out whatever it is that's bothering you."

Barbara and Fran exchanged knowing glances. Allie was lying about her little "domestic spat." Surely even her parents could see that. Sam's tight-lipped expression said clearly that he knew Allie wasn't telling the whole truth. Laura must know this was more than her daughter tried to make it sound, but she was putting a good face on it, at least for now. All right. If the three of them wanted to play out this little game, Fran and Barb would go along.

"Allie's right," Barb said in the small silence that followed. "You and Daddy go on up to bed, Mother. The three of us can clear up this cyclone in no time flat." She grinned as though everything was normal. "Where's the new baby going to sleep, by the way?"

"I thought we could make him a little bed in the kitchen."

"Give you odds he'll cry all night," Fran said.

"No, he won't," Barbara declared. "He's going to be a model child. And to make sure, I'll put an old alarm clock in his bed. They say the ticking reminds them of their mother's heartbeat and keeps them quiet."

"My sister the veterinarian," Fran laughed. "By the way, Mother, what are you going to call him?"

Laura cuddled the puppy. "I haven't the faintest idea. Anybody have a suggestion?"

"How about 'Spoiled'?" Sam said. "That sure is what he's going to be."

"Maybe 'Goldie'?" Alice suggested. "For the anniversary and his color?"

"He looks more carrot than gold right now," Barb said.

"But he's a fourteen-karat little beast." Fran smiled. "Why don't you call him 'Karat,' Mother? With a 'K' as in 'Killer.'"

"Or 'K' as in 'Krazy,'" Barbara added. "Which probably is what I am for giving you something that's going to be such a bother. Are you sure you and Dad want to keep him? I won't feel hurt if you decide not to."

Laura looked at her husband.

"Of course we're going to keep him," Sam said. He took the puppy from her. "Come on, Karat. Your old man's going to fix you a nice warm bed."

The three of them went about clearing up the living and dining room and kitchen after their parents went upstairs, Laura protesting that she really shouldn't leave them with all the work. They shoo-ed her off lovingly and changed into robes, except for Allie, who'd left hers at the hotel. "No matter," she said cheerfully. "I'll just stay in my bra and girdle and put one of Mother's aprons over me." The effect was hilarious. They laughed at Allie's girdled derriere exposed from the rear. They laughed at Fran in her two-hundred-dollar silk robe stacking dishes to carry to the sink. It was all suddenly warm and fun and girlish, as though they'd turned back the clock and were "the Dalton girls" of their youth. As they worked, they gossiped about the guests.

"Aunt Mamie is impossible," Barb said. "She had me cornered with a lot of self-righteous blather about the joys of marriage! Heaven help Uncle Fred. Imagine living with that!"

"How about the dour old aunts from Denver?" Fran asked. "Poor Mother. She has to cope with them. Daddy runs, I gather, even though they're his own sisters."

"And Uncle Earl," Barb said. "The perennial bachelor. Do you think he could possibly be gay?"

Fran collapsed with laughter, leaning against the kitchen table. "Gay? He wouldn't even know the meaning of the word! Listen to her, Allie. She's clearly out of her head."

Alice tried to join in the bantering, but she was much too troubled. Barb's flippant remark reminded her of Chris. Chris was gay. What would they think if they knew that? What would they think of Janice with her don't-give-a-damn attitude? Of Spencer with his psychotic behavior? What would my sisters say if they knew my whole life was a melodrama?

Fran was chattering on. "What did you think of that dreary little wife of Buzz Paige's? I remember her from school. She was always peculiar. Never did fit in. I wonder why on earth he married her."

"Oh, listen, Mother gave me a rundown on that," Barb said, suddenly remembering. She proceeded to tell them the gossip about the Paiges. Fran looked thoughtful.

"So he had an affair and left home once," she said. "That's very interesting."

Her sisters looked at her sharply.

"Fran, don't start anything," Barbara said. "You know we discussed that."

"That was before I knew all this. And before I saw him again. He's still damned attractive. And if you'll forgive my immodesty, I know he thinks I am too."

Barbara was suddenly angry. "Don't you dare try any of your tricks with Buzz! For God's sake, Fran, you'll ruin his marriage and then take off to some other part of the world leaving a wrecked home and a couple of unhappy people! That's loathsome! That's more rotten than screwing around with a waiter!"

Alice looked puzzled. "A waiter? What are you talking about?"

"Nothing," Barb said. "Forget it."

"Oh, don't be such a damned prude, Barbara!" Fran was angry, too. "Allie's a big girl. I'm not ashamed to tell her." She turned to Alice. "Your little sister is referring to the fact that I picked up a waiter at LaFitte's and went to bed with him last night. Big deal. A one-night stand. What's so earth-shaking about that? I've had a hundred of them. A thousand. They don't mean a thing. They're more fun and less habit-forming than sleeping pills." She smiled. "Are you shocked, Allie? Barb is. Haven't you ever cheated on Spencer? Or am I the only immoral member of this trio?"

Her sister didn't answer. Finally, Barbara said, "Look, Fran, I'm not condemning you. I'm the last one to sit in judgment. But don't fool around with Buzz. You're not serious about him. You broke his heart once. Isn't that enough?"

"People's hearts don't break, pet. They just chip a little around the edges."

"That's not true," Allie said slowly. "Mine broke when I had to give up Jack Richards and his baby."

There was a long pause before Fran said with surprising gentleness, "Poor Allie. You've had it tougher than either of us, haven't you? You're still having it tough with old Spencer, aren't you? What's the story behind tonight? Have you left him for good?"

"I don't know. I'd like to. But there are so many things . . ." Her voice trailed off. "I can't talk about it just now. Maybe later. Maybe you two can advise me what to do about Spencer. And other things."

Fran tried to lighten the atmosphere. "You certainly couldn't pick two better marriage counselors. One who'd had three strikeouts, and the other who's had none at all."

"But you're both so much more determined than I," Allie said. "They couldn't have done to you what they did to me. Not that I blame them. It was my fault. I should have fought them."

Who are "they"? Barbara wondered. Mother and Daddy? The Richardses and Jack? Aunt Charlotte? Or were "they" Allie's husband and children—that snob she married and the son and daughter none of them really knew anything about? Fran was right. Allie had had it tougher than the other two. And she was less able to handle it.

Fran's been bruised, Barb thought, but she's so basically selfish she's survived. And I've never had to go through anything that tore me to pieces. Her train of thought took her to Charles. Why hadn't he called since she'd been in Denver? They'd agreed she'd never call him. Certainly not at home. And not even at the office unless it was a real emergency. But it was strange she hadn't heard from him. She missed his voice. Even when they couldn't meet, he telephoned her every evening, telling her how much he loved her, how unhappy he was that he wasn't in her arms. It had been three whole days since she'd heard. That wasn't like him. Maybe he's ill, she thought, panicked. I'd have no way of knowing. My God, if he died, I'd read it in the papers! Pull yourself together. You're letting your imagination run away with you. He's probably been busy. He'll call tomorrow.

A strained silence had fallen after Allie's last remark. There was nothing to say. Not until she felt able to talk. Then we'll help her any way we can, Fran and I, Barbara thought. She's our sister. She's part of us.

John Peck couldn't keep his eyes off the young woman draped so casually in a chair in his living room, one trousered leg slung over the side. Janice Winters was pure class. She had the kind of assurance that came with money and breeding, the relaxed attitude of the rich who could afford to wear jeans and a sweater to dinner at the home of a stranger. He felt overdressed in his dark-blue suit. Middle class. Even Carol's "hostess gown" seemed fussy and wrong. They were "squares" next to this easygoing, confident young pair.

Are you my half-sister? John wanted to ask. Do we have the same mother? Is something important going to come out of this hastily arranged evening with Clint Darby and his girl? He felt terribly nervous. Carol didn't. At least she gave no sign of being ill at ease. She chattered brightly about the advertising business, about John's marvelous job, about everything except what he was dying to know: Was Alice Dalton Winters the woman who'd given birth to him and the exotic young creature across the room?

Not that he or Carol would come out and ask. But dammit, why didn't his wife steer the conversation toward some area that might produce a clue? She was in a better position than he to get into that without creating suspicion. Stop pressing, he told himself. Carol is right. Let the evening take its course. At some point we'll slide gracefully into the subject of Janice's family.

It was not until after dinner that the moment arrived, and then it was Janice who provided him with the opening he sought. While Carol and Clint discussed an upcoming advertising campaign, Jan turned her attention to her host.

"Is Boston your home?"

"Yes. I was born and raised here. You, too, I gather."

Jan nodded. "I'm a native. Not Mother and Dad, though. Mom comes from Denver and Dad's originally from Chicago." She laughed. "Not that he chooses to remember. He'd like everyone to think he was brought up with the Cabots and the Lodges. Old J. B. Thompson, the Lord High Executioner of my father's law firm, still firmly believes that no civilization exists west of Massachusetts. I think he's convinced that Illinois is still peopled by pioneers living in log cabins. So, darling Daddy has become more Bostonian than the baked bean."

"Have your parents lived here long?"

"Oh, sure. Forever. Mother came when she was seventeen. And Dad got his first job here, right out of law school."

Careful, John. Don't seem too interested. "Your mother was seventeen? What made her move to Boston at that age?"

"My Aunt Charlotte kind of adopted her. My great-aunt, really. Tiresome old lady. She's my grandmother's sister and she was widowed early with no children of her own. I think she talked Mother's parents into letting her raise their little Alice. Probably promised more 'advantages' than she could have in Denver. My grandparents aren't very well off. I mean, they're not poor, but I guess in those days, with three girls to raise, they probably thought they were doing the right thing for Mother, sending her to a rich relative."

"I see. How long ago was that?"

Janice calculated. "Well, let's see. Mother's forty-eight, so it was about thirty-one years ago. Around nineteen forty-five or six. She married my father in nineteen fifty-one. They just had their

twenty-fifth anniversary. I came along in nineteen fifty-five, two years after my brother Chris. He's gay, by the way." She tossed in that last, gratuitous piece of information as casually as though she were saying that her brother was six feet tall, or married, or a lawyer. Jan looked at him impishly and he realized she'd wanted to see whether he'd be shocked. John smiled.

"To each his own," he said easily.

Jan nodded approvingly. "Exactly. But you couldn't sell that to my father. Mother accepts it, more in sorrow than in anger, but the Old Man is outraged. He's practically disowned Chris. It's like an insult that this could happen to *his* only son."

"So there are just the two of you. You and Chris."

"Yep. What about you? Your parents living? Any brothers or sisters?"

"I'm an only child. At least I guess so. I was adopted when I was an infant. I was never told who my real parents were. The people who raised me were killed in an automobile accident when I was twenty-one."

Jan's face softened with pity. "How awful for you!"

"It was a shock, but one gets over everything."

"I meant about being adopted. Not that there's anything wrong with that, but it must be an odd feeling not to know anything about your real mother and father. I'm so sorry for people who'd like to know and can't find out. I think the laws are wrong. Records should be opened to adoptees when they're old enough to know. Don't you agree?"

He weighed his words carefully. "Yes. There's nothing worse than wondering. It used to bother me a lot."

"I don't doubt it! It would drive me up the wall! Not that I'm so crazy about what I drew, but at least I know what kind of people they are." She realized he'd used the past tense. "It used to bother you," Jan repeated. "Doesn't it any more?"

"Sometimes. But you can get obsessed with that kind of thing if you don't watch it. The people who raised me were so good to me that it seems kind of disloyal to think about the others. My adopted mother, especially, was a wonderful woman. I was very close to her." He almost held his breath. "Are you close to your mother?"

"Not really. I mean, I like her a lot. She's a super lady. Pretty

and kind and patient as hell with Dad and me, but I don't go along with some of her thinking."

She obviously wasn't going to elaborate. At least I know that much about Alice Dalton, John thought. He was even more convinced this was the right one. He even imagined he saw some faint resemblance between this girl and himself. And he knew now he had to see his mother. Even if she turned away, he had to meet her once, face to face.

"Didn't I read somewhere that your parents are in Denver?"

"Yes. Dad came home yesterday. Mother decided to stay a few days. They went out for her parents' fiftieth anniversary."

"You and Chris didn't want to go?"

"I think Chris would have liked to, but he isn't on speaking terms with The Pater. I couldn't care less about any of them. The Denver relatives, I mean. I don't even dig great-Aunt Charlotte. She's a whiny old lady who never lets you forget that her husband was *the* Carlton Rudolph, the architect who built so many of the old Back Bay houses. As if anybody cares."

Carlton Rudolph. Charlotte Rudolph raised Alice. John filed away the information carefully in his head. She might be the route to Alice. Alice who'd been sent to her rich aunt for "advantages." Alice who'd arrived in Boston the year John was born. It was too coincidental not to be the answer he'd searched for so long and hard.

"Telephone for you, Barbara," her mother called out late the next morning.

Thank God! It must be Charles. She hurried to answer, but another man's voice responded to her breathless "Hello."

"Barbara? I hope you remember me. It's Jack Richards."

She was incredulous. "Jack? Well, this is a surprise!" Even as she said it, Barbara thought that was the understatement of the century. As Laura said, since the day Alice left, no one had spoken that name. Even when Barb was growing up, she was forbidden to speak to him or his family, and of course she'd not attempted to contact them on her visits home in the past years.

"I'm sure you're wondering why I'm calling."

"Well, yes. Of course I am. It's been so long." She paused. "Mother told me about your wife, Jack. I'm sorry."

"Thank you. She was a lovely girl. I wish you'd known each other."

Barbara waited. What on earth was he getting at?

"I ran into Buzz Paige this morning at the bank. He told me you were home for your parents' anniversary party last night. You and Fran . . . and Allie." He sounded nervous. "I'd like to see her again. Allie, I mean. It's been so many years and I'm so ashamed of what happened. I'd like to try to make her understand why I let her down. Do you think you could arrange it, Barbara? Would you?"

She was puzzled. "I suppose I could, Jack. But why? What's the point? Allie's married, you know. She has two children by Spencer Winters."

"I know. Believe it or not, I've kept track of her."

"Then you must know she had to give your son up for adoption." Barbara's voice unconsciously hardened.

"Yes. That's part of what I want to talk about. I'm trying to make up for so many wrong things I did when I was young. Lucy's death hit me hard. She suffered so long before she died and she was so brave about it. It made me see what a weak, selfish man I've been all my life. How many rotten moments I've given other people. Allie most of all."

"Aren't you a day late and a dollar short? What good is your repentance now, Jack?"

"I want more than her forgiveness, Barb, if she can be big enough to offer that. I thought . . . that is, I hoped maybe I could find our child. Maybe do something for him, if he needs it. At least provide for him after I'm gone. I've done pretty well, and Lucy and I couldn't have children of our own. That boy, wherever he is, is all that will be left of me."

So that's it! Barbara thought. You don't want to make up for your mistakes. You want to enjoy a son you didn't care enough about to give your name to. My God! When she answered, it was coldly.

"Why are you calling *me*, Jack? Why don't you call Allie? I can't answer for her. I don't know whether she cares to speak to you again."

"That's just it. I was afraid she wouldn't come to the telephone. And I don't want to get her into trouble with her husband. I know he's here, too. But I'd like to see her. Just for a few moments. Please, Barb. You and I used to be such good friends. Won't you help me, for old times' sake?"

Such good friends. Barbara almost laughed. I worshiped you. I thought you were the most wonderful thing that ever drew breath. Even after you deserted Allie, I still felt sorry. Amazing. Even when I was nine I realized you weren't strong enough to fight the pressure your family put on you.

"I don't know," she said. "I don't think you should put me in the middle of this." She started to tell him that he could perfectly well call Allie; that Spencer had returned to Boston and her sister was right here at home. She'd already gotten her personal belongings from the hotel and come back to the house. In fact, she was sitting in the next room. But the wiser thing was to discuss it first with Allie. Barbara had no idea how she'd feel about seeing Jack Richards.

"Give me a number where I can reach you. I'll find out whether Allie wants to get in touch with you."

"Thank you, Barbara. I'm really grateful." He gave her his home and his office numbers. "I'll wait to hear from you or Allie. You've always had so much heart, Barb. Even when you were a kid you seemed to understand more than the grown-ups."

Sure, Barb thought as she hung up. I've always been the understanding one. The patsy. The fall guy. My big sisters manipulated me like a toy on a string. Even now, I'm the one who stays in touch with the family, pulls together the reunion for "us girls." And what do I get for it? Damned little. But what do I want for it? Nothing, really. Anything I've ever done I've done because I wanted to. So quit blaming the world, Barbara. You are the way you are.

She had no idea how to approach Allie on this. Straight out, she supposed, was the only way. Just repeat the conversation and hand over the phone numbers and let her make the decision. Jack Richards couldn't matter to her any more. But the child must. Maybe she's as anxious as Jack to find out what happened to their son. Or maybe she never wants to think about it. Perhaps she couldn't face that abandoned baby even if they were to find him. Could I, in her place? Could I stand the accusing eyes of a child I gave to strangers?

Damn. Why did this have to happen? Alice has enough problems with Spencer. She doesn't need one more. She hasn't come out and said she wants to leave her husband, but that surely is in her mind. And she never talks about her children. Not really.

It's about time she leveled with us, Barb thought. We can't help her if she keeps us in the dark.

Chapter 12

He wasn't surprised to see Fran drive up to the Ford showroom. It was as though he expected her this afternoon. They'd barely spoken last night after the initial encounter at the party, and yet Buzz knew she'd be here. Just as he knew there'd be a scene with Dottie when they left the Daltons'.

God, how he hated arguments! And fighting with Dot was as unproductive as trying to reason with a drunk. She didn't listen. She stormed and cried and accused and heard nothing he tried to say. She knew he was going to go to bed with Fran, she'd said. Hadn't she seen for herself the way that woman looked at him? And the way he looked back? What did he think she was—a blind fool?

Buzz had protested gently at first. Her outburst was ill-founded. Of course he admired Fran. She was a beautiful woman. And, yes, he remembered how much he'd cared for her once. But it was over long ago.

"Dottie, dear, Fran and I have nothing in common any more." He tried to be reasonable. "There's no reason for you to be so insecure. I won't even see her again while she's here. You know that."

"I know nothing of the kind! You probably can't wait to get to the office tomorrow to call her!"

He finally exploded. "Don't be an ass! I have no intention of getting in touch with her. Or vice versa! You'll drive me crazy with your jealousy! Your damned possessiveness! Listen to yourself! Everything you're saying is a figment of your imagination!"

It was as though he hadn't spoken. She kept on and on for hours, comparing herself unfavorably to Frances, dragging up old wounds, including his supposed affair with Stacy Donovan, accusing him of a hundred infidelities he'd never even thought of, much less committed.

He finally put the pillow over his head, trying to shut out the sound of her voice. At that moment he could have killed her. And yet he felt sorry for her. She was so unknowingly self-defeating. The more she talked about her "old rival," the more Buzz thought about seeing Frances. Poor Dot. If she'd just stay cool, they'd both be happier. But she had to torture herself with these fantasies and put ideas in his head that probably wouldn't otherwise be there. She deserves what she gets, he thought savagely. It would serve her right if I did just what she expects. But he didn't plan to. What point pursuing something dead and buried? Why try to bring it back to life for the few days Frances would be in town?

But he knew, even as he denied it, that he would see Fran again. He'd not initiate it, but it would happen. Only this morning he'd told Jack Richards all about "the girls" being home. Which meant Frances was very much on his mind.

He almost expected the little rented car to pull up at dusk. She saw him through the big plate-glass window and lightly tapped the horn. He went outside and leaned on the open window on the driver's side.

"Hi," he said. "What brings you here?"

"Curiosity. How are you, Buzz?"

"Fine. That was a nice party. You looked gorgeous. I'm sure every woman in the room hated you."

Fran looked innocent. "Really? Anyone we know?"

He pretended not to understand. "*Everyone* we know. You made the rest of them look like last year's models."

"I presume you mean cars, not mannequins." She was flirting with him.

"Of course. Cars are my business. New and used."

They smiled at each other, their faces only inches apart. Buzz had an insane impulse to lean in and kiss her. Really kiss her. Not just a little social peck on the cheek. He pulled back. What the hell did she want? Diversion? A few kicks? Or did she need to prove she could still have him any time she wanted? It occurred to him that Fran, for all her glamor, might be as unsure of herself as the nervous little woman who was his wife. The anxiety of middle age, Buzz thought. The moment when we wonder whether we still have it. He knew the feeling. He'd experienced it lately himself. But Fran? With her money, her position, her three ex-husbands? What reason would she have to bother with a small-time car dealer from Denver? How could he possibly imagine she ever lacked confidence in herself? Still, she'd come looking for him. She hadn't been merely driving by. Come on, Frances, he thought. Make your move. Damned if *I* will.

"What time do you get off from work?"

He laughed. "Fran, dear, I'm not an employee. I own this franchise. I set my own hours. Sometimes I go home at four. Other times it's eight or nine."

She actually blushed. "I'm sorry. I didn't meant to sound patronizing."

"It's okay. How would you know?"

She drummed on the steering wheel with her long, perfectly manicured fingernails.

"I came by to see whether you'd buy me a drink. We didn't have a chance to talk at all last night."

He wasn't going to make it easy. He'd waited thirty years for this moment.

"I'd be glad to buy you a drink, but what do we really have to talk about? I'm sure you're not interested in what's been going on here since you left, and I certainly can't relate to the people you run around with now."

She sounded almost petulant. "You said last night you wanted me to tell you about myself."

"As I recall, I said you must tell *us*. Would you like to come to the house and have a drink with Dot and me?"

"Damn you, Buzz Paige!" Fran didn't hide her annoyance. "What do you want me to do? Come right out and say I'd like to spend some time with you? Say I still find you attractive? All right. If it gives you any satisfaction, that's the truth. I don't want to visit with you and your dreary little wife. I want to . . ."

"What?"

"I don't know. Get to know you again, I guess."

Suddenly he didn't want revenge. He spoke gently. "What's the matter, Fran?"

"Everything. Nothing. Never mind. It doesn't make any difference." She started the engine. "I was crazy to come here. Forget it, Buzz. It was nice seeing you."

"Fran, wait! We can be friends, can't we?"

She looked at him slowly. "No. We can't. I don't have men friends. They're either acquaintances or lovers. And you don't qualify as either." She'd regained her composure. "Now that I've made a fool of myself, I'll just take off and go home to the family. Thanks for putting me straight. I'm glad to know you've turned into such a faithful husband. It's nice to know somebody has one."

He reached in and took her face between his hands. This time he kissed her, deeply, passionately, not caring who saw. Slowly he released her and looked into her eyes.

"All right," Buzz said. "Do I qualify now?"

The answer came in a whisper. "Where can we go?"

It was semi-dark in the motel room. The only light came from the one he'd left on in the bathroom, enough light for him to see the quiet, naked figure beside him, enough to see by his watch that it was ten o'clock.

"You all right?" Buzz asked.

"Mmmm. Delicious. You?"

"Stunned."

"I take it that's a compliment," Fran said.

"You know damned well it is."

She reached over and touched him. "I was such a fool, darling. Why did I ever let you get away?"

"You didn't, remember? You were the one who left me."

"Stupid of me. But your fault, really. If you'd made love to me then I'd never have gone. Why didn't you? It would have changed the course of history."

"I wanted to marry you. I respected you."

Fran laughed. "Oh, my God! Buzz, my love, you were always much too good. Much too idealistic. Didn't you know I was sleeping around even before I ran off with Stuart Mills?" She suddenly sounded sad. "But I never loved any of them. Not then, not later. I never loved anyone but you."

"Then why did you leave me?"

"Who knows? Adventure, I suppose. I was afraid of getting married and settling down in a house like the one I grew up in. I had all kinds of delusions of grandeur. Thought I'd be a great actress, be rich and famous. Material things seemed more important than love."

"And now?"

"They're not worth a damn."

He smiled. "That's because you have them. I can't imagine you living here. Not any more. You'd hate this life. It would stifle you."

She was quiet for a moment. "Not if I had you. I'd be happy anywhere with you, Buzz. We wouldn't even have to live here, for that matter. I have plenty of money. We could travel. Live in Paris. Take the Concorde across the ocean. Oh, darling, it would be wonderful!"

He sat up on the side of the bed. "I can't, Fran. You know that. It's too late for us."

She snapped on the bedside lamp. Even tousled and with her lipstick smeared she was still ravishing.

"Too late? It's never too late."

"For us it is. I'm married. Good God, I'm a grandfather!"

"So what?"

"I couldn't walk out on Dot."

"You don't love her. You love me."

He didn't answer.

"Am I wrong about that?"

"No, you're not wrong. I don't love Dot, but I'll stay with her. She's helpless and unhappy and she needs me. I couldn't desert her."

She stared at him. "You don't love me after all, do you? What was this all about? Some kind of revenge? Why did you bring me here? Why did you make love to me? To show me what I missed? To laugh at me?"

"You know better than that. I love you. I wish I didn't. These past few hours have been more than I've ever dreamed of. You're like some kind of goddess to me. Unattainable. A creature beyond my grasp."

"Oh, for Christ's sake! You're talking like somebody in a Victorian novel! Buzz, don't you see? We've found each other again! We can have years of happiness. You're entitled to your life. You don't owe it to Dorothy. You've given her twenty-nine years. You even left her once before. What do you think she'd do if you left her again? Kill herself?"

He spoke very quietly. "Yes, I think she would. She tried it that other time."

"But she didn't make it. People who don't succeed at suicide don't want to die. They just want attention. Anybody will tell you that!"

"I'm sorry, dear. I couldn't take that chance. I couldn't live with that on my conscience."

"So you'd rather be half alive, is that it?"

"If that's what you think it is, yes. I guess I'd rather go on living as I have than be haunted every day of my life." He took her hand. "I'm not trying to be a martyr, my love. I just know myself. I'm fifty years old. I can't chuck my responsibilities and run off like some selfish, lovesick kid. It wouldn't work."

"I hate you." It came out in a monotone.

"You probably have every right. But I didn't propose marriage to you this time, Fran. I just wanted to go to bed with you. As you did with me. I'm sorry if you thought it was a commitment."

She began to laugh. "Oh, God, this is funny! The thousands of men I've been with just for sex, and I never took one of them seriously. It had to be you I wanted to believe in! The one I thought I was in love with!" She was almost hysterical. "No fool like an old glamor girl, is there? Nothing more pathetic than a washed-up beauty grasping at straws. How marvelous this must be for your vanity, Buzz. How you'll smirk over it later!"

"Fran, don't! It isn't like that at all."

"The hell it isn't! Get out of here. Go home to your damned dependent wife and your drooling grandchildren. Dear Dorothy doesn't have to worry about me. I never want to see you again as long as I live!"

"Fran, please! Calm down!"

"I'm calm. Boy, am I calm! Calm, cool and collected, that's me. Go home, Buzz."

"I won't leave you like this."

"Why not? I'm not the suicidal type. And I know how to let myself out of motel rooms. I've done it often enough before. But surely you've already thought of that."

He got up and slowly dressed. Fran lay still, staring at the ceiling, smoking a cigarette. When he was ready to go, he came to the bed and looked down at her.

"I do love you, you know, whether you believe it or not."

Frances shut her eyes. "As we say in Gay Paree, dear boy, *merde*."

"So you came home. What's the matter? Didn't she want you?"

His wife's voice assaulted him from the living room as soon as he opened the door. Buzz pretended innocence.

"What are you talking about? You know I had dinner with Al Farmer from Detroit. I called and told you I wouldn't be home."

"Don't lie. I can't stand it. You were with Frances."

"Don't be ridiculous." He yawned. "I'm beat."

"I'll *bet* you are."

Buzz didn't answer.

"Well, how was she?" Dorothy asked. "As marvelous as ever? Better, I should think, after all the practice she's had."

"Dot, I'm too tired for another fight tonight. I'm still tired from *last night's* fight. I'm going to bed. You coming up?"

"I tried to call you at the office ten minutes after you phoned me. Charley said you'd left half an hour before. He also said Al Farmer wasn't in town."

"How could Charley know? I don't report the visit of every company executive to my salesmen! What's this all about? It isn't the first time I've spent the evening with one of the people from Ford. All right, I called you from Al's room at the Hilton. I'm sorry I didn't make it clear that I wasn't calling from the office. What was on your mind? Why did you want to reach me?"

Her voice was calm. Dangerously calm. "What I wanted wasn't important. You weren't with Al Farmer at the Hilton. He isn't registered there or at any other hotel in town. I called them all."

She paused. "And then I called the Daltons. Fran was mysteriously 'out for the evening' too."

"So what? What does Fran's social life have to do with me? As for the Hilton, they were wrong. Farmer is registered there. They just screwed up."

Dot narrowed her eyes." "All right, let's call him."

The bluff wasn't going to work, but he kept on with it. Anger was his best weapon. "Godammit, Dorothy, I'll do nothing of the kind. I'm not going to make an ass of myself by calling Al Farmer just so you'll believe he's there! What do you want me to say? That my wife is checking up on me? I've told you where I was. The subject is closed!"

"No, it isn't. You were with her, Buzz, weren't you? Where did you go? To some sleazy little motel? Did you lie there laughing at me? Was she very amused when you told her how jealous I am? It must have been a wonderful evening. Was she sympathetic? So sorry for you, having to live with a neurotic, nagging wife? 'Poor Buzz.'" Dorothy's voice dripped with sarcasm. "'Poor, long-suffering Buzz, saddled with a dreary woman who can't control her emotions. How brave and noble you are. How self-sacrificing.' I can hear it now."

"You're crazy!" It was he who was yelling while Dorothy recited her accusations without raising her voice. "You're really crazy! I never heard such a bunch of circumstantial hogwash! You're so obsessed with the idea that Fran is after me that you've put a lot of crazy coincidences together and built a case of infidelity in your mind. Just as you've done before! I've had enough of this, Dorothy! I don't want to hear any more about it! As God is my judge, if you go on with this, I'll . . ." He stopped. He was getting dangerously near the breaking point. If he kept talking, he'd tell her the truth. He'd say that he'd give anything to leave her and go off with Frances. That he was tired of being patient and responsible. That his life was mediocre and his marriage nothing.

"You'll leave me?" Dot finished the sentence for him. "Is that what will happen if I go on with this? Well, why don't you? You did before."

Buzz forced himself to calm down. "Yes, I left once before. For exactly the same reason—your hysterical accusations. I can't live like this, always suspect in your eyes, always worried that some slight deviation from my everyday pattern is going to set off one of these outbursts. We're reliving that nonsense with Stacy Donovan. It's incredible! Have all these years of psychiatry been for nothing? Are you never going to stop this paranoid behavior? Every time I make a business engagement in the evening am I going to come home to this kind of inquisition?" His voice was rising again. "How much can I take, Dot? How often do I have to prove I'm faithful? How *can* I prove it when you choose not to believe it?"

"You can't prove it because it isn't true. You were unfaithful tonight. With Frances Dalton."

It was too much. Everything was too much. He didn't care.

"All right, I was! I've been in bed with her all evening! You're right. Now are you happy?" His rage was ungovernable. "And I'll tell you something else. She begged me to go away with her and I refused! I told her I owed you too much. That I couldn't leave you because I was afraid you'd harm yourself. That I wasn't able to walk out on my responsibility to you after twenty-nine years! Yes, I made love to Fran Dalton tonight and it *ended* tonight! She never wants to see me again. She thinks I'm a spineless hypocrite. And she's right. I am because you've made me one!"

In a split second, Dorothy changed. In one of her meteoric turnabouts, the coldness turned to sniveling fear, the sarcasm became a plea for survival. Tears spilled down her face as she choked out her words.

"I don't blame you," she sobbed. "I know what hell it is to live with me. I can't help it. I've tried to be different, but I love you too much. I'm so afraid. Always. Afraid of losing you. Afraid of being alone. I know I drive you to these things, Buzz, and I hate myself for it. I'm sorry. It's my fault, not yours. It's a vicious circle with no beginning and no end."

He was filled with remorse. "No, it's not your fault. I'm the one who should be sorry. And I am. I was wrong tonight, Dottie, and I beg your forgiveness. It won't happen again. I promise you."

She nodded. "We won't talk about it any more. You got it out of your system. I'm not a child. I knew you had to. I'm almost glad you did. And I'm thankful it's over."

It was impossible to believe she really meant that, but Buzz tried to tell himself it was true. One thing certainly was true. He wouldn't be with Fran again. But only because she made it clear she had no use for him. Maybe, he thought hopefully, Dot really is becoming mature. Maybe all the therapy is finally taking and she can handle the truth better than she can cope with lies. The confession was apparently more important to her than the fact of his unfaithfulness. He didn't understand, but he gratefully accepted this "new Dorothy." He felt tenderness for her for the first time in years. Crazy. He'd just left the passionate embrace of the woman he really loved and he was feeling warmth and gentleness toward the one he didn't.

I did the right thing, he thought. Right to have told Fran I couldn't leave my wife. Right to have confessed what I did tonight. Driving home, he'd regretted the first and had no intention of doing the latter. He'd called himself all kinds of a damned fool to throw away what Fran offered, had thought perhaps she was sensible in her appraisal of his situation. He'd almost turned back to the motel to tell her he'd changed his mind; that she was more to him than his damned code of ethics. He was glad now he hadn't. Just as he was glad he'd made a clean breast of it with Dorothy. Perhaps things would change at home after this. He'd behave himself. The funny part was, despite Dot's belief, he always had, until tonight. But in the future he'd be more caring, more considerate. If Dot could forgive, so could he. Besides, she couldn't live without him. And Fran could.

It was a good act, Dorothy thought, watching him from behind her handkerchief. He really thinks I blame myself. He believes I forgive him. I hate him. I hate them both. And I'll get even.

Chapter 13

Barbara decided to wait until after dinner when the relatives left and Sam and Laura retired before she told Alice about the call from Jack Richards. She wasn't sure how her sister would react to the news that her childhood sweetheart wanted to see her again. Or, more surprisingly, that he wanted to search for the son he'd never acknowledged. As they cleaned up the dishes, Barb tried to lead up to the subject as easily as possible.

"Kind of a boring evening, wasn't it? We do have a batch of dreary aunts and uncles. No wonder all their kids moved away."

Allie smiled and didn't answer. She just kept washing plates and putting them into the draining rack for Barbara to dry.

"I think it was rotten of Fran to fink out on us," Barbara went on. "Mother and Daddy were really upset that she wasn't here. I'm sure they didn't believe her story about running into an old girlfriend and deciding to have dinner with her. Who'd buy that last-minute excuse? Honestly, she's hopeless. I can't help loving her, but she's to drive you mad! Do you think she went back to that waiter? I can't believe the whole scene!"

"You know Fran," Allie said. "She's restless."

"And selfish."

"Yes, I suppose so. But in a way I envy her. She keeps trying to find something right for her. She doesn't seem to make it, but at least she never stops searching. I give her credit for that, even if it's sometimes selfish and thoughtless, like tonight."

"You've never been selfish and thoughtless in your life, have you?" Barbara spoke slowly, wiping a platter, not looking at her. "You're so good, Allie. So much nicer than Fran and I."

Alice turned abruptly from the sink. "Bull!" she said unexpectedly. "I'm anything but nice. I'm full of hate, Barb. I hate myself and other people. I nurse grievances and I put up with things no woman with an ounce of dignity would stand for. Nice? No, I'm not nice. I'm gutless." She suddenly pulled down the shoulders of her caftan. "You need proof? Look at this."

Barbara stared at the big, ugly, purple-green bruises on her sister's upper arms. "My God! Where did you get those?"

"Where I get them all. All the bruises and black eyes and broken arms. From Spencer. From my lovely, respectable husband. This morning when I went to the hotel to get my clothes, he beat me. But only around the shoulders so nobody will see the marks." Allie's lip curled. "Nice of him, wasn't it? He probably didn't want to 'embarrass me' in front of my family. That's why he showed such 'restraint.' Otherwise he'd have kicked the living hell out of me for staying here last night instead of going home with him."

"Allie! I don't believe this! He beats you?" Barbara was horrified. "Why? Why does he do such a terrible thing?"

"Because he's sick. That's a lot easier to understand than why I've put up with it all these years." She pulled the gown back up to cover the evidence of Spencer's sadism. "That's what I mean about being gutless, Barb. Why do I stay with a man who has so little regard for me that he treats me like a possession he can abuse at will? Why have I done that for so long?"

Barbara was almost speechless. "For your children? Have you stayed because of Christopher and Janice?"

"That's what I told myself in the beginning. But that was wrong, and I recognized how wrong it was even when they were small. It's a crime to bring up children in a house full of cruelty. I couldn't hide it from them once they reached the age of understanding. I did a terrible thing to them, letting them grow up in that atmosphere. The way they've turned out proves it. Chris despises his father and God knows he has no use for marriage. He's gay, Barb. And no matter what the doctors say, I'll always blame myself for shaping his character in that direction."

"You shouldn't. Nobody's ever proved that homosexuality is a result of environment."

"And nobody's proved it isn't. In any case, it's been his revenge on Spencer. He taunts him with it. It's the one thing he knows his father can't handle."

Barbara sighed. Christopher's sexual preferences did not shock her. They didn't even dismay her, except she knew that to Allie it must represent one more proof of her failure.

"What about Janice? She must hate Spencer too."

"It's not the same with her. She despises him, but she has more scorn for me as a woman. Jan's very 'together,' as they say these days. She goes her own way and doesn't brood about things the way Chris does. She's having an affair with a young art director named Clint Darby. She seems quite happy, as long as she doesn't have to spend too much time at home. And God knows she doesn't."

All this explains so many things, Barbara thought. Allie's obvious unhappiness. The fact that she's kept pretty much to herself, only visiting Denver every three years or so, discouraging contact between us even though we live quite close. She's ashamed. She hasn't wanted any of us to know. But it still doesn't explain why she hasn't left Spencer. Her children are grown. If there was nowhere else to go, she could always come home. Why does she put up with this? She's still attractive and she's not mercenary enough to stay for the "comforts" Spencer provides.

"Why, Allie? Why don't you divorce him?"

"Good question. Why do thousands of women stay with wife-beaters? There must be a different answer for each one. Maybe some really love these bastards. And some are afraid they can't make it on their own. And I suppose a few masochists enjoy the punishment. Or think they can reform the monsters. Who knows? I only know it's not rare. I used to think it was unique with a man of Spencer's intelligence and social standing. I thought wife-abuse was something confined to the poor and ignorant. Not so. The world is full of Spencers. Rich, smart, successful men. And it's also full of Allies. Willing victims for one reason or another." She shrugged. "All I know is that the beaten must be as demented as those who beat them."

"You're not demented."

"I think I am. This started when I told Spencer about Jack Richards and the baby. He was outraged. He felt he'd been tricked into marrying a tramp. Why did I tell him, unless subconsciously I wanted him to punish me?"

"But even if I accept that, Allie, even if I accept that as the motivation, does the punishment never end? Do you pay the rest of your life?"

"I was resigned to that until I got here. Being with you and Fran again, feeling I was with people who cared for me . . . well, it started me thinking, Barb. I wish we could all have more than a week together. That we could talk a lot. About life. About our lives. Maybe I'd get the courage I need to tell Spencer Winters to go to hell forever. I think I'm pushing out of the fog. Just a little. I can breathe here. I'm almost happy. I was happier those two days before Spencer arrived than I've been in years. It's you, Barb. You and Fran. You're my sisters. And my only friends. God, it feels so good to confide in somebody! I'm sorry to burden you with this, but I've been wanting to say it ever since we all arrived. I'm not looking for sympathy. Everything I've done is my own fault. What I'm looking for is strength. Some of yours and Fran's, if you're willing to lend it to me."

Barbara put her arms around Alice. "Willing? Need you ask? If I can help you now, you know damned well I'll do anything. So will Fran. I know she will. She may seem self-involved, but you were right in what you said earlier: She's a fighter. And she'll fight just as hard for you as she would for herself. You can count on both of us, Allie. We'll talk a lot. You need to get this thing out in the open. Fran can certainly stay on awhile. For that matter, so can I. My boss will understand a 'family emergency.'" Barbara smiled. "And nobody could say this isn't one."

Allie was on the verge of tears. "You don't know what it would mean to me. It's horribly selfish, but I don't know when the three of us will be together again."

"Exactly. Good Lord, we've waited thirty years for this reunion! Wouldn't it be silly to end it in a few days?"

"You're really great, Barbara. I love you."

"I love you, too, silly." Forgive me, Charles, she thought silently. I want to be back with you more than anything in the world, but my sister needs me. We have years to be lovers, but she has only a few days to make up her mind about the rest of her life. If only Fran will help. But she will. There's a heart under that veneer. She'll be happy to make up for some of the neglect she's been guilty of too.

That thought brought Jack Richards back to mind. Absorbed in this startling story of Allie's life, Barbara had nearly forgotten about the man who really started it. The one who claimed he was anxious to atone. Was he serious? Could he help Allie now? Or would he only complicate her life and her thinking and make matters worse?

"Allie, I've been waiting all evening to tell you something." Barbara took a deep breath and told her about Jack's call. Her sister's face was a study in astonishment.

"Jack wants to see me? He wants to find our child?" Allie was incredulous. "Why? Why now?"

"I guess he's a changed man since the death of his wife. At least that's what he says. I don't know whether it's true, but somehow I believe him. Losing someone dear to you can do that, I imagine. Make you realize how precious life is and how sorry you are for your mistakes. But it's up to you. I have his phone numbers. I told him I couldn't make that decision for you." She watched Alice carefully and saw an almost ecstatic look come over her face.

"Oh, Barb, if you only knew how I've wondered about that baby! If you could imagine what it's like not to know whether he's well and happy! Whether he's even . . . alive."

"I could guess," Barbara said quietly.

"I've thought about him every day since they took him away. Every single day. I know nothing. Not where he went or who the people are who took him. Aunt Charlotte handled the whole thing. I just signed papers. I was so young and dumb and scared. I knew I had to give him life, but I was too frightened to keep him. Girls didn't do that in those days, you know. Society is much kinder to them now." She looked at Barbara with hope in her eyes. "Do you think Jack could find him? How would he start? Aunt Charlotte won't tell him anything. To this day she won't tell me. Says it's history and should be forgotten. I'm not sure she even knows any more."

Old bitch! Barbara thought. How dare she refuse to tell a grown woman about her own child! She's punishing Allie, just as Spencer is. I could murder both of them!

"Maybe you should give Jack a chance," she said. "I don't see that you have much to lose."

"What if he finds Johnny and my son hates me?" Alice seemed frightened by the prospect of the very thing she'd prayed for.

"Darling, he won't hate you. Nobody could hate you. But let's face the worst. Suppose Jack can find him and you discover that he resents you, that he wants no part of you? At least you'll *know*, Allie. Isn't that better than spending the rest of your life wondering?"

"Yes." The answer came slowly. "Anything is better than that."

They heard the front door open. This time Fran had had the foresight to borrow a key from her disapproving parents. Barbara and Alice went into the hall. Fran looked terrible, as though she'd been crying.

"What's wrong?" Alice asked. "Are you all right?"

"Terrific." Fran quickly put on the mask of bravado. "What are you two doing lurking around the foyer?"

"We've been talking about important things," Barb said. She glanced at Alice, who nodded confirmation. "We need your help, Fran. Feel like listening?"

"Sure. I'm a whiz at other people's problems." She laughed, a brittle, disenchanted little laugh. "Shall we get into our 'jammies and make hot chocolate and talk about boys?"

While the mother and father he had yet to meet were separately considering a search for him, John Peck decided to make his own move. The evening with Janice Winters had reinforced his belief that he was the son of Alice Dalton Winters and some unknown man. It all fitted. Not only the name but the circumstances and time of her arrival in Boston, her own mysterious, unlikely "adoption" by a childless aunt. He surmised, accurately, that an unmarried Alice had "gotten into trouble" in Denver and been packed off to the East before people discovered her condition. She'd probably been unhappy and frightened. He felt sorry for this stranger whom he was prepared to love. But what of his father, whoever he was? Obviously, the man was not Spencer Winters, who married Alice five years after she came to Boston. Had he fathered her first child, he'd have married her then and there. Whoever my father is, John decided, he must be a sonofabitch to get a girl pregnant and not marry her. Maybe the man was already married when Alice took up with him. Or, more likely, he ran out on her when he found out about me.

Jan said her father had come home without Alice. Good. That meant John could look up Daltons in the Denver telephone book and call Alice at her parents' house without Spencer Winters' knowledge. His pulse raced as he realized that within a few minutes he could possibly be talking to his mother. But what if he was wrong? What if this was yet another false lead? Carol continued to urge caution, even after the meeting with Janice.

"There still isn't much to go on, darling," she said. "I know how much you want this to be it, but I can't stand to see you get your hopes up and be disappointed again. Isn't there anything else we can do before you call Denver? Any other confirmation we can get?"

"The only other link I have is an elderly lady named Charlotte Rudolph. She's Alice's aunt. The one she came to live with when she was seventeen. She'd know, of course, whether her niece had a baby here and gave it up for adoption." John shook his head. "I doubt she'd admit anything, though. She's Mrs. Carlton Rudolph, widow of the architect. If you think 'high-toned people' like the Winters wouldn't admit to all this, can you imagine the dowager Rudolph confirming it?"

Carol whistled. "You have picked the upper crust for a family, haven't you? Carlton Rudolph's widow! Spencer Winters' wife! Sure you can't tie yourself into the Saltonstalls? Or maybe the Kennedys?"

He had to laugh. "Honey, I haven't picked anybody. You're the first one to say this might be just another pipedream. But I don't think so. I'm approaching the truth. What the hell, maybe I'll have a go at 'Aunt Charlotte' anyway. She might surprise me. And then I could call Denver with some degree of confidence."

"What will you say to her?" Carol sounded worried.

"I'm not sure. I'll have to play it by ear."

The next day he called Mrs. Rudolph's residence in Back Bay. A woman answered the phone.

"May I speak with Mrs. Rudolph, please?"

"Whom shall I say is calling?"

"John Peck."

He held on while she went to inform her employer. In a few seconds she came back on the line.

"I'm sorry, Mr. Peck, but Mrs. Rudolph says she doesn't know anyone by that name. I'm her housekeeper. Could you tell me what it's about?"

If I did, John thought humorously, you'd faint dead away. "I'm a friend of her great-niece, Janice Winters. It's purely a social call. I'd appreciate it if Mrs. Rudolph would spare me a minute or two."

"Hold on, please."

There was a period of silence and then an older, higher-pitched, more querulous voice came over the phone.

"This is Mrs. Rudolph."

He literally felt his knees knocking, but he tried to sound casual.

"Mrs. Rudolph, my name's John Peck. I'm a friend of Janice's."

"I already know that," Charlotte said tartly. "What is it you want?"

"I . . . I'm looking for some information about your niece, Mrs. Winters."

"Information? What kind of information? Who are you? Some government person from the tax bureau? Or are you selling something? What is your affiliation, Mr. Peck?"

"None," John said. "I mean, none of those things. That is, it's something personal. Mrs. Rudolph, could I come and see you? This is a very private matter and I'd rather not discuss it over the telephone."

"Come and see me? I don't entertain strangers, Mr. Peck. I'm a very old lady and in poor health, and even if I were not, I certainly wouldn't open my door to someone I've never heard of. I haven't the faintest idea what it is you're after, but if it has to do with Mrs. Winters, then I suggest you call her husband. Goodbye."

"Wait! Please don't hang up! Mrs. Rudolph, it's about something that happened thirty years ago. About a baby."

There was silence on the other end. John thought perhaps she'd already hung up.

"Mrs. Rudolph? Are you still there?"

"Yes. But I'm quite at a loss. I don't know what you're talking about."

"I think you do," John said quietly. "I'm the child Alice Dalton gave up for adoption."

"You're obviously mad, Mr. Peck." But the voice was less arrogant now. John felt a surge of joy. He'd shaken her. He was right. Her tone betrayed her surprise and dismay. He pressed his advantage.

"I think we should have a quiet talk, Mrs. Rudolph. Otherwise, my next call will be to Mrs. Winters at her parents' house in Denver."

This time he heard an intake of breath. But she was admitting nothing. She simply said, "I find this all quite extraordinary! Obviously a case of mistaken identity. However, if you wish to call at five o'clock I will receive you." She paused. "And I strongly advise that you do not embarrass yourself by calling my niece. There's no need to involve her in this mix-up."

"Of course. Thank you, Mrs. Rudolph. I'll be there at five."

She hung up without another word. John stood looking at the receiver in his hand. He couldn't help smiling. Aunt Charlotte was a tough old bird, but he'd have her eating out of his hand in another few hours.

Promptly at five, he rang the doorbell of the big old house on Huntington Avenue. A competent-looking woman in a white uniform, presumably the same person he'd spoken to on the phone, admitted him and ushered him into the drawing room, saying that Mrs. Rudolph would be with him in a moment.

While he waited, John looked about him, aware that this was his first real contact with his past. This is where she lived, he thought. This is where she hid out during her pregnancy. He imagined her sitting in this room with its stiff Victorian furniture, all dark carved wood and red velvet upholstery. He touched the three-tiered walnut whatnot in the corner, covered with silver boxes and miniature paintings on tiny easels, wondering whether Alice had wandered around in boredom, touching them too. Had she gazed at the dark landscapes on the wall, dwarfed by their ornate gold frames? Or stood in front of the oil painting over the fireplace, examining the portrait of a man with kind eyes who'd posed stiffly in his "Prince Albert" morning coat? He was so absorbed that he didn't hear Mrs. Rudolph come into the room. He almost jumped when she spoke to him.

"Mr. Peck? I'm Charlotte Rudolph."

He turned to face a tiny woman with penetrating blue eyes. She

wore a plain black dress and leaned heavily on a silver-headed cane. At her throat was a cameo, and her wrinkled hands were bare except for a plain gold wedding band. My God, thought John, she couldn't be a more typical matriarch if I'd ordered her from Central Casting! He gave an unaccustomedly formal little half-bow and said, "Thank you for seeing me. I wouldn't have imposed if it hadn't been terribly important."

Charlotte seated herself in an armchair and motioned him to the facing settee.

"Would you care for tea, Mr. Peck? I don't serve hard liquor."

"Nothing, thanks."

"Very well. Shall we get on with it? What is all this about you and my niece?"

He wondered how to approach her. As briskly and impersonally as she addressed him? Or should he try to ingratiate himself, play on her sympathy, beg for her help? Not that he really needed it now. He could always call Alice directly. But it would be easier if he had the background before he confronted his mother. No. No use trying to win over this hostile old lady. The best he could hope for was a few more scraps of information. He came right to the point. He told her about discovering his adoption papers after the death of the Pecks, how he'd searched for the Alice Dalton listed as his mother, how he'd finally seen the maiden name of Alice Winters in the society column and had met her daughter Janice. He told Charlotte of the meshing of dates and places and of his firm conviction that he was the child of Alice Dalton Winters.

Charlotte listened impassively, without interrupting. When he finished, she looked almost sympathetic.

"Poor Mr. Peck. What a sad story. How dreadful not to know who one's parents are. I was not blessed with children, but had I been I'd never have been so heartless as to part with them under any conditions. Nor," she said pointedly, "would *anyone* in my family. I'm sorry to disappoint you, but once again I'm afraid your search is futile. My niece came to live with me when she was a young girl because I was widowed and lonely and I could give her advantages my sister could not. Alice was introduced to the best people in Boston and eventually married well and had two children. But I assure you, Mr. Peck, she had no children before then,

and she certainly gave none away for adoption. I'm sorry," Charlotte said again. The last words had the ring of dismissal. "I do hope you'll find your mother one day."

"I *have* found her, Mrs. Rudolph. I know she's your niece."

Charlotte flushed with anger. "Are you presuming to say I'm not telling the truth? Are you accusing me of falsehoods, young man?"

John spoke quietly. "I'm afraid I am. I know you're not the kind of woman who's accustomed to lying, but in this case I believe you'd resort to that to keep an old scandal buried. I can understand. You want to protect my mother's reputation. You don't know anything about me. For all you know, I might have come here to blackmail you. But please, Mrs. Rudolph, please believe that all I want is to meet my mother. I don't plan to make a public outcry about any of this. I won't even tell Mr. Winters, if he doesn't know. Not anyone, except my wife. I don't want anything from you. Not even recognition by the world at large. I simply want to meet the woman who gave birth to me. To know about my father and the circumstances of that birth. I've lived all these years with questions. There'll be no peace for me until I get answers. Can't you understand that?"

"All I can understand is that you indulge in wishful thinking. You have nothing to go on but a not-too-unusual name and a series of unrelated events. I've never heard such nonsense! You had best leave now, Mr. Peck. And I warn you, if you have any ideas of stirring up trouble in this family we shall take steps to stop you."

"You leave me no choice," John said.

"And what, exactly, does that mean?"

"You can't believe that I'm going to stop now. Not when I'm so close to the answers. I don't plan to 'stir up trouble,' as you call it, but I do intend to call Denver."

Charlotte's eyes flashed. "And just where do you think that will get you? Mrs. Winters will no more confirm this silly supposition of yours than I will!"

"I hope you're wrong about that. I hope my mother will be happy to hear from me."

"Stop that! She's not your mother! How many times must I tell you?"

"You could tell me a million times and I'd never believe it until I heard it from her. Maybe," John said sadly, "not even then, if she's as unwilling to accept me as you are."

Charlotte stared at him. Somehow, she'd always known one day it would come to this. It was the thing she dreaded. One read about it every day in the newspapers: adopted children looking for their natural parents. She'd always feared Alice's illegitimate child might be one of those. That he'd turn up on their doorstep, demanding his birthright.

For that matter, it hadn't been easy after the first few years to keep Alice from trying to locate *him*. She wanted to find that Richards person's son as much as he now wanted to find her. Charlotte had had to be very firm, lying even then, denying she knew the name of the adoptive parents. Alice never believed that story, of course, but she had to accept it because her aunt was immovable.

And now it was here. All the old trouble, the old disgrace. This determined young man was dead-set on injecting himself into their lives, howling for his identity as loudly as he had howled with his first breath of life. Charlotte tried one last time.

"Look here," she said pleasantly. "I understand your obsession with your problem. I'm sure you're honestly convinced you're on the right track. But you could create some very upsetting gossip that would distress Mr. and Mrs. Winters. And to what avail? I assure you, Mr. Peck, my niece is not your mother. Why, after all this time, would I deny it if it were true? My heavens, it's so many years ago! If my niece had had you and given you up, there'd be no reason for her not to admit it to you. I'd admit it to you myself. Times have changed. She's a middle-aged woman with grown children of her own. She's perfectly safe and secure, much too firmly entrenched in society to be bothered by a youthful indiscretion," Charlotte paused to let the next words sink in, "*if it were true*. But it isn't true. If you pursue this, you will force Mrs. Winters into a public denial which will be unattractive for her and humiliating for you. Take my word for it, Mr. Peck, and drop this whole pathetic idea."

"I'm sorry, I can't. I don't wish to embarrass anyone, least of all my mother, but I won't stop now."

Charlotte became angry again. "You've accused me of not telling the truth. Very well. I now accuse you. I think you know very well that this is a complete fabrication. You probably have read about Spencer Winters and somehow managed to meet his daughter. You have the ridiculous idea that you can blackmail us by threatening ugly publicity. You mentioned that very word when you arrived. Blackmail. I don't know why it took me so long to understand why you're really here. It's money you want, isn't it? You're nothing but a low, conniving thief! I should call the police. That's what I should do. But that would make distasteful headlines. That's what you're counting on. All right, Mr. Peck, or whoever you are, I'll give you money. I'll give you a check for a thousand dollars right now and you'll sign a paper saying Alice Dalton Winters is no relation to you. Then you'll go away and never bother us again."

John rose from the settee and stared down at her. She was a good bluffer but she'd overplayed her hand.

"Thank you, Mrs. Rudolph, for making that offer. You've finally told me what I needed to know."

Charlotte watched him walk out of the room. Too late, she realized her mistake. Offering money when she had no need to was all the confirmation John Peck needed that he'd stumbled on the truth. What an old fool she was! How could she have fallen so easily into a trap! Spencer Winters would be furious. He might not let Alice ever see her again. And Laura would be so upset that the secret was out after all this time. Heaven help her, what had she done? Why did she ever agree to see Alice's child? I'm too old for this, she thought. Too old and too tired. She crouched over like a frightened animal and wept with regret and frustration.

Chapter 14

In his bedroom in Washington, Charles Tallent threw a clean shirt and a change of underwear into an overnight bag. Andrea watched him calmly, leaning against the door in that appraising stance he knew so well.

"I'll be back tomorrow night," he said. "It's only a two-hour flight, but the Candidate wants me to stay over."

"Do you think the rumor's true that he's going to offer you the job?"

Charles shrugged. "Secretary of Agriculture? I don't know. He's just interviewing possibilities. But you can't say he's not confident. Not even elected and he's already picking out his Cabinet."

"But he will be elected."

"Probably. All the polls point to a landslide."

"You'd be a very important and prominent man," Andrea said. "You'd have to change your lifestyle. Drastically."

"I don't see why. I'm already a public figure."

"Oh, Charles, for God's sake, stop acting! I'm not the only one who knows about your little Georgetown love nest. I'm sure the future President is well aware. In fact, I'm amazed he's even considering you. I hear he's going over possible appointees with a fine-tooth comb, looking for any *hint* of political or personal scandal. He can't afford to take chances. He's not going to name a man whose private life won't bear scrutiny."

Dammit, Charles thought, I've been wondering the same thing ever since I got the call. He must have heard about Barbara. It doesn't square with his pious image to choose a cabinet member with a mistress. It's probably just routine, this meeting. I don't have a chance. I'll be led to believe I'm "under consideration" because he wants my support in the House, now and later. That's all this is. Just window dressing. But I won't admit that. Not to Andrea, who must be getting great satisfaction out of knowing that my "outside interest" will do me out of something I'd give anything to have. She wouldn't mind being a Cabinet Wife. But she probably is enjoying her revenge even more.

"Well, we'll just have to see what the Senator has on his mind, won't we?" Charles sounded almost disinterested. "I'm sure as hell not flying to the Cape for a yachting trip at this time of year."

"Too bad you aren't meeting him in Denver."

Charles ignored her.

"I know where she is," Andrea went on. "I always know where she is. You've been home early every night for almost a week, so it's a fair guess your lady-love is not available. But I don't even have to guess at such things. Miss Dalton's landlady and I have become very good friends. She's quite meticulous about reporting to me. For a price, of course. She's a greedy, vulgar little woman, but she does have good eyes and ears."

He was furious. "That's disgusting! Spying on me as though I were some criminal! What for? You've known about this for years! I haven't lied to you. I haven't ever publicly embarrassed you. Why would you do this to Barbara?"

"Why would she do what she's done to me? *She*'s had no scruples. Why should *I?* One day, my dear Charles, I'll get some information that will open your eyes. Believe me, I'll bet your precious paramour is not the faithful lover you imagine. No woman in her right mind would put up with that kind of situation forever. She'll stray. You'll see. And I'll be the first to know. And the most delighted to tell you."

"You miserable . . ." Words failed him.

"It's a little absurd for you to play the injured party, isn't it? You're going to pay for the years that I've swallowed my pride and pretended to be above it all. What a pity your wonderful Miss Dalton is visiting her parents right now. It deprives you of the chance to strut like a peacock in front of her, instead of having only me to tell that the next President of the United States is interested in you." Andrea laughed. "Not that he is, of course. We both know that. This is a political ploy. You have too many strikes against you, Congressman. You'll flunk Agriculture. And every other important offer in your life. Because of her. I hope she's worth it."

On the plane, Charles still felt the sting of her words. She was right, of course. He'd worried, every election, that some word of Barbara would get to his constituents back home. But it never had. Anyway, his people loved him. Even if they heard it, they'd never believe such gossip.

The Cabinet post was another matter. The Candidate had no blind devotion. He dealt in facts. Hard facts. And the fact was that even though Charles Tallent might be the best man for the job, he'd never get it while Barbara Dalton was in his life. Not Charles's qualifications nor his personal popularity would make the hard-nosed Yankee Senator lay himself open to criticism about the caliber of men he chose to surround him. But he must know, Charles thought again. What could he have in mind?

He found out within an hour of his arrival at the big old sprawling New England house where the Candidate rested briefly between his nonstop campaigning. The Senator and his wife and their five children greeted him cordially and then he was conducted to the study. His host offered him a drink and chair in front of the fireplace, where a bright blaze crackled more for atmosphere than for warmth on this October afternoon.

The nominee of his party smiled companionably, asked briefly after Andrea and then got right to the point.

"I'm going to be elected, you know."

"Yes. I have no doubt."

"Neither have I. That's why I want the team ready. From the Vice President all the way down."

Charles felt his heart leap. Tom Schneider was the vice-presidential candidate, but none of the "team" had been named. Wouldn't be until after the election, of course, but The Man was a planner. Between now and January, he'd act as though he were already elected and inaugurated. Every detail in place. The smoothest victory and transition the country had ever seen.

"Very wise of you," Charles said. "Gives you time to find the best people for the top posts."

"Exactly. I'd like you in one of those posts, Charles. Agriculture, I thought. That's where your strength is. With the farmers. You'd be a good Secretary."

Before Charles could answer, his companion went on. "You leave the rest of your competitors in the dust as far as political savvy is concerned. But there's something else. Something the press would jump on. Something that could embarrass both of us. I don't have to spell it out, do I?"

Charles reluctantly shook his head.

"Lovely girl, Barbara Dalton. Always found her amusing when we met at parties. But she's bad news for you. That's obvious. Hell, Charles, you're not the first man in government who's been indiscreet." He smiled. "Between us, there were a few incidents early in my life that I wouldn't exactly want publicized either. We all sow the proverbial wild oats at one time or another. The point is we can't still be sowing them when we go into high office. People will forgive the past, overlook the little indulgences and human weaknesses you've put behind you. Assuming they find out, which we'll try to avoid. But even if there's talk, it wouldn't matter a helluva lot, as long as the affair was over." He paused. "Unfortunately, it's not over, is it?"

"No."

"But it could be? If something really big came along?"

Charles hesitated. "I don't know whether you understand. This is not some fly-by-night thing. It's a long-standing relationship. Andrea knows about it. She and I haven't been man and wife in years. We only stay together for the sake of the children. I love Barbara. I'd marry her tomorrow if I could." He stopped. "What if I did? What if I got a divorce and married her?"

The Candidate frowned. "No good. Too late in the day. Too obvious. It's not a divorced man I'd object to. We've had a lot of those high up in government. But they don't get divorced and quickly marry another congressman's secretary just before a new President appoints them to the Cabinet. That would cause worse talk. No, Charles, that won't work. The post is yours if you want it. But it comes with the image of a long-time devoted husband and father. We'll try to keep the other thing quiet. The press has been damned good to you in the past. But you were only a congressman. This is something else. We'll hope it won't come up when we announce the appointment, but if it does, there won't be one bloody thing to link you now to another woman. They can speculate, but as long as you're clean they can't prove anything. I assume Miss Dalton could be counted on to keep her mouth shut? She seems like a decent girl."

Charles said nothing for a moment. Then, "Yes. She's a very decent girl."

"Good. Then it's worth the risk in order to have you with me. Assuming, that is, you want the job."

"I want it very much. I'm complimented that you want me, but . . ."

"But it's a high price to pay, giving up the lady? Yes, I suppose it is. It depends on where a man's priorities lie. What he hopes for in his own future. You're still comparatively young in this business. No telling where you could go in, say, another eight years."

"There's no way we could resolve this? Are you sure the divorce idea isn't practical? My children would get over it, and Andrea doesn't give a damn."

"No, the timing's wrong. Good Lord, man, you know the press! I couldn't have this coming down around me at this particular time! Every nervous housewife in the country would blame *me* for your leaving your family and marrying your mistress! Sorry, Charles, but it's either/or. A big political future without Barbara, or damned little future at all."

Charles was torn. "Can you give me a little time to think? This means a great deal to me. All of it. The appointment and Barbara."

"Sure. I'm sorry to be unfeeling. Sometimes it's tough to be a realist. But look at it this way. Maybe after a few years, when you're well-established in the new job, you *can* get a quiet divorce, wait awhile and marry again. It won't attract so much attention then." The Senator was compassionate enough to lie. "I know it's difficult, but I need a decision before you leave tomorrow."

"Yes. Of course. Thank you very much."

"I hope you'll make the right one, for both our sakes."

In the guest room, Charles paced back and forth. Giving up Barbara was unthinkable. But so was refusing this great chance. "A few years," the Candidate said. What a laugh. As though Barbara would wait a few years, never seeing him. No. If he accepted the offer it was finished with the woman he loved. He couldn't imagine life without her. He couldn't bear to think how crushed she'd be. But she'd understand. She'd want this for him. She'd never stand in the way of his future. He might even be President. The Senator had hinted about "eight years"—implying that one day it might be Charles standing on that platform, listening to the cheers, accepting the party's acclaim. If only it could be Barbara and not Andrea standing next to him. But it couldn't, wouldn't be.

He knew his decision had been made even before he left the study. Andrea will be delighted on many counts, he thought bitterly. It solves all her problems. And she'll enjoy knowing what it cost me.

But what of Barbara? How can I face her? Can she understand that ambition sometimes is more compelling than love?

I'll fly out to Denver tomorrow, he decided. I've got to be man enough to tell her face to face, but I'm not strong enough to do it when we're alone in her apartment. There are too many memories there. Too many tender reminders of all the years. I couldn't stand saying goodbye to her in that dear, familiar place.

In the morning I'll tell the Senator I accept his offer. And I'll phone Andrea and tell her I'm going to Denver. And why. I don't give a damn what kind of fuss she makes. She's finally won. The Candidate has won. The loser is Barbara. And probably me.

The "loser," unaware of her impending loss, looked serious as she brought Fran up to date on the evening's developments. Allie sat quietly as her younger sister recounted the unexpected call from Jack Richards and her older one listened intently.

"So, he wants to find their son," Barb concluded. "He wants to see Allie again. He sounds like a changed man. Like he has a lot to make up for."

"You better believe it," Fran said. "More than a lot! But why the hell should he use Allie to purge himself of his sins? Why at this late date? For God's sake, it's been a closed chapter for a hundred years! Who needs him now? Him and his long-overdue remorse! I never heard such garbage! Tell him to get lost! Men! Always thinking of themselves! They don't give a damn how their actions affect anybody else as long as *they're* happy! If Allie sees Jack Richards again, she's a bloody fool. As for that crap about finding their 'long-lost child,' that's a convenient excuse if I ever heard one. He's probably bored and lonely and looking for a little heat from an old flame. I know the type. Probably thinks she's still in love with him, still wants him. And all *he* wants is some temporary action!"

Barbara stared at her, remembering the way Fran looked when she came home a few minutes earlier. She's not talking about Allie, she's talking about herself. Barbara was certain of it. Was it Buzz? Had Fran seen him tonight? Maybe made a play for him and been turned down? That's what this was all about. It had nothing to do with Allie and Jack. She opened her mouth to accuse Fran of voicing her own cynicism, but before she could say a word, Allie spoke up.

"I know you two are trying to help, but I get the feeling that I'm not in the room, the way you're discussing my problem. Look, my dears, it is *my* problem. I have to make the decision. I don't mean to sound ungrateful, but you're turning this into a debate, as though I can't speak for myself." She smiled. "I can, you know. You're both so strong, so sure of yourselves. I'm a mouse, but I can squeak when I choose to."

The quiet voice temporarily silenced her sisters. Then Barbara said, "I'm sorry, Allie. You're absolutely right. We are talking about you as though you aren't here. I guess . . . I guess Fran and I are seeing this from our viewpoints rather than yours. That's wrong, of course. Our attitudes aren't necessarily yours. What do you want to do about this?"

"I'm going to call Jack tomorrow." Alice's tone was firm. "I do want to see him. Wouldn't you want to see someone you were once desperately in love with? Even if it was 'a hundred years ago'?"

Fran reddened. It was as though they knew about her and Buzz. What a complete ass she'd made of herself, throwing herself at him, sure he'd jump at the chance to leave his wife for her. And how humiliating it had been to be rejected. She shut her eyes, as if to blot out the memory of that scene in the motel room. It never happened, she told herself. I didn't mean any of it. I wouldn't have that stupid little car salesman on a bet! But she would. He seemed to represent all that was solid and sane in a world gone berserk. And he *was* solid and sane. So much so that he'd never get mixed up with her again. He's smart, Fran thought bitterly. He knows what he has. He's not going to take a chance on what he might get. He must have sensed her desperation and recognized it for what it was: the reach for the last chance; fear of loneliness, not love of him. She glanced at Barbara, who seemed equally thoughtful. What's Barb's life really all about? she wondered. In its own way I suspect it's as precarious as mine. Allie's wrong about one thing. She's as strong as we are. Stronger, maybe.

"Okay," Fran said, "so you're going to see him. What then?"

"I don't know. Nothing, probably. Between us, I mean. But if he can help find our boy . . ."

"Oh, Allie, darling, don't count on that!" Barbara was distressed. "See him if you want. But don't hope for miracles about the other thing."

"I live on hope," Allie said. "I have for years. Hope that that baby is now a happy man. Hope that my other children will always be all right." An edge of bitterness crept in. "I've even hoped that one day Spencer will change. Or that I will." She turned to Fran. "I told Barb tonight what it's like to live with a man who beats you for any reason or for none at all. That's been my life for twenty-five years, Fran. Always in fear, always waiting for the unpredictable. Hiding the evidence, pretending my husband isn't psychotic, hoping, hoping he'll change. Or that I'll finally find enough courage to be done with it. I've been totally faithful to Spencer. I haven't so much as looked at another man since the day we got engaged. But this trip has made some kind of difference. Seeing Mother and Dad. Seeing you and Barb. Feeling cared about. It's renewed me. Strengthened me. And maybe seeing Jack will help restore some of the self-esteem I haven't had since I was a girl."

Fran hardly heard the last part. "Beats you? Spencer Winters beats you? And you stand for it?" As Barb had been, Fran was horrified, outraged. "Why, Allie? For God's sake, why?"

"It's too long a story for now. Let's just say he's a sick man. And I'm pretty mixed up myself to live with his sickness."

Fran took a deep breath. "You're not counting on Jack Richards to save you, are you? That's storybook stuff, Allie. The knight in armor riding in on the white charger to rescue the maiden in distress. Maybe you ought to settle one problem before you take on another."

"I told you I don't expect anything significant to happen between Jack and me. Nothing permanent or even momentary. But I do believe in fate, Fran. There must be some reason for his coming back into my life after all these years. Maybe our son is the reason. I don't know. I just know I'll see him, and whatever will be, will be." Allie gave an embarrassed laugh. "You must think I'm crazy, both of you. Talking about predestination. But I do believe in it. For all of us. I think heaven and hell happens right here in our lifetime, and that everything was meant to be." She sobered. "If I didn't believe that, I couldn't exist."

"Maybe so," Fran said. "But whoever drew up my plan was a lousy architect. And from what you've said, Allie, and from what I suspect about Barb, they should have gone back to the drawing board when they were mapping out our lives."

"Things could always be worse," Barbara said. "Bad as they may be, there are always people with more terrible troubles. Fran, nothing's perfect."

"Tell me," Fran mocked. "Listen, kid, I wasn't twenty years old before I discovered *that.* I've lived my life with one comforting piece of knowledge: There's always a broken window in the Taj Mahal."

The flippant remark broke the tension. Suddenly they were laughing, momentarily forgetting their disappointments and disillusionments, locked together in the warm and comforting embrace of womanly understanding. The same thought was in each mind: They're my sisters and they'll stand by me, no matter what. It was a precious realization.

Upstairs, still awake in her bed, Laura Dalton heard the beautiful, sudden sound of her daughters' laughter. What good girls they are, she thought sentimentally. Warm and loving and devoted. True, they were not "dutiful" in the accepted sense. It was embarrassing sometimes to explain to friends why her children came home so seldom. Why, indeed, her eldest hadn't returned, until now, since the day she left. Why her youngest managed only an annual visit and her middle girl came to see her parents so infrequently. For that matter, it really was inexplicable. Not unique, perhaps, but rare, especially when families had not had an obvious "falling out."

She couldn't say to the world that Sam had virtually banished Alice and that the old wounds had never really healed. She couldn't admit that Frances had run from a "middle-class existence" of which she did not wish to be reminded and that she might never have come back if there'd not been a Golden Anniversary. One that Barbara had probably bullied or shamed her into attending. And Barbara herself was so involved with her congressman and her glamorous Washington life that she couldn't be expected to spend much precious free time in Denver, doing nothing.

I understand, the mother thought. And then, almost angrily, No, I don't. Why do I think of them as "devoted"? Because they send occasional letters and gifts and phone now and then? They're not devoted. Not the way other children are. They don't really want to see us. They stay in touch out of duty. Or, she shuddered, pity. They've made lives without us. Without our help or our approval. Almost in spite of us. They give us nothing. We seem more ancestors than parents.

Immediately, she was ashamed of herself. Those were the thoughts of a self-pitying, aggrieved mother. The stereotype of the deep-sighing, neglected parent. She had no right to think that way. She and Sam had no claims on these women simply because they'd given them life.

We gave them damned little else, Laura thought. We fed and clothed and housed them, but we didn't think it necessary to really know them or let them know us. We stayed aloof from them as human beings, even while we smugly assumed ourselves to be "good parents." We expected love. We didn't know we had to earn it.

And knowing that, they left us, not only physically but emotionally. Why *should* they come home? Because it's expected of them? Because it's the thing children are supposed to do? Where is it written that one must frequent scenes of boredom? We bore our children. She smiled at the unconscious little play on words. I bore them and we bore them. But it wasn't funny. It was sad. Parents and children should be friends. There should be a desire to see each other, to exchange ideas, compare worlds, have adult-to-adult conversations. But such congeniality was a two-way street, she told herself. And Sam and I know only one way.

It would be different, she supposed, if one of us were alone. If she died or Sam died, the girls would feel obliged to pay more attention to the survivor. But that was wrong too. They're not responsible for us, Laura mused. I hope neither of us makes them feel that way, because we are as much to blame for the separation as they. Early on, they invited us to visit and we never did. Sam didn't want to. He felt they should come home. I suppose I did too. I'm as bound up as he in the conventional attitudes. I grew up in an age when respect was demanded and the elders received it. Or thought they did. Did I respect my own parents? Maybe not. Maybe not really. I never thought about it. I was so thoroughly conditioned to "honor" them that it never occurred to me it might be nice to like them as well.

And when my children were born, I made sure that Sam's parents and mine saw them often. "Duty calls." Aptly titled. We dutifully took the girls to see their grandparents. They probably hated it. Maybe that's why Alice doesn't insist her children come to see us. And of course Sam and I are too stiff-necked and thin-skinned to go and see them.

So, year after year goes by and I talk of my family and sometimes brag about them and always pretend I'm so "modern," that I accept their absence without hurt or question. But I don't. I wish I were more interesting to them. I wish we could share. I'm a little in awe of them, I suppose. All so efficient and poised and in charge of their lives. I wish they felt me worthy to enter the doors behind which they live.

The laughter stopped and she heard the sound of them coming upstairs, the whispered goodnights, the gentle closing of the two bedroom doors. Where was Fran earlier tonight? Why is Allie staying on without Spencer? What will become of Barbara if that married man leaves her one day? Where are my daughters headed in this life? So many questions. So few answers.

Sam snored loudly at her side. Lucky man, Laura thought. No nagging doubts nibble at his mind and disturb his dreams tonight.

Chapter 15

Spencer Winters was still seething when his flight got into Boston's Logan Airport. The past two days had been full of surprises, and he didn't like surprises. They threw him off stride, took control of the situation out of his hands, and Spencer didn't care for that. He hated it when it happened in the courtroom. When some unexpected witness for the prosecution appeared or some damned fool jury brought in an unlikely decision. Things were supposed to be predictable. Of all things, his wife was supposed to be. And she hadn't been, last night or this morning.

He felt his anger rising again as he remembered Alice's calm declaration, the night of the party, that she was staying at her parents' house. It had been humiliating to leave alone. She'd made an ass of him in front of other people, and even though there was no one there Spencer gave a damn about, he was still furious with her for that. This morning, he'd given her a little taste of what to expect when she came home. And she'll be home, he thought grimly. That uncharacteristic burst of independence won't last. She can't stay away from her precious children, for one thing. And for another, how would she get along? He'd not give her a red cent. She'd tire pretty quickly of living in her parents' run-down house without a penny to spend. God knows that dreary father of hers couldn't afford to support her. The man probably had a couple of hundred dollars a week, if that. And Alice wasn't likely to go back to work either. At her age, what would she do? Sell at the

Denver Dry Goods? Hardly. After twenty-five years of luxury, she was far too spoiled.

Ungrateful bitch! She should be on her knees thanking God that a decent man had married her. Instead, she'd openly defied him at the hotel when she'd come to collect the few things she had there. He suddenly realized how few there had been. Allie had left most of her clothes at her mother's. She'd never intended, right from the start, to spend a week at the Hilton. She knew damned well he wouldn't stay in Denver, and all along she planned to be there without him. She was some actress! All that carrying on about his leaving early! Pretending she was disappointed he intended to go home the day after the party! She knew he would. She was hoping for it.

Well, she got her wish. And a few nice fat bruises to remind her that disobedience would not be tolerated. She'd get worse in a few days, when she came crawling back. Spencer would not soon forget the things she said the morning he left.

He'd started raising hell that morning, the moment she walked into the hotel room. He was still furious that she hadn't come back with him the night before, that she'd had the temerity to say he should tell J.B. to go to hell!

"You filthy little nobody!" Spencer had said. "How dare you behave as you did last night! Making a spectacle of me! What did those people think when I went home alone, a man whose wife preferred to sleep with her sister!"

Allie was dismayed to find he was still in the room. She thought he'd left. The desk said he'd paid his bill. "I don't think people noticed, Spencer." She tried to remain calm. "There was nobody there you cared about. Nobody important to you."

"That's not the point. Your place is with me."

"Why?" Her voice was flat.

Spencer was incredulous. "Why? Because, God help me, you're my wife. That's why! Because you belong to me. Because, like it or not, I own you."

"You really believe that, don't you?"

"You bet I believe it! I more than believe it: I *know* it! Every dress you put on your back, every mouthful of food you eat is thanks to me. Every person who knows you accepts you because you're Mrs. Spencer Winters, and don't you ever forget it!"

"I've never been allowed to. Not in twenty-five years."

Her calmness only added to his anger. "You're going back to Boston with me this morning. Call your mother and tell her to pack your things. We'll pick them up on the way to the airport."

Allie stared at him. "Yesterday you said I could stay as long as . . ."

"Never mind what I said yesterday! Yesterday my wife was behaving like the dutiful, respectful woman she's supposed to be. Today I've changed my mind. I don't want you hanging around out here, letting those sisters of yours put ideas in your head. Oh, I know what happened. Don't think I'm a fool, Alice. They've encouraged you, those tarts! And you're so stupid you listened to them. I suppose you've told them everything about our life. About our pansy son and our immoral daughter. I'm sure you've even told them about our fights, without explaining that you deserve what you get!"

"I've told them nothing!" Alice's face was becoming as flushed as his own. "I'd be ashamed to tell them I'm married to a sadist. I'm not ashamed of our children, but I'm mortified for you. What kind of a man hits a woman? Any woman? And *deserve* it? My God, Spencer, even you can't believe you're entitled to beat your wife!"

He'd approached her then, his fists upraised. "It's the only thing you understand—a good whipping. You don't have brains enough to accept reasoning. Yes, I have a right to hit you anytime I damn well please because it's the only way to knock any sense into your head! Like now. You're going home. Willingly, if you're smart. Forcibly, if you make it necessary!"

Alice backed away. "No, Spencer. No, I'm not going. I'm staying here for a while. Long enough to decide what I should do."

He came closer. "It's not for you to decide. Do as I tell you."

"No." She was trembling, trying to step away from him, hopelessly looking for escape from the room. If only she could get to the door. But he'd come after her, follow her down the hall, maybe knock her around out there where anyone could see and hear. "No," she said again, placatingly. "Please, Spencer, let me stay. You said I could. I just want to visit with my family awhile. I'll come home in a few days. I promise. I didn't mean all that about deciding what I should do. I need a rest, that's all."

"I'll give you a rest! In the hospital, by God, if you don't stop this nonsense!"

He'd backed her up against the wall. She saw his clenched hands come down with terrible force, striking her shoulders. She covered her face, tried to remain upright, but the strength of the attack knocked her onto the bed. She lay there; trying to shield herself as he struck her again and again on her upper body, accompanying every blow with a filthy word; calling her every kind of ugly name. She could only sob in pain and terror until he stopped. Then he straightened up and looked at her with disgust.

"That's all you know how to do, isn't it? Whimper and snivel. You miserable excuse for a woman! Beating's too good for you."

Abruptly he turned away and picked up his overnight bag. Allie lay on the bed crying quietly, feeling the soreness begin in her arms and shoulders and yet also realizing a strange sense of victory. This time I won, she thought. I stood up to him for what I wanted. This time even his violence couldn't make me obey. Maybe I can make it, with the help of Barb and Fran and Mother. Maybe I never have to go back again.

She said nothing, nor did he. An almost unbearable sense of relief came over her as Spencer left, slamming the door behind him. She lay still for a few more minutes, fearful of his return, but nothing happened. At last she rose and slowly, painfully, packed her small bag. I could never tell them what he says to me, Alice thought. I couldn't use those words. But I'll tell my sisters about his cruelty. And I'll ask their advice. There must be some other way for me to live. I'm entitled to a life as free and independent as theirs. Coming back here has made me see things in a different light. I'd forgotten there was a world in which Spencer Winters is not king.

Spencer hailed a cab at Logan Airport and was home in a few minutes. To his surprise, Janice was in the living room.

"Well! To what do we owe this unexpected honor?"

His daughter smiled casually. "Hi, Dad. Just dropped in to pick up a few clean clothes. What are you doing home? I thought you were going to stay longer. Where's Mother?"

"Your mother is still in Denver. I permitted her to stay on for a few days."

"You *permitted* her?" Janice snorted. "My God, you make her sound like some kind of a galley slave! Why don't you get with it, Pops? It's nineteen seventy-six. Husbands don't *permit*; they *respect*. She's a person, too, you know. Not a possession of yours."

"Don't call me 'Pops.' It's vulgar. As for the rest of your ridiculous conversation, Janice, I choose to ignore it. You're a silly child who doesn't understand a mature relationship."

"I would if I saw one. I never have, around here."

It was too much. First Alice defying him and now this impertinent girl telling him how to handle his own wife. Damn women anyhow! Damn all this new independence. He hated the way the world was going. He was only following the rules he grew up with in his own parents' house: Wives were submissive, and if they were not, they occasionally got a cuffing to keep them in line. Children were seen and not heard, and unfailingly respectful of their elders. Daughters were obedient and sons manly. The values he cared about and believed in, including the domination of the home by the father, were threatened, and Spencer Winters was infuriated by the knowledge.

"Janice, be quiet! I won't be spoken to that way!"

She grinned. "Aye, aye, sir. Yessir, Captain Bligh. Anything you say."

He wondered why he loved her. She was the only thing he did love. And yet she mocked him, ridiculed him, offended his "sense of decency" in every way. Spencer sighed.

"I suppose you're off again right away. You wouldn't consider having dinner here with me tonight?"

"Sorry, we can't. Clint and I are busy."

"I didn't ask Clint."

"Oh? I just assumed it. We come as a pair, you know. A matched set, like bookends." Janice was enjoying his discomfort. "When's Mother coming back, by the way?"

"I'm not sure. In a few days."

"How was the party?"

"You should have been there."

"It was that good, huh?"

"No, but it would have been respectful for you to show up."

"Hell, Dad, I hardly know those people! I wasn't about to fly all the way to Denver for a hokey reunion with some relatives I don't give a damn about."

"*I* did."

"Okay, I'm sorry." She smiled winningly. "You were a good sport to go. I'm sure Mother appreciated it."

He relaxed a little. "Anything happen around here?"

"Not much. Aunt Charlotte called a few minutes ago. She was looking for Mother. I reminded her you planned to stay a week. She'd completely lost track of time. She really is dotty, you know." Jan looked at him speculatively. "By the way, why didn't you stay? You and Mother have a fight?"

"Your mother and I don't fight, Janice."

"Oh, no, Dad. Neither does Muhammad Ali."

Shuffling through his phone messages, he pretended not to have heard. "Did your Aunt Charlotte want anything special?"

"I haven't a clue. She just said Mother was to call her as soon as she could. That it was urgent."

"I see. Well, maybe I'll give her a ring later and see what's on her mind. I know neither you nor your brother has checked in. There was a note when I was in Denver, saying you hadn't."

"Oh, for God's sake! She must have written it before Mother boarded the plane! I was going to call her tomorrow. Honestly, she's impossible!"

Charlotte sounded even more distracted than usual when he got her on the phone.

"Alice won't be home for a few days," he said. "Is there something you need?"

"No. That is, well, not really. I mean . . . Oh, dear, Spencer, I do think I've done something frightfully unwise." The moment she said it, Charlotte knew she'd made another mistake. She hadn't intended to tell Spencer anything about that upsetting visit from John Peck. Quite the contrary. She'd simply wanted to secretly warn Alice that the young man intended to make trouble. And now she'd given Spencer an opening he'd surely pursue until she told him the whole story. He'd be so angry with her, the way she handled it. Why was she so stupid! I'm old, Charlotte thought defensively. My mind doesn't work as quickly as it should any more. She heard her nephew-in-law's impatient intake of breath.

"All right, Aunt Charlotte, what have you done? Alice isn't here, so you might as well tell me."

She's probably done something idiotic, like firing the housekeeper, Spencer thought. Old fool! As though it wasn't difficult enough to get servants of any kind these days, and nearly impossible to find one willing to live in with an eighty-year-old woman. Why the hell didn't she answer him? He could hear her nervous breathing on the other end of the line.

"Aunt Charlotte? What is it? I asked you what you've done."

"Nothing, Spencer dear. Nothing important. It can wait until Alice comes back. No need to trouble you."

"I'm not sure exactly when Alice will be back." He was beginning to sound annoyed. "Now, you wanted something, surely. Otherwise, why the urgent call?"

She tried to think of a reasonable evasion but she was too upset. "It's John," she said. "He's looking for Alice."

"John? Who's John? What are you talking about?"

Once started, she blurted out the whole story. Spencer listened, trying to make sense out of the rambling account. For a moment he was too surprised to be anything but incredulous, and then the full impact hit him. Alice's goddamn illegitimate brat had turned up! He'd somehow found out where his mother was! And this ninny had thoroughly fumbled the situation, offering him money to go away and keep quiet, confirming that he'd stumbled on the truth! Spencer could have cheerfully wrung her neck. He tried to control himself. Tried to think how to handle it. It was too late for recriminations but he couldn't resist them.

"What on earth made you do such a damned-fool thing? Why did you receive him in the first place? Don't you realize how embarrassing this can be for all of us? My God, have you any idea the trouble this can cause?"

She'd begun to weep. "I know, Spencer. I knew you'd be angry. I was so frightened when he called. He sounded . . . evil. He was. He was threatening. I was in fear of my life!" She began to embroider the picture of a menacing, desperate man. "I . . . I thought a person like that would take a thousand dollars and go away without harming me. For all I knew, he might have had a gun!" She was whining now. "I'm an old, unprotected lady. Facing someone who might kill me. Don't you see, Spencer? I was terrified!"

"All I see is that you're even more stupid than your niece! How could you have made such a mess of things?"

"I'm sorry. I wish I'd gone to Denver! This never would have happened to me!"

To you, Spencer thought. Who the hell cares what happens to you? It's the future I'm thinking of. What will people say if they find out Alice has a bastard child? What will J.B. think? He'll think my wife is a whore. And he'll think me crazy for having married one. It's not fair. I've worked so hard for that partnership, and with a man like J.B. this could blow the whole thing. He won't tolerate scandal. None of us can forget how he fired Tyler Parke when he found out Parke's wife was an alcoholic. "Bad for the firm's image," J.B. said. Jesus! What will he make of this?

Be calm, Spencer told himself. Maybe you can solve it somehow. Think, man. There must be a way out. He forced himself to sound composed.

"All right, Aunt Charlotte. It's done. It can't be helped. What we have to do now is make sure this John Peck leaves us alone. He didn't take the money, is that right?"

"No." Her voice was almost a whisper.

'Too bad, in a way. I might have been able to threaten him with extortion. Scare him off with the idea of a criminal charge. But he's too smart for that, obviously. He's gambling for higher stakes."

"I think he just wants to find his mother," Charlotte said meekly.

"Don't be naïve! He thinks he's blundered into a good thing. We're not even sure he is who he claims to be. What proof does he have? Unfortunately, that's even less important than the trouble he threatens to make. It's the publicity we don't want, and he knows it."

"He said if he could just see Alice he'd never tell anyone."

Spencer turned sarcastic. "And of course we should believe him. He's just a poor little waif searching for his long-lost mother! Doesn't want a thing out of it except a kiss from her! Really, Aunt Charlotte! Even you couldn't swallow that!"

"I think I have to hang up now, Spencer. I'm feeling quite ill."

"Wait! Did he say where Alice could reach him?"

Charlotte searched her memory. "No. I don't think so. But there was something else besides the thing he read in the paper. Now, what did he say that made me think . . ."

"Try to remember! It's important that I have every detail."

"Just give me a minute, Spencer." There was a pause. "Oh, yes, I believe he mentioned Janice when he telephoned. Yes, he did. He said he was a friend of hers."

Spencer was stunned. "A friend of Janice? Are you sure?"

"Yes, quite sure. He began the conversation that way."

"But he didn't give you his address or telephone number. You're positive."

"No, he didn't. Perhaps Janice knows."

"We'll see. All right, Aunt Charlotte, I guess that's it for now."

"I'm so sorry, Spencer," she said again.

"You bloody well should be."

In his characteristically methodical way, Spencer went to his desk in the library and organized his thoughts on a yellow legal pad. In his precise handwriting he wrote on the left side of the page "Possibilities" and on the right "Solutions," numbering each:

POSSIBILITIES	SOLUTIONS
1. Peck may be a fake.	1. Make him prove he isn't.
2. P. may be A.'s child.	2. Have A. disclaim him. Tell J.B. we're being blackmailed.

Under this, Spencer made another heading:

PROCEDURES AND ALTERNATIVES

1. Inform Alice immediately.
2. Find out from Janice who P. is.
3. Say nothing and find him myself.

He studied the list carefully. Too bad this isn't a gangster movie, he thought. I could have a "contract" put out on this goddamned John Peck and end the thing forever. Sometimes the underworld had the right idea: move swifly and silently and expeditiously to get rid of your enemies. He thought of Peck as an enemy. A threat to Spencer's well-ordered life and carefully planned future. Of course, murder was out of the question. Reason or, if necessary, threats would have to prevail with Peck. And force with Alice.

He realized he instinctively believed this intruder was his wife's

Chapter 16

She was as nervous as an animal in a windstorm. During the night, after the talk with her sisters and Allie's incredible admission of the abuse she took from that no-good Spencer Winters, Fran impetuously decided to leave Denver early. Get away from all of them. They made her feel so obligated: Allie with her marital problems, and now this business with Jack and the child; Mother with those damned haunting eyes that seemed to see right through her; Dad with his pathetic acceptance of old age. Even Barb, who had whispered to her on the way upstairs, "We may have to stay on a few days longer, Fran. Allie needs us."

The only one who didn't make her feel duty-bound was Buzz. He'd made her feel foolish, and that was even worse.

She'd lain awake until all hours, smoking cigarettes in the dark, thinking about them. And this morning she knew she wanted to run and wouldn't. Not from the family. Not from a man who'd rejected her. The nerve of him, that two-bit auto dealer! Men didn't do things like that to her. Ironically, she'd never felt about one as she did about Buzz. She wondered if, after all these years, she'd fallen in love for the first time. Idiotic fancy! And yet she'd never been so depressed over any lost lover. Perhaps because none had ever so gently but firmly pushed her away. His firm but tender dismissal only increased Fran's desire. She felt trapped and unable to free herself.

It had been almost dawn when she fell asleep, and after eleven child. God knows what the man actually said to Charlotte. Probably more than she remembered. He considered his options, immediately discarding the idea of telling Alice anything now. He was equally reluctant to question Janice. Perhaps she already knew about it. It seemed certain she did, if the man really was a friend of hers. Of course, he might not be. He could have also made up that part of the story if he'd "researched" the Winters family. He could have read Janice's name somewhere as easily as he'd read Alice's. But if that were true, how had he made the connection to Charlotte Rudolph? No. Peck knew Janice, all right. Not that that proved anything. How much does Janice know? Spencer wondered. She takes such pleasure in tormenting me. Maybe she knew all about this even while we were talking today. Maybe she was laughing inside, knowing what I'd hear when I called Charlotte. Damn that girl! I won't give her the satisfaction of asking her help. Not unless there's no other way.

He reached for the Boston telephone directory. There was a long list of "Pecks" and a number of "Johns" and "J's." I don't even know whether he lives in Boston, Spencer thought. He could be in a nearby town. Andover. Lexington. Concord. Anywhere they circulated the Boston *Globe*. I'll just have to assume he lives here. Tomorrow I'll have my secretary start calling every "J. Peck" in the book. She won't have to know what it's about. I'll simply have her ask for the gentleman who contacted Mrs. Rudolph.

If that doesn't work, I'll have to go to Janice. And I'd better move quickly. Peck said he was going to call Alice in Denver. I hope I can stop him before he does that. She'd be sentimental and crazy enough to see him, probably acknowledge him. It wouldn't matter a damn to her how that would affect me!

He paced angrily through the empty apartment, nursing the rage he felt once again at having been "tricked" into marrying what he thought was a virgin. What a young fool I was! I could have had any girl I wanted and I chose this one because I found her exciting. Exciting! You bet she was exciting! She had enough experience to know how to be. Good thing for her she isn't here right now when all this dirty business has come full circle. Yes, a damned good thing she isn't. I think I'd kill her.

when she woke. Barbara had written a note and shoved it under the door.

> Fran, dear, Allie spoke to Jack this morning. I'm driving her over to meet him. Borrowed your car. Hope it's okay. The Parents know *nothing!* (They've gone marketing.) See you later. Luv, B.

More nonsense! Fran thought. If Alice wanted to meet her old boyfriend, why on earth did she drag Barbara along? Obviously, Jack couldn't come here, but why didn't Allie drive herself? She probably needed "moral support." That was an apt phrase. Demure little Alice, the "weakest" of the three, turned out to be the one with the juiciest problems. God knows her pregnancy out of wedlock and her sordid married life were more dramatic than Fran's affairs and divorces. Probably more than Barb's life, too, whatever it was. Her "baby sister" was tantalizingly close-mouthed about her life in Washington. Well, I haven't gone into much detail about my own, Fran thought. Before we scatter, it would be interesting to swap stories. Who knows? It may be years before we see each other again.

The deserted house seemed shabbier than ever, its worn oriental rugs and frayed old furniture mercilessly spotlighted by the morning sun that streamed through the windows. Fran wandered out to the kitchen. They'd left coffee on the stove for her. While she drank it, hot and black, her mind went back to Buzz. He'd be in his office now. Was he thinking of her? Did he regret throwing away that second chance she'd offered? It would be easy enough to pick up the phone and find out. You can't really believe he doesn't want you, can you? she asked herself. No, she answered. I can't. I don't take kindly to defeat.

En route to Jack's apartment in Stoneybrook, Barbara chattered nervously to a silent, introspective Alice. "Every time I come back I remember so many things we all did together. It's amazing what stays tucked away in your head. Like 'special occasions' when Mother took the three of us to lunch at Daniels and Fisher's tearoom. Remember what a treat that was? These days Mother goes to lunch at The Lookout Room at The May Company D and F, out in University. Once a week. With her 'girlfriends.' I think they even sneak a cocktail." Barb shook her head. "We grew up here a million years ago, didn't we? Everything's changed. Even the elm trees have died off from some kind of blight. . . ."

"Barb," Alice interrupted.

"Yes?"

"I know what you're trying to do: distract me. Get my mind off this meeting. Thanks, honey, but it really isn't working. I'm scared out of my mind. Even hearing his voice this morning gave me a sinking spell. I was so in love with him once. I'd have done anything for him." She gave a little laugh. "In fact, I did."

Barbara concentrated on the highway. "You were too young, Allie. Both of you. You made a mistake you couldn't handle. You can't go through life torturing yourself for it."

"I suppose so. I haven't had to. Spencer's done that for me."

They were silent for a moment and then Allie said, "I wonder what Jack is like now. He sounded the same on the phone." She looked at her sister. "Do you think I'm wrong, Barb? Going to see him, I mean? I don't know what I expect of this visit. I know he can't find our baby. I really do know that, in spite of what I said. I understand why he wants to see me. I guess that whole business has weighed on his conscience all these years. You wouldn't remember, but he behaved abominably. He lied to me, promised everything would be all right. What a dumb little thing I was to believe him! I was so disappointed in him I thought I hated him, but I never have. There's something about the first man in your life you never forget. Not even when he's also your first disillusionment. Women. We're such sentimental fools." She brushed at her eyes with the back of her hand. "Good Lord, I hope I don't start bawling when I see him! I mean to be calm and collected. I keep trying to imagine how Fran would handle this."

Barbara half-smiled. It was such a naïve statement. Fran would never find herself in such a spot. She'd always been too self-protective to be vulnerable to the kind of "sweet talk" that had been Allie's undoing. Fran was born knowing it all, Barb thought. I'm sure she was selfish in the sandbox. "You'll handle it better than Fran would," she said reassuringly. "You'll be yourself. Here's the turnoff to Stoneybrook. What was that number again?"

Allie consulted the little slip of paper in her hand. "South Yosemite Street. 8675. Apartment 108."

They pulled into the driveway and Barb switched off the engine. "Sure you don't want me to wait for you in the car? I don't mind. It might be easier for both of you if there's no third party present."

Something like panic came into Allie's eyes. "No! Please, Barb. You promised you'd be with me."

"I will, of course. I just thought . . ."

"That I'm a grown woman and should be able to handle this alone. I know. I am a grown woman. I shouldn't need support, but I do."

"Okay. You've got it."

They crossed a little stone path and climbed a flight of wooden steps to the front door of number 8675. The condominiums were more like small houses rather than apartments, each one with a "front porch" and an outside entrance. Alice hesitated for a fraction of a second and then rang the bell. The door was opened almost immediately and she stood looking up into the handsome face of Jack Richards. He's so much older! she thought involuntarily. The silly reaction made her smile. Of course he was. What had she expected? That nineteen-year-old who'd made love to her in the back seat of his car? He must be going through the same shock. But there was nothing but pleasure in his face as he reached out and took both her hands in his.

"Allie. I can't believe it. I'm happy to see you." The voice was the same. So were the clear brown eyes, though there were little crisscrosses of lines at the outer edges of them. He'd put on some weight and there was a touch of gray at the temples. But he hasn't really changed that much, Alice realized. He still has the magnetism that fascinated me from the day we met.

"I'm glad to see you, Jack. You're looking well."

"So are you. You haven't changed."

She was still smiling. "You're very gallant, but I know better." She gently extricated her hands. "You remember Barbara."

For the first time he noticed the other woman. "No! Not that kid who always wanted to tag along!"

Barb laughed easily. "If you say I haven't changed, I'll scream.

Last time you saw me I had pigtails and braces on my teeth. But I'm still 'tagging along.' How are you, Jack?"

"Fine. Just fine. Come in, please. Both of you. This is wonderful!"

They followed him into a spacious apartment, the airy living room set three steps below the foyer. It was lovely, painted white, furnished with soft, flowered chintz sofas and chairs, the walls hung with delicate paintings and exquisite framed petit-point designs. Beyond, they glimpsed a small dining room and stairs leading to the bedroom floor of the duplex. It was all simple and cheerful and in impeccable taste.

"What a charming place!" Barbara said.

"It's nice, isn't it? Lucy was very talented. She did the paintings and the needlepoint herself." He spoke calmly but there was an undercurrent of pain. "I suppose it seems a little out of character for a man's apartment, but I haven't really wanted to change it."

No, of course you haven't, Alice thought. Lucky you. You must have been very happy here with your Lucy. "We were so sorry to hear . . . about your wife."

They were seated now, Jack and Alice on the couch, Barb in a chair pulled up beside it.

"Thank you. It was rough. She was so young. And she suffered so much." He stared at the floor. "She made me ashamed of my weakness. I was the one who fell apart when we knew she was dying. She was more concerned for me than she was for herself. You'd have liked each other, Allie. In many ways she was very like you." He looked up. "I told her about you. About the child. She always wanted me to get in touch with you, see if we could locate the baby. She couldn't have any and she'd have loved to have adopted mine. Ours." He stood up and began to walk back and forth. "I didn't think it made sense, so I didn't do anything much about it. Oh, it was easy enough to find out where you were. I hired a search outfit for that. But when I heard you'd had a boy and given him for adoption, I gave up. I figured it was too late." He stopped pacing. "No. That's a lie. The real truth is I wanted to forget the whole thing. I've always been so ashamed of the way I acted when all that happened. I couldn't face you. Not until Lucy died. That made me take a hard look at everything. It's what I told Barbara on the phone. I'd like to right some of the wrongs.

I know you're married and have other grown children. I have no one. I was hoping I could find the son they made you give up, maybe make up to him now for what I should have done thirty years ago. Will you help me, Allie?"

She looked stricken. "I can't Jack. In the early days I tried to find out where he'd gone, but I never could."

"But there must be a way! He's grown now. He surely wonders who his parents were."

"I don't know," Allie said. "I don't even know whether he's alive."

"Of course he is! He has to be! Allie, I'll spend every nickel I have trying to find him. Tell me everything you know. Any clue may help us."

She shook her head. "I don't know much. He was born in Massachusetts General in Boston on November tenth, nineteen forty-six. He was a big beautiful boy and I named him John. After you. I only saw him once, right after he was born. They never let me see him again. I don't know where he is or even what he's called." Alice's eyes filled with tears. "Oh, Jack, why now? Why didn't you come for me when I needed you so?"

I can't stand it, Barbara thought. I don't belong here. Why on earth did I agree to come? I'm an intruder. It's indecent for me to be in the same room with these people who are torturing themselves and each other. They were oblivious of her presence, but that didn't help the way she felt. Quietly, unnoticed, she slipped out of the apartment and went to sit in the car. When she left, Jack and Allie had their arms around each other, she crying on his shoulder, he trying to comfort her.

It was almost an hour before he brought Alice out to the car. They were both red-eyed and subdued. And they were all embarrassed.

"I'm sorry, Barb," Jack said. "We didn't mean to make you uncomfortable."

"I shouldn't have come. It's too private a matter."

"It was my fault," Allie said. "I apologize, Barbara."

There was an awkward pause and then Jack helped Allie into the front seat. "Call you tomorrow," he said.

"Yes."

" 'Bye, Barbara. And thank you for bringing her."

"Goodbye, Jack."

They drove for five minutes without saying a word. At last Alice said, "I'm sorry I put you through that. I wasn't thinking how it might be for you."

"It's okay. It was dumb of me not to realize it myself."

"I told him everything, Barb. All about Spencer and me. He . . . he wants me to leave Spencer. He wants to marry me. He says we'll find Johnny."

Barbara almost drove off the road. "Are you serious? He's still in love with you? He wants you to marry him?"

"Is that inconceivable?" There was a faint smile on Allie's face. "Am I that far over the hill?"

"No. Of course not! But, my God, Allie, you were only together for an hour or so after all these years! He's a stranger, really. Isn't it a bit rash to talk about marrying a man you haven't seen since you were a girl? You don't now anything about him. Not what he is today, I mean."

"I know as much about him as he does about me. But I haven't said I'm going to marry him. I just said he wants me to. Barb, dear, you know I'm much too timid to make such an important decision on the spur of the moment. That's the kind of thing Fran might do, but not me." Despite her quiet protest, Allie seemed more serene than she had since her arrival. "I'm going to see him again, though. Tomorrow. We have a lot of talking to do."

"Allie, he can't find your child. You must remember that."

"I know. I don't expect him to. For once I'm thinking of myself. Funny. I've felt all along there was some big purpose for this trip. Something made me stand up to Spencer for the first time in my life. It's as though I knew this was coming. Maybe it's a chance, Barb. Another chance."

"I hope so, dear. If that's what you really want."

"I don't know. I don't know what I want."

As the cab sped along the highway that skirted the Potomac River and wound its way past the Lincoln Memorial and up through Rock Creek Park toward his home, Charles Tallent thought he must be the world's most easily persuaded man. First it was the Candidate who made it all sound so logical and sensible to sacrifice his personal happiness for his career. Then it was Andrea on the phone, cool and dispassionate, pointing out that it would be unkind to Barbara to tell her in Denver that their affair was over. His wife had discussed the matter as clinically as though she were analyzing the problems of a stranger.

"If you have any feeling for that woman," his wife had said, "you won't humiliate her in front of her family. My God, Charles, you don't have an ounce of sensitivity! What makes you think it's right to burst on the scene out there and announce it's all over when her family probably doesn't know the whole thing exists? I hold no brief for Barbara Dalton. I should be the last to care how she feels. But if I were in her shoes, I certainly wouldn't want to be publicly renounced."

"I wasn't planning to do it in front of the State Capitol," Charles said bitterly.

"No. You're just going to fly into town unexpectedly and call her. You'll meet in some bar and tell her. Terrific. What do you expect her to do? Go home, smiling bravely? I hate the woman. But I'd give my worst enemy a better shake than that."

He'd wavered. It was weird. Why should Andrea give a damn for the feelings of her husband's mistress? He'd expected her to be angry that he planned to fly to Denver, but he'd not been prepared for this unlikely consideration of Barb's feelings.

"I don't get it," he said. "Why this sudden compassion?"

"Perhaps I know how it feels to be a victim," Andrea said. "Or maybe I can afford to be magnanimous in victory. Whatever. I simply know how any woman would feel in that situation. You'd be rotten to do it that way, Charles."

Maybe she's right, he'd thought. God knows she has no reason to want me to postpone telling Barb. Quite the contrary. There must be a little milk of human kindness in her, a little sympathy for the woman who's been her enemy all these years. She's won. She has me back. She'll be a Cabinet Wife. She's picked up all the marbles. I suppose she feels sorry for Barbara, in a superior way. I don't understand the working of the female mind. If the tables were turned, I'd want her to rub the other man's nose in this kind of rejection.

"I think I owe it to her not to let her read about the appointment in the papers. The Senator will be making an announcement. She's been around Washington long enough to know what that means for us."

Andrea sounded very patient. "Charles, you know he can't announce his Cabinet until he's elected. Presumably she'll be home long before. There'll be a more suitable time and place."

"Why do you care?" he asked again. "I can't understand your concern. Frankly, it isn't like you. Hell, it isn't like any woman!"

"I told you. You don't understand us. Come home, Charles, before you make a fool of yourself, as well as her."

He'd reluctantly agreed, ashamed to realize he was grateful for a reprieve. There'd be no announcement for a few weeks. Meantime, he'd figure just the right words to say to Barbara. Thank God he'd made her financially secure. Not that she'd prefer a trust fund to him, but it was some consolation to know she'd be all right for money. Maybe it was all for the best. What kind of life was it for her, tied to a man who'd never marry her? Maybe some unselfish part of him had always known this was better for her. He simply didn't have the strength to let her go. It had to be taken out of his hands. Like a guy who doesn't have enough guts to kill himself and wishes someone would murder him. They'd done it for him, the Candidate and the Party. They'd probably done Barbara a kindness in the long run. He had to believe that. He loved her so much. But he supposed, human nature being what it was, he might even have come to resent her if he'd turned down this opportunity for her sake. I'm too old for idealism, Charles told himself. I've passed the stage where a man renounces everything for love. The bitter, ugly truth is that the only ultimate satisfaction is power. It's been called the greatest aphrodisiac, and, God help me, it is.

I've pulled it off! Andrea was triumphant as she hung up the telephone. Charles was so weak, so manageable, so stupid, really. All he'd have to do is be in the presence of that woman and he'd probably change his mind about accepting the post. Barbara was smart. She'd use everything she had to talk him out of it if he went to see her. I know I would, in her place. This time, Andrea Tallent was going to outsmart her. Outsmart them both. Charles had been gullible, willing to believe she cared a hoot in hell about his mistress's feelings. How could he have fallen for that? Easy.

He wanted to. There was a flash of unsettling comprehension. He was delighted to be off the hook, even temporarily. I gave him a way to postpone doing what he dreads. It really was funny in an unfunny way. Andrea frowned. She could end up outsmarting herself. By the time that bitch got back to Washington, Charles would have figured out some way to keep her *and* the job. He was no fool after all. Right now he was confused, upset, snowed by the Senator's flattery. He was ready to call off his affair and she'd stopped him. She'd been wrong. She should have let him go to Denver while he was fired up by the excitement of the big offer. Nothing Barbara could have said would have changed his decision. She saw that now, too late. But who knew what could happen when he'd gotten used to the idea of becoming Secretary? She'd given him time to scheme. Damn! The strategy she'd decided on when he said he was going had been a mistake. But she couldn't call him back and say she'd changed her mind. Not after the "humane" case she'd made.

He mustn't have a chance to think it through, and that's just what I've given him! He'll manage to keep Barbara tucked away somewhere, out of sight of the new President, away from the prying eyes of the press. When he's mulled it over, he'll never give her up. I blundered, Andrea thought. I acted on impulse, not reckoning with power of time to clarify things for Charles and let him get the whole situation in perspective. I can't let him spend these next few days figuring out how to get around a sticky situation. Because he will. I know he will. Unless I move first.

She went to her desk and pulled out a scrap of paper. Barbara's landlady had obligingly given her the forwarding address her tenant had left. Unhesitatingly, Andrea selected a piece of her personal notepaper and began to write.

"Buzz? This is your impetuous, headstrong friend."

The call surprised him. He'd been certain, after last night, that he'd not hear from her again.

"Hello, Fran. How are you?"

"Embarrassed. I don't usually make a fool of myself."

"You didn't. You were being sweet and honest. It was a wonderful few hours. I'll never forget them."

"Neither will I. I didn't mean it all to get so heavy." She

laughed, a self-conscious little laugh. "I came on too strong. I guess I got carried away. Old longings. That kind of thing. Anyway, I called to apologizc and tell you how much I admire you. You're terrific."

He didn't answer for a moment. Then, "No need for apologies. It was something we both wanted."

"Yes, I suppose it was, but I almost wish it hadn't happened. What you haven't had, you can't miss." She paused. "Oh, hell! There I go again. Sorry. I'd better quit before I make things even worse. 'Bye, Buzz. Take care."

"Fran! Wait! Don't hang up!"

"What is it?"

"Look, we shouldn't leave it this way."

"Do we have a choice?"

"Yes. Now that we both know where things stand, it would be different. For both of us. A few more hours while you're here, that's all. We're entitled to that."

She pretended to hesitate. "I don't know . . ."

"Please! We're not hurting anybody."

"Well . . ."

"I'll be at the motel at six. Will you?"

"Yes," Fran said. "I'll be there."

Chapter 17

"I suppose I have to tell Mother and Dad."

"Don't see how you can avoid it." Barbara parked Fran's rented car in front of their parents' house and sat still for a moment, looking at Alice. "I don't know why you should even worry about it. It's not nineteen forty-six. You're not a kid living under their roof. For heaven's sake, you have a perfect right to do anything you please with your life, including marrying Jack Richards, if that's what you decide you want."

"I know. Childhood hang-ups are hard to get rid of. Wouldn't it be nice if you could send old guilts out to The Thrift Shop, like old clothes?"

"You bet. We'd all have a helluva tax deduction. But I don't think it'll be as grim as you imagine. Dad may still harbor a grudge against the Richards family, but Mother doesn't. She told me so."

"She did? When?"

Barbara repeated her earlier conversation with Laura and a smile of relief came over Allie's face. "I'm so glad. It'll make things easier."

"Easier still if you told Mother and Dad the truth about the way Spencer treats you."

Alice shook her head. "I don't want them to know about that. Why upset them any more than I will now? Spencer has nothing to do with this."

"Like hell you say! If you had a happy marriage you wouldn't give Jack a second thought. And if they knew what you'd been living through all these years they'd have nothing but sympathy for this situation. They don't know anything about your life, Allie. They barely know Chris and Janice. And even though they've been tactful about it, I'm sure they're hurt and disappointed that your children didn't come out for their anniversary. To tell you the truth, I'm curious about that part myself."

"I didn't encourage them," Alice said. "Jan didn't want to, but Chris would have. He'd really like to know his grandparents."

"Then, why on earth didn't he come with you?"

"He and Spencer don't get along. Besides, I was afraid Mother and Dad would suspect."

"Suspect what?"

"What he is. Oh, he isn't flagrant about it. I mean, he's not a stereotype. Anything *but*. He's strong and very manly. I don't suppose the casual observer would know, but I was afraid to chance it."

Barbara was silent.

"I'm not ashamed of Chris," Allie went on. "I simply wouldn't want him or Mother and Dad or anyone to be embarrassed. I don't think the folks would understand. They haven't been exposed to that kind of thing."

"It does bother you."

"Of course it bothers me! My God, Barb, I'm only human. And I'm a mother, with a mother's natural instincts. Don't think I'm blithe about it. I've accepted it because it's his choice. Who has the right to decide what's 'normal'? Not I, of all people. No 'normal' woman would go on living with a wife-beater. No, I don't condemn Chris, but I do condemn myself. I told you before. Nobody will ever convince me that what he saw and heard at home didn't turn him off marriage forever."

"Did it turn Janice off too?"

"Maybe. She's too thick-skinned to admit anything bothers her, but how could she not be affected? How could any child not react to such an environment?"

"Allie, you mustn't blame yourself."

"Oh, but I must! I've done everything wrong all my life. I'm a born loser, Barb."

"Don't be ridiculous!" But even as she said it, Barbara reluctantly agreed. Allie did seem to make one mistake after another, always seemed to get the short end of things. Barbara wondered what the outcome of this reunion with Jack Richards would be. They didn't know him any more. What kind of man was he? As warm and kind as he'd seemed a little while before? Or was he playing some kind of game with Allie? The world had gone crazy. All this, and Fran's odd behavior and no word from Charles. None at all.

"We'd better go in the house," Allie was saying. "If they saw us arrive, they'll be wondering why we're sitting in the car so long."

"Right. You plan to tell the family right away?"

"I guess so. Why postpone the inevitable?"

They found Laura and Frances having a cup of tea in the kitchen. Sam, fortunately, had gone back to his garden. It's better this way, Allie thought. Mother can tell Dad. I won't have to. God, I am "chicken"!

Fran looked up knowingly, a hundred questions in her eyes. But it was Laura who brought them to the subject.

"Well, where did you girls run off to? Fran said you borrowed her car for an errand."

Behind her mother's back, Fran silently mouthed, "I didn't say anything."

Allie took a chair at the table. "Mother, I have something to tell you."

Throughout the recital, Laura listened carefully, not interrupting.

"He wants to find our son," Allie said at the end. "He . . . he thinks we should get married."

Her mother exploded. "Married! Allie, you *are* married! What are you saying? My dear child, don't go searching for the past. You have a different life now . . ."

"A lousy one," Fran interrupted. "Mother, you don't know what Allie goes through with that maniac! He beats her, for God's sake! He's sadistic! Do you want her to stay with that?"

Laura's eyes widened. "Is that true, Alice?"

"Yes. I didn't want you to know. I'm terribly unhappy with Spencer. I have been, almost from the day we married. He's a sick man, Mother, just as his father was. He thinks of a wife as a possession he's entitled to abuse."

"And you've lived with that all these years? Oh, Allie, why? Why didn't you come home long ago?"

"I was ashamed. Also, soon there were the children to think of. And I wasn't sure you'd want me, after the disgrace I brought you."

Laura sighed. "We knew there was something wrong with your marriage. Your father and I sensed it. But in our wildest imagination we never pictured anything as terrible as this. My poor baby." She went around the table and hugged her daughter. "How can we ever make it up to you? If it hadn't been for us, these awful years wouldn't have happened."

The roles reversed, Alice began to comfort her mother. "You're not to blame, neither you nor Dad. You did what you thought was best."

"We were so wrong, so terribly wrong." Laura returned to her chair. "Don't go back to Boston, Allie. Stay here with us. Your children are grown and independent. You've been through enough. At least we can offer you peace."

"That's what Jack promises me." Alice gave a little laugh. "I don't know. I don't know whether I want peace. Maybe I don't deserve it."

Barbara jumped into the conversation. "That's crazy talk! Snap out of it, Allie! You've worn the hair shirt long enough. Mother's right. Stay here, at least until you decide about Jack. You can't go back to that life in Boston."

"Seems like I can't go back to any life. Mother says I shouldn't search for the past. What's here for me except the past?"

"How about a future?" Barbara asked. "That could be here, with or without Jack Richards."

Allie didn't answer.

"Do you still love him?" Laura's voice was gentle. "If so, Allie, you should go to him. I was wrong about searching for the past. Maybe you can find it together. You've both suffered so much. Perhaps it's the Lord's will that it comes out this way."

"I'm not sure how I feel about Jack. I don't want to use him as an escape from Spencer. That wouldn't be fair. And I don't want to be influenced by the hope of finding our son. I don't know. It's all so mixed up in my mind. I can't bear the idea of going back to Spencer, but I don't want to be separated from Chris and Janice, either. They're my life, Mother. Just as we're yours. I don't want to leave them the way we left you."

"Your situation is quite different," Laura said. "You can't compare this separation to ours."

"I suppose not. I just don't want to hurt innocent people. Chris and Janice have their own lives, and yet I know they count on me. At least, I like to think so. Spencer and I gave them such a rotten childhood. They hate him. I don't know why they don't hate me, but they don't. In a funny way, they need me as much as I need them."

"I'm with Barb," Fran said. "You're talking crazy. Your children are adults. You're not deserting a couple of innocent babes. Good God, Allie, are you going to be martyred the rest of your life? It's dumb. Really dumb. The only thing to think of is yourself. Haven't you spent enough time repenting? What the hell do you think you are, some kind of saint? Stay here. See Jack Richards. Go to bed with him. Find out if the old magic is still there. And stop being such a pious bore!"

"Frances!" Her mother was shocked. "Don't talk to your sister that way!"

"Somebody had better talk to her that way," Fran said. "All this hand-wringing and sympathy aren't what she needs. What she needs is a damn good shaking up. A nice big jolt to make her see how stupidly she's behaved for years!"

"I won't have you say such things to her!"

"She's right, Mother," Allie said. "I have been stupid. My thinking is as warped as Spencer's. I wanted that punishment. I'd almost come to think of it as a way of life. Until I came here and realized how happy I was without him. I'm not going back. Not for a while. Maybe not ever. I'll explain it as best I can to Chris and Jan. They'll understand."

Barbara took her sister's hand. "What about Jack?"

"We'll have to see. I think Fran's advice is good." Allie smiled. "I've already had one affair with him. Why not another?"

Laura looked unhappy. "I don't know whether that's the answer Allie."

"Neither do I. But it's positive action for a change."

"Your father . . ."

"Will blow his top." Alice finished the sentence for her. "He won't have to know just yet. What's the point in upsetting him? We'll skip the gory details about Spencer, and we don't have to tell him anything about Jack. We can just say I've decided to stay on here for a while, can't we?"

"I don't know, dear. Your father is more aware than you might imagine. We'll have to give him some explanation."

"All right. We can say I'm unhappy with Spencer, without going into the sadistic part. And I won't let Jack come near the house."

"Denver's a small town in its way," Laura said. "It's bound to come out if you start seeing Jack."

"Not if we don't appear in public." Alice was suddenly filled with confidence. "I feel so free! Just thinking of the miles between here and Boston makes me happy. To be with my family. To have a breather. You can't imagine what a relief that is."

"You're safe here, darling," her mother said, "and welcome for as long as you want to stay."

"It's not going to work, you know," Fran said to Barbara when they managed a few minutes alone. "Grown-up daughters can't go back to living under their parents' roof. There's the conflict of two women, each used to running her own house. They'll drive each other mad in two weeks."

"Then what's the solution? She can't go back to Spencer."

"She could be on her own in some other city, the way you and I are."

"Fran, you know that's not possible. How would she live? You have money from an ex-husband and I have a job, but Allie isn't trained to support herself and she hasn't a nickel of her own."

"Then Jack Richards could keep her. What the hell, she doesn't have to marry him, she could just move in."

"Dad would die! Even Mother would have a fit! Allie 'living in sin' right under their noses? No way!" Barb paused. "Anyway, she's much too conventional for that. She's not like me."

Fran raised her eyebrows. "Am I to infer from that that you're being kept in Washington? And I thought you were the poor little working girl only Heaven is supposed to protect!"

"I'm not. Not being kept, I mean. But I've been involved for a long, long time."

As she had to her mother, Barbara confided her affair with Charles Tallent. When she'd finished, Fran sat back and looked at her.

"You're a bigger damned fool than any of us. Giving up your life for a guy who can never marry you? What kind of half-assed idea is that?"

Barbara's indignation made her sarcastic. "I didn't realize you were so moral! At least *I* don't go around picking up waiters for one-night stands!"

"That's a helluva lot smarter than tying yourself up permanently in some impossible situation."

"Look who's stumping for holy matrimony! It hasn't seemed to work out so well for you."

Fran laughed. "Touché. But that doesn't mean I don't believe in it. Listen, my little friend, no matter what you hear, marriage is still the most desirable state for women. It's convenient and comfortable. I know a lot of couples are living together without benefit of clergy these days. Fine. I wouldn't object if you were doing that, openly, but you aren't. You're playing second fiddle, Barb. You have all the disadvantages of marriage and none of the benefits. Hell, I wouldn't care if you didn't marry your congressman if you could live with him and be accepted. It's the dreary little catch-as-catch-can life that's such a nothing. You get the scraps from Mrs. Tallent's table. You're too damned good for that. I thought Spencer Winters was a selfish beast, but this one is worse. He's just plain greedy. And you're a dope."

"You don't understand," Barb said. "Charles often tells me how unfair this is. I'm the one who won't let go."

"Okay. Have it your way. Just be braced for the kiss-off when it comes. It always does in these deals."

"Not in this one," Barbara said stubbornly.

"Sure. You'll be the Romeo and Juliet of the geriatric set."

"How can you be so cynical? I'm sorry for you, Fran. I don't think you've ever loved anyone in your whole life."

"You know, I think I would have bought that until a couple of days ago." The tough mask dropped and Frances was suddenly soft and appealing. "Barb, I'm in love with Buzz Paige. We were together last night and we're going to be again tonight."

"Oh, no! Fran, you can't! I said it before: You'll get him crazy for you and then take off. That's terrible!"

"I don't mean to take off. Not alone, that is. I'm taking off with Buzz when I go."

"You're insane! His wife won't divorce him. I'd bet on it. Do you realize what you're saying? You're planning the very thing you've been criticizing me for: living with a married man."

"Wrong. He'll get a divorce and marry me. He doesn't think so now, but he will. But, okay, let's say he couldn't. I'm still better off than you. I'll be with him full time, not sneaking a few hours here and there. It won't be a secret, the way your affair is. We can have friends, go out together, be a 'couple' even if it's not legal."

"I don't believe he'll do it. He has too much integrity."

"Oh, come on, Barb! You sound like Buzz. He thinks that too. But I know something he doesn't: His strongest urges are not in his head. He's found something he won't be able to give up. Believe it. I may be forty-nine, luv, but I know how and where to hook a man. Just watch me."

"That's despicable."

"No, pet. That's life."

While she made conversation with her parents and her sisters the rest of that day, Barbara's mind was far away. Strange she hadn't heard from Charles. Why so strange? she asked herself. She'd been away only a few days, and he probably was wildly busy. Why was she making so much of this? It was an uneasy feeling. Almost a premonition that something was wrong.

Damn Frances! she thought. She and Mother make me think about things I don't want to dwell on. I know all the disadvantages of relationships like Charles's and mine, and it's still worth it. It was just that, at times like this, she wished she could call him at his office. But she'd have to give her name before the secretary would put her through, and it was foolish to be so indiscreet. Not that they didn't all know anyhow, no matter how careful she and Charles tried to be. But it still seemed ill-advised.

I'll hear soon. I'm sure of it. If I don't, I'll write to him, a letter marked "Personal," to say I'm staying on for a few more days. Barb realized she hadn't informed her own office of this change of plan. She'd better call in. For a few minutes she hesitated. She wasn't sure why she was staying on. It was pointless, really. There was nothing more to be done for Allie, now that she and Jack had gotten together. Those two adults could work it out.

She allowed her mind to drift to Jack Richards and her sister. It would be strange if they got together after all these years. Stranger still if they could locate their child. But more peculiar things did happen. Barb smiled, remembering what she'd told her mother about her schoolgirl crush on Allie's beau. It had been odd, seeing him again. She was almost as nervous about it as Allie. And he hadn't been a disappointment. He'd become an enormously attractive man, better looking now than he'd been in his youth. She felt a small pang of envy that Jack still worshiped Allie, that he wanted to marry her. Nobody wants to marry me, Barb thought.

What nonsense! Why am I feeling sorry for myself? I don't want to be married. Don't you? a little voice inside replied. Wasn't there a moment earlier today when you wished it was you Jack Richards loved?

The disloyal thought shocked her. How could she even entertain such an idea? She loved Charles. And Jack belonged to her sister. He wasn't interested in her now any more than he'd been when she was nine. It was Allie he wanted, and Barb was sure Allie ultimately would decide to marry him. That was probably as it should be. Probably? Why on earth did she say "probably"? It was the rare "happy ending" that people only dream about: the long-lost-lovers' reunion. And they deserved it. Deserved to be together. If she was going to spend her time worrying about anybody, she should be worrying about Fran. This thing with Buzz was a hideous mistake. God knows where it would lead. Fran's so spoiled, she thinks she can have anything she wants. I don't believe Dorothy Paige will give up so easily, even if Fran convinces Buzz to go away with her.

Barbara recalled Dorothy as she'd been the night of the anniversary party. She'd seemed apprehensive, clinging to her husband's arm. It was not at all difficult to believe she'd had a nervous breakdown. Could Frances live with the idea that her actions might push this woman over the edge?

It was extraordinary, everything that had gone on since their arrival. No one could have foreseen that this "quiet family reunion" would create such highly charged side effects.

It's as though we were all brought here to act out a drama, Barb thought. As though we were programed. A slight shudder ran through her. I'm afraid, she realized. I'm scared to death of what's ahead. I don't know why, but I have an awful feeling the worst is yet to come.

Jack Richards paced the floor of his living room, also deep in thought. He'd been so sure of his course when he was talking to Allie, as though he somehow expected to find she was unhappily married, that it was the right moment to make contact with her. And now that he had, he didn't feel the elation that should have been part of his discovery. Alice was lovely. Kind, gentle and still beautiful. All a man could want in a wife. The right replacement for the dear creature he'd lost. But something was missing. Excitement. Alice represented peace, which is what she deserved, and what he'd promised her. But peace was not what he wanted. He still felt young, vital and eager for life, now that the pain of Lucy's death was diminishing. There'd be no heights with Allie. She'd gone through too much, been too beaten down for too long. She'd forgotten how to be gay and reckless. Why did I ask her to marry me? The silent question came on a note of panic. I want to find our child, but why did I think I wanted to marry his mother? I'm devoted to Allie but I'm not in love with her. I lied, out of guilt and remorse, out of the feeling I did her an injustice? Good God, what have I done?

Ashamed, he realized he hoped she wouldn't marry him. He needed someone brighter, more independent, younger. A playmate after all the months of agony, watching Lucy's life slip away. He longed for a companion to make him laugh aloud, after the long days of silently tiptoeing around a sick room; a passionate woman after so many nights with an invalid too frail to make love.

Allie isn't any of the things I want in a wife, Jack thought. But if she says yes, I'll marry her. I owe her that. Dammit, I owe her much more than that!

Chapter 18

Now that he was so close to the truth, John Peck was uneasy. His interview with Mrs. Rudolph had eliminated any lingering doubts he might have had about the identity of his mother. It was Alice Dalton Winters all right. No question. But instead of elation, he was experiencing a sense of anxiety. If his great-aunt was so dismayed by his appearance, would his mother also be appalled and frightened? I couldn't stand it, John thought again. Maybe I should leave well enough alone. Is there any real need to see her, even though I've dreamed of it all these years?

He did nothing for a full twenty-four hours after his meeting with Charlotte. He didn't even tell his wife he'd seen his great-aunt. Carol would be upset, angry that the imperious old woman had tried to buy him off. Strangely, John wasn't angry. He could understand the reaction even while he deplored it. It must have been a terrible shock to have the abandoned child appear out of nowhere, demanding to be recognized. Like some ghost rising from the grave, some creature they never expected to see again. Poor old Mrs. Randolph. He was sorry for her, but he was glad they'd met. At least he knew what to possibly expect when he saw his mother. He was glad, too, that Carol had insisted he wait until Mrs. Winters returned to Boston. She'd been instinctively right. This was not the kind of thing one announced in a long-distance call. He recognized that now.

Only a few days more. Janice had said her mother would be

back soon. Janice, my half-sister. The idea seemed impossible but it was true. And Chris, the man she so flippantly said was gay, is my half-brother. I've suddenly walked into a full-fledged family. There's even a stepfather I know about, though I don't know my real father.

It was incongruous. He'd found them all and they probably wouldn't want him. Where would he find courage to intrude on these strangers? He was not an aggressive man. In a way, it was distasteful to push in where he feared he'd not be welcome. But I must, John thought. I won't rest until I've seen my mother, no matter what the outcome.

Janice was surprised to receive a call from her father. He never telephoned the office. It must be important.

"Yes, Dad?"

"Are you coming to the house this evening, Janice?"

"I hadn't planned to. Why? Is something wrong?"

"No, there's nothing wrong. I want to talk to you, that's all. Please make it a point to be here."

There was something going on. She could hear an unusual note of agitation in his voice.

"All right. I'll drop in after work."

"Fine." He hung up abruptly without saying goodbye.

Mr. Loveable, Janice thought. Mr. In-Charge. There's not a shred of affection in him. I might as well be some underling he's summoned for a business conference. She shrugged. Who cared? She'd long since given up the idea of having a father like other people's. He was a machine. Driven. Violent. Tyrannical. How did her mother stand him? Janice could never comprehend that. Since she'd been old enough to realize what went on, she'd been puzzled by her own family. Why had they married in the first place, these two incompatible people? And even more unfathomable, why did they stay together in an atmosphere of such open hostility? She shrugged, indifferently. It was their generation, she supposed. Early conditioning made them unable to recognize the fact that there was an alternative.

As she entered the house, it crossed her mind that this summons from her father might have something to do with Aunt Charlotte's "urgent" call. God, is he going to ask me to go see

that old biddy? I can't stand her. Always patting my cheek and telling me what a lovely young lady I am, and how fortunate Mother is to have me. She makes me sick.

Spencer was already home. She saw the light in the library and went in. Her father was working at his desk, as usual. She dropped into a chair beside it.

"I'm here."

"So I see. Very generous of you."

Janice was impatient. "Come on, Dad. Does every conversation have to start out like World War III?" She lit a cigarette. "Can't we skip the sarcasm and get to the point?"

"Can't you say two words without lighting a cigarette?"

Jan sighed. "All right, I smoke too much. I'm going to die of lung cancer or a heart attack. Is that what you brought me here to say?"

"No. I need some information about a man who says he knows you. Peck. John Peck. Claims to be a friend of yours."

For a minute she couldn't remember who John Peck was, but then she recalled the evening with him and his wife. Dreary. She and Clint had decided not to see them again.

"I know him casually. His wife is a free-lance artist. Clint and I went to their house a couple of nights ago. He's not really a friend. More an acquaintance. Why do you ask?"

"I'm trying to find him. A business matter. Miss Perrone couldn't locate him through the phone book. I thought you might be able to give me his number."

Jan laughed. "Miss Perrone couldn't find the oars in a rowboat. I don't know why you keep such an incompetent secretary, just because she's been with you for twenty years. I take that back. I do know. Men resist change of any kind. They'll hang on to a useless secretary because it's too much trouble to break in a new one. Just as they'll stay in a loveless marriage because it's too much bother to end it. Women are much more adventurous and optimistic. They always think things could be better; men always presume they'll be worse. It's the difference between the sexes. *Vive la différence!*"

Spencer looked annoyed. "I fail to see what all this pseudo philosophy has to do with my question. I merely want to know if you know where to find John Peck."

"Of course I do. I told you I had dinner at his house. What kind of business matter would bring The Great You in contact with a lowly bank manager?"

"Never mind. That doesn't concern you. He lives in the city?"

"Yes."

"He must be unlisted. Miss Perrone called all the John Pecks in the Boston directory. She couldn't find the right one."

"Of course she couldn't. Honestly, how dense can she be? He works. So does his wife. Nobody would answer the phone during the day at his apartment. My Lord, she must have had a million 'don't answers' among her calls."

Spencer consulted the list in front of him. "Four, to be exact. That's very astute of you, Janice. I should have called myself, in the evening. I didn't think of it. However, since you know which of the four is your friend, I can spare myself that tiresome chore."

Her curiosity was rising. "Why do you want to find John Peck?" she asked again.

"I told you. A simple business matter."

"Then, why don't you reach him at his office?"

"It's personal."

"So why can't you tell me? If it's personal, you won't be violating any lawyer-client confidentiality."

He was reaching the end of his patience. "Janice, I do not choose to discuss my affairs with you. This has nothing to do with you, so stop playing childish games and give me Peck's number."

She took a wild guess. "Does it have to do with Aunt Charlotte's call to Mother?"

Spencer momentarily was taken off guard. His surprise showed in his startled reaction.

"How did you figure that out?"

Jan smiled her win-father-over smile. "I'm a witch. Didn't you know? Come on, Dad. If it's a family matter I'm a big enough girl to be let in on the secret. Maybe I can help with the problem, whatever it is."

Maybe she can at that, Spencer thought. She can charm her way into anything when she chooses. Or out of anything. Neither of the children knew about Alice's past. He'd die before he confided in Christopher. But this girl was something else. Maybe she knew something about Peck that would be useful. She might

even be able to disprove his claim. Or talk him out of pursuing it if it were true. It was a gamble, but it might work.

"All right, Janice. I'm going to tell you something very few people know. Your mother had a child out of wedlock before we were married. A boy. She gave it up for adoption. Of course I knew nothing of the matter until much later." There was a touch of righteous indignation in his voice. "It all happened thirty years ago and nothing has been heard of the matter since. Until this John Peck person went to see your Aunt Charlotte. He claims to be your mother's child."

Janice stared at him, open-mouthed. "You're putting me on! Mother had an illegitimate baby? I can't believe it!"

"Unfortunately, it's true. What we don't know is whether this man is that child or simply a con artist." He repeated Charlotte's rambling story of how John had tracked down "Alice Dalton." "I'm not sure the whole thing isn't a hoax," Spencer said, "but I can't afford to take a chance. That's why I must reach him before he starts any unpleasant publicity. I don't want your mother or anyone else to know about this, Janice. You do undersand that."

"I sure do," Janice said slowly. "I understand a lot of things I couldn't figure out before."

Spencer ignored that. "What kind of person is Peck? Does he seem like a smooth operator?"

"I hardly know him. We only talked a few minutes, but I got the feeling he was kind and honest. He spoke very warmly of his adoptive parents."

"I'm sure he tried to pump you about us."

"Maybe. He didn't seem to be prying, but I volunteered a lot of information. I didn't think anything of it at the time, but I told him a lot of things. About Mother's background and about Aunt Charlotte. I even told him about Chris."

"Good God! You set it up for him! You made it easy for him to approach Charlotte with that trumped-up story."

"Are you so sure it's trumped up?"

"No, but what difference does that make? Damn! I'm sure he's after money. Much more than Charlotte offered. Well, I have a surprise for him. I won't be blackmailed. I'm not going to buy his silence and be bled dry the rest of my life. Where do I reach him, Janice?"

Reluctantly, she gave him the address. "I think he could be telling the truth."

"What if he is? You're being as sentimental and gullible as your mother would be if she heard about this. Thank you for your help. I'll take it from here."

She didn't answer. For once, Janice was subdued and thoughtful. This extraordinary disclosure explained a great deal about her parents. She could imagine a frightened young Alice, pregnant and "disgraced," coming to Boston. She saw how her mother might have married Spencer Winters to escape Aunt Charlotte. She realized now why her father was so cruel to his wife, and why she endured her punishment all these years. Poor lady, Jan thought. They brainwashed her into a low opinion of herself. She suddenly felt warm and loving toward her mother. It's unfair. She's suffered so much at so many hands. I wonder who fathered her child. Some "childhood sweetheart" in Denver who abandoned her, no doubt. She must have been remorseful ever since. I'd be. Guilty as hell if I gave away a baby. It's wrong to deprive her of this knowledge. If this man's her son, she has a right to know.

She tried to recollect John Peck's face. Did he look like her mother? Was there any family resemblance to her and Chris? No, as she recalled there was nothing in his appearance to tie him to Alice. Yet she was convinced he was telling the truth. It was gut reaction, but she was certain of it.

"What are you going to do?" she asked Spencer.

"See him. Set him straight before your mother returns. Let him know we're not frightened by this scheme. Get rid of him once and for all."

"What if he won't go away? Suppose he insists on seeing Mother?"

"He won't when I'm through with him. I'm used to crooks. I meet them every day in my business."

"Dad, I don't think he's a crook."

"Frankly, Janice, I don't care what you think. My instincts are better than yours. So is my judgment." Alarmed, he realized she might interfere, make things more difficult. It had been a mistake to tell her. "You stay out of this, do you hear? Don't go near John Peck. And don't say a word to anybody, least of all your mother."

The old, defiant Janice returned. "I'll do whatever I please. You can't order me around the way you do her!"

"I can and I will." Spencer's quick temper rose. "I won't tolerate impertinence from you, young woman. You'll do as you're told or . . ."

"Or what? You'll beat me up too? Mother's afraid of you. I'm not. You're a bully. I know the only way to handle bullies is to stand up to them. You won't touch me. I won't allow it."

In a quick movement, Spencer crossed the room and slapped her hard across the face. "You'll show some respect! You'll obey my orders! I'm head of this house and I'll take no nonsense!"

Janice stood very still. Her cheek stung but she didn't cry or move away from him. When she spoke, it was with scorn. "You're a big man, aren't you? It must make you feel wonderful, slapping women around. You're pathetic. So uncertain of your manhood you have to use force to prove how macho you are."

Enraged, Spencer raised his fist. Jan stared at him. Then she said, "If you hit me, I swear to God, I'll kill you. You're not dealing with Mother." She picked up a letter opener that lay on the desk and held it like a dagger. "I'm not kidding. You lay a hand on me again and I'll stick this in your rotten heart!"

He lowered his hand. "Get out!" he said. "Get the hell out of this house and don't come back!"

"Don't worry. I don't intend to." She started for the door, still holding the weapon. "I would have used this, you know. I wasn't bluffing. I'm going to get out of your house and out of your life, the way Chris has. And if I have any influence, I'll make Mother do the same."

She was gone before he could answer. Goddamn women! Spencer thought. I hate them all, the evil, conniving bitches. Good riddance to my ungrateful daughter. She'll go to her lover. Let her. She's nothing but a whore, the way her mother was, the way *my* mother was! Scheming whores, all of them, good for nothing but messing up a man's life. He glanced down at John Peck's address. There's the perfect example of the trouble women cause. Another inconvenience to be disposed of. I'm always washing Alice's dirty linen.

He reached for the phone and dialed Information.

Carol looked at him curiously when he came back from the phone. "Who was it?"

"Spencer Winters."

Her eyes opened wide. "Spencer Winters! Calling you? What's going on?"

John Peck sat down on the sofa and put his arms around his wife. "Winters wants to meet with me. Honey, I've been holding out on you. I didn't want to upset you."

He told her of his meeting with Charlotte Rudolph and, as he anticipated, Carol was furious with the old woman. She was also slightly annoyed with John.

"Don't you think you moved a little too quickly? I know we talked about Mrs. Rudolph, but I thought we agreed that you'd wait until your . . . until Mrs. Winters got back."

"We did, but after I got that lead from Janice I decided to follow it up. I said I might."

"But you didn't tell me you had." She looked hurt. "I didn't think we kept secrets . . ." Abruptly Carol stopped and smiled. "I shouldn't say that. I've been keeping one from you. Johnny, we're going to have a baby."

"Are you serious?"

"Very. Almost three months serious. I held out on you too. I thought it would be compensation if you were disappointed about your mother again. Or a double celebration if Mrs. Winters turned out to be the one."

He kissed her. "Darling, it's wonderful! I'm so happy! And it is a double celebration!" He laughed. "My God, that lady has some surprises in store. Not only a son but a grandchild!"

Carol was very sober. "You're sure? That she's really your mother?"

"Completely. Mrs. Rudolph's performance confirmed it. And now this call from Winters. They're taking it seriously, that's obvious. I wonder what he'll have to say."

"When are you meeting him?"

"Noon tomorrow. At his office. I'll take an early lunch." He frowned. "It seems wrong to talk to him instead of my mother. Maybe I should call Denver."

Carol was about to advise against it when the phone rang again.

This time Carol answered, and after a few seconds she called John.

"It's for you. Janice Winters."

He was trembling as he took the receiver. So much was happening so fast. The whole Winters family was in the act.

"I'd like to talk to you," she said without preamble.

"Of course." He couldn't tell from her voice whether she was friendly or hostile.

"I know everything that's happened," Janice went on. "You're going to be hearing from my father."

"I already have. I'm seeing him tomorrow."

"It figures. So we'd better talk tonight. May I come over now?"

"Certainly." He hesitated. "Janice, I don't intend to make trouble for anybody. I'm really not devious, though you might be thinking so. I did have something in mind when we asked you to dinner, but I hope you know it was just because I was so anxious to get at the truth."

"We'll talk about it when I get there. But meanwhile, put your mind at ease. I'm on your side."

He relayed the conversation to Carol. "She says she's on my side, whatever that means."

"I think she'll help you, darling. She's nice. And I'm glad she's coming over. You got an icy reception from 'Aunt Charlotte' and I doubt Spencer Winters will be better. Worse, probably. We can use a friend at court."

Chapter 19

Laura Dalton came in with the mail. "Letter for you, Barbara," she said.

"Hallelujah!" It was here, the longed-for letter from Charles. She hugged it to her without even looking at it, smiled at her mother and disappeared to her own room to read, in private, the love words that had come at last. But the handwriting on the envelope was not Charles's familiar scrawl, though the return address was his. She sat down on the bed and slowly took the thin parchment paper from its envelope. Disbelieving, she began to read Andrea Tallent's message:

> Dear Barbara,
>
> This is a most awkward letter for me to write, but one of utmost importance to Charles and therefore worth the difficulty on my part and, I'm sure, the distress on yours.
>
> Until this past week, we have all managed to be civilized and live with a distasteful but apparently unavoidable situation. The roles you and I have assumed have not been pleasant ones. You must feel a sense of shame equal to my humiliation, but we have both endured for the sake of a man we care for. You and I are enemies, Barbara, but we are also conspirators in the mutual effort to make Charles happy. Now we must collaborate to make him powerful and famous as well.

The Candidate, who is almost certain to be the next President, has offered Charles the Cabinet post of Secretary of Agriculture, with the proviso that he rid himself of the potential for scandal. You, of course, represent that potential in an administration which will pride itself on honesty and openness.

It is difficult for me, as a woman, to admit that the choice was a hard one for my husband. His devotion to you persists. And it is not easy for Charles to discard any obligation, particularly one of long-standing. However, he has decided to take the sensible and practical route which could lead him to a place in history, perhaps even, one day, to the highest office in the land.

You must be wondering why you learn this from me. Charles intends to tell you when you return to Washington, but my feminine intuition says that knowing what is in store may make you wish not to return to a place of haunting memories. It seemed kinder to let you make that decision now and avoid a wrenching scene whose outcome is already determined. Charles feels it is his duty to tell you his decision in person. He does not reckon, I fear, with the sensibilities of women's emotions. I have tried to put myself in your place. Were I in this situation, I would choose to close the book on a happy chapter rather than be left with a degrading finale. I cannot help but believe you will feel the same.

I bear you no ill will. Indeed, I feel sympathy for you. I do not doubt that you love Charles and that, given a choice, you would in any case have set him free to go on to the greatness of which he is capable. Like many other women in the backgrounds of important men, you will be comforted by the knowledge of the contribution you have made and, aware that the time has come to step aside, putting his and the nation's need above your own desires.

You will make things a great deal easier for Charles if you pretend you know nothing of this matter but have simply decided, given the perspective of time and distance, to end the relationship. It is a final kindness and one that will relieve his conscience and allow him to face his new responsibilities with a free mind and a lighter heart.

Sincerely,
Andrea Tallent

A numbness came over Barbara. It was cruel, unbearably cruel, to hear from her lover's wife that the only thing she existed for had been taken from her. I won't accept it! she thought. I don't believe it! It was a trick of Andrea's, cleverly contrived to get her husband back. But this was no threatening letter from an enraged wife. It would be too easy to disprove with a single phone call. It must be true. Charles has accepted the job and the conditions that go with it. The knowledge stabbed her. How could he? How could he give up the lifetime they planned to share? Could he put a job, no matter how important, above the happiness he found with her? Andrea's wrong. If he'd let me share in the decision-making I'd have made him see that no amount of fame can make him content if he doesn't have me. I'd have talked him out of it. Maybe I still can. I'll call him. I'll beg him to change his mind. Or I'll fly home tonight. I won't let him go. I can't.

But even as these thoughts raced through her head, Barbara knew it was useless. Even if she reached him, even if she persuaded him to decline the job, it had gone too far. The day would come when he'd hate her for depriving him of this chance. That would be worse than anything. Worse than this.

She threw herself down on the bed and let the tears come. Tears of misery and loneliness. Tears of regret for what would never be again. In her mind she relived their hundreds of times together, felt his touch as though he were in the room with her. I never thought it would end, she told herself. And it has, as suddenly and hideously as an amputation.

She stopped crying after a while and lay back, staring at the ceiling. Slowly, a feeling of resentment crept over her. Why didn't he come straight to her and tell her himself? Wasn't he man enough? Was her lover weak and cowardly, when she thought him strong and courageous? For a moment she felt revulsion, but it quickly passed. He didn't know about the letter. He did plan to break this news to her. It would have been terrible for him, but he'd have done it, trying to be gentle, hating himself for his ambition and begging her to understand.

And I'd have let him go, Barbara thought dully. I wouldn't have stood in his way. I know it. Andrea knows it too. We want for him everything he wants for himself. We want to make it easy for him because we both love him.

Strange that at this moment she felt a kinship with her old adversary. They worshiped at the same altar.

There was a tap on the door and she heard her mother's voice. "Barbara? Are you all right, dear?"

She wiped her eyes and sat up. "Come in, Mother."

Laura approached the bed, a look of concern on her face. "Is anything wrong? You've been up here so long."

The sympathetic question brought a lump to Barbara's throat and she felt the tears coming again. Wordlessly, she handed her mother Andrea's letter. Laura fished in her apron pocket for her glasses and read, shaking her head as the meaning came clear. When she finished she put the pages down and faced Barbara, her own eyes swimming.

"My poor Barbara. My poor child."

"Don't. Please don't feel sorry for me, Mother. It only makes it worse. Tell me what a fool I've been. Tell me he isn't worth this pain. Tell me he's a weak, selfish man. That's what I need to hear."

Laura shook her head. "No, dear heart, I can't tell you that. If you loved him, he was all that you believed. You're unhappy now and disappointed in him, but if I know you, Barbara, you wouldn't have liked yourself if he stayed with you because you made him feel he should. Maybe in time you'd even have respected him less for running away from this awful choice. Or maybe he'd come to resent you for depriving him of a great future."

"I know. I've thought of that. But it's so hard, Mother. So terrible to think of life without Charles. I'm hurt. I can't help it. And I'm angry with myself for being such a fool all these years."

"You were no fool darling. You had more than a dozen years of joy. Even your sisters can't say that. All right, perhaps you would have been better off if you'd never met Charles, never tied up so much of your life to him. But you did and there's nothing to be gained by regretting. Remember the lovely times, Barbara. They can never be taken away from you. He was part of your experience and there's no such thing as a wasted experience, dear. We learn from everything that happens to us, good or bad. You've become a wiser, more tolerant, loving woman because of Charles. And I'm sure he's a better man because of you. Let him go gracefully, Barbara, without bitterness or hatred. You will let him go, won't you? You won't try to change his mind?"

Barbara shook her head. "No, I won't put him through that. Or myself, either. It would be wrong." She sounded wistful. "I think I could handle it better if I'd heard it from him, though."

"Possibly. But his wife says he plans to tell you." Laura sighed. "I wish I were Christian enough to think she meant well by writing that letter. I'm afraid it gave her pleasure. She's only human too. But I think her suggestion is right, if you're big enough to accept it. It would be a great gift to Charles if you wrote him, pretending to know nothing of this and breaking things off yourself."

"A gift to him? Letting him think I'm the one who's decided to end it? Good Lord, how much do you expect of me?"

Laura patted her head as though she were a child. "I expect a great deal of a woman as generous as you. I think you can do this one last thing in the name of love. Spare him, Barb. He must be in enough agony as it is."

"Agony of his own making. He didn't have to accept the post."

"You know that isn't true. He had to accept it for his own self-respect. He sounds like a man who couldn't turn his back on success. He'd be incapable of it. Washington's full of men like that, isn't it? If they didn't have drive, they wouldn't be there in the first place. It's not a god you love, Barbara, it's a human being torn between two different kinds of desire. If you could see this unemotionally, you'd know that the temptation would be too strong for him."

"Or his capacity for love too weak."

"I don't think you believe that," Laura said. "You're not a cynic. Don't let this make you bitter. We all suffer disappointments, some greater than others. But we keep our illusions and our belief in the basic goodness of people. He's made you unhappy, but that doesn't cancel out all the times he made you very happy indeed."

Barbara reached for her hand. "You're a wise lady."

"No. I've just lived a long time and seen a lot of grief. Some of it my own. You won't get over this today or next month, Barbara, but you'll get over it, and you'll be glad you handled it with dignity." Laura smiled gently. "I know that's easier said than done. You'll have some bad times, but they'll pass."

"I dread going back to Washington. I'm bound to run into him. Into them. Maybe I should stay in Denver."

"Don't make that decision quite yet. Your father and I would love to have you here, but that's something to think about when you're calmer. There's a lot of life ahead of you, and nobody pushing you to decide right now how to live it."

"Right now there doesn't seem to be very much to live *for*."

Laura was desperately sorry for her youngest. But Barb was right. It was no time for commiseration.

"Self-pity doesn't become you, Barbara. It's a trait the world quickly becomes weary of. You're an intelligent adult. You've had a bad shock, but you must have known this might happen one day." Her voice softened. "I'm sorry, darling. I hurt when you do. But I can only be glad this happened while you're still young enough to start over. It didn't have a future, that kind of relationship. It almost never does."

"Young enough?" Barbara's laugh was hollow. "Forty's hardly young, Mother."

"When you're seventy, it seems like nothing. You'll see."

Another thirty years of nothingness? God spare me, Barb thought. My job, my home, my life in Washington are meaningless without Charles. She allowed the tears to come again. I don't know what to do. I wish I were dead.

In contrast to the bleakness Barbara felt that morning, Fran's mood was optimistic. She was pleased with the way things were going with Buzz. Calling to "say goodbye" had been the smartest thing she'd ever done. It always worked with men. Just let them think you were going to walk away and they couldn't be without you. It was Buzz who was doing the pleading now. Buzz who, last night, had been grateful she'd agreed to meet him again, had begged her to give him a few hours every night as long as she stayed.

She'd shaken her head when he said that. "We can't, Buzz.

Dorothy might find out. It's too risky. You've made it clear that you won't leave her. We'd better stop now, while we can."

He'd reached for her again. "No. There's no need. I know you're going to go away again. Let me store up as many memories as I can." He began to make love to her for the second time. "You're so incredibly desirable. I can't have you forever, but for now . . ."

Fran responded with genuine passion. She'd not expected him to be such an expert lover. I'm tricking him, she thought for a moment. I'm lulling him into a false sense of security. He really believes I'll let him go. The hell with it. I know what's best for him. All's fair . . .

This morning she was blissfully exhausted. They'd been very late leaving the motel, almost midnight. She'd been honestly concerned for him.

"Will there be trouble when you get home?"

"That's not for you to worry about, my love. Tomorrow night? Same time, same place?"

She laughed. "What do you think we are, teen-agers?"

"Yes. I feel like one. I haven't felt this young in years. Maybe never. I could make love to you all night."

"I'd like that." She allowed a wistful note to creep into her voice. "Do you think we'll ever have a whole night?"

Buzz hesitated. "I don't know why not. Why not a weekend? We could go to Vail or Aspen."

"Oh, Buzz, really? Could we? No. We couldn't. There's no way you could manage that."

It was all the challenge he needed. "I can manage it. This weekend, if you like. But what about you? How will you explain it to your family?"

"I don't have to explain, darling. There's no one to ride herd on me."

"Then it's a date."

"You're sure?"

"Damned right I'm sure. Dorothy doesn't know how lucky she is that I'm not taking off forever!"

Now Fran smiled, remembering last night, thinking of tonight and of the weekend. It was going perfectly.

"I'm glad somebody has something to smile about this morning."

Laura's voice surprised her. Her mother had come into the room, looking upset and unhappy.

"What's wrong? Are you still upset about Allie?"

"No, it's Barbara. I don't know whether she's told you about her friend in Washington . . ."

"She told me. And I told *her* she's being an idiot. I didn't know you knew about it, Mother. But since you do, I'm sure you agree she's wasting her life."

"Not any more," Laura said. "She had a letter this morning."

Frances was aghast as she heard about Andrea Tallent's letter. "My God! That poor kid! What a way to be brushed off! And that bastard Tallent! Not enough guts to tell her himself!"

"In fairness, he planned to."

"Oh, sure. I'll just bet he did. Like hell. He probably is behind the whole thing. I wouldn't be surprised if he suggested his wife write. What a smart move, loading the responsibility for his damned future onto Barb's shoulders! She's well out of it, is all I can say."

"I suppose she is, but it's hard for her. She loves him, Frances. He's been her whole life for a long time. I don't say it's right. I don't approve of any woman taking another woman's husband. But I feel sorry for her. She's almost destroyed by this. She's even talking of staying here, never going back to Washington. I think she'll change her mind about that, but right now she's at rock-bottom. Poor thing, she's paying for her sins."

"And he's getting off scot-free. A big important job. Back to the little woman and the kiddies. Where's the damned justice in this world? Isn't he supposed to pay for *his* sins? Or is it only women who get the short end of the stick?"

Laura shook her head. "No. They've both been wrong. I'm sure he's suffering too. He must be a fine man if Barbara loves him. This can't be easy for him."

"Oh, for God's sake, Mother! He's had all the kicks and none of the kicks-in-the-behind! He's not the one who's had to hide out. He hasn't had to sit by the phone like some damned beggar waiting for a handout. Barb's been a fool. She should have had better sense. But that's no reason why she should continue to make it all so easy for him. If she writes that letter, I'll kill her!"

"What would you have her do, Frances?"

"I'd make him sweat. I'd stop being such a pushover and give him and that smug wife of his a hard time. Damned if I'd let him off the hook so easily!"

Laura looked at her curiously. "And what would that prove? What good would it do to threaten a lot of trouble?"

"None, probably, but *I'd* feel better."

"You and Barbara see life differently," Laura said.

The implied criticism angered Fran. "Not all that differently, Mother. Neither of us has any qualms about going after a married man if he's what we want." She threw discretion to the wind. "While we're on the subject, I've been seeing Buzz Paige. I'm crazy about him and I'm going to take him away from that dreary wife of his."

"Frances! What are you saying?"

"I think it's pretty clear. I had first claim on him. He's never loved anybody but me. He only married that stupid girl because I left him. Well, I was wrong. I want him now and I'm going to get him. I'm sorry if that shocks you, Mother, but I only have one life and I'm going to get as much out of it as I can."

"Even if its means hurting an innocent woman?"

"Would you say that to Barb? She hurt one. She just wasn't smart enough to do the job thoroughly. I won't live any trashy little secret life with Buzz. The break will be clean. To me, that's more admirable than sneaking a few hours while you try to fool the public. I say, if you're going in for adultery, then for God's sake have the courage of your convictions. Otherwise, you end up like Barbara."

Laura covered her ears. "I don't want to hear this! How can you be so hard? Frances, you mustn't break up Buzz Paige's marriage! It's wrong! It's a mortal sin!"

Fran quieted down. "I'm sorry, Mother. It probably was wrong of me to say those things to you. But, dear, I am going to do what I said. If Dorothy can't hold her husband, that's not my fault. Why should he stay in a marriage he doesn't want? I can make him happy, and I will."

"No, Frances. Please. Let him alone."

"Darling, I can't. I'm just as glad you know about it. Now I don't have to make up an excuse for going off this weekend. We're going to have a couple of days together to make sure we want to make it permanent."

Laura wrung her hands. "And Buzz agrees to this?"

"Yes. He doesn't know about it yet, but he agrees." Fran put her arms around her mother. "We give you terrible troubles, don't we? All of us. I wish we didn't. I wish we were what you deserve." She released Laura. "I think I'll go talk to Barb. Maybe my kind of selfishness is just what she needs."

Laura sank wearily into a chair. "Maybe so. I can't handle these things any more. I feel so totally useless. Your father and I. We're . . . we're outmoded. I used to think I was still part of today. I couldn't understand why he'd abandoned all the activity he used to love. But *I* feel that way now. You and Buzz. Allie and Jack Richards. Barbara and this married man. It's too much for me, Frances. I can't cope with it. I want to run away and hide."

"We'll be all right, Mother. You can't protect us, darling. No mother can shelter a child forever, much as she might like to. We don't live hermetically sealed, dear. We're going to have our tragedies, make our mistakes. We have in the past and we will in the future. Don't think it's a reflection on anything you have or haven't done. We're women, Mother, not girls, but don't think of us in terms of yourself. You'd never do any of the things we've done. You're much too good. You and Dad. Much too moral."

"Our friends' children haven't caused them such grief." Laura couldn't resist. "They stayed here, married, settled down, had children of their own. Most of your friends are grandmothers, Frances." She stopped. "That's wrong of me. I'm sorry. I'm trying to make you feel guilty because I'm guilty myself. You did what you had to do, all three of you. I'd give anything if you hadn't had to pay so dearly for it."

"It's okay," Fran said. "None of it's your fault."

Laura didn't answer. How I wish I could believe that, she thought.

Chapter 20

Janice was hardly inside the Pecks' apartment when she came right to the point. "Are you on the level?" she asked John. "Did my mother have you before she was married?" But there was no hostility in the businesslike way she put her questions.

John answered in the same, unemotional vein. "Yes, I'm on the level. This is no con game, Janice. I'm sure I'm the child Alice Dalton gave up for adoption. I know Mrs. Rudolph believes it, and I think your father does too."

"Aunt Charlotte's an addled old woman. Dad's something else. He'll demand proof. Do you have any?"

"I have my birth certificate. I know my mother's name and the date and place I was born. It all fits with the time of your mother's arrival in Boston."

"It's damned slim," Jan said. "My father's a lawyer. He'll shoot holes in that circumstantial evidence."

"I'm sure he'll try. But how could I invent such a story? Besides, what about your aunt? She practically admitted I was right. She even offered me money to go away and not bother any of you again. She knows I'm the one. She knows the Pecks adopted me."

Jan shook her head. "I told you. She's a crazy old lady, and scared witless of my father. He'll make her deny everything, and if it comes to that, it'll be the word of a well-coached dowager and a prominent Boston attorney against yours. Bad odds, John. You have no idea what you're dealing with when you try to fight

Spencer Winters. There's nothing he won't do to protect his bloody 'impeccable reputation'—including making mincemeat out of you and your story."

John was silent for a moment and then he said, "You believe me. Why?"

"I'm not sure. Call it a hunch. No, it's really more than that. I don't think you could invent it. And it explains some things I've never understood. Like why he beats up on Mother. And why she stands for it."

"Beats up on her?" John was horrified. "You mean he literally hits her?"

"Always has. Knocks hell out of her. Maybe this is why. Maybe he's punishing her for you, and she takes it because she's been conditioned to feel worthless. I don't know. I don't have anything to go on. No more than you do. We're both operating more from instinct than hard facts. But I do believe you. It's a shame we don't look anything alike. That might help. You don't look anything like Chris either." An idea struck her. "You wouldn't, by chance, have an identifying birthmark, would you? Some nice heart-shaped thing on your shoulder that would clinch it?" Jan smiled. "If this were a mystery story, you'd dramatically open your shirt and produce proof."

He tried to return her smile. "Sorry. Nothing. Not a blemish on my beautiful body."

"Too bad. I don't know how you're going to make your story hold up. I don't know much about adoption, John, but it even seems unlikely to me that Aunt Charlotte would know the name of the people who took you. I thought that was known only to the adoption agency and the court."

Carol, who'd been listening quietly, suddenly spoke up. "I think that's true, Janice. I haven't wanted to upset John, but I've wondered all along about that. And yet, apparently, she does know. The way she reacted to John's visit indicates that." She hesitated. "Unless . . ."

Her husband looked at her. "Unless what, honey?"

"Maybe you weren't placed through an agency at all. If they wanted to keep everything so secret, maybe they managed it another way. Like through the obstetrician. I've heard of that. Doctors sometimes know couples who're eager to have a baby and can't get one through regular channels. Could the Pecks have been one of those, John? Could they have gotten you through Mrs. Rudolph and the doctor who delivered you, without going through an agency? Was there any reason why they'd have been turned down if they'd followed the usual procedure?"

"No. They were good, honest, hard-working people. A lot older than the parents of my friends, but . . ."

"How much older?" Janice asked.

John realized what the question meant. "They were well into their fifties when they adopted me. Maybe more. My God, I never thought of that! They'd have been considered too old to adopt a newborn baby, wouldn't they? I haven't thought about it for years, but I remember my father telling me they'd tried to have their own children for twenty years before they got me! Do you think that's it? Could Carol be right? If they applied to an agency and were turned down because of age, maybe they paid the doctor to get them a baby! Sure. It makes sense. He'd have known the circumstances and put the proposition to Charlotte. He'd have told her about the Pecks! She could tell us who the doctor was. Or we could find him! That would prove it!"

"Slow down, darling," Carol said. "From what Janice says, Mrs. Rudolph's not likely to tell us anything. And it's been thirty years. The doctor could be dead by now."

His surge of hope disappeared. "I suppose you're right. It's just another unprovable idea that won't help with Spencer Winters."

Janice lit a cigarette and exhaled slowly. "I'm suddenly wondering why we're worrying about Dad and Aunt Charlotte. You don't give a damn whether they accept you or not, do you? There's only one person you want to convince. Seems to me we're making this too complicated. If you believe you belong to Alice Winters, why the hell don't you go and talk to her?"

"That's what I've wanted to do all along," John said, "but I guess I've been afraid. I keep looking for things to make sure she believes me."

"I've held him back," Carol said. "I was afraid he'd be disappointed again."

"He might be," Janice said. "We don't have a clue about how much Mother knows of what happened to you. She was a young, dumb kid when you were born. Maybe Charlotte dealt her out of the whole thing after she had the baby. But she's the only one who can answer your questions. Or, rather, the only one who *will*, if she can."

"Will she, Janice?" John sounded eager. "Will she see me and tell me what she knows?"

"She's a lady, whatever else she is," Jan answered. "She may be mixed up and full of guilts, but she's loving and honest. You get to her, John. Here." She pulled a scrap of paper out of her handbag. "I brought the address and phone number of my grandparents in Denver. Call Mother. Or get on a plane and go out there. The sooner the better. I don't know how long she's going to stay, and you sure don't want to meet her with Dad around."

"I'm supposed to see your father in the office tomorrow."

Jan laughed. "Forget it. Stand him up. It'll be good for him."

The plane came in low, making its approach to the Denver airport. John's face was pressed to the window, his eyes taking in this first impression of the land. It was checkerboarded from the air, like most countrysides, in brown and green squares that he assumed were farms, with an occasional speck of building dotted here and there. It seemed quite ordinary, almost dreary, until he saw the mountains. They rose in the distance, an imperious, snow-topped, breathtaking white-capped contrast to the drab flatness between. Like Sarah Peck's kitchen floor on the days she cleaned it—an expanse of unremarkable tiles edged with a dramatic border of billowing soapsuds. The unlikely comparison made him smile. Comparing the Colorado landscape to a Boston kitchen floor! I must be going mad, he thought. I *am* mad, flying here with no advance warning to the woman I plan to confront, telling no one except Carol and Janice what I decided in an instant to do. He glanced at his watch. Even now, Spencer Winters would be wondering what had happened to his twelve o'clock appointment. Let him. He'll probably call the apartment again, but Carol won't be home. And even if he suspects that Janice had a hand in this broken date, he'll have a hard time getting anything out of her.

He felt his anger rise again. The three of them had talked far into the night, and at some point Janice had told Carol and him about the earlier part of the evening when her father struck her.

"He's out of his mind," she said almost without concern. "I'll never see him again. Never speak to him if I can avoid it. I'm not going back to that house and I hope to God Mother won't either. You talk her out of it, John, when you see her. Make her understand there's no reason she has to live with that."

Make her understand, John thought now. There's so much I hope she understands before I get to that. He'd felt sick when he heard of Spencer Winters' cruelty. What possessed such a man?

"Does Chris know?" he'd asked.

"About Dad hitting me? No. Chris already hates him enough for what he's done to Mother. Why should I give my brother one more thing to be unhappy about? He's a nice fella. Much more like Mother than I am. You'll like each other."

The plane set down gently, and as he made the long walk from the gate to the taxi entrance, John realized he didn't even know where he was going to stay. He had only one piece of hand luggage. This wouldn't be a long trip. He couldn't stay away from his job more than a few days. Carol was going to call the bank and say he was sick. They'd thought of that, but they hadn't even discussed hotel reservations. Maybe I had an idea I'd call from the airport and be invited to my grandparents', John thought. Crazy! I have to check in somewhere and prepare my mother for this shock. He hailed a cab.

"Yessir. Where to?"

For an instant, he was tempted to give the Carona Street address, but instead he said, "I don't have a hotel reservation. Can you suggest one?"

"Town's pretty crowded. Always is, these days. We're getting to be a big convention center. Your best bet is the Hilton, I guess. They might have a single."

"Fine." John settled back as they pulled away from the airport. "By the way, how far is the Hilton from South Carona Street?"

"Fifteen, twenty minutes, maybe. The Hilton's right downtown. Carona's out near Washington Park."

"Nice neighborhood?"

"So-so. Not tops, but okay. Working people area, I guess you'd call it. You got friends there?"

"I hope so."

"How's that?" The cab driver looked at him in the rearview mirror.

"I mean, I have relatives there. I've never seen them." John managed a laugh. "I sure *hope* they're friendly."

"Most people here are. It's a friendly town. If you can't get a room in the hotel you can always bunk in with your folks, right? Maybe you want to go there instead?"

"No. I'll try the Hilton."

Allie smiled nervously at the man across the luncheon table. "Barb suggested we eat here at the Promenade Cafe when she and Fran and I came to Larimer Square a few days ago, but we went to LaFitte's instead. This is pleasant."

Jack Richards nodded. He was as ill at ease as she. "It is nice. I like dining outdoors. What made you change your minds?"

"Fran changed them for us." Her smile broadened. "You know Fran. So conscious of her looks. She refused to sit in the sunlight."

"No, I don't know Fran. I haven't seen her since she was a girl, remember? I hadn't seen Barb either until yesterday."

Or me, Alice thought. You haven't seen any of us. Or we, you. We have to start all over. Can we? Is that what we really want? It was hard to believe this was the boy she'd loved, whose child she'd borne. He seemed a pleasant, attractive stranger. Yesterday's meeting had been emotional, dramatic for both of them. Today she sensed she was not the only one who was uncertain about a reconciliation.

"How is Barb, by the way?"

Alice hesitated. She didn't feel close enough to him to say that when she'd gone up to their room to dress for this luncheon date she'd found Barbara lying still as death on her bed. Alice had asked her what was wrong, but her sister had just smiled a pathetic little smile and said it was nothing, she wasn't feeling too well. It was an obvious lie, but whatever was troubling Barb, she didn't want to discuss it. I should have stayed and talked, Allie realized. I've been so absorbed in my own life I haven't even asked about hers. But Fran had come in just then, and her older sister had shaken her head as if to say, "Don't bother her now."

"I said, 'How's Barbara?'," Jack repeated.

"What? Oh, fine, I guess. She was resting when I left."

"You should have let me come to the house and pick you up. It was foolish for you to take a cab down here."

"I couldn't, Jack. Not yet. I don't know what Dad's going to say when he finds out you and I are meeting again." She seemed embarrassed. "Even Mother was upset when she heard, and she's much more sensible about ancient history."

He was quiet for a moment. "Your father's going to have to know, Allie. About us. You're not a child. He has no say in your life any more. Not like he did years ago."

"I know."

Jack suddenly reached over and took her hand. "You don't want to marry me, do you? Our reunion yesterday was romantic and nostalgic, but you're not sure you want to make it permanent, are you?"

She met his eyes squarely. "No, I'm not sure, Jack. I'm desperately unhappy in my marriage. I don't think, after this visit home, I can go on with it. But I don't want to make another mistake. That wouldn't be fair to either of us." A note of desperation crept into her voice. "I'm so afraid of everything. I wish I weren't. I long to be like my sisters, but I'm not. I can't make hasty decisions or take chances with your life or mine. You're lonely. You miss your wife. And I hate my husband. That's the truth of it. That's our bond."

"No, that's not all of it. You may be right. I won't try to rush you into anything, Allie. But you're overlooking the strongest tie beween us: our son. We both want to find him. We have that in common. We needn't decide about us. Not now, at least. But we have to resolve the other thing, or neither of us will ever know peace of mind."

"How, Jack? I want to find him as much as you do. I always have. But where do we begin? Realistically, how can we track down someone you never saw and I saw only once in my life? There's no place to start. No clues. It's hopeless."

"Nothing is hopeless. I'll get those private detectives again. They'll go back to the beginning. We'll find him. Doesn't your mother know anything? Didn't your Aunt Charlotte ever tell her who took the child?"

Allie shook her head. "I don't think so. Mother and Daddy didn't want to know. They left it up to her."

"Then, dammit, she's the key! She'll have to tell you."

"She won't. She's too afraid of Spencer. So am I. He'd be in a rage if my illegitimate child showed up and caused a scandal in his well-ordered life."

"To hell with him! He's there and you're here. He can't do anything to you, Allie. And what's he going to do to an eighty-year-old woman? We have to make her realize how important this is!"

"You just don't understand. She's kept the secret all these years. I'm not sure she even remembers the details any more. She's getting senile, Jack. Even if she wanted to tell us what arrangements she made thirty years ago, I'm not sure she could."

He looked grim. "I won't accept that. If we can't find out what we need to know through Charlotte, we'll do it some other way. People don't just vanish. Our son is out there somewhere, Allie, and I damned well am going to find him, with or without her help. And there's one thing more. We have to talk to your parents. I can't believe they still hold a grudge against me. And I can't believe they know nothing. It just isn't possible that they could wash their hands of the whole matter. Your mother, particularly. She has to have been told what was done with that baby. My God, that's her grandchild! Her flesh and blood! Wouldn't she have cared what happened to him?"

Allie looked at him hopelessly. "Tell me, Jack. Did you?"

He stopped. "That's a low blow, Allie."

"I'm sorry. I suppose it is. But it's true, isn't it? Everybody wanted to forget the whole thing. Your parents. Mine. Even you. Oh, I don't blame any of you. I was the one who should have stopped it from happening. I wanted that child enough to have him. I should have been strong enough to keep him. I'm not surprised nobody inquired about what Charlotte did with Johnny. I never made much effort myself, and I was his mother."

"Don't, Allie. Don't punish yourself this way."

"Who else should be punished? I caused the trouble by refusing an abortion. I thrust this problem on other people. I wasn't willing to go through with what I started."

"You were young. Frightened. Alone."

"That's no excuse. I asserted myself once in my whole life, and wouldn't you know I picked the wrong time? Insisting on having that child! What a stupid little fool I was. I should have known

I'd never have enough backbone to take care of him. And I've spent the rest of my life repenting, and wishing I could see him, or even know he's alive."

Jack held her hand more tightly. "You will darling. You'll see him again. I make you a solemn promise. You'll see he's well and happy. Please don't cry. I don't know what will happen with us. We'll let that develop as it will. But we'll find your son. Our son. You believe that, don't you? Say you believe it."

She looked up, tears streaming down her face. "Say I believe in miracles? Is that what you're asking?"

"If that's what it takes, yes. But we won't trust to miracles. We'll make it happen. That's what I want you to believe."

"I'll try," Alice said softly. "I'll really try."

John Peck sat in his hotel room staring at the telephone. Just a local call. Dial nine and the number and you'll be talking to your mother. His palms were sweating as he picked up the piece of paper on which Janice had written the Daltons' telephone number and address. Very slowly he dialed and heard the telephone ringing in a house he'd never seen. It was three o'clock in the afternoon.

He felt as though he were choking as he asked, "Is this the Dalton residence?"

"Yes. Whom do you want?"

"Ah . . . Ah, I'm trying to reach Mrs. Winters. Mrs. Spencer Winters."

"This is Mrs. Winters. Who is this?"

The blood rushed to his head and he could feel his heart pounding. "It's John," he said. "John Peck." He stopped, wondering what to say next. The name would mean nothing to her. There was a pause and then Alice said, "I'm afraid I don't know anyone named Peck. You have the right number, but . . ."

"You don't know me." John was stammering. "That is, you do know me, but not really. I mean, it's all rather complicated."

There was a suspicious finality in the cool voice at the other end of the phone, yet the woman remained polite. "I don't understand. I'm sorry. Perhaps there's been a mistake."

"No! Don't hang up, please!" He was suddenly terrified, so frightened that he blurted out words he'd been prepared to lead

up to carefully, cautiously. "It's John. I'm your son. At least I think I am. That is, I *know* I am. You haven't seen me for thirty years."

There was a terrible silence. My God! What have I done? John thought. Maybe she's fainted. Maybe I'm not even . . . I must be insane, telling a woman this kind of thing on the phone! He waited, cursing himself for his impulsiveness. Perhaps she had hung up. The silence after his outburst was almost unbearable, but finally Alice said, disbelievingly, "Johnny? You say you're Johnny?"

"Yes."

"But how . . . ? Where . . ." She sounded almost frightened and then her voice grew stronger. He could imagine her pulling herself together, wondering, no doubt, if this was some kind of hoax. "You believe we're related? What makes you think that?"

"It's a long story. A crazy set of coincidences. I've talked with Janice and Mrs. Rudolph . . . and your husband." Like Alice, he now struggled to sound calm, almost matter-of-fact. "I don't think there's any doubt," John said gently. "I'm sure I'm the child you gave up for adoption."

There was a quick intake of breath. "Where are you calling from?"

"I'm here in Denver. At the Hilton. I flew in today from Boston."

"Boston? You've been in Boston?"

"All my life. Since the day of my birth, November tenth, nineteen forty-six, at Massachusetts General."

"Oh, no!"

He couldn't tell whether she was happy or horrified. Or even whether she believed him. Probably she didn't know that herself. She was too much in shock, understandably unable to absorb the full impact of this incredible revelation.

"I'd like to see you as soon as possible," John said. He managed a little laugh. "That's an understatement. I've been waiting years to see you, Moth . . ." His voice trailed off. He didn't know what to call her. "Mother" was impossible to say, but he couldn't bring himself to call her "Mrs. Winters" or, even less suitably, "Alice." He hesitated, disconcerted, but finally he said, "Can we meet somewhere this afternoon?"

"I . . . I don't know." She sounded dazed, and John felt the return of his old fears. She didn't want to see him, didn't want him to exist. But then she said, "Yes, of course. I'd ask you to come here, but I think it's better that we talk outside the house. You're at the Hilton, you said? Why don't I come there? There's a little sort of cocktail lounge at the end of the lobby. Would that be convenient?"

"Perfectly. Thank you. I'll be waiting. Do you remember the name? It's Peck." He felt foolish saying that, but in her bewilderment she might have forgotten.

For the first time, she sounded half-amused. "I remember. I'll ask for you." There was another small pause. "I may bring someone with me. Jack Richards. Is that all right?"

No, John wanted to say. Come alone. If there's to be a reunion it's yours and mine, no one else's. He felt almost angry that she was being so cautious. Richards probably was her lawyer. She was bracing herself to cope with a possible phony, an impostor and extortionist, perhaps. "If you want to bring your friend, that's entirely up to you, but I assure you you're perfectly safe. I certainly mean you no harm."

"It's not that. If you are whom you say, you'll want to meet Jack Richards. He's your father."

It was John's turn to be stunned. He'd been so obsessed with finding Alice that he'd hardly given a thought to his other parent. Both of them? Here in Denver and presumably close? Good God! Who would have thought? He stammered something, hopefully civil, and hung up. In less than two hours he'd see her. *Them.* It was like a dream. Too nervous to sit still, he showered and changed, hoping he looked well, praying it would turn out right. He regretted their meeting in a public place, but there was little choice. She was right. He couldn't burst into his grandparents' house, and his modest hotel room was unsuitable, even if she were "chaperoned" by Jack Richards. He repeated the name to himself. Jack. Nickname for John. Alice had called her son after his father. I'm John Richards, Jr., he thought, staring into the mirror. I finally know who I am. Now I need to know how I came to be.

Alice gently replaced the receiver and sat gazing blankly into space. It couldn't be. It simply couldn't be that the child she and

Jack had discussed finding would ring up an hour after their luncheon conversation about him. Things like that didn't happen. It was some dreadful mistake. Another disappointment in her life, which already seemed to have been a series of them.

And yet she dared to believe because she so desperately wanted the "miracle" she'd spoken of an hour before. Don't! she told herself. Don't get your hopes up! Things don't fall into place so easily. Not after thirty years. But how wonderful if it were true! What joy to be reunited with the child she'd given up! He'd surely accept her. Of course he would. If he wasn't prepared to forgive, he'd never have sought her out. And she yearned to put her arms around him, to try to make him understand the desperation of his young parents, to tell him he'd always been loved and wanted, despite how it must seem to him.

She glanced at her watch, silently giving thanks that none of the family was within earshot. She couldn't stand a skeptical, advance examination of this amazing development by anyone. Except Jack, who'd share her optimism and her joy. Quickly she dialed his office, and when he answered she said, "Something incredible has happened. Can you pick me up at four-thirty to go to the Hilton?"

"Sure." His voice was filled with curiosity. "What's going on?"

"We have an appointment at five o'clock." Suddenly she began to weep. "You won't believe it. I can't believe it!" The words came between sobs. "I've just had a phone call from Johnny. He's here, Jack. Our son has come to find us!"

From the moment she saw him, Alice knew this was her child. She and Jack approached the cocktail lounge at the hotel and Jack asked the hostess where Mr. Peck was. Before the young woman could answer, a tall, well-built stranger rose from a chair nearby and said, "I'm John Peck."

Alice's knees went weak. It was like looking at Jack Richards thirty years ago. There was no mistaking the resemblance. Even the smile was his father's. She stared at him, speechless, and then glanced at Jack, whose stunned expression confirmed her own instant reaction.

"My God!" Jack said as the three of them stood awkwardly looking at each other. The hostess gawked, openly curious. Crazy things went on every day in a hotel, but these people looked as though they'd all been struck by lightning. Finally, the young one regained his composure.

"Shall we sit down?" he asked courteously. "This nice young lady has been kind enough to save us a quiet corner over by the window."

The older couple followed him. In that first moment they'd simultaneously reached for each other's hands and they held on tightly as they made their way to the table. Even when they were seated, Jack and Alice's fingers remained entwined as though they were giving strength to each other. The hostess watched them. They all looked as though they were going to burst into tears. It seemed, she thought idly, like some kind of reunion, and yet they obviously were strangers. The young man had even had to introduce himself. It was a mystery. She saw the waitress take their drink orders and withdraw and finally, before she had to turn away, she saw they'd begun to talk. She was always telling her boyfriend about the nutty things that happened during her working day. The pick-ups, the arguments, the drunks, the solitary boozers, the silly groups of conventioneers, all were good for a laugh. But there was something sad and serious about this trio. Well, she'd never know. It probably was nothing at all. But why did they keep staring at each other that way, like skittish animals? Hell, who cared? It wasn't her business.

The hostess would have been even more intrigued if she'd managed to eavesdrop on that meeting. They gave their drink orders and sat silently for a long moment. Finally, Jack Richards cleared his throat nervously and said, "Let's get right to the point. What's this all about?"

Johnny couldn't take his eyes off his mother. She was so beautiful, so dignified, and yet she seemed frightened. He'd tried so long to picture this moment, imagined it full of drama, not sure whether it would be tears of joy or cold rejection but certain it would be emotional. And here they were, like three well-bred strangers, waiting for their cocktails, sizing each other up, finding it almost impossible to speak. They were going to leave it up to him to prove himself. Except for that first startled exclamation of Jack's, there'd been no outward indication that they were ready to accept what he knew to be true. All right. He'd carry the ball. Slowly, calmly, he began to tell the story of his search. Of finding the papers with Alice Dalton's name on them. Of tracking down a hundred futile leads. And of finally coming across the society item which led him to Janice and Mrs. Rudolph and a phone conversation with Spencer Winters and this precipitous flight to Denver.

"That's it," he ended, flatly, looking straight at Alice. "I've searched for you all my life. And now I've found you. I can't prove anything really. My adoptive parents are dead. To my knowledge, only your aunt knows the truth. Unless your parents do. Or unless we can find the doctor who delivered me and probably arranged the adoption 'under the counter,' so to speak." He kept looking at Alice. "But I know you're my mother. I knew it when you walked in. I think you know it too."

Alice was too overcome to answer, but Jack Richards made one more effort to be "businesslike."

"How can we be certain, John?" he asked not unkindly. "Just a few hours ago we talked about ways of finding our son. We had one. Alice has already told you that. We'd planned to explore every avenue that could take us to him, but to have you suddenly appear this way, so insanely coincidentally, is almost too pat. This is the most important thing in all our lives. We must be sure, all of us. Absolutely sure."

"Can you ever be?" Johnny answered. "Where will the proof come from? There's only one place I know: from Mrs. Rudolph, who can confirm that the Pecks took your baby. I know my mother's name is Alice Dalton." He smiled bitterly. "But there are a lot of Alice Daltons and I've contacted most of them in the past ten years. No, I can't prove who I am. I can only believe it."

Impulsively, Alice reached across the table and touched John's cheek. "You're Johnny," she said softly. "Look at you. Look at your father. Can either of you have any doubt?" Her eyes glistened with tears. "I don't need proof. I don't need a 'confession' from poor old Aunt Charlotte. I know you're part of me, part of us. I know it as surely as I'm sitting here. Oh, God, you don't know what this means to me! The years I've dreamed of you, the hours I've spent reproaching myself for ever letting you go, the wondering where and how you were. That was the worst, the not knowing. Johnny, Johnny, can you forgive me? I didn't want to let you go. I had no choice. I couldn't care for you. Nobody would help. I had to let them take you."

They were all weeping now, Alice openly, the men trying to brush away the tears with the backs of their hands.

"I want to know all about it," John said. "How it happened and why. But even before, I can tell you that there's never been any need for forgiveness. I always knew you wouldn't have given me up if you'd had a choice. I clung to that belief. It's why I never stopped searching. I wondered about you just as much as you did about me. I knew you'd be as sweet and warm as you are." He reached out and touched her cheek as she had his. "You're everything I dreamed you'd be. You're my mother."

They were so intent upon each other they nearly forgot the other person intimately involved. His voice brought them back to the moment.

"If there's any forgiveness, it must be for me," Jack said. "I'm the one who walked away. I'm the stupid, selfish kid who let her go through this alone. There are explanations, of a sort. Alice has found it in her heart to forgive me. I hope you will, too, when you hear the whole story. It's a long one, son. A terrible one, especially for you and your mother, but I want you to know it all, and I pray you'll understand and accept me. You see, I came late to this kind of love. So many years later than I should have. But that doesn't diminish what I feel . . . for both of you."

His parents looked at him, waiting for his answer. "You're my family," John said. "I finally know who I am, and I can only believe I'm lucky to belong to people like you."

"We're the lucky ones," Jack Richards said. "We have so much to talk about, Johnny. When you hear it, you'll realize how lucky we all are."

Chapter 21

Like envy, greed or even misguided love, the desire for revenge is an ugly, all-consuming passion more destructive to the one who nurtures it than to its target. Seldom sweet, as popularly supposed, revenge is, in fact, an empty, useless exercise in self-indulgence which feeds like a cancer on its carrier, destroying logical thought and discipline. There is a sick joy in the anticipation of it, but a sense of futility in its achievement. Yet there are those who cannot live deprived of hate. It sustains them, occupies their every waking thought, pervades their dreams and becomes as necessary as breathing.

For years, Dorothy Paige had nursed an irrational desire for revenge on "the Dalton girls." From adolescence she'd despised their beauty and easy confidence, their popularity and their strict but adoring parents. Her own mother and father were cold, undemonstrative people whose prime interest in Dorothy seemed to be in her scholastic achievements rather than her happiness. They approved her high marks in school, expected her to be (as, indeed, she was) Valedictorian of her high school class. They did not see, or they chose to ignore, the fact that she had few friends and fewer dates and that her peers looked on her as a "grind," useful only when they faced a test for which they were not prepared and for which Dorothy had the answers. Eagerly, pathetically, she came to their rescue at such times, basking for a few moments in their admiration and friendship, hoping it would continue and knowing it would not. Frances Dalton was guilty of this unconscious cruelty time and again. So was Buzz Paige, for whom Dorothy had a secret, unrequited passion. She could not hate Buzz. But she grew to despise Fran and the sisters who were an extension of her: Alice, sought-after in her own group, with Jack Richards as a steady beau; even little Barbara, child that she was in those long-gone days, showed promise of being as pretty and popular as her older sisters. They seemed bathed in sunshine while Dorothy sulked in the shadows of loneliness and hated them.

Frances, of course, was an obsession, the focus of her envy. Fran and Buzz and their friends speeding by her house in his open car, en route to some picnic or party from which she'd been excluded. Fran and Buzz jitterbugging at the prom and dancing soulfully, cheek to cheek, as the band played "Goodnight, Sweetheart." Fran and Alice giving parties at the Dalton house for the "gang," sometimes inviting her out of pity but making no effort to see that she had a good time. Not that there was much they could have done about it. Dorothy was moderately pretty. She dressed as well as the others, did her hair and make-up in imitation of theirs, but she was shy and inarticulate and the boys found her boring.

Even when, once or twice, she talked her parents into letting her have a party of her own, it was a dismal failure. She had the same ingredients as Fran and Alice did—the latest phonograph records, the space cleared for dancing, the fruit punch into which someone would sneak a bottle of gin. But she was a nervous and inept hostess with no natural gift for entertaining, unable to project that indefinable enjoyment contagious to guests. Her parties broke up early and she went to bed in tears, knowing the others were off to a drive-in for hamburgers and malteds, glad to escape from the heavy atmosphere of the Kravett house and the stilted attitude of the Kravett daughter. She did not know then what was missing in her. Even years later, when she had her "nervous breakdown" over Buzz's imagined infidelity, she could not see what the psychiatrist tried to guide her into discovering: she lacked the capacity for unselfish love. She wanted to possess, to be totally necessary. She did not know she thrived on her injured feelings. She thought she loved her husband and her sons, but in fact she did not. She strove to be indispensable to them, playing on their sense of duty or pity or guilt. And they responded with outward kindness and patience and with hidden resentment of her devouring qualities.

When Fran ran off with her actor, Dorothy was the only person in town who rejoiced. The Daltons were shocked and grief-stricken, unable to handle this new blow coming so soon after Alice's disgrace. Buzz was like a man in a fog, morosely moving away from the group of which he and Frances had been a part, drinking to escape his memories, ripe for someone totally different from the girl who'd betrayed him.

Dorothy was clever enough to know she could be that someone. She "moved in" with gentle persistence, in the form of invitations to plays for which she'd "accidentally" received tickets. She sent him notes and small, silly, thoughtful gifts. Buzz was grateful for this unthreatening new companionship. He appreciated her kindness, seeing her as he'd always seen her, an attractive but dull young woman who people said was a born "old maid."

Later, he did not know how it happened, he went to her house one night for a quiet evening and ended up seducing her on the living-room couch after her parents had gone to bed. He'd been drinking heavily from the bottle he sneaked in, and Dorothy was suddenly someone he'd never seen before—a passionate, reckless girl who threw herself, literally, at him. Before he realized it, he'd been aroused. She offered no resistance. On the contrary, she invited him to destroy her virtue.

It was an inexpert and unsatisfactory coupling, for Dorothy was a virgin and Buzz, for all his seemingly worldly ways, had had little experience. After it was over, he was covered with remorse and yet he felt tenderness toward her, and when she lay quiet, looking at him with her big eyes and saying, finally, "I love you," he heard himself anwering, "I love you too."

From that moment, she took it for granted that they were engaged. And Buzz, too guilty to fight it and too unhappy to care, went along with her assumption. They were married a few months later in a big church wedding at which some of the guests privately remarked that the groom looked hangdog and the bride had the smirk of a cat who'd devoured a canary.

It was, in the beginning, not too bad a marriage. Dorothy was not a sparkling companion but marriage seemed to mellow her. She was a good wife, an excellent homemaker and a surprisingly passionate bedmate who produced three strapping sons, the joys of Buzz's life, in four years. He was never in love, but he was reasonably content. His business flourished and kept him away from home for long hours. He enjoyed his children and gradually slipped into the role of satisfied husband, devoted father and active member of the business community, joining all the businessmen's clubs, serving on the advisory committee of several charities and taking an active role in church affairs. If his life was dull, he refused to think about what it might have been with Frances. And in time he could think of her almost without pain, as though she were some high-spirited shadow from his past. Only when he accidentally ran into the Daltons did he remember how much he'd adored their daughter.

It was not until she was forty that Dorothy reverted to the neurotic, withdrawn, frequently unpleasant creature of her youth. Whether the fact of becoming forty was traumatic, or whether she was undergoing premature "change of life," Buzz did not know. She'd been angry when the boys married early, though they chose nice girls who wondered among themselves how that attractive Mr. Paige had ever chosen such a dreary wife. Whatever the reason, for the next few years Dorothy made life hell for everyone around her, culminating in her ungovernable jealous rage about her husband's supposed affair with the widow. He stood it as long as he could and finally moved out. It was a relief to be free of her. He'd have liked never to return, but the pressure came from all sides—from his parents and hers, from the sons who sympathized with him but felt sorry for their unhappy mother, from the daughters-in-law who had no love for her but saw the terrifying possibility of his children following in his footsteps someday. Most of all, the plea to return came from a seemingly chastened Dottie, who was dutifully undergoing therapy and apparently trying hard to change, vowing tearfully that she could and would.

So he went home and made up his mind to live with this still unpredictable woman whom he no longer even pretended to love. And he would have allowed this lethargy to carry him along forever if Frances had not come back into his life, offering herself and freedom and the kind of heady excitement he'd not known since the day she left. She was temptation incarnate. He could think of a dozen selfish reasons to run off with her: There were too few good years left to him. He'd always adored her. He'd fulfilled his obligations to his children, who now were grown men with families of their own. He'd been trapped into this sometimes dull, sometimes stormy marriage by his own youthful ignorance and Dot's shrewd, scheming mind. And Dot herself was still mentally unstable. But that last reason, which should have been the decisive one in favor of his defection, was, perversely, the same one that kept him from throwing caution to the winds and leaving town with Frances. He couldn't abandon Dorothy, he told himself. He couldn't be that cruel to a woman who was not responsible for her acts. And yet she drove him out of his mind with her nagging, her accusations, her air of being put-upon in every situation. He'd even been so undone that he'd confessed to sleeping with Fran! What had possessed him? And why had she reacted in that strange way, almost humbly and yet with a flicker of triumph, as though she was glad to have her suspicions confirmed. In a way, he wished Frances had never come back. And at the same time he gloried in knowing her as he never had, even if it was to be only a brief and dangerous interlude. She'd be leaving soon, but he was determined to arrange that weekend he promised. He wanted it as much as she. To wake up with her for two mornings was not too much to ask after a lifetime of longing. But this time he'd not indulge in some foolish confession. Dorothy wouldn't know. Nobody would. It would be a little difficult to invent a business trip over the weekend, but he'd manage. And then suddenly he thought, Why does it have to be a weekend? Fran can come and go as she pleases and it will seem much more logical if I have to go out of town during the week. Mentally, he arranged it for Tuesday and Wednesday of the next week. They'd go to Phoenix. He'd find a small, romantic hotel where they'd make love and sleep and talk and be at ease instead of sneaking into a shabby motel room which they knew they must leave in a couple of hours. It's not wrong, Buzz told himself. Nobody will be hurt. And two people will be happy.

He underestimated the workings of Dorothy's warped mind. The confession of his infidelity which she appeared to accept only rekindled the fires of revenge which had simmered within her all these years. To have captured Frances' first love was not enough for Dorothy. Frances had to pay for her lifelong disregard of other people's feelings. God had brought her back to face her punishment for all the early hurts, and He'd appointed Dorothy His avenging angel. She felt almost euphoric. It was her duty to make Frances Dalton repent her wantonness, past and present. I'll have peace then, Dot thought. The peace that's always eluded me. In her troubled mental state she saw Fran's return as a sign from the Almighty. This was a new religion and it was called revenge.

She smiled calmly and nodded when Buzz told her he had to fly to Phoenix for a couple of days next week to look into a new dealership.

"How long will you be gone?"

"Oh, two, three days at the most. Will you be all right?"

"Of course. I'll visit the boys. And maybe have lunch with Laura Dalton." Dot's expression was innocent. "I imagine the girls will have left by then and she'll be feeling lonely. Besides, I should repay her for that nice party."

He glanced at her suspiciously. She and Fran's mother had had lunch before. They saw each other frequently at church. But even if this were coincidental, it would not do to have Dot get in touch with Laura and discover that Fran had gone away "for a couple of days." There was only one way. Fran would have to leave Denver for good when she went off with Buzz. She could fly back to Paris or wherever when they parted. That way, Dorothy could be assured that Frances really had left and Buzz's trip was legitimate. God, it was getting complicated! For a minute he wavered. Maybe all the cover-up wasn't worth it. It was too tricky. How did he know Fran was ready to leave Denver? But she was. She'd said she was only staying a week and it was almost that already. He'd tell her how it had to be when they met tonight at the motel. He couldn't bear to think of losing her again. But he had to. There was no future for them with the specter of Dorothy haunting him wherever he went. Fran accepted that. She was willing to settle for the only thing within reason. What a fabulous woman she's become, Buzz thought. Realistic but not cynical, passionate without possessiveness. There'd be regret, not for what they'd done, but for what they'd never have again.

Chapter 22

After the initial, devastating effect of Andrea Tallent's letter, Barbara fell into an uncharacteristic mood of helpless resignation. She seemed to have none of her usual spirit or buoyancy, no instinct to fight back for what was dearest to her. It was as though she'd always known one day it would come, this end to her happiness, and now that it had, though not in the way she could have imagined, she seemed to accept her defeat more in sorrow than in rage.

She stayed in her room that whole day and evening, feeling disembodied, detached from reality. She knew now what people meant when they said that in times of tragedy they felt they were outside of themselves, watching their own grief in an almost clinical way as though this terrible thing was happening to someone else. It was a protective trick of the mind, she supposed. A curtain between the truth and one's unwillingness to face it. It was merciful, this feeling of being dead. That's how she felt. Dead. Emotionless. Incapable of action or even of anger.

After the tears, after the talk with her mother and later with Fran, she went into this introspective state. She did not question the truth of what Andrea reported. Not the fact of the probable appointment or the accurate reporting of Charles's feelings. She was sure he was suffering the tortures of the damned, looking for an "easy" way to end this with as little hurt as possible. Poor Charles, mistaking cowardice for compassion. Like most men, he dreaded unpleasant confrontations. Barb could not hate him, could not summon up bitterness. She understood why he was postponing the terrible moment when he'd have to tell her the one thing neither of them wanted to hear.

If it hadn't been so terrible, it would almost have been funny, Barb thought. Ironic. I thought I was the one in this family who "had it made." I pitied Allie with her terrible husband and her awful guilts about the abandoned child. I saw Fran's life as useless and petty, a lonely life in spite of its material comforts. I even felt sorry for Mother and Dad, stuck in this mediocre existence with nothing to look forward to. I thought I had it all: a man who adored me; a busy, interesting life in the capital of the world; my independence and my tiny but nourishing sense of importance. Now, in the space of a week, I've become the one with no hope and no future and no one to cling to. The people I secretly patronized are working out new lives while mine is coming to an end.

She walked to the window and saw Allie running down the front steps, her movements as graceful and excited as a young girl's. Jack Richards waited in a car at the curb. Four-thirty. Where were they going? And how had Alice suddenly found courage to let Jack pick her up at the house? What difference did it make? Alice had been reunited with the father of her baby. That was all that mattered. He still cared for her. He could take her away from that awful life in Boston. It was too much to hope they'd find their son, but they'd have each other.

Barbara turned away. Even Fran has found something again, she thought. I don't know how she really feels about Buzz or what she seriously plans to do about him. But that doesn't matter either. Her ego has been restored. She knows she's still desirable. She'll be able to take him, if she decides to. She'll hurt poor, pathetic Dottie Paige, but so what? In this world it's every woman for herself, Barbara thought bitterly. God knows I've found that out today.

She paced the room. Even Mother and Dad aren't the sorry creatures I once thought them. Their life seems unutterably boring to me, but why do I presume to put my feelings into their heads? They feel safe here where they've always lived. Comfortable with their house and their neighborhood and their friends and each other. Each other. That was the bottom line. That's what it eventually came down to: having someone to care about, some life to share. I should have realized that long ago. I thought I did, in my own, peculiar way. I thought Charles and I were the exceptions who could break the rules. We care for each other. But we never shared. Not really. Not, as Fran says, publicly. That still matters. Not marriage so much, but honesty. She's right. If I didn't want to marry, I should have had the wit to find a man who could openly be my lover. Why did I feel I could go on forever walking the tightrope, balancing an existence halfway between wife and mistress? I thought I was the smart one. The sensible one. And all the time I was a sloppy, sentimental dope. It is a laugh. A very bitter laugh. Well-adjusted Barbara is a bigger fool than her mousy sister or her cynical one. At least they recognize their failings. I've been so high and mighty, overconfident and stupid. Wonderful me. Miss Know-it-all. Advising everybody else. And now I don't know what to with my own life.

She heard noises in the next room, but she didn't want to see Fran again just then. Their earlier talk had only confused her further. It was so diametrically opposed to what their mother had said. Laura had urged her to step aside, to move off with dignity. Fran had taken just the opposite view when she'd come in to see her sister.

"Don't be a bloody damned fool!" Fran's voice was harsh. "Are you really going to hold still for this? Are you going to let him brush you out of his life like some piece of dirt that messes up his career? For God's sake, Barbara, where's your backbone? The man owes you!"

"He's . . . he's provided for me. We always thought, in case he died . . ."

Fran literally shook her. "I'm not talking about money! Hell, nobody likes it better than I do. I married for it once. I'd despise being without it. But you've never cared about it. You don't care about it now. He's 'provided for you,' you say. Well, I should hope so! But he hasn't provided for what you care about. He's used up most of your good years and now you're supposed to roll over and play dead because you're in his way. You're supposed to give up without a struggle. Be ladylike and well-mannered and subsist on the knowledge that you made some kind of contribution to his success. I never heard such garbage!"

Barbara looked at her helplessly. "I don't know what you think I should do. He's always said he couldn't marry me. He's been honest about that."

"But you never really believed it, did you?"

Her sister's shrewd insight startled Barbara. Fran knew her better than she knew herself. Inside, deep inside, she'd stifled the belief that somehow things would work out for her and Charles. She could deny it forever, even to herself, but it was true. She remembered how angry she'd been when her mother cautioned her. How vehemently she protested that she was content with things the way they were. But it was a lie she'd almost managed to make herself believe.

"All right, maybe I did hope. Unconsciously, at least. But what does that matter now? I have to let him go, Fran. I couldn't hold him even if I tried."

"No? My dear little sister, you are in a position to make things heavy for the good congressman. You could blow his life sky-high if you chose. He knows that. So does that bitchy wife of his. Listen, Barb, I can't stand to see you get the short end of this deal. You love him. And I suppose he loves you. A little less than power, maybe, but more than any other woman. Well, something's got to give. And why should all the sacrifice be on your side? To hell with Tallent's big Cabinet job and his dazzling future! Don't accept this. Tell him when push comes to shove it's up to him to find a way out, but in any case you don't plan to disappear. Not now or ever."

Barbara was aghast. "I couldn't do that to him! My God, Fran, I wouldn't blackmail a man I love! And I'd never force myself on someone who didn't want me. What happiness could there be in that? He'd resent me forever."

"Oh, get off it, baby! Can't you see what that letter really means? Andrea Tallent is scared to death that her husband loves you so much he'll change his mind when he sees you. She's just dying to have you play the long-suffering heroine and kiss Charles off before he has a chance to realize what he's giving up. Well, you just beat her at her own game, kiddo. You get your fanny back to Washington pronto and remind the great man that it's damned uncomfortable to sleep with a Cabinet post. You won't have to threaten him. I know that's not your way. It's unfortunate that this came up while you weren't around to stop it, but it's not too late. You want him, Barb. For God's sake get in there and fight for him. That's what I'm going to do about Buzz!"

Remembering, Barb shuddered. There was a great deal in what her sister had said. But she couldn't do it. It wasn't in her to scheme or demand or to play games. Charles was weighing the problem. She was certain of that. Nothing would happen until she either wrote the letter Andrea suggested or went back and made him tell her his decision in his own words.

I don't know whether to write the letter, Barbara thought. I can't really go with Fran's tough attitude. I won't keep him from the thing that will make him happiest, if only I were sure he knows what he wants. Fran doesn't think I should suffer because Charles is ambitious. Well, I don't think he should pay the price of my blindness, my childish, oblivious attitude toward the hard facts of life.

Absorbed as she was with her own problems, she suddenly recalled Fran's parting words about Buzz, a statement on which she'd not elaborated. Obviously, Fran *had* come to a decision about him, probably had a specific "game plan." I envy her the ability to justify everything she does, Barb thought. She's right. Grab what you believe belongs to you and don't think about the long-range results. I'd like to live for the moment, as Fran does. And then, contradicting herself, Barbara rejected that idea. She couldn't. Couldn't be blithe about destroying someone else's life for some selfish pleasure which might or might not endure. God knows, she was no saint. In her parents' eyes, she'd been "a fallen woman" all these years, but she'd never felt she was hurting anyone. Not even herself. She couldn't change now. Her automatic rejection of Fran's suggestion that she make things difficult for Charles came from a gut instinct. Much as I'd like to be a different kind of woman, Barb thought, I never will be. I might as well reconcile myself to that. As they grow older, people don't take on new attitudes; they only become more of what they've always been.

The acceptance of that made her suddenly stand very straight and tall, alone there in the room. Okay, Barbara Dalton, she told herself. Enough self-pity. You'll grieve. You'll regret. You'll damned near die. But you're your mother's child. Laura was right. It was time to let go, to do one last thing for someone she loved so much. Charles had been nothing but good to her. She wouldn't go out of his life with shrieks or whimpers. She'd leave quietly, knowing his memories would be as sweet and poignant as hers. The empty feeling would lessen in time as the anguish would diminish. Life wasn't over, as she'd so dramatically told herself. It might stop for a while, might seem futile and meaningless, but she'd endure. She didn't want pity from anyone. Not from Charles or from her family. Certainly not from herself. Before she could change her mind or be swayed by Fran's persuasiveness, she sat down at the desk where years before she'd done her homework and began to write the most difficult letter of her life.

My dearest Charles,

I've missed you so this week. There have been few moments when you have not been in my mind, as for all these years you have been in my heart and in my arms. You have given me hours of indescribable joy, a euphoric sensation of being endlessly submerged in happiness. You made me feel beautiful and invincible, as though nothing was wrong with the world and never could be as long as I was with you. You are an extraordinary man, the one I dreamed of and never hoped to find. A sensitive, brilliant, giving human being, your intuition is incredible in one so manly, so virile and strong. I've clung to you, Charles. I've grasped at you, clutched you to me fiercely to save myself from going under, from being swept away in a tide of loneliness.

I thought we could drift together, not wanting rescue, not wishing to step foot on the sands of reality. But since I've been home, I've seen that I have a need for firm ground and solid footing. I've watched my parents who've traveled fifty years over the rough road of marriage, clasping each other's hands, sharing the same triumphs and tragedies, holding their heads high, secure in the knowledge that they will be together in all things sad and wonderful. I want that too, Charles, for whatever time is left to me. This golden anniversary has made me think deeply about my own life. About you. About us, my darling. About the make-believe life we live.

It hurts to call those precious years 'make believe.' But

they have been. They are. Our chemistry has no real continuity. Our passion no permanence. Our love no future. Not, at least, in the sense of an enduring commitment for all the world to see.

Coming home has made the ancient verities all too clear to me. I shall never have a fiftieth wedding anniversary, but selfishly I want a fifth, or a tenth, or even a first. The basic insecurity within me has come face to face with jealousy of those who have the security of an avowed love. The selfishness that has always been just under the surface can no longer settle for a secret love, deep and true as I know it is. Only a fool is compelled to state the obvious, but I am foolish enough to say I must give up something romantic because I need something real.

I can see you now, my dearest love, reading these words with bewilderment. Or perhaps not. You have always known, I think, that someday I would want the whole of you I cannot have. You have understood my need better than I understood it myself. You have warned me about this very moment, even as I denied it would ever come.

Barbara paused in her writing. It was a blatantly unbelievable letter. Charles knew her too well to buy this story of "sudden realization." He'd recognize it as a tissue of lies and demand the truth. That's what I really want, she thought. I've put down this nonsense about the fiftieth anniversary bringing a flash of comprehension because I want him not to believe it, because I want him to tell me I'm a fool and reassure me that our love can go on. That's what I want. And that's what I must not allow. I must be more convincing. Fighting back the tears, she wrote the ultimate, convincing finale.

You must be wondering, though, why my painful decision to end the thing between us comes so suddenly. You are entitled to know before anyone else that I've met someone here in Denver who wants to marry me and give me the kind of security and shelter a drifting, forty-year-old spinster should have. I cannot say I love

> him as I love you. No one will ever have that place in my heart. No one ever could. But he is a good man, a kind and patient one.

She stopped again, not knowing how to paint a convincing picture of this fictitious suitor. Tears forced themselves past her will to contain them, as she tried to think how to go on. Let me visualize someone, Barb thought. Anyone. Buzz Paige? No. Not even in imagination could she picture herself marrying Buzz. Jack. Yes, Jack Richards. Not that she could love him, or he, her, but he was a prototype Charles could understand. She began, again, to write.

> I've known this man since I was a little girl. I had a terrible "crush" on him even when he was taking out my older sister. He's a widower now and childless, as alone as I. He's intelligent and successful and devoted. I've told him there's been someone else in my life for many years. He does not condemn that. He is not interested in the past, only in a future which involves me. We will make our home here and travel a good part of the year. I do not expect the ecstasy you've taught me, but I hope for peace and serenity in the declining years which are coming all too quickly.
>
> Forgive me, my darling Charles. I could not bring myself to tell you this in person, coward that I am. Indeed, I will not be coming back to Washington at all. Am I afraid to risk seeing you? Of course I am. But I know this is right for all of us, and the nearness of you must not cloud the clear course I am determined to follow.
>
> I will be happy. I know you care about that most of all. And, dearest, you will be happy too, for the generosity of spirit which is so much a part of you will want what is best for me—as it always has. Just as I want all that is good and wonderful for you—and always will.
>
> Barbara

She reread it, hoping against her real desire that Charles would accept it. She even prayed he'd be relieved, bitter as that thought was. It solved his problems and left no room for guilt.

Fran would think she was an utter fool. Perhaps she was. But this was how she had to handle it. Only this way could she live with herself, knowing she'd always have Charles's love even though she renounced it. The other way, Fran's way, was futile. She might get Charles but she'd lose his love, if not right away, certainly in time when he'd look back and regret the abandoned chance for a place in history.

Slowly, sadly, she addressed the envelope to his house. What did it matter if Andrea saw the letter arrive? But I hope she won't read it, Barb thought. I'd hate to think of her triumph, but even more, I'd hate to have anyone but Charles see these lying, loving words which are meant only for him.

"Where is everybody?" Sam Dalton looked curiously at the three empty places at the dinner table.

"You're really getting terribly spoiled," Laura teased. "We haven't had a full house in thirty years and now you expect one every night!"

"Well, dammit, those girls are only here a short time and I've hardly seen them. They don't seem to spend much time at home. I don't understand this younger generation. They finally come back for an overdue visit and all they do is gad around day and night! I thought the whole purpose was to see us."

"It is, dear," Laura said soothingly, "but you can't really expect them to be underfoot every minute. You're not around that much yourself, you know. You're either tinkering in the basement or working in the garden."

"I'm here at mealtimes and in the evening. And I see all the comings and goings. Who was that who picked up Allie this afternoon? Some man in a car."

Laura was genuinely at a loss. "I have no idea. I was in the kitchen about four-thirty when she called out and said she was going out for cocktails and might not be home until later."

"What about Frances? Where does she go until all hours? And why has Barbara been in her room all day?"

Laura hated lying to him. She never had, but she couldn't tell him about Buzz and Frances. Any more than she could let him know about Alice and Jack Richards, who, now that she thought about it, must have been the man who came for her today. Or Barbara with her smashed "illicit" romance. Dear Lord, it had all gotten so out of hand! Sam would never understand. He still thought of their middle-aged daughters as "the younger generation." He'd be outraged by all of it. He loved his girls and in spite of his actions, past and present, thought they were wonderful. It would break his heart if he found out what had happened to them, what tragedies they'd lived through, even those of their own making. And he'd go out of his mind if he had any idea of what had transpired this week. He wasn't young. It might affect him physically as well as emotionally. Heaven knows it had taken its toll on her. She felt a hundred years old.

"Well?" Sam was staring at her.

Laura tried to think how to answer him without outright lies. "Sam, dear, Frances has friends here. You remember the night Spencer took us to dinner? She was meeting one of them that evening. I suppose she's catching up with a lot of acquaintances." She hoped he wouldn't pursue the subject of Allie. She couldn't think how to avoid telling him about Jack Richards' renewed interest. "As for Barbara," Laura hurried on, "she hasn't been feeling well today. I thought she should stay in bed and rest."

"What's the matter with her?"

"Nothing serious. She'll be all right."

Sam didn't pursue it. Woman trouble, he supposed. Not the kind of thing he cared to discuss. Besides, he wasn't worried about Barbara. She was always fine, always cheerful. It was the other two he didn't understand. Alice staying on without her husband, and with apparently no intention of leaving. Frances out every evening. Laura was lying. Frances was up to something. She wouldn't have stayed this long in Denver if she wasn't. And he still fretted about Allie and that snob she was married to. He'd bet there was something really wrong in Boston. For a moment, he felt angry with all of them, with his daughters and his wife. He sensed the girls had confided more in Laura than she was willing to admit. Dammit, why didn't they think they could talk to him? Was he such an ogre? Did they think their mother was more understanding or more intelligent than he? Secrets! He hated them. He could smell them. And right now the scent of hidden knowledge was all over Laura Dalton. He knew her too well not to recognize when she had something on her mind. Something she was keeping from him. Sam was sure that was the case right now. His questions made her nervous. She kept picking at the bread crumbs on the table, avoiding his eyes when she answered. Hell, for all he knew there was something going on with Barbara too. He'd never known that girl to spend a day in bed since she was a child and had measles.

"Maybe I'll look in on Barb after dinner." He watched Laura's reaction. It was much too hasty.

"Oh, no! I mean, that isn't necessary, Sam. She's perfectly fine."

"Like the other two are fine?"

Laura didn't answer.

"Come on," Sam said quietly. "You might as well let me in on what's happening around here. I'll find out sooner or later."

It was an almost irresistible temptation to tell him everything. The burden of her knowledge was almost more than she could bear alone. Besides, he had a right to know. They were as much his children as hers. But she couldn't. Not just yet. Not until the girls found solutions to their problems. It would be much easier for everybody concerned if Sam stayed out of things right now. She could imagine his rushing over and telling Jack Richards to leave Allie alone. Or raging at Fran for her promiscuity with Buzz Paige. Or, worst of all, being faced with the fact that his favorite, his baby, had been involved in a long-term liaison with a married man. What would upset him more? Laura wondered. The fact of Barbara's affair or the knowledge that the man planned to walk out on her?

"There's nothing to get upset about," Laura finally said. "Really, Sam, I think your imagination is running away with you. These aren't babies we're dealing with, you know. They have a right to be out for dinner without your permission." She smiled. "You still think of them as little girls, don't you? Never mind. So do I. I guess we always will. No matter how old they get, they'll still be children to us." She came around the table and hugged him from behind. "Now you stop fretting, Sam Dalton! You'll just get yourself worked up over nothing."

He patted her arm. "All right, Mother, if you say so."

Chapter 23

It was as though some all-powerful playwright was building toward a third-act climax in the four separate dramas taking place in Denver that day.

For Alice he chose the moment of grateful happiness in the reconciliation with her son. For Barbara, frustration and a sense of unbearable loss. And for Laura, bewilderment, anxiety and a bad conscience about the secrets she kept from Sam. But it was for Frances that the director of our destinies reserved the moments of terrible tension which ultimately would propel her down a predetermined path of reckless destruction.

The evening began, as had those few before it, on a note of passion made all the more exciting by its illicit overtones. Within minutes of each other, Fran and Buzz slipped into the motel room and almost without words gave themselves to the devouring act of love. Each time there was more sexual satisfaction as each came to know the preferences of his partner. Each time there was less inhibition and more desire, a strengthening on Fran's part to have this man with her always, a mounting dread in Buzz at the thought of losing her.

When they finally rested, exhausted, Fran flung her arms over her head and sighed with contentment, stretching her still-beautiful body in sensuous relaxation.

"Darling, are we going away next weekend? Have you decided where?"

Buzz felt his muscles tighten. He'd known, driving to the motel, that he'd have to tell her of the change in plan. He assured himself once again that she'd accept the inevitable. God knows he didn't want it any more than she, but this thing had to end. Tentatively, he began to lead up to it.

"We have to talk about that, sweetheart." Stalling for time, he lit two cigarettes and gave her one. "The weekend thing isn't going to work too well, I'm afraid."

All of Frances' senses came alert but she didn't move. "Why not? You were the one who suggested it."

"I know. But it's getting pretty complicated. How about going off together for a couple of days in the middle of next week, instead? It doesn't matter which days, does it? I thought maybe we could fly down to Phoenix and lie around in the sun, like maybe Wednesday and Thursday. How does that suit you?"

She took a deep drag of the cigarette and exhaled slowly. Something was wrong. There was something more than a switch from a weekend to a midweek escape. Go slow, Fran, she warned herself. He's holding back. Whatever is making him nervous has to be carefully handled. She pretended to be perfectly amenable to the idea.

"Fine with me. Wednesday is as good as Saturday, but why Phoenix? I thought we were going to rough it in the mountains."

Lying next to him she could feel the tension in his body. She was right. This was no petty complication.

"Godammit, Fran, I can't lie to you. Dorothy's scaring hell out of me. She's too quiet, too agreeable. I recognize the symptoms. It's the calm before the storm. She knows we're still meeting. She has to. I've never been out night after night in our whole life. But she's never said a word since the first night. Not, that is, until I told her I had to go away for a couple of days. Then she said she'd probably have lunch with your mother, because, to quote her, 'Laura will be lonely with all the girls gone again.' She didn't mention you by name, but I know what that meant. She was fishing. She suspects I'm going away with you and she'll confirm it when your mother says you're out of town for a few days."

Fran propped herself up against the headboard. "I'm not quite following this, darling. Perhaps I'm dense, but I don't get the drift. I gather you decided on weekdays because they'd be less suspicious for a 'business trip' than a weekend. And I take it you chose Phoenix instead of Aspen or Vail because if you had to be reached, you conceivably could have business there. But I still don't see how all that changes anything. Mother will tell Dorothy I'm away at the same time you are." She paused. "Or do you expect Mother to lie and say I've really left town for good? That won't wash, you know. First of all, Mother won't lie. And second, when I come back to Denver, Dorothy will know it."

In the dim light, Buzz looked miserable. Finally he said, "Fran, darling, I know your mother won't lie. She'll be telling the truth. My idea is that you'll fly to Paris from Phoenix. Oh, Dorothy will still suspect that we've been together, but she'll accept it as she has this past week, knowing this was a last fling before your departure."

Frances stared at him in disbelief. "What the hell do you mean, 'a last fling before my departure'? Is that what this is to you? A fling? And what gives you the right to decide when I'll stay or go? Do you really think I'm going to arrange my life to suit that sniveling little creature you married? Do you honestly think I'm going to let her run me out of town? Tell me, Buzz, have you believed for one minute I'm going to give you up? I've known all along that one of us would have to be the heavy in this, and I knew when the chips were down it would be me. All right. If you're so damned scared of Dorothy, I'm not. I'll tell her we're in love and that we're going away together. I hadn't thought we'd have to break it to her quite so soon, but apparently we must. And since you can't, I will."

It was Buzz's turn to be startled. "What are you talking about? I told you I'd never leave her. I can't. I don't know what she'd do. Something desperate. I can't live with that on my conscience, no matter how much I want you. Fran, darling, we both knew from the start it couldn't last. We agreed to take our little bit of happiness and be grateful for it. I'll think about those days in Phoenix the rest of my life. I'll think about you the rest of my life. But that's all I can do—think and wish and dream."

She pulled him to her, letting her body remind him again of what he was losing. "No, my love, that's not all you can do. Neither of us can live on wishes and dreams. There's too precious little time left. I won't let you martyr yourself this way. I won't let you throw away your happiness and mine for no reason." She kissed him gently. "I'm sorry I got so angry. I was hurt that you planned to push me out of your life this way. I realize you don't want to hurt Dorothy. I admire you for that. But you're too blinded by pity to see that you do the woman no favor by staying with her when your heart is somewhere else. What a wonderful, gentle man you are, dearest. You care for others so much you're willing to sacrifice yourself. But it's misguided loyalty. I promise you it is. You've given so much and gotten so little in return. This is your last chance, Buzz. Mine, too. I'll never want anyone except you."

The persuasive voice flowed over him, the body pressed itself against his. She was so positive this was right. And he wanted it so much. He heard the soft words going on.

"Have you thought of me in this, dear heart? You know I'm not the hard-shelled creature the world thinks I am. I can be hurt too. Desperately hurt. Don't you care what will happen to me if you leave me? Dorothy has her children and her grandchild, her place in life. But until I found you, I had nothing. No roots. No love. No reason for being." She allowed a half-sob to escape. "I'd never threaten. That's not my style. I panicked when you told me you wanted me to leave. I won't go to Dorothy. You know that. That's your job, darling. A man's job to protect the woman he loves. And that's what I'm asking of you now. If I'm the woman you love, protect me. Live with me and love me forever. Let me make you as happy as you deserve to be."

He felt he was in some kind of terrible war, the victim of a conflict not only between two women but of an even more frightening one within himself. He wanted to hear all the things Fran said. Wanted to believe them. Wanted to take charge of his life and hers. But there was Dorothy who'd have to pay the price for this selfishness. And how would she exact that price? On him? On their children? On herself?

As though she read his mind, Fran said slowly, "I know you fear what she might do if you leave her. We talked about that before. But she won't do anything, Buzz. I promise. I know women like that. They use their weakness as their strength. In her own way, she's more selfish than I. She's holding someone through the helplessness she pretends. She plays on duty and pity. That's a tenuous thread, but it can cut deep. I know it has cut into you all these years, dearest, and in time it will destroy you. I won't let that happen. I can't. I love you too much."

For the first time that evening she heard hesitancy in his voice. "I don't know. I don't know what's the right thing to do. God knows I love you. It's taken every ounce of courage in me to say we've got to end it. I don't want to. You know that. But we can't go on this way, Fran. You can't stay on here, meeting me in motels, sneaking off for a day or two. That's no life for you. And I can't handle that forever either. As for Dot, I see the breaking point coming. I told you before. I'm frightened for her. I can't push her much further."

"No, of course you can't. It would be cruel. Crueler than telling her the truth. You must tell her, darling. It will be hard for you, but it's best for everyone concerned. I give you my word. In the end you won't regret it. You only have one life, my love, and you've dutifully given most of it to your family. They don't need you any more. But I do. I need you beyond anything I can tell you. And you need me." Abruptly, Frances moved away from him and got out of bed. It was time for a change of strategy.

"Where are you going?"

"Home. To my parents' home, that is. But only for a few days. I'm not going to Phoenix, Buzz. Those two days will only haunt me if you go back to Dorothy. I'm going to leave you alone, darling. I won't see you or speak to you until you've had time to think things through once and for all. I'll wait a little, Buzz. But if you don't want to come to me totally and irrevocably, I won't wait forever. I'm strong, my love, but not that strong."

He watched her dress, watched every gracefully calculated movement. Fran was the only woman who could put on clothes with more seductiveness than other women could take them off. Troubled as he was, he felt desire starting again as he looked at her. God help me, how I want this woman! She means more to me than anything. More than my conscience, my honor, my sense of right and wrong. I don't care what happens. I don't care about anything but her.

"Stop!" he said suddenly.

Half-naked, she slowly turned to look at him, The Question in her eyes.

"You're right, I can't let you go. Not now. Not ever." He held out his arms to her.

Triumphant and hiding her victory under easy tears of joy, Fran went to him, half-laughing, half-crying. And that night, as though to seal the bargain, neither of them went home at all.

The hours slipped by unnoticed as Alice and Jack talked with the stranger who was their son. To them and to John Peck, it was the fulfillment of an impossible dream. In one evening they could not hope to bring three lives up to date, much less fill in the searing background, but that did not matter. They had years ahead, they told each other. Years to be a family.

"Don't think I didn't love my adoptive parents," John said at one point. "I did. I loved them dearly. They were as good as any two people could be. It hurt them to know I wanted so much to find you, but I think they understood that everyone needs to know who he really is and where he comes from. Maybe they felt they were protecting me by not telling me anything. I don't know. But they never did. I didn't find the first clue until after they died."

"Perhaps they weren't sure how you'd be received," Alice said reluctantly. "After all, how much confidence could anyone have in a woman who'd give up her child?"

"Don't," Jack Richards said softly. "Don't keep punishing yourself, Allie. You've done that long enough. It's over, my dear. That part of your life is over. You've more than paid your dues."

John nodded his agreement. "He's right. Janice told me what Spencer Winters has put you through all these years. It was because of me, wasn't it? He made you feel worthless, didn't he? That damned sadist! It's a wonder Jan didn't kill him when he tried the same . . ." John's voice trailed off when he saw a look of horror come over Alice's face.

"Spencer threatened Janice? Oh, my God! He didn't hurt her, did he?"

"No, but he slapped her. I'm sorry. I didn't mean to tell you that. They had a terrible row when he was trying to find me, but Janice stopped him cold. That's when she came and told me where to find you. She's quite a girl."

"He's mad," Alice said. "He's a maniac, but I never thought

he'd lay a hand on Janice. She was the only one he ever cared about. Probably because she's the only one who wouldn't be intimidated by him. He drove Chris away and he made my life a living hell, but he could never get to Janice. She wouldn't let him dominate her. I think he admired that. Spencer admires strength, even when it gets in his way."

Jack interrupted. "Forgive me, but I don't think this is a night to rehash Winters' mental problems. As far as I'm concerned, he's out of our lives. Not worth talking about. There's the future to think about now, isn't there? We want to meet Carol first thing. Imagine, Allie. We not only have a son but a daughter-in-law and a grandchild on the way!" He shook his head. "It's almost beyond comprehension."

Alice brightened at the reminder of the unknown other family in Boston. "Oh, yes, we can't wait to meet her, Johnny! Could she fly out right away?"

"I don't know. I really hadn't thought that far ahead. Lord, I haven't even called her! She doesn't know how everything's turned out. She must be frantic, wondering. Jan, too. They're the ones who really made this happen."

"We'll get to a phone as soon as we leave," Jack said. They'd lingered for hours over dinner, hardly touching their food. "We can call from my place. By the way, wouldn't you like to move in with me instead of staying at the hotel? There's plenty of room for you and for Carol, if she comes."

"Yes, I would. I'd like that very much." John waited. When would he be asked to meet his aunts and his grandparents? Alice had told him about them but there'd been no mention of a meeting. John realized this was a delicate area, at least where Sam and Laura Dalton were concerned. This was where he might not be so warmly received. It was understandable, he supposed. These were the people who'd sent his mother away when she was carrying him. But could they possibly resent him now? Yes, he answered himself, they could. That generation didn't change. To them, he'd probably be a reminder of an old "disgrace." During the course of the evening, he'd been amazed to learn that his mother and father had not seen each other for years and that Jack Richards had not entered the Dalton house since the day Alice left. It was incredible, the whole thing. He hadn't been surprised to discover he was an illegitimate child. He'd assumed that. But he hadn't known until tonight that his parents had not been in touch with each other for more than thirty years, that their reunion only slightly preceded his appearance. He wondered what they would do. Marry, finally? He couldn't repress a sudden smile. If his real parents got together after all this time, he might be his father's best man at his wedding to his mother. What was that old riddle from his childhood? "Brothers and sisters I have none, but this man's father is my father's son. Who is he?" And the answer of course was "Me." What unexpected turns this hoped-for discovery had taken! Childhood sweethearts meeting again. Long-lost children appearing out of nowhere. Grandparents nursing old grievances. Whole families, never dreamed of, springing into existence. It was more than any of them could grasp. But the wonderful thing, the blessed, almost inspirational thing, was that Alice Winters and Jack Richards had unquestioningly accepted him for what he was. They'd taken him on faith, welcomed him with an intensity of joy that matched his own. There still was no hard and fast evidence that he was their child, but they needed none. They knew. Just as John knew these were his real parents.

The minor things, and they were minor compared to the miracle of finding his mother and father, would sort themselves out. There were a thousand things to discover, a dozen difficult problems, large and small, to solve, and yet John knew that answers would come. How strange it all was. He didn't even know what to call them. All evening, he'd never directly addressed them, feeling awkward and unsure what they wanted.

"I'd like to ask you both something," he said almost shyly. "It seems silly, but I . . . well, I don't really know what you want me to call you. I mean, what's the precedent for this? When a thirty-year-old child suddenly meets his parents for the first time, does he call them by their first names?" He gave a little laugh. "I hardly can call you 'Mrs. Winters and Mr. Richards,' that's for sure. And it feels funny to say 'Alice and Jack.' I guess what I'm asking is whether it's okay to call you Mother and Dad. That is, if it doesn't bother you . . ."

Jack and Allie exchanged glances of understanding. It wasn't quite the ridiculous question it seemed. This sensitive young man was trying to tell them, politely, that it would have been different if they were a married couple. Knowing their strange story, he was diffident about linking them this way.

"Johnny, dear," Alice said, "we *are* your mother and dad. There were other people who had those titles for many years, but I'm sure they never wanted to hear them any more deeply than your father and I do."

"I've been waiting all evening to hear you call me that," Jack added. "I thought maybe *you* didn't want to. What your mother says is true. For years Mr. and Mrs. Peck were your parents. I was afraid you'd think we were trying to take their place if we suggested it." He sounded happy and slightly wistful. "Nobody's ever called me Dad. It has a mighty nice ring."

They sat silently for a moment. Such a little thing and yet so important to all three. It made it all real, somehow. Natural and warm and permanent. Allie's eyes were shining and Jack felt a suspicious moisture in his own. Brusquely, he cleared his throat. "Well, that's settled. Now, shall we go to my place and call Carol and Janice?"

Much later, Alice let herself into her parents' house and went quietly up the stairs. It was nearly midnight. There was no light under Fran's door. Maybe she's asleep, Allie thought. She's been out every night but she's always home and awake by now. She softly opened the bedroom door. The room was empty and the bed untouched. Allie felt a little let-down. She was so eager to share her wonderful news with both her sisters. I hope Barb's awake. She'll be amazed and delighted. And then she remembered the strange state Barb had been in earlier in the day. What a selfish thing I am! I've hardly given her a thought. It's been such a full day. First the revealing lunch with Jack and then, less than an hour later, the phone call that sent her rushing, not daring to believe, to the meeting with her son. But I should have found time to see whether Barb was all right. I shouldn't have dashed out this noon when there obviously was something wrong.

The room they shared was dark but Allie sensed that her sister was awake in the other bed.

"Barb?" she whispered. "You awake?"

"Yes. Hi."

"Mind if I turn on a light?"

"Go ahead. I haven't been asleep."

Alice switched on the lamp between the beds and sat down on her own. Barbara looked different, somehow. The usually cheerful face was expressionless as it turned to meet Alice's eyes. I know that look, Alice thought. It says everything's pointless and life is just one long, unfunny joke. I've seen it too often in my own mirror.

"What's wrong, baby? I knew something was going on when I left, but Fran shoo-ed me out before I had a chance to find out. What's happened, Barb?"

"I don't want to talk about it now, Allie. In the morning, okay? Did you have a good day? How's Jack?"

This was no moment to recount her own happiness. "My day was fine," Alice said quietly. "I'll tell you all about it. But right now, I want to know what's happened to make you look so miserable. Please tell me. Maybe I can help."

"Nobody can help."

"Don't be so sure."

Barbara sat up suddenly, almost angrily. "All right. Help me. Tell me how to solve this, if you're so smart!" She snatched Andrea Tallent's letter from the bedside table and threw it across the small space between them.

Alice read the cool, cruel words slowly, her heart sinking as she absorbed their meaning. When she finished she stared blankly at the woman who sat gazing into space. No wonder Barbara sounded so filled with hate! Right now she must hate the world, Allie thought. I know that feeling too.

"I'm so sorry." Such inadequate words, but she could find no others.

"Thanks. Me, too."

It was like listening to a stranger. Is this what the end of her love affair will do to Barbara? Allie wondered. Is she going to become hard and impossible to reach? Will this turn her into another Fran, embittered and distrustful of everyone and everything?

"I know how it hurts," Alice said. "I don't blame you for being angry. It's unfair. Hideously unfair. It's no consolation, but these things happen to nice women. It's the price you pay for giving so much of yourself, darling. All you can do is pick up and go on. And you will, Barb. You're not one to indulge in self-pity."

"You should be an expert on that! You've been pitying yourself for years!" Barbara stopped, aghast at what she'd said. "Oh, God, I must be out of my mind! Allie, forgive me. I didn't mean that. You know I didn't. You've been anything but self-pitying. You've been the bravest person I've ever known. I'm so sorry. I don't know what made me say such an awful thing to you, of all people. I thought I was under control. I even wrote a letter to Charles, pretending *I* was breaking off with him. I thought I was going to be able to handle it, for his sake. But I can't. I've been lying here for hours, going over everything in my mind, telling myself how I've been used and what a fool I've been and what an idiot I am to let him go. Fran thinks I shouldn't. She thinks I should make it tough for him, that I might even keep him if I fight." The words came tumbling out. "I don't know what to do, Allie. Should I send the letter? I'd convinced myself it was the only decent thing to do, but now I'm not sure. Everything seems so futile, so meaningless. You're right. I am drowning in self-pity and I should be killed for taking out my own stupidity on you. Please forget what I said. I'm not making any sense. You just happened to be the first target for all the spite and venom that's been building up inside of me tonight."

"It's all right. I understand. I truly do, Barb. There've been so many times I wanted to lash out at the first person I saw. Darling, I know how you feel about me. The same as I do about you. Those silly words aren't important. I'll never think of them again. What matters is you. I want you to come out of this the same generous, loving woman you've always been. I don't want to see you become disillusioned and distrustful of any relationship. And most of all, I want you to do what you know inside is right for you. Whether that means sending the letter or making a fight for Charles, I can't answer. Only you can decide what you can live with. That's what it finally comes down to, Barb. A compromise, at best, but hopefully an endurable one."

"I can't do it Fran's way. I have to let him go, Allie. But it's so hard. It's my whole life."

"I know," Alice said again. "I've been there. We all have, one way or another. But we survive." She went to Barbara's bed and stroked her head as she might have soothed Janice. "Try to get some sleep now, okay? We'll talk more tomorrow."

Barb nodded. "Thank you. I mean it. If you can live through what you have, I can live through this."

"You'll live. You may even come out the better for it, though I know you can't believe that now."

In the darkness, Alice lay awake, pitying the woman next to her. She'd never been through anything exactly like it, but in a way she'd felt the same terrible despair when Jack Richards deserted her for his own future. The situations were not comparable but each was terrible in its own way. It had taken years for Allie to shake her grief and her suppressed anger. In fact, she'd not felt truly happy until tonight, the night she'd been so eager to tell Barb and Fran about. God knows it was no moment to tell Barb how wonderful life had suddenly become. That would have been rubbing salt in an open wound. Tomorrow, she thought. Tomorrow I'll tell them all, including Mother and Dad. I'll tell them about Johnny and about Jack. Except I don't know what to say about him. Do we love each other? Should we marry? Neither of us is sure. But I am sure of one thing: I'm never going back to Spencer. If I had any doubt that he's a madman, it was dispelled tonight.

Chapter 24

Insomnia was an unusual affliction for Sam Dalton. Normally, he was a "good sleeper" even when he had things on his mind. Laura always marveled at his ability to rest soundly for nine or ten hours, not even waking during the night as she and most of their contemporaries did.

But this morning, the day after he'd tried to question Laura about the girls, Sam was up and in his garden at six o'clock. He'd had a terrible night. His mind simply wouldn't stop asking the questions his wife tried to make light of. She didn't fool him, though he let her think he was satisfied with her reassurances. As the hours crawled by he lay wide awake in the darkness, trying not to turn and toss and disturb Laura. Maybe he dozed off for an hour or so. He couldn't be sure. But at four o'clock he was wide awake and impatient to get out of this uneasy bed. He forced himself to stay put until five-thirty. Then he quietly slipped out of his side of the old four-poster, pulled on a sweater and pants and went down to make coffee.

The house was completely quiet, but Karat greeted him joyfully as he came into the kitchen. The puppy playfully nipped at Sam's gardening shoes and yapped happily as he ran in circles around his new master. Sam regarded him with sudden affection. He hadn't been too delighted with Barbara's gift, but he had to admit the little dog was a beauty.

"All right, Karat. Easy does it. Don't wake the whole household. You want to go outside? Okay. Come on. But don't get the idea I'm coming down here every morning at this ungodly hour!"

The early October morning air was chilly, but it felt good. He took a few deep breaths of it while Karat raced madly around the yard, finally stopping to "attend to his duties."

"Good boy!" Sam patted the dog's head. He hoped the little animal would be easily house-trained. The kitchen floor was covered with newspaper, much of it shredded by Karat, who'd obviously spent a good part of the night playing with the papers and tearing them into small pieces.

"You sure did more harm than good," Sam said wryly when they went back inside. "You're supposed to *use* the papers, dummy. Not tear them up! And how on earth did you manage to do your business wherever the papers *weren't?* Lord, what a mess!"

While the coffee perked, he cleaned up the kitchen floor and spread fresh paper. "There's where you go," Sam said, picking up Karat and setting him down firmly on the front page of yesterday's *Post.* "Until you learn to wait to be let out, you're supposed to use *these,* not the spaces in between!"

The small golden ball of fluff looked up at him so impishly that Sam couldn't help laughing. "You're a lucky little beast, you know. That lady upstairs is going to spoil you like a baby, and you'll take outrageous advantage of her. Everybody does, so why should you be different?" He finished his coffee. Breakfast would wait until Laura came down in an hour or so and fixed him a good meal. I'm spoiled too, he thought. I picked the best woman in the world. I wish our children had her serenity. Damn! The cloud of mystery that hung over his house made him uneasy. Why didn't they let him in on whatever was going on? Sam felt another surge of resentment. But in the next breath, he grudgingly admitted to himself that he hadn't always been the most sympathetic audience, especially where the girls were concerned. Not as understanding and forgiving as Laura, that was for sure. She'd have let Alice stay home and have her baby if I'd agreed. She'd have gone to visit Frances when we were invited, years ago. But I acted like some bloody biblical patriarch disowning an ungrateful child. Two ungrateful children. I tried to put them both out of my mind, and when I did think of them I made myself remember how they'd repaid us with immorality and selfishness.

He supposed he'd been unfair to all of them. Too strict, too demanding even while he was too much removed. He'd let Laura handle the children while he gave ninety per cent of his thoughts and energies to that damned job. He loved the girls, but he hadn't been much of a companion to them. It wasn't his way, even now. He felt so much affection inside, but he was incapable of projecting it as their mother was.

The stupid job. It had been his life. He resented anything that took his attention away from it: Alice's pregnancy, Fran's "unladylike" behavior. When circumstances demanded his attention, he felt put upon, impatient to be rid of family problems, anxious to find the easiest solutions with little thought of their consequences. He hadn't helped them when they needed it. Why did he think they'd come to him with their troubles now? Even Barbara didn't want him to know what was bothering her, and he was closer to her than he was to her sisters. By the time she was growing up, he'd mellowed a little. But, obviously, not enough.

So much for old mistakes. Sooner or later he'd find out what the mystery was all about. Nothing he could do about it now, but if these girls were in trouble he'd be more understanding, more compassionate. Funny. When you knew you were coming close to the end of your life you began to see the value of things you'd always taken for granted. Like the love and respect of your children. And the endless patience of your wife.

"You hungry, Karat?" Sam asked. "Me, too. Don't worry. She'll be down to feed us both soon."

He left the dog in the kitchen and went back outdoors. Six o'clock was a fine hour. You could feel the world waking up, yawning. There was almost nobody on the street. A paper boy down the block. A woman in curlers and a coat over her nightgown, walking a silly-looking little Yorkshire Terrier. He picked up the rake and started gathering fallen leaves into a neat pile near the front steps. I'm probably making a big fuss over nothing, he told himself, almost believing it. It's the whole business of having them all here at once after so many years. My routine is upset and I'm such a crusty old codger I can't stand having my pattern disturbed. Wild horses couldn't drag it out of me, but the honest truth is I'll be glad when they go away again. Too many women. Too many temperaments. They make me nervous.

He was so deep in his thoughts he didn't notice a car pull up to the curb. Fran was halfway up the walk when he saw her.

"Hi, Dad!" The voice was cheerful. "Lovely morning, isn't it?"

He was so surprised that, for a moment, he couldn't answer the breezy greeting. His eldest daughter was glowing. Fran never got up this early. What was she doing out at this hour? When had she left the house? And then he realized she was just coming home from wherever she'd spent the night. Sam's lips tightened.

"Where have you been, Frances? What is the meaning of this? It's six o'clock in the morning!"

"Is it? Good lord! So there really are two six o'clocks in every day. Imagine that!"

Her flippancy infuriated him. "Don't get smart with me! What will the neighbors think, seeing you come home at this hour?"

Fran refused to be ruffled. "What are the neighbors doing up at the crack of? For that matter, Dad, what are you doing out so early?"

"Never mind me. It's you I'm interested in."

"Really? Ah, that's sweet, dear. I never thought you cared. Now, if it had been Mother . . ."

"Stop that! Answer me!"

Her smile faded. "Why, Dad? Why should I answer you? What business is it of yours where I spend my nights?"

"It's my business because you're under my roof! I won't have you disgracing us again with your running around! I don't give a damn how old you are, Frances, while you're in my house you'll behave like a lady, not like a tart!"

"Again?" she repeated. "Disgrace you *again?* Is that the way you feel? That I've disgraced you before?"

Angered, he snapped back at her. "Yes, that's the way I feel. Running off with that actor! Three divorces! All kinds of gossip about you in every unsavory newspaper! I hoped at your age you'd settled down. But no. You never will. You're as selfish and reckless as you were at eighteen. You don't care for appearances? Fine. That's your business when you're somewhere else. But in Denver, you'll behave yourself or, by God, you can just pack your bags and be off again!"

Frances leaned casually against the porch railing. "Nothing changes with you, does it? We were always guilty until proved innocent. You're doing the same things you did thirty-odd years ago. Jumping to conclusions. Damning me before you know the facts. What's so terrible about coming home at six in the morning? And why do you assume I couldn't have been spending the night with a woman friend? Or maybe alone in a hotel to get away from this stifling, dreary house? You're all over me like some bloody nemesis! And you don't even know whether I've 'disgraced' you or not!"

He was still furious but he tried to control his temper. "All right, Frances. Where were you?"

"I told you. None of your damned business! I can take care of myself. I always have. It's not *this* daughter you should be worrying about. Why don't you devote your righteous efforts to finding out why Allie is a battered wife? Or why Barbara has had an affair with a married man for the last dozen years? Why don't you take some interest in what's going on around you, Father dear? Or do you prefer to know nothing? Is it easier that way? Of course it is. Let Mother worry about us. That's always been your attitude." She stopped. Sam's face had gone gray and he suddenly looked old and helpless. "Oh, hell, I'm sorry," Fran said. "I had no right to go blabbing all those things to you just because I was so defensive about being questioned. I really am sorry, Dad. You're right. When we're in your house you have a right to know what we're doing. I'll tell you where I've been. You won't like it, but you're entitled. I spent the night with Buzz Paige."

Sam rallied. "You *what?*"

"I've been with Buzz. We're in love. He's going to tell Dorothy this morning. We're going away together. When she gets the divorce, Buzz and I will be married." She looked at him appealingly. "Please try to understand. He's the only man I've ever loved. I was foolish once, but I'm so fortunate to discover he still loves me. We're going to be happy, Dad. I've waited a long time to be happy."

"Get out!" Sam spoke quietly but his teeth were clenched in rage. "Go pack your bags and get out of this house right now! 'Tart' is too kind a word for you. You're a monster. An evil, conniving woman who's set out to destroy a good marriage. Well, I won't let you do that. Not while you're here. No child of mine will have my approval to wreck a happy home. I can't control what you do when you leave here, but I don't want you around one more day. Not one more hour! You've been trouble since the day you were born. You've broken your mother's heart. Enough is enough!"

Frances looked straight at him. "Yes. Enough is enough. You're certainly right about that. You've never attempted to understand the fuzzy areas of life. It's all good-versus-evil to you, and anything you don't approve of is evil. Poor Father. How incredibly naïve you are. 'Wreck a happy home.' Don't you know that's an impossibility? The unhappiness is already there, for God's sake! I couldn't take Buzz away from his wife if he hadn't been unhappy for years! But you wouldn't understand that, would you? My happiness doesn't mean a damn to you if it violates some middle-class, moralistic code. Yes," Fran said again, "I've had enough. Enough of wishing I had a father who cared more for me than for his damned pride. I'll leave. No problem. They still have hotels in this town. But I won't leave Denver until I leave with the man I love." She started for the door and then turned to face him once more. "I take it back. I'm not sorry I told you about Allie and Barb. Mother's out of her mind with worry about them, but she wouldn't let you know. She's used to protecting you from unpleasantness. Or perhaps she knows, as I do, that you and your moral judgments would only make things worse. Goodbye, Dad. I didn't say it before but I can this time. Goodbye and good luck."

He stood staring at the door after Fran vanished through it. He had to do something. Get to Buzz Paige before he talked to his wife. Jump in the car and go over there right now. Tell Buzz it was a mistake. That Fran left town. Anything. But even as he thought it, he knew there was nothing he could do. He had no authority. He was not dealing with juveniles. Sam sat down weakly on the front steps. All those things Fran said about herself. About her sisters. About him. God help him, was that what the mystery was all about—Allie married to a wife-beater and Barb in love with a married man? Was he to blame for any of it or, somehow, for all of it? Dimly, he heard Laura's voice from the doorway.

"Sam? What's the matter? Are you all right?"

He turned slowly to look at her, to see the genuine concern in her eyes. He got up like a very old man, and when he spoke it was with the voice of defeat.

"I think we'd better have a talk, Laura. There seem to be a few heavy crosses you've been carrying alone."

We were born fifty years too soon, Laura thought, as she finished her "confession" to Sam and saw the pained, incredulous look on his face. If only we could face these problems by today's standards, we wouldn't find it so horrifying that we have a thrice-divorced daughter about to run off with a married man. It happens every day. A man leaves his family for another woman, usually a younger one than Fran, but people accept it because it's become too prevalent to shock any group except us "senior citizens." She shuddered involuntarily at that phrase. Why do those of us in our late years have to call ourselves "senior citizens" or "gray panthers" or "elder statesmen" or anything except what we are—old people. We act as though it's indecent to have lived a long time. It isn't indecent. But sometimes it's damned inconvenient. We just can't accept the changes all around us. We cling to the old standards, the old values, stubbornly rejecting the new ones.

It's the same with Barbara and Alice's problems. These days, it's unsophisticated to be shocked when two mature people have an affair. Or even when it's discovered that your son-in-law is one of thousands of deranged men who regularly beat their wives. But Sam and I are old-fashioned. Such unorthodox behavior doesn't happen in our family. It's something you read about in magazine articles. Something that happens to other people. Like cancer or heart attacks or strokes. We don't believe they'll ever touch us. Scandal is in the same category, as far as we're concerned. Not so terrible, perhaps, but equally unacceptable.

And it is unacceptable. No matter how casually younger people treat infidelity and immorality, Sam and I cannot support it. Not when it comes to one of our own. Remembering her own anguish when she heard these stories from her girls, she was sympathetic to Sam's stunned reaction. It was like receiving a rapid series of body blows. You reeled from them, dazed, incapable of fighting back. Sam sat immobile at the kitchen table for a long moment after Laura's recital. And then he slowly shook his head in unmistakable bewilderment.

"What are we going to do?"

At least he isn't going to rant and rave. Laura thought with relief. It tore her apart to see him so defeated, but it was better than the monumental anger she'd expected when he finally found out what she'd known for days.

"I don't see that there's much we can do, dear. They're grown women. We can't direct their lives. We never could, really. Not even when they were young. But certainly not now. All we can contribute is our presence, I suppose. Perhaps it helps to know that we love them, even if we don't really understand. We'd best stay quiet, I think. Let them work things out for themselves with our silent support."

He gave a short, mirthless laugh. "Too late for that, at least where Frances is concerned. I caught her coming in at six this morning. She told me she'd been with Buzz Paige and that he was going to get a divorce and marry her. I told her to pack her bags and get out."

"Sam! You didn't!"

"Afraid I did. We had a whale of an argument. She said I'd never been much of a father to any of them. She's right. I never was. I never took time to find out what they were thinking. It didn't occur to me that they needed both of us. Maybe if it had, they'd have turned out differently."

"That's nonsense," Laura said. "You've always been a good father, a good provider. You can't blame yourself for what's happened to them. If you believe that, you have to blame me even more. I was in a better position to influence them. You were busy. Your job was elsewhere. Do you blame me for the way they turned out?"

"No, of course not. You're a wonderful mother."

"And you've always been a good father. Sam, dear, we tried to give them a good foundation. That was all we could do. All any parents can do. I don't hold with this business of people blaming their troubles on their early lives. I'm sure it's not always true. There comes a time when they have set their own course of action and they're influenced by all kinds of outside things." Laura sighed. "All you can do for children is try to teach them what you believe is right and decent. If they don't apply your standards to their own lives, it can't be helped. I love them as you do. I'm terribly disappointed in the way their lives have turned out. My heart breaks for them. But I can't solve their problems and neither can you."

Sam frowned. "But I have to do something about Frances. What she's doing is wrong. Terrible. It makes me ashamed. But I took the wrong approach with her. I see that now. She might have responded to reason, but I didn't even try that."

"I'll go up and see her," Laura said. "I'll explain that you were just terribly upset, and that we don't want her to leave this way. She'll understand. She's an intelligent, worldly woman."

"No. You've been doing that for almost fifty years, making excuses for my stubbornness, smoothing over problems I've caused. I can't let you do that any more. I'll talk to Frances myself. Don't worry. I won't fly off the handle. I hate what she's doing because it is wrong. No one can convince me otherwise. But I have to let her know that no matter what she does she always has a home here. All of them do." He took a deep breath. "What's going to happen to the others? What's Barbara going to do now that that man has thrown her over? And Allie. We can't let her go back to that sadist."

Laura patted his hand. Such a big hand with strong, blunt fingers roughened by endless work in the garden. Once Sam's hands were smooth and soft when they touched her. "White collar hands" they were, belonging to an executive. Now they were as tough as a laborer's, and it had been a long, long time since they'd stroked her. Odd I should be dwelling on that now, she thought. Crazy that a woman in her "sunset years" should be thinking of romance long gone. It was simply that the change in Sam's hands reminded her of the changes in the man himself: As his will to live weakened, his body became stronger. Physically he had toughened, but emotionally he was spent. All this is killing him, she realized. In many ways he's more devastated than I, more filled with remorse.

"We're all going to survive," she said at last. "You and I and the children, as long as the Lord allows. The girls will find their way out of their situations. Ways they can live with. We just have to try to accept what they do." She smiled sadly. "We can't play God, Sam dear. We don't know enough to even try."

The slamming of dresser drawers in Fran's room a little after six in the morning awakened her sleeping sisters. Neither of them had slept well after their talk. Allie, almost ashamed of her new-found happiness, was sensitively reluctant to announce her good fortune when Barb was so miserable. That was silly, of course. No one would be more thrilled for her than her younger sister. Convincing herself of that, she'd finally drifted off to sleep.

Barbara dropped off at last from sheer exhaustion. She had no idea what time it was when she closed her eyes in merciful unconsciousness, but it must have been only a couple of hours before the racket next door awakened her. She and Allie sat up almost simultaneously when the noise began.

"What on earth is going on?" Allie asked. "What's Fran doing crashing around at this hour?"

For a moment, Barb forgot her own troubles. She got out of bed and put on her robe. "Let's go see."

The two of them entered their sister's room. All Fran's suitcases were out and she was feverishly packing, the contents of the closet and bureau making the place look like some elegant but disorganized dress shop. She didn't even look up when the other two came in.

Allie stared at the disarray. "What's happened? Where are you going?"

"To a hotel. I've had it with this house. I hated it before and I hate it now. I can't wait to get the hell away from all this goddamned middle-class morality!"

Barbara and Alice looked confused. Of course Fran wasn't at home here. Neither were they. But there was more than that to this precipitous departure.

"To a hotel?" Barbara repeated. "I don't understand." For the first time she noticed Fran's untouched bed. "You must have just gotten home. What *is* all this?"

"All this," Fran said acidly, "is that once again I'm getting out of here to live my own life without being told I'm a tramp and a tart and all those other attractive things. Who needs it? I'm going on fifty years old, for God's sake!"

"Calm down," Allie said. "Let's make some sense out of all this, Fran."

"Who can make sense out of a crazy old man who thinks he's still living in the nineteenth century? *Your* father is the same sanctimonious, self-righteous bastard he always was! He's ordered me out of the house. How do you like them apples? Caught me coming in a few minutes late again and did a rerun of 'Orphans of the Storm.' Too bad I'm not penniless or that there isn't a blizzard he can toss me out into!" She sat down suddenly on the bed. "I'm sorry," she said more quietly. "I'm behaving like an Italian soprano. The fact is, I spent the night with Buzz. We're going to be married. I ran into Dad on my way in and told him. He's turned my picture to the wall. Again. It wasn't a very pretty scene on either side, but it was inevitable. Tom Wolfe was right: You sure as hell can't go home again. Anyway, I'm leaving, kids. Sorry to run out on you when you both have troubles, but I'll be sticking around Denver for a little while until Buzz can get his affairs in some kind of order, so we'll be able to meet away from here. That is, if you want to stay friendly with the black sheep of the family."

"Don't, Fran," Barbara said. "Don't do it. It'll kill Mother to see you leave this way. You know Dad. He flares up. He'll come around when he's had time to think it through."

"I'm sure he will," Fran said sarcastically. "Maybe he'll let me come back to celebrate his Diamond Jubilee. No, Barb. Sorry. No go. He doesn't want a 'fallen woman' under his roof. Might contaminate him, ruin his respectability. God forbid he should harbor a strumpet who sleeps with somebody else's husband! They'd probably drum him out of the Kiwanis!" She stopped, seeing the pained expression on Barbara's face, remembering what she'd said to Sam. "Oh, Jesus, I've blown it for both of you too, I guess. I'm afraid I said more than I should have about Tallent and Spencer. He's probably getting the story of our lives from Mother right now and will come charging up here like the wild bull of the pampas. I'm really sorry about that. I shouldn't have involved anyone else."

Alice was trying to absorb what she'd heard. Fran and Buzz Paige were going to be married? It was incredible. She had no idea her sister was contemplating such a thing. Apparently it was not surprising to Barbara.

"Are you sure, Fran? Sure this is right for you, I mean." Barb looked pleadingly at her sister. "It's a fierce responsibility you're taking, separating a man from his wife and children, asking him to chuck everything for you. Are you so sure he won't regret it? Or that you won't?"

She's thinking of herself, Fran recognized. She's decided to let that selfish congressman go because she's afraid he'll regret it later on if she doesn't. She was tempted to say something cutting to the younger woman, make some cynical crack about stupid self-sacrifice. Barb was wrong. She was too much the idealist, too considerate of others at the expense of her own happiness. Or maybe she was just too weak and frightened. But whatever the reason, Fran couldn't be cruel enough to add to her sister's misery.

"Who knows how any of us will feel in the future, Barb? We each have to do what we think is best at the moment. We don't have to agree, you and I. Our skins are not the same thickness, but that doesn't mean we don't respect and love each other." She stood up and put her arms around her sisters. "We're quite a trio, aren't we? The three sisters. Very appropriate title for us. Remember your Colorado history? In this neck of the woods 'The Three Sisters' refers to an avalanche area up in Loveland Pass!" Fran laughed. "That's us, all right. Three avalanches crashing toward our individual ends. We're coming down from the mountains. Down to the flatlands in one hell of a rush!"

"I'm no avalanche," Barb said quietly. "Right now I feel more like a stagnant pool."

"You'll be okay. Time works wonders, honey." Fran was reassuring. "What about you, Allie? Which direction are you taking?"

This was the moment to tell them about Johnny. They'll be glad for me, she thought again. I haven't sorted out my life, not in terms of Spencer or Jack, but at least I'm at peace about the one thing that's haunted me all these years. "I have some news," Allie said. "Yesterday afternoon . . ." A knock on the door interrupted her.

"Frances? May I speak with you, please?" The voice from the hall was low-pitched, calm. Without waiting for an answer, Sam opened the bedroom door. "Oh, I'm sorry. I didn't realize you girls were in here. I wanted to talk to Frances for a minute. I can come back later."

"No, it's all right," Alice said. "We can come back when you're finished." She was actually relieved by the reprieve. It was still hard not to feel guilty about her good fortune amid so much misery. "Come on, Barb."

"Wait!" Fran's voice was cold. "There's no reason for you and

Barb to leave. Everybody here knows the whole story. Whatever you came to say, Father, certainly can be said in front of all your children."

Sam took a deep breath. She wasn't going to make it easy for him, but perhaps she was right. He owed each of them an explanation, an apology. Perhaps through Fran he could speak to all three.

"Your sister is right. There've been too many secrets in this family. Too much you didn't want me to know. I'm not blaming you for that. You were right to think I wouldn't understand. I haven't had much time for understanding in the past. Or maybe no use for it. But I've been wrong and I hope I'm enough of a man to admit it. I want you all to know that I'm sorry I've been so rigid, so uncompromising, so sure my judgment was always right. I did a bad thing to Allie years ago. I couldn't find forgiveness in my heart when Fran ran away. Later I even resented you, Barbara, for wanting to leave me. Those things were wrong. Stupid and blind and un-Christian, and I regret them and all the things I've said and thought and done in the years since. I hope it's not too late to be a friend to you, even if I'm not much as a father. I want you to know that I love you and want you here if this is where you want to be. And if it isn't, I'll still try my best to see your side of things." He paused and looked first at Barbara. "I'm sorry about what's happened to you, child. I know you're miserable now, but as your mother says, you've had a lot of years of happiness. As for you, Allie, there aren't words to say how I regret causing you so much anguish." His gaze came to rest on Frances. "We had some hard words this morning. I'm not going to pretend I approve of what you're planning, any more than I can condone what Alice did years ago or what Barbara has been doing in Washington. But I'm going to try not to set myself up as judge and jury for you or your sisters. I hope you won't leave, Frances. Not like this. You are very dear to me. Very important. All of you. More important than the strict code of behavior I set for myself and tried to impose on you."

This extraordinary speech was met by silence from his children. They're not going to forgive me after all, Sam thought. One contrite confession, hard as it was to make, isn't going to wipe out all the resentment I've created. Why did I think it might? He turned to leave, but Fran caught his sleeve.

"Don't go," she said. "I know that was the hardest thing you ever had to do in your life. And maybe the best. We all love you, Dad. We do. No matter how we act, we couldn't stop being your daughters or admiring you more than any man we've ever known. Don't you see? Each of us has been searching for you in the men we chose. That young, lonely Allie thought Spencer had your dependability. And Barb saw the tenderness and consideration in Charles that she always got from you. And me, even crazy, mixed-up me, was always looking for someone with your sense of decency. I found it in Buzz. He's you. Honest and responsible and terribly guilty right now. As you would be in his situation. I think I can speak for all of us. We don't expect you to change your beliefs, Father, but we respect you for saying what we've always wanted to hear."

His gaze rested lovingly, lingeringly, on all his girls. Barb and Allie were crying softly, nodding their heads in agreement. He felt his own eyes fill with tears. I finally made it, he thought humbly. I finally found the humility to admit what a pig-headed tyrant I've been. He was suddenly overcome with emotion. He had to escape. He smiled and awkwardly threw them a grateful kiss before he left the room.

Laura was still sitting at the table when he went back to the kitchen. There was no need to voice the question.

"I did it," Sam said. "I talked to all three of them. Funny. It wasn't as hard as I thought it would be. The words just seemed to come tumbling out, almost like I couldn't have stopped them if I wanted to." He looked as though some terrible weight had been lifted from his shoulders. "I'm proud of them, Laurie. They're fine women. I said I couldn't approve of what they did, but I love them and I'd try to understand. And they—that is, Frances—said they loved me."

Laura was as relieved as he. She'd been afraid of what might happen when Sam went up to talk to Frances. They were so alike, these two. Stubborn, strong, opinionated. She'd been afraid there'd be another clash of wills. But it had turned out better than she dared hope, not only with Frances but with all their daughters.

"You've wanted to do that for a long time, haven't you? Tell the girls how much you care, I mean. I'm so glad you finally did. It means so much to all of us."

Sam nodded. "I wish I'd done it years ago. Why didn't I, Laura? Why couldn't I ever open up with them?"

"We do things when the time is right, I guess. There's no other explanation. But that's not important. What matters is that they know they have your sympathy and support. *Our* sympathy and support, whatever they do."

The daughters were quiet for a moment after he left the room and then, wordlessly, Frances began to put her clothes back in the closet.

Chapter 25

Martha Perrone enjoyed being the center of attention. Spencer Winters' drab, middle-aged secretary pretended to disapprove of the curiosity the other secretaries were showing about her boss, but secretly she reveled in their attention. Usually, they paid little heed to her. She was older than most of the girls in the law firm and far more prim and proper. To know something they did not filled Martha with a heady sense of importance.

"Come on, Martha. What's turned that walking icicle into a towering inferno?"

"Yeah, Martha, what gives with Mr. Cool? Is he in hot water with the big boss? Or is it something juicier, like trouble at home?"

She looked at the interested faces of the secretaries to Wallingford and McClean. J. B. Thompson's secretary, lofty in her post as confidante of the senior partner, would not deign to join the group at Martha's desk, but Martha knew she was curious, equally intrigued by Mr. Winters' odd behavior in the past week. And J.B.'s secretary would love to find something she could report to the head of the firm.

"I'm sure I don't know what you mean," Martha said with just enough lack of conviction.

"Like hell! He's been in a rage ever since he got back from Denver. Snapping and snarling at everybody. And a while ago, he rushed out like his tail was on fire!" McClean's secretary lit a forbidden cigarette. All the executives were out of the office. "Come on, Mart. What's gotten into old Spence? You know he's always tried to win a popularity contest with the partners. He's even buttered-up us poor slaves, trying so hard to be the perfect heir to the throne! And now, all of a sudden, it's like he's mad at the world. We even hear him yelling at you these days, and Lord knows you don't deserve that," the girl said ingratiatingly. "You've always been the indispensable right hand."

It's true, Martha thought, nursing her injured pride. He has no right to be so mean to me just because he's having personal problems. I've given him years of loyalty and he repays me by calling me incompetent and stupid. It's not fair.

"Well," she said almost in a whisper, making sure she couldn't be heard by Thompson's secretary, "it seems there is some trouble at home." She hesitated. It was unprofessional, unethical to tell anyone about Spencer Winters' private life, but the temptation to hold the spotlight was too strong. Besides, she really did feel put-upon. She didn't care what the widowed mother she lived with said about job security. She didn't have to take this kind of abuse.

"What kind of trouble?" Wallingford's secretary urged her on.

"It started the day he got back from Denver," Martha said. "First, he had me call every 'John Peck' in the phone book, trying to locate one who'd been in touch with Mrs. Carlton Rudolph."

"That's his wife's aunt, isn't it?"

Martha nodded. "Yes. She raised Mrs. Winters. Anyway, I couldn't find the right John Peck, and Mr. Winters was furious. He said I was incompetent and stupid. As though it was my fault, the man wasn't listed or was one of the ones who didn't answer the phone!"

The others looked sympathetic.

"But the next day I saw penciled in an appointment on his calendar for noon. It was just initials. 'J.P.' Of course I knew who *that* was."

"He sure wasn't making a date with a Justice of the Peace," Wallington's secretary said.

The other girl laughed. "Maybe it was a meeting with himself and he wrote in 'Just Perfect.' Go on, Martha. What then? Did John Peck appear? Who is he?"

"He didn't appear. Mr. Winters waited a whole hour and then he got his daughter on the phone. That's Janice, you know."

"Sure. The snappy one who lives with the art director."

Martha blushed. "I suppose she does. Anyway, Mr. Winters raised Cain with her and she was very fresh to him."

"How do you know?" McClean's secretary wagged a playful finger at Martha. "Don't tell me you listened in, you naughty girl!"

"Well, yes, I did. Mr. Winters wanted to know where John Peck was, and Janice said, 'How should I know? Am I my brother's keeper?' And then she laughed and said something about wasn't that funny, she never thought she'd be able to use that line and mean it."

Martha's audience was growing more intrigued, and she grew expansive under their rapt attention.

"The next thing I knew, there was a long-distance call from Mrs. Winters in Denver. That was just this morning. I never heard her sound like that. She's always so quiet, you know. Such a lady. But she was screaming at him, something about him beating up Janice the way he always beat *her!*"

The other two gasped. "You're kidding!" McClean's secretary said. "She actually said that? That he beats her? The sonofabitch! What a lousy hypocrite!"

"Shhh. Keep your voice down." Martha glanced nervously toward J.B.'s office. "I'm not so happy with Mr. Winters, but I don't want him reported to the head of the firm."

"Okay. Don't stop now. What else did she say?"

Spencer's secretary paused dramatically. "Then Mrs. Winters said—and her voice was enough to give you goose bumps—that she was never coming back to Mr. Winters because she'd found her long-lost child and she was going to make a new life for herself." Martha waited, enjoying the stunned reaction before she went on. She was having a fine time now. These snippy girls who made fun of her behind her back were truly impressed.

"You actually heard her say that? What do you think she meant, that stuff about a long-lost child?"

"I think," Martha pronounced, "that Mrs. Winters had another baby, not by her husband. I also think Janice knew something about it and wouldn't tell her father. That's why he hit her. And furthermore," Martha added, warming to her subject, "I think this mysterious John Peck knows something about it too. He was probably trying to blackmail Mrs. Winters through her aunt."

"Good God! It's better than a movie!" Wallington's secretary was fascinated. "No wonder old Spencer's been so steamed! Talk about scandal! J.B.'d toss him out on his can if he knew! Imagine, our teddibly respectable Mr. Winters a wife-beater! And that nice, sweet woman he's married to having an illegitimate kid!"

"Wait just a moment," Martha said. "I never said Mrs. Winters had an illegitimate child. I said I thought she had one by someone else. Maybe she was married before."

"If she was, why all this mystery about John Peck and Janice and blackmail? Why would she talk about a long-lost child? Come on, Martha. Don't try to pretend you think there are no skeletons in the closet."

Martha was silent. They were right, of course. She'd continued to eavesdrop on that phone call from Denver and there was much more. Things so terrifying she didn't dare repeat them. She'd probably said too much already. It had been foolish to let these nosey girls know any part of this. She'd been flattered by their attention, lured into telling things she had no right to disclose. She hoped they wouldn't repeat them. A dim hope. This was much too good not to be whispered around the office and it surely would get back to the big boss. Oh, Lord, what had she done? Mr. Winters would kill her!

The thought reminded her of the rest of that conversation, the part that really made chills run down her spine. When his wife said that about the child, he'd gone quite mad, calling her every kind of terrible name and then he'd said, evenly, "When I get my hands on you, Alice, I'm going to kill you. You and that goddamn bastard of yours. You've lied and cheated and made my life hell for too many years. You don't deserve to live."

Martha shuddered, remembering the cold, ominous quality of those words. I believe he could kill, she thought. He'd sounded insane with fury. But Mrs. Winters had calmed down and her level tone matched his own.

"You're not going to kill anyone, Spencer. You're much too cowardly, much too consumed with self-preservation. If you were going to murder me, you'd have done it long ago. But you always stopped just short of that. You may not think my life is worth anything, but you're too selfish to trade your own for the pleasure of destroying it."

"Don't be so sure of that. There's a limit to what a decent man can endure. And you've finally gone too far."

Alice hadn't answered that. She'd simply said, "Goodbye, Spencer. You'll hear from my attorneys."

That had been only a few hours ago. Immediately after the call, Spencer had slammed out of his office, only stopping long enough to say, "Miss Perrone, get me a plane ticket to Denver."

"Yes, sir. What day?"

"Tomorrow."

"Yes, Mr. Winters. Will you want a hotel reservation too?"

"No, I thought it would be more fun to sleep in the park. Of course I want a hotel, you idiot!"

She hid her resentment under the impassive face of the perfect secretary. "How long do you plan to stay? I have to tell the hotel."

"Oh, Christ, I'm not sure. One night. Two, maybe. That should be plenty of time."

"Yes, sir."

"And I probably won't be back in the office before I leave. Send the air tickets and hotel information to my house by messenger."

"Very well."

He'd shot out the door without another word, leaving her angry and frightened. "Plenty of time," he'd said. For what? To drag Mrs. Winters home? To settle things with her? Or, God forbid, to carry out his threat?

Automatically, Martha called the travel agent and specified his needs. Then she sat back and wondered what to do. Perhaps she should call Mrs. Winters at her parents' home and warn her. Or get in touch with Janice and tell her that her father might be on his way to do something terrible. But how could she do that without disclosing what she knew? And what if she was wrong? What if these theatrics were just Spencer's way of frightening his wife into submission? It's none of your business, Martha, she told herself. Don't get involved.

A short time later the girls had started asking questions. They'd seen Winters' angry departure, the culmination of several days of bad temper which, unusually, he hadn't bothered to hide. She'd told them as much as she dared. She couldn't bring herself to reveal the rest, though she'd liked to have asked their advice. Poor Mrs. Winters, she thought. Imagine having to live with that! Martha had had only a week of watching his Jekyll and Hyde personality. What could it have been like for Alice to have endured it for twenty-five years?

When the girls finally drifted back to their own desks, Martha picked up the morning paper and began to read the "Help Wanted" ads. She'd be sorry to leave this job, but she couldn't work for a monster. And she didn't want to be around when he finally, inevitably, cracked up.

Alice was trembling when she hung up on her furious husband in Boston. At the same time she felt an enormous sense of relief. It was over and done with, this nightmare life with Spencer. She'd declared herself, and though she feared the consequences, not only for herself but those most precious to her, she also had a sense of freedom and peace. Only now did she fully realize how much of her life had been devoted to needless self-reproach and contrition, how masochistic she'd been. Johnny was fine. Had been, all along. The fact did not absolve her from her feelings of guilt about letting him go, but it was comforting, at last, to know that he'd grown up in a good home and had turned into a son to be proud of. Another son. She'd always be proud of Chris too. And of her daughter. They had the courage of their convictions. More than she could say for herself, even now.

She frowned, troubled by thoughts of her future. It would be sensible to divorce Spencer, marry Jack Richards and settle down in Denver. Even though the children—hers and theirs—would be thousands of miles away, they'd be a family. Johnny would have the real parents he'd searched for, and her other two would be happy to see her safe and well-treated. But the truth was, she wasn't in love with Jack, and instinct told her his feelings toward her were more dutiful and nostalgic than romantic. They were both trying very hard to re-establish the old magic. And it wasn't working.

We're trying too hard, Alice thought. We've changed too much, or perhaps not enough. He's still weak, almost sanctimonious in this new, penitent role of widower. He's now trying to please a dead woman. Just as years ago he tried to please demanding parents. And I'm just as bad. I can't shake the habit of thinking first of what would make other people happy. I allowed myself to be sent away to accommodate my parents. Now I'm thinking of going into a life which will put my children's minds at ease.

It's wrong. Middle age is the time to start thinking of yourself. When you've done all you can for those who have real or imagined demands on you, it's time to be selfish. Healthily selfish. But what is it I really want? I want to be free, Alice told herself. Free as I never have been. I'd like to live in sunshine year round, after so many bitter New England winters. I'd like not to worry about housekeeping and social obligations and appearances. I'd like to be a slob when I feel like it. Sleep as late as I like, stay up all night reading if I decide to, eat a peanut butter sandwich for dinner if that's what I want. I'd like to be an old droput. A late-blooming hippie. The idea made her smile. It was so totally unlike the proper Alice Winters the world knew.

She couldn't do it, of course. She had no money to support even a simple life. Neither could she return to Boston. But she didn't want to stay in Denver, though she knew her parents would gladly give her shelter. She'd made a move without thinking out a follow-up plan. She'd burned her bridges with Spencer and mentally rejected Jack, and she had no idea where she was headed. Oddly enough, she didn't worry. Perhaps, Alice thought ruefully, I have begun to believe in miracles. If Johnny could reappear as he did, anything is possible.

After they dropped Alice off, Johnny and his father talked most of the night in Jack's comfortable living room, shoes off, feet propped up on the coffee table, can after can of beer in hand. They'd told each other the stories of their lives, more like two friends than like father and son. It was a revelation to both men. Johnny had not expected the bonus of finding his father as well as his mother. And Jack was still filled with wonder at the return of his child.

"I'll be able to meet all the family while I'm here, won't I?" Johnny asked at one point.

"Of course. All your mother's family, that is. Her parents and her two sisters. I don't have any family left. I was an only child too, and my mother and father have been dead for years. But Alice makes up for it." Jack grinned. "She can trot out assorted, eccentric old aunts and uncles if you have need for such things."

"I wonder when she'll tell them about me."

"Remembering how close those sisters always were, I'd venture to say she's already told Barb and Fran, even if she had to wake them up to do it. She'll probably tell Mr. and Mrs. Dalton in the morning."

Johnny toyed with his beer can. "How do you think they'll take it?"

"The girls will be delighted and your grandmother is not the sort of woman to hold grudges. I suspect she'll be overcome with joy for you and your mother."

"But Mr. Dalton will be a problem." It was more a statement than a question.

"Could be," Jack said. "He's always been painfully righteous. He's a good man, Johnny, but unbending. Time may have softened him enough to let him accept the child he never wanted to see or hear of. But we can't be sure. Look, Son, I haven't seen any of those people in more than thirty years. Except your Aunt Barbara." An odd note came into Jack's voice. "She's lovely, Johnny. I can't understand why she's never married. She must have had dozens of chances."

John Peck glanced sharply at his father. He sounds like he's in love with Barbara! The unwelcome thought disturbed the younger man. He'd had it all worked out in his head. Alice would divorce that bastard Winters and marry her childhood sweetheart. He'd have a mother and father living together. He could bring his own child to visit his grandparents. More fantasy. Why did he think this whole thing was going to work out like a fairy tale, with everybody living happily ever after? He suddenly wondered whether Alice loved Jack Richards. He assumed she did. Was she going to be hurt again, after all she'd lived through? He felt himself becoming unreasonably angry, but he hid it under a seemingly casual question.

"Do you think you and Mother will get married when she's finally rid of Winters?"

Jack took a swallow of beer, stalling for time before he answered. "Getting rid of Spencer Winters isn't going to be all that easy. From what I know of the man, he could be vengeful, and your mother has your half-sister and half-brother to think of. Not to mention that poor old aunt of hers in Boston who's scared to death of the man, with good reason. Oh, Alice will eventually be free. We'll see to that. We're never going to let her go back into that situation again, but it may take a long time to work out."

He's deliberately ducked my question, Johnny thought. He's talked about the difficulties of the divorce, but nothing about remarriage. All right. It's none of my business. I can't tell them how to run their lives. It's enough that I've found them and that they're such good people. Other adopted people haven't been so lucky. He remembered the tales he'd heard, the stories he'd read. Some children were rejected by the parent or parents they finally found. Others discovered whores for mothers or drunkards for fathers. I'm blessed just knowing them, just finding out about myself. They've given me the identity I always needed. They owe me nothing more.

The Dalton girls were uneasy all morning, following Sam's unexpected emotional apology to them. It was not that they weren't happy about this new understanding, but each recognized that while unity was a supportive thing, the fact of its existence did not settle their individual problems.

Alice had not yet told them about Johnny. Even after she telephoned Spencer in midmorning, and then spoke to Jack and their son, arranging for them to come over late in the afternoon, she somehow couldn't find the right words to announce this wonderful news. What if they didn't believe Johnny was who he claimed to be? There was no proof. Just her instinctive certainty, and Jack's. She couldn't bear it if they doubted, and she was afraid they might. So she waited through the morning, longing to tell them and ridiculously afraid they'd try to burst her bubble.

Barbara dressed and came quietly downstairs, the letter to Charles in her hand. It was like issuing her own death warrant to put this final communication into the mailbox on the corner, but that's where she was headed. She slipped out of the front door and walked slowly down the familiar block, kicking at the fallen leaves in her path. She could imagine Charles's face when he read her words, but she could not hazard a guess as to his reaction. There'd be some response, of course. Either a vehement rejection of what she'd written or a sad but unwillingly thankful acceptance. There was nothing to do but wait for the next development. Wait in frozen despair for the verdict. But, bitterly, she was sure what it would be. She had no need to hazard guesses.

And what would she do then? Run? Hide? She didn't know that either. She couldn't anticipate her own course of action. Emotionally, she wanted to stay as far away as possible from any chance encounter with the man she loved. But sensibly, maturely, she should go back to her job in Washington. To her pretty apartment and her good friends. Life didn't end when a love affair did. Like millions of other disappointed women, she'd pick up the pieces and go on. But nothing would ever be the same. The realization stung her, and her hand trembled as she lifted the metal flap of the mailbox and slowly, reluctantly slid the envelope into its gaping jaws.

Fran paced her room, smoking endless cigarettes, waiting for the phone call from Buzz that would tell her he'd done what he promised. As the hours wore on, she became more apprehensive. What if he hadn't found the courage to tell Dorothy? What if that crazy woman had done something violent? My God, she was capable of anything! Maybe she had a gun. Maybe she'd killed Buzz! Nonsense. She, not Dorothy, was behaving like a lunatic. It took time, these things. After twenty-nine years you didn't just walk in the house, announce you were leaving forever and then run to the telephone and call your beloved. There'd be a lot of talking and arguing and angry accusations in the Paige household. Poor Buzz. Between his own conscience and the things that demented woman probably was threatening, he must be going through hell. Never mind. She'd make it up to him. For once in her life, she'd devote herself utterly and entirely to making a man happy. It had taken a long time and a lot of experiences she didn't even want to think about. But she'd come full circle. She was a woman in love. At last. Never mind if it took all day, she'd hear what she wanted to hear. There were years ahead to rejoice in this lovely new feeling of being a totally happy, totally fulfilled woman.

The five of them squeezed around the kitchen table for lunch, a reunited family. But only Sam seemed completely content, as though he'd purged himself of all the hatred and prejudices he'd held for years.

Men are so easily satisfied, Laura thought. It was wonderful beyond belief that Sam had been able to reach out to their daughters, to humble himself as she'd never seen him do. The fault wasn't all on his side, but he'd been willing to make it seem so, and she loved him for it. But having made one touching speech, he now acted as though all their troubles were behind them. And of course they weren't. All that had been accomplished was to keep Fran from leaving in anger, and assure her and her sisters that they could count on the devotion and support of both parents.

The girls were so quiet. Laura realized it was a troubled stillness, broken only by Sam's jovial monologue and his endless repetition of how wonderful it was that they all finally understood each other. She wished he'd be quiet. He was overdoing it with all those clichés about blood being thicker than water. Couldn't he see that his daughters were deep in their own thoughts? Why on earth did he have to rattle on so? She wanted to tell him, rudely, to shut up, but of course she wouldn't do that. He was so happy. So full of good will. She hoped they'd all hurry up and finish lunch so they could escape from this heavy atmosphere. Midway through the meal, Alice interrupted her father.

"Dad. Mom. All of you. I have something to tell you."

Sam stopped talking and four pairs of eyes fixed their attention on Alice. No one spoke until she finished the story of her reunion with John Peck. They listened, wide-eyed, as she told them the remarkable story of the past twenty-four hours. Only Sam did not know that Alice and Jack Richards had seen each other, but none of them was aware of how drastically Allie's life had changed since the previous day.

"They're coming over this afternoon," she said. "I want you all to meet Johnny and him to meet you. Jack's bringing him." Alice faced her father, almost challenging him to go back on the generous words he'd spoken early that morning. "It's a blessing, Dad, that we all can count on your strength and understanding. It makes things so much easier to know you share my joy."

Sam Dalton's face went dead-white. It was one thing to try to forgive Fran for her selfishness in breaking up another woman's home, or attempt to understand how Barbara could have been involved in a love she was unable to deny. But welcome Jack Richards and the illegitimate child he'd fathered? Here, in his own house? No, Sam thought. That's asking too much. That man violated my young daughter. He brought us disgrace. And that boy! How dare he come back after all these years, demanding to be recognized! He felt them all watching him. Laura and the girls had not spoken, waiting for him to be first. They were happy, of course. Sentimental women. Ready to forgive and forget and have a good cry over a story with a "happy ending." Even Allie. How could she stand to look at the man who betrayed her or embrace a son who was a stranger to her? He looked at his middle daughter. Her eyes pleaded with him to remember what he'd said in Fran's bedroom. Sam gave a great sigh.

"That's wonderful, Allie dear!" he said. "Amazing! We'll welcome Jack and the boy."

As though he'd pulled a cork out of a bottle, the voices of the women bubbled forth, delirious with relief. Her mother and sisters kissed Allie and hugged her close, exclaiming in surprise and happiness, wanting to know more details, eager for every tiny scrap of the story. In their pleasure for her, they forgot their own difficulties and for a few minutes the kitchen was filled with the excited questions of Laura and the girls and the lyrical responses of Alice.

So be it, Sam thought. At least they wanted my approval. Only one thing's wrong. Nobody's mentioned what Spencer Winters is going to do about all this.

Chapter 26

It has been unreal, Jack Richards thought later. Unreal to walk into the old house on South Carona Street and find the living room exactly as he remembered it, down to the very last Maxwell Parrish print on the stucco walls. He'd shaken hands with a reserved but cordial Sam Dalton and a gently smiling Laura, and greeted Alice's sisters, a surprisingly subdued Barbara and a restless Frances. Most of all, it had been unreal to hear Allie introduce her family to her son.

The past blended with the present in those two awkward hours of "reunion." At one moment Jack was a callow kid, nervously hearing his parents and Alice's angrily accusing each other's child of immoral behavior. Even now, he remembered the horror on Allie's face that night so long ago. Fran, he recalled, had been out somewhere and Barbara was a little girl, banished to her room, out of earshot of this ugly exchange. It had been devastating. He'd wanted to speak out, say he was man enough to assume his responsibilities, young as he was. But he hadn't. He'd sat silently, letting his mother and father bail him out of the mess, letting Allie carry the burden alone. He'd been weak. He supposed he still was. Even Lucy had been stronger than he, not only in those last months when they knew she was dying, but all through their married life. Gentle, adoring Lucy had made his life easy, provided a quiet, comfortable home, bolstered him through his early struggle in business. It was Lucy, not he, who wanted to find the child he'd fathered, willing to accept another woman's baby because she could give him none. Yes, his wife had been strong and he missed her strength as much as he missed her love.

Allie had never really been strong, except in that one moment when she fled the scene, refusing to have any more of their undignified accusations. The only forceful thing she'd ever done was to reject the abortion and decide to have the baby without a father. That was her one moment of heroism, Jack thought. Before and after that she presented herself as a target for everyone's abuse.

I suppose that's why I never really loved her, never fought for her, he realized. It's why I don't want to marry her now. I need a strong woman. Not tough and brittle, like Fran, but confident and compassionate, like Barbara. Even as quiet and remote as she was this afternoon, Barbara exuded strength. She was like Lucy in many ways: composed, clear-headed. A woman a man could turn to for support and sensible advice.

He was nervous when the Daltons received him again and were introduced to their grandson. But John Peck handled himself well, not overeager or too deferential. In an awkward situation, he spoke easily and honestly, telling them how grateful he was to have found his parents and his mother's parents. He'd been warm and well-mannered, showing no sign of resentment or hostility toward any of them, not even toward Sam Dalton.

Alice had an almost worshipful attitude toward this young man who did her proud. Her eyes never left John's face as he told his grandparents and aunts of his early life, praising his adoptive parents as fine, upstanding people, smiling affectionately as he mentioned his wife and his forthcoming child. It was John who dominated the conversation and who was more at ease than his elders. Jack, for the most part, remained silent, uncomfortable in the presence of Sam and Laura, disquieted by Barb's stillness and Fran's inattentive attitude. He couldn't tell whether the sisters were distracted by their own thoughts or simply bored by this strange gathering. Fran's not a lovable woman, Jack thought, watching her fidget. Certainly not a serene one. She had none of Allie's kindness or Barbara's composure.

It's true that people don't change, he realized. In maturity, we continue to be what we always were. Fran was always volatile and

Alice acquiescent. Barbara, even as a child, had grace and assurance. With every passing year, inherent characteristics become more pronounced: the nice get nicer, the selfish more self-involved.

On the whole, it had been a remarkably uneventful coming together of diverse individuals. They'd had tea and discreetly examined one another's reactions, subtly probing, seeking some common ground. There was none, really, except for this young man who'd torn a family apart before his birth and now sought to bring it back together for his parents' peace of mind and his own.

At the end of two hours, each of them was anxious to escape. The emotional intensity of Jack and Alice's meeting with their son was missing in this quiet, strained, "official" reunion. It was like a ritual they had to go through, and once done, they would go their separate ways, having merely tied up some loose ends. *Some*, indeed, Jack thought. John Peck had his own family, a wife and a child to come. Satisfied, after so many years of search, it was unlikely that he would stay close to any of them. It was too late, no matter what Allie thought, to become a "family." The Senior Daltons seemed to accept this presentable young man, but it was clear from their courteous but restrained manner that they expected to see no more of him than they did of Alice's legitimate children. Fran would soon go on her wandering way, he supposed, and Barbara would return to her life in Washington. So much for loose ends. That left only him and Allie to decide where their futures lay. She couldn't return to Boston—not, at least, to Spencer. It would be sensible for all concerned if she'd stay here, remain with her aging parents, live quietly and contentedly, free from fear. It occurred to Jack that Allie, not Barb, should have been the unmarried, dutiful daughter. She was the best suited for it, the most passive and undemanding of the three. He wondered again what was really in her mind. He'd marry her, if that's what she wanted. She wasn't in love with him any longer. Maybe she never had been. But Alice needed protection, especially now when she'd found courage to tell Spencer Winters she was through with him. And Jack was her only recourse.

And what about me? Jack wondered. Marriage to Allie wouldn't be a bad life. Quiet, predictable, almost foreordained, as though it were a debt he was destined to pay. But it wasn't what he wanted. If only she were Barbara. The thought shocked him. He was attracted to Alice's sister. He'd marry her tomorrow if he could. He knew nothing about her life. He really knew nothing about her at all. And yet, after two brief meetings in their adult lives, he was half in love with her. Perhaps she was in love with someone else. She had to be, an attractive woman like that. And she hardly noticed Jack. She'd quickly left his apartment the day he and Allie talked and she'd barely glanced at him through these past hours. He was thinking like a fool. Like the adolescent he still was. Barbara Dalton had no interest in him, and God knows even if she had he couldn't pursue it. Hadn't he hurt Alice enough?

At the end of the afternoon, Laura said, softly, "We all have so much to be grateful for, haven't we? We have our health and we have each other." She smiled at John. "And now we have a fine new grandson to take into our hearts."

For the first time, John Peck lost his composure. "I . . . I want to thank you," he said. "All of you. I didn't know what to expect. I didn't dare hope to find such warmth and kindness. That is, you've made me very happy, accepting me this way. It's . . . well, it sounds trite, but it is a dream come true."

"For all of us, Johnny," Alice said.

Sam Dalton cleared his throat. "We hope you'll come back, John. Often. You too, Jack. Bygones are bygones. We all made mistakes, but it looks as though we've profited by them."

Laura glanced at him affectionately. It was as close as he could come to apologizing to this fine young man and to the unhappy woman who'd been separated from him. It was also his way of telling Jack Richards that he was sorry for the years of bitterness that lay between then and now. There was a moment of embarrassed silence and then Laura said, briskly, "Well, who's hungry? My goodness, it's almost dinnertime! Just give me a few minutes and I'll . . ."

"Why don't you let Alice and Johnny and me take all of you out to dinner?" Jack said. "This certainly calls for a celebration, Mrs. Dalton. We don't want you standing over a hot stove this evening."

Laura looked at Sam, but the older man shook his head.

"Nice of you, Jack, but I think not. It's been a good afternoon, but Mother looks a little tired, and to tell you the truth, I am too." He smiled. "Guess we're just not used to so much excitement. Maybe Frances and Barbara . . ."

"Sorry," Fran said. "I appreciate it, Jack, but I have to wait for a phone call."

"I have to beg off too," Barb said. "It's sweet of you, but you three go along and celebrate. How long are you staying, John? We'll see you again, won't we?"

"I hope so. I'll be leaving in a day or two, I guess. Otherwise, I won't have a job or a wife."

Alice sounded disappointed. "Carol can't come out?"

"Afraid not, Mother. She's working on a rush job for the agency. But she sends her love and looks forward to seeing you and Dad in Boston."

The unfamiliar, intimate terms came as a shock to his grandparents and aunts. It was startling to hear Alice and Jack referred to that way. More than anything that had been said all afternoon, it established what they had been almost unable to grasp. But Alice seemed blissfully unperturbed as she said, "I don't know when we'll be in Boston, Johnny, but we'll see Carol. Certainly when the baby comes, if not before."

"We," Jack thought as they prepared to leave. Well, that's what it is now, isn't it? *We* have a son. *We're* going to be grandparents. *We* have to figure out the next move.

Dorothy, fully dressed, was sitting in the living room when Buzz let himself into his house shortly after six o'clock that morning. He didn't see her as he quietly entered the hall and headed for the kitchen. The prospect of going up to their bedroom, of facing an enraged woman who would demand to know where he'd been all night was more than he could handle at the moment. He'd promised Frances he'd take the step he both wanted and dreaded, but the thought of speaking those final words made him almost physically ill.

His wife's surprisingly calm voice stopped him in his tracks.

"Good morning."

Buzz turned, startled, toward the living room and saw her in her usual chair, her face quite impassive except for a dangerous glint in her eyes.

"Hello, Dottie. What are you doing up at this hour?" The words were so trite, so silly, but they came automatically.

She sat as though frozen. "I haven't been to bed. Too bad you can't say the same."

Buzz sat down in the chair facing hers. His chair. The one he'd sat in nearly every evening for twenty-nine years, reading his paper, having a small drink after work. He'd actually missed that chair when he'd moved out for a short time. He'd miss it when he left for good. It represented his place in the household, as comfortable and familiar as an old friend. Odd what trivial things one thought of at moments of crisis. He was about to break up his marriage, abandon his wife, probably alienate his sons and bring down the wrath of the community in which he'd lived all his life. And he found himself regretting the loss of a sagging piece of furniture.

"We have to talk," he said wearily. "I won't lie to you. I couldn't if I wanted to. You know where I've been, not only last night but every evening for a week. I'm sorry, Dot. I didn't mean to hurt you. I didn't mean it to go this far. It just happened."

"Affairs don't just 'happen.'" Dorothy's voice was scornful. "You wanted it to happen. So did she. You couldn't wait to get at her, like some prowling tomcat. I knew it before you saw her. I knew, just as I knew about that other woman. Men!" She made the word sound like a curse. "Evil, lecherous old fools, always running after something new and different, and then expecting to come home and find all is forgiven. How dare you do this to me? How dare you expect me to excuse you?"

"I don't expect you to. You'll never believe there was nothing between me and Stacy Donovan, but there wasn't. There's never been another woman in twenty-nine years. Until now. Until Frances."

Dorothy's control vanished. "Don't mention her name in this house! That whore! That disgusting, vulgar tramp! I never want to hear of her again! Never, do you hear?"

He'd never seen such hatred on anyone's face. The sight of Dorothy's twisted mouth and blazing eyes repelled him, even while he felt pity for her and shame for what he had to do.

"We have to talk about her, Dorothy. I . . . I want a divorce. Fran and I are going away together. There's no way to put it kindly. God knows I wish I could spare you, but I have to tell you the truth. Frances and I love each other. We're going to be married as soon as we can."

There was no answer. She simply stared at him for a long moment. She'd planned to make him pay for this insult. Planned to make Frances pay too, somehow, for sleeping with her husband. But she hadn't anticipated this. She hadn't really believed Frances would want Buzz permanently. She'd thought the woman would tire of the affair and take herself back to the glittering international world she preferred, leaving a chastened Buzz to be magnanimously but slowly forgiven. Divorce? A dazzled, flattered Buzz might think he wanted that, but it was wrong for him. In a few months Frances would leave him, as she'd left the others. She doesn't love this ordinary, middle-aged man, Dorothy thought. And I do. In spite of everything, I love him enough to save him from himself. The anger drained out of her. She felt like his mother, protective and much wiser than he. The rage generated by the affair gave way to a feeling of superiority as Dorothy realized she must keep her husband from making a fatal mistake.

"No, Buzz," she said gently. "No divorce. I'm not thinking of myself. I can't let you do such a foolhardy thing. Frances is not for you. Where would you fit in her world? Are you prepared to be a gypsy, never putting down roots anyplace? Can you handle her fancy friends? Speak their language? Will it make you happy to be a kept man? You'll live on her money, you know. You couldn't begin to earn enough to support her way of life, not even if you started over. You think you're in love. You're not. You're caught up in old memories, old dreams. You're a grandfather, Buzz. Not the dashing young man in the convertible. No," Dorothy repeated, "I won't divorce you. In fact, I won't even let you go. This is where you belong. Here, with your own kind. And here is where you'll stay." She rose from her chair. "I'll never forgive you for this humiliation, but I won't let you humiliate yourself by becoming a lapdog for a selfish, pampered, oversexed woman like Frances Dalton."

He couldn't believe his ears. This was not the unstable, emotional, hysterical Dorothy he knew. He'd expected a hideous scene, uncontrolled fury, threats. Anything but this clinical, almost dignified discussion of his future. What did it all mean?

Dorothy was not the self-sacrificing, concerned person she was pretending to be. She was using the frighteningly clever deliberateness of a madwoman. Perhaps, at this moment, she really thought she was speaking the truth, but she was not. She was schizophrenic, and the role she was playing was the other side of Dorothy, the "authority figure" she sometimes practiced on her children, rather than the helpless, dependent personality she normally projected for Buzz.

He stood too, his face inches from hers. "I'm sorry, Dottie, but you can't keep me here. You may not divorce me, but there's no way you can make me stay."

There was a strange smile on her lips. "Isn't there? I think there is. I think I know how to save you from making a fool of yourself. Forget about marrying Frances Dalton. You never will."

Buzz sank slowly back into his chair when she left the room. He felt chilled, fearful of the unknown. He was dealing with a sick and devious woman. Her reasonableness was much more terrifying than the wild outburst he'd anticipated. She's going to hurt Fran! he thought. She's crazy enough to try to kill her! For a moment he considered calling the Dalton house and warning Frances, but then he thought better of it. She'd think he was insane, would laugh it off and reasonably ask whatever had put such an idea in his head. He couldn't give a sensible answer to that. It was just something he felt. Some terrible threat that had no name.

He heard Dorothy in the kitchen. My God, she's preparing breakfast as though none of this ever happened! Suddenly he couldn't bear this house, couldn't bear the sight of his wife. Tired as he was, he went upstairs, showered and changed his clothes. He'd take a long drive up in the mountains and think things through before he called Frances. He had to be clear about this, had to try to make some sense out of Dorothy's implied threat. Fran was perfectly safe at her parents' house. She wouldn't be going out until she received his call. Nothing could happen to her. And he needed time to shake off this awful sense of impending doom. The crisp, fresh air made him feel better as he slowly drove along the winding roads. With each mile he put between himself and Dorothy, his terror receded until at last he told himself he was being stupid. Dorothy might not divorce him, but she couldn't keep him in Denver. He'd provide for her. He'd sell his agency and put the money in her name. He and Fran didn't care whose money they lived on. They were too mature for that. All they wanted was to be together and happy.

By noontime, he was in control of himself but exhausted. There'd not been much sleep the night before. The memory of those hours brought a smile to his face. They made love as though they were in their twenties. And they would, for a long, long time. But he wasn't twenty, and now he was weary.

Ahead, he saw a small, decent-looking motel. He pulled in and asked for a room. The owner looked at him dubiously.

"A room? For a few hours? You alone?"

Buzz laughed. "Believe it or not, I'm just tired."

It was dark when he awakened, and glancing at his watch he saw it was six o'clock in the evening. Good lord, Frances would be furious that he hadn't called her all day! He supposed Dorothy was wondering where he was too. That didn't matter any more. Still, he owed her the courtesy of checking in.

The man at the desk got Buzz's house on the line for him. To his surprise, his eldest son answered.

"Larry? What are you doing there?"

"Dad, where in God's name have you been? We've tried calling everywhere!"

Buzz felt his spine turn to water. "What's wrong?"

The younger man's voice broke. "It's Mother. She . . . she called me at noon and said I'd better come over as soon as I could. When I got here an hour later . . ." the voice turned into a sob, "she was dead."

"Dead?" Buzz repeated the word stupidly. "She can't be dead."

Larry was crying openly now. "She hanged herself, Dad. I found her in the basement." He struggled for control. "The police were here. They've taken her away. I didn't let them see the note. It was sealed and addressed to you. Why did she do it? For God's sake, why did she kill herself?"

"I'll be home as soon as I can," Buzz said. "I'm a few hours away, but I'll be there, Son. I'm sorry you had to go though this, Larry. Finding her like that, I mean. I . . . I'd better leave now."

In a daze he raced back to the city, his mind accepting with terrible clarity what he'd not understood that morning. This was how Dorothy planned to keep him from marrying Frances. She knew him well. Knew there'd be no happiness for him with her rival while the specter of the suicide they'd caused hung over his head. The price of her own life was not too great for Dorothy to pay if it meant the final, ultimate revenge she was determined to have. He could not yet feel sorrow for her death. He did not know, would never know, that her deranged mind saw her final act as a sacrifice for him. He knew only, with bitterness, that the self-destructive destroy the lives of the living. Dorothy had destroyed his. No logic, no persuasion would take away his guilt. His whole life would be spent in self-reproach for the selfishness which had sent a woman to her last moments in the basement of their house.

He let out a great sob. The brief thread of happiness he'd reached for had turned into an ugly, unforgettable noose that would sway forever from the rafters of his mind.

After Allie and Jack and John Peck departed and Barbara wandered off to her room, Frances paced the downstairs of her parents' house, listening every minute for the phone, wondering angrily why she hadn't heard from Buzz all day. A little before six, she couldn't stand it any longer. To hell with what Dorothy thought. By now, if Buzz hadn't told her, she would. She dialed the Paiges' number and a young man answered.

"Is Mr. Paige at home?"

"No. This is his son. Who's calling?"

Frances hesitated. "I'm a friend. It's a personal call. Can you tell me where to reach him?"

"No, I can't. We've been trying to find him all afternoon ourselves. Who is this?" Larry asked again.

"Frances Déspres. I was Frances Dalton. I'm an old friend of your parents. If your father isn't there, may I speak to your mother, please?"

The voice shook. "I'm afraid that's impossible, Mrs. Déspres. My mother died suddenly this afternoon. That's why we're trying to locate my father. He doesn't know yet."

Fran was speechless for a moment and then she said, "Died? How can that be? She wasn't ill. What happened?"

"I'm sorry, but I can't discuss it now. Please forgive me. Good-bye."

The phone clicked into place and Fran sat staring at the receiver. Dorothy dead? Had she had a stroke or been in an accident? And where was Buzz? Why didn't he know about this? Why hadn't he called her all day? What in God's name was going on? She flew up the stairs to Barbara's room and burst in. Her sister was sitting quietly in a chair by the window. One small light burned on the dresser but Barbara was gazing out into the darkness, lost in her thoughts.

"Barbara! I just called Buzz's house. Dorothy's dead!"

The younger woman turned, startled out of her reverie. "What are you talking about?"

"It's true. I just spoke to one of their sons. Buzz isn't there. He hasn't been home all day, apparently." Fran was suddenly conscious of the darkness. "For God's sake, why are you sitting here in the gloom? This room is like the black hole of Calcutta!" Fran quickly turned on two more lights. "There. That's better. What do you think could have happened?"

"I have no idea. It's terrible! I can't believe it!"

Frances suddenly looked frightened. "He was going to tell her about us. My God, you don't suppose they got into an argument and he killed her!"

"Frances! What are you saying? What a horrible idea! Of course that didn't happen! How could you even think such a thing?"

"Well, where is he? Why haven't I heard from him all day? Why is his family looking for him?"

"I don't know, but I know it isn't that. Buzz could never harm anyone. She must have had a heart attack, something totally unexpected like that."

"You mean as a result of Buzz saying he was leaving? That's all I'd need! Buzz blaming himself for her death. Oh, Jesus, why doesn't he call?"

"Pull yourself together!" Barbara's voice was commanding. "We don't know anything yet. We'll just have to wait until we hear. Let me get you a drink. Sit here quietly and try to compose yourself and I'll be back in a minute. You have a bottle in your room, haven't you?"

Fran nodded. "Top right-hand drawer. Thanks. I could use one."

As she got the whiskey from Fran's bureau, Barbara couldn't repress an actual feeling of dislike for her sister. She has no heart, Barb thought. Not an ounce of sympathy for that poor, dead woman. Only the fear that Buzz might be a runaway murderer or that Dorothy's death might somehow interfere with their plans. That's all she cares about—her own convenience. It's all she's ever cared about.

She took the drink back to Frances, who gulped it gratefully and sighed. "Maybe it's all for the best. Her dying, I mean. It solves a lot of problems, after all."

Barb stared at her in horror.

"You know what I mean," Fran went on. "I know Buzz didn't kill her. You're right about that. He could never do such a thing. And if she did have a heart attack, he won't be stupid enough to hold himself responsible. I'll see that he doesn't. That's an act of God, after all. No one can blame himself for that." She glanced up at Barbara. "You don't have to look at me that way. As though I'm some heartless monster. I can't pretend to be sorry she's gone. She contributed nothing to anyone, not even to herself. At least Buzz will be free, and I'll make him happy. I really will, Barb. You'll see. I love him."

"No," Barbara said slowly, "you don't. You don't love anyone. Not even yourself. In fact, I think you hate yourself, Fran. You've been on a self-destruct pattern all your life. I never realized it before, but everything you touch turns bad. You *make* it turn bad."

"What the hell are you talking about?"

"You don't give a damn how your running away from home affected Mother and Dad. You used your first husband to escape and married your second for money. And God knows what the third was like, but you must have driven him away too. Now you come back here and mess up the lives of some perfectly normal, contented people. You get Buzz crazy and worry Mother and Dad to death and now . . ." Her voice trailed off.

"And now," Frances said angrily, "I suppose you think I'm somehow responsible for Dorothy Paige's death. Wonderful! What lovely, sweet, sisterly devotion! You probably wish Charles Tallent's wife would conveniently die. Oh, you'd never admit it!

You're far too goody-goody for that! But you'd be just as relieved if that happened as I am right now, and if you had an ounce of honesty in you, you'd admit it, instead of going through this nauseating self-sacrificing renunciation! Don't talk to me about loving! When I love, I take what I want. I'm not some hypocritical little martyr who sleeps with a woman's husband and hasn't enough guts to stand up and fight for him! Okay. I might be all the things you said, but I'm not the phony you are. I'm glad Dorothy Paige is dead. I'm glad I can have her husband. I'm goddamn grateful for the way it's worked out, for his sake and mine. And I don't feel guilty, little sister, for any part of it. Guilt is not an emotion I enjoy."

Barbara turned away. "How could you enjoy it? You don't know the meaning of it."

Fran walked to the door. "It must be lovely to be a living saint, but isn't it painful to have headaches from your halo?"

"Get out of this room!" Barbara screamed. "Get out of my life! I'm ashamed that you're my sister!"

Chapter 27

The call Frances waited for did not come until midmorning of the day after Dorothy Paige accomplished her "ultimate revenge." By the time Buzz telephoned, the morning paper already carried a small obituary notice, noting only the fact of his wife's death, "suddenly, at her home," and listing the surviving husband and children. Funeral services, it said, would be private.

At the breakfast table, Laura, who religiously read this page first, let out a gasp that made Sam look up from the sports pages.

"What's the matter?"

"I can't believe it! Dorothy Paige died yesterday!"

"You don't mean it! How?"

Laura shook her head. "It doesn't say. I can't imagine. How terrible, Sam! She was only forty-nine. Dear Lord, I wonder what happened! Poor Buzz!"

For a moment, both the Daltons had forgotten the Paiges' connection with Frances. The realization dawned almost simultaneously, and they looked at each other, the same question in their minds. Laura gave voice to it first.

"I wonder if Frances knows."

"Doubt it."

"She was awfully quiet at dinner last night. Hardly touched a bite of her food."

"No more quiet than Barbara," Sam said, "but it did occur to me that except for the party it was the first evening Frances stayed home since she got here." He frowned. "I also thought she'd been drinking. Did you?"

Reluctantly, "Yes."

They sat in troubled silence for a few moments, communicating wordlessly in the way of people who've lived together most of their lives. Humanly, shocked and sorry as they were to hear about Dorothy, their thoughts were of their daughter. What would this mean to her? Would it clear the way, after a respectable period of mourning, for Buzz and Frances to decently marry? Was it, terrible thought, some kind of divine providence that would keep them all from another scandal? Each knew what the other was involuntarily thinking and was ashamed.

"I'd better tell Frances," Laura finally said.

There was, as she soon discovered, no need to tell Frances. Newspaper in hand, she walked into her daughter's bedroom and found her sitting up in bed, wide-awake and smoking a cigarette. The full ashtray beside her was mute evidence that she'd been awake most of the night. Before Laura could speak, Fran said, "I know about Dorothy Paige, Mother. I called the house yesterday afternoon, looking for Buzz, and his son told me."

Laura sat on the foot of the bed. "How did it happen? Had she been ill?"

"Not that I know of. I don't have a clue what happened. And Buzz hasn't had the good grace to call."

"Frances! What do you expect of him? The man's wife has just died, suddenly. He hardly could be expected to be on the telephone himself informing his friends!"

Frances stubbed out one cigarette and lit another. "I'm not exactly a 'friend,' Mother. Remember? I'm the woman he was leaving his wife for. That would seem to put me in a very special category, wouldn't you think?"

"I don't know what to think," Laura said. "I can't even imagine how this could have happened."

"There are all sorts of possibilities." Fran reached for her robe. "Anyway, I presume I'll hear something this morning."

Like Barbara, Laura was appalled by Fran's coldness. "How can you be so detached about this, Frances? A very nice woman has died too young. Her husband and children must be shocked and grieving. I know you and Buzz planned to go away together, but this puts a different light on things."

"Does it? Only a more respectable one, I'd think. Instead of running off, we can get properly married right away." Fran turned from the mirror where she was brushing her hair. "Or do you think we're going through those silly, outmoded gestures of waiting a year and pretending Buzz is mourning for a wife he didn't love and was ready to leave? Really, Mother! This isn't the turn of the century, you know. I'm sorry Dorothy's dead, but I can't pretend I consider it a great tragedy. And I'll be very surprised if Buzz turns out to be so hypocritical that he'll act the part of the bereaved husband."

"He's a decent man, Frances. He'll do what's expected of him."

"And what is that, may I ask? Should he go about weeping for twelve months, pretending Dorothy was the greatest woman who ever lived? God, if there's anything I can't stand it's the widow or widower who's been unhappily married and suddenly begins to act as though the person who died was a saint! I see it all the time, especially with women married to absolute stinkers. Just let those men die and you'd think they'd been paragons of kindness and virtue! It turns my stomach. Death doesn't automatically beatify a rotten human being. And Dorothy Paige was a rotten human being. If Buzz pretends otherwise, I'll spit in his eye!"

Laura was momentarily speechless. "I've never heard such terrible talk!" she finally said. "How can you be so heartless?"

"It isn't heartless, Mother. It's realistic. People don't wear black and refuse invitations any more. Men especially. It's a good thing Buzz's future is already planned. If this had happened before I came back, every widow and divorcee in Denver would be after him twenty minutes after the funeral. And thirty minutes after *that* he'd be out enjoying his new role as an eligible man. It's a different world, dear. One you can't understand."

"I suppose not. I'm not sure I want to. Do Barbara and Alice know what's happened?"

"Alice doesn't, as far as I know. She went out after that peculiar get-together yesterday, remember? But Barb knows. I told her, after I talked to Buzz's son yesterday." Fran shrugged. "We had quite a set-to, as a matter of fact. She thinks I'm as much of a vulture as you do."

"I never said anything of the sort, Frances."

"Darling, you don't have to. I can read that anxious look from across the room. Don't worry. I'll play the game for a little while. I'll go to the funeral and look appropriately stricken if that makes everybody happy. I'll be respectful about my 'dear old high school friend' and no one will ever know what was in the works when she died. I'll put on a good show, but none of this changes Buzz's plans or mine."

"I see. You're very sure of yourself and of Buzz, aren't you?"

"Of course. Why shouldn't I be? He doesn't have to live with his crazy guilt about leaving her. The one obstacle I feared has been providentially removed. I'd be a liar if I said I was sorry."

"We still don't know how she died, Frances."

"Does it matter? It must have been quick, an end all of us devoutly wish for ourselves. Buzz wasn't even home when it happened. Dammit, I wish he'd call!"

In midmorning he did, sounding totally unlike himself. When Fran picked up the phone, Buzz said without preamble, "I know you've heard. Larry told me you called here yesterday evening."

"Darling, I'm so sorry! I've been frantic, waiting to hear from you. Are you all right?"

"Yes. As well as could be expected."

Oh, no, Fran thought, slightly annoyed. He's not going to pretend to be crushed. Not with me. She kept her tone gentle and solicitous. "What happened, dear? I know you weren't there. Was it her heart?"

"No. She did it herself after I left the house. We talked. She didn't seem hysterical. In fact, she was reasonably calm but more determined than usual. She said she'd never let me go. I was afraid she meant to do something to you. I never dreamed she planned . . ."

Fran was suddenly shaken. She'd thought of everything from an accident or a massive stroke to the unlikely and quickly dismissed idea of murder. But suicide had never crossed her mind. It took a moment for the implications of such an act to sink in. Dorothy Paige knew what unbearable remorse her husband would feel. Much worse than if he'd left her. This was her way of making sure he'd never marry Frances. In her crazed mind, Dorothy conceived the one deterrent to Buzz and Fran's plans. If her husband felt he and his mistress were responsible for his wife's suicide, he'd never forgive himself. As for marrying "the other woman," the idea would be impossible. She'd be there every day, reminding him of the tragedy they'd precipitated. Damn you, Dorothy Paige! Fran screamed inwardly. Damn you to eternal hell! She willed herself to be calm. She was stronger than Dorothy alive, and she'd be stronger than Dorothy dead. She'd beat her yet.

"Buzz, dear, that's horrible! Horrible for you and your children. Thank God you knew she was not able to think rationally. The poor woman didn't know what she was doing. I'm so sorry for all of you, having to go through this. What can I do? Can I be of any help?"

"No. No, thank you. Everything's being taken care of. The boys and their wives have been wonderful. I'm afraid I haven't been good for much. But thank you for offering."

So polite. So distant. As though she were some old acquaintance offering sympathy and friendly assistance. Fran felt cold inside.

"I'd like to see you, as soon as you feel up to it."

"Yes, of course. In a few days when everything is . . . over."

"A few days when everything is over," Fran thought. My God, he's already dismissed me. Us. No. I won't let him. I'll give him time to come out of shock. Then I'll talk to him gently, sensibly. I've always been able to make him see things my way. I will again.

"Of course, dear. I understand. We'll all, the family I mean, see you at the services."

Buzz hesitated. "They'll be private, Fran. Just our family. But after that . . . well, I'll be in touch."

"I see. That's probably better. I'll wait to hear from you." She paused, uncertain whether to say it. "I love you, Buzz."

There was a moment of silence on the other end. Wrong, Fran thought. Wrong thing to say at this moment. Damn. She was stupid.

"Goodbye for now, dear," she said.

"Goodbye."

In Washington, Charles Tallent picked up the mail from the box outside his house and wandered back, sorting through the bills, the "junk," the letters for Andrea, who kept up a voluminous personal correspondence with old friends. At the bottom of the stack was an envelope in familiar handwriting. He'd seen it hundreds of times on love notes left in the Georgetown apartment, little notes to greet him when he occasionally got there ahead of Barbara, messages pinned to his pillow on those rare times when he could stay overnight and awaken to find his darling making breakfast while he slept. The sight of the round, honest handwriting and the Denver postmark gave him a little jolt of joy. And then, almost as though he knew the contents were not happy, he dropped the other mail on the hall table, pushed the letter into the pocket of his robe and went into his study to read it in private.

He sat for a long time after he finished, trying to sort out his emotions. It was a phony. He knew it was. It came from Barbara, all right. No doubt about that. But it wasn't the truth. He knew her too well. This was not a woman who suddenly would have a "revelation" about her life, certainly not in the space of a week. She'd been home many times before, and the sight of her parents' companionship had never made her feel differently. If anything, those visits had only seemed to reinforce her happiness about her life with him in Washington. She'd always been so glad to come back, so lightheartedly grateful, in a kind way, to have escaped the dull, predictable routine of so many of her contemporaries in Denver.

"Thank God I got away!" Charles could hear her saying. "What if I'd married one of those hometown boys and been doomed to a life of diapers and drip-dry dresses!"

And now she was trying to make him believe that all she wanted was security and serenity with some nice middle-class life-companion. She was trying to fool herself. Or more likely, she was trying to fool him. For some reason, Barbara was making it easy for him. Could she conceivably have heard about the either-or offer of the Candidate? No way. No one knew except the Senator and his closest advisers. And Andrea.

Intuitively, he knew there was no "other man." No stalwart protector who'd suddenly come into her life to rescue her from a futile future. That was as much bunk as the nonsense about the happiness of her parents or the "make believe" world she and

Charles had shared for years. The whole letter was a loving sham. Somehow Barbara did know how he was suffering over the selfish decision he had to make. This was her way of letting him off easily, caring for his happiness more than she did for her own. Someone had gotten to her, had made her feel it her duty to step aside, to spare him the terrible task of telling her that the wonderful thing they shared was over. Someone who knew she could not stand in his way because she loved him too much. And that same someone knew he might be unable to go through with the ending of his affair if he came face to face with the woman he adored.

There was only one person that knowledgeable, that devious and selfish. Only one that bitter. And he was married to her.

He started toward the door, to find Andrea and accuse her, but a rush of emotion stopped him. It would demean Barbara to discuss her letter with his wife. Damned if he'd give Andrea the satisfaction of knowing her plan had worked. And it was her plan. She knew where to reach Barb, and reach her she had, as certainly as his name was Charles Tallent. Who are you, Charles Tallent? he asked himself. Or, more aptly, *what* are you? Some wind-up toy who marches stiffly in any direction strong and clever people care to send you? Some helpless piece of putty to be manipulated to please others? It had pleased the Candidate, no doubt, to find him so quickly amenable to the idea of changing his whole life. It must have been sweet to Andrea to know that she had outwaited, outlasted and finally outmaneuvered Barb. My God, what is happening to me? Charles wondered. Am I so caught up in this power-crazed city that I'm willing to give up the only thing in the world that makes sense to me? What little shred of importance, or even what remote dreams of the future make me think that life is worthwhile without the only human being I really care for? Who could even remember the names of past Cabinet members? What real chance did he have of ever stepping into the Senator's shoes eight years from now? Damned little. He was a very low man on the big political totem pole. And even if he were not, how did all this stack up against what he'd pay for temporary prominence, or even for a possible place in history?

He knew suddenly why he'd let Andrea talk him out of going to Denver with her rational "Don't embarrass Barbara" arguments. He knew why he dreaded facing his love. It was wrong, and he'd known it all along. His whole life was wrong. A half-life which seemed enough until he was faced with losing even the small, wonderful part he had.

A feeling of peace came over him, as though he'd mercifully been relieved of a terrible burden. Andrea had done him a great favor. Ironic that her great coup had backfired. She must have spent so much time working out the convoluted, intricate scheme. He smiled. All he had to do was abdicate. Other men had given up much more for women they desired. What were those touching words spoken by a truly powerful man almost forty years before? Something about "I cannot faithfully discharge my duties without the help and support of the woman I love." I'm no king, Charles thought, but I know how he felt. It took courage. It would not be without some small twinge of regret for what might have been. But this was nothing compared to the knowledge of how lonely and pointless it would be with no one to share his triumphs, whatever they might be.

He glanced at the desk clock. Eight-thirty. Six-thirty in the morning in Denver. Too early to awaken a sleeping Dalton household, even for this. Besides, he wanted to put his declaration in writing, even if it were only on the yellow page of a telegram.

Charles picked up the phone. "I want to send two wires," he told the Western Union operator. "The first is to Miss Barbara Dalton, 1016 South Carona, Denver, Colorado. And the second is to Senator Wilson Dermott, Horizon Manor, Burlington, Vermont."

Janice moved her head gingerly on the pillow, but the movement was enough to awaken Clint.

"Good morning." He reached out and tenderly stroked her brow.

Jan groaned. "A matter of opinion. Darling, would you mind not doing that? This morning, even my hair hurts."

"Hung over, huh? You deserve it."

"Thank you. I shall go to my grave remembering those sweet, understanding words."

"You're a terrible grouch when you wake up."

"Right now I wish I couldn't wake up for about forty-eight hours." But then she grinned. "It's worth it, though. That is, I'm trying to tell myself it is. It was a great evening, wasn't it? Super-special."

Clint Darby returned her smile. "It was an extraordinary evening, to say the least. You and I and your nice gay brother and his friend and your half-brother's pregnant wife all celebrating the reunion of your mother with her illegitimate child. Now that, I would say, is a rare combination of people and circumstances. I think that's what I love about you. You come up with such inventive gatherings. So sophisticated."

"Don't make it sound like something out of Noel Coward. It was sweet. The way Chris and Carol took to each other was nice. Really nice. I like her, you know. She's a helluva woman when you get to know her. She was so happy for John and Mother. I mean, we all were, but especially Carol. She's some crazy for her husband. And so pleased about the baby. It's a damned shame she can't go to Denver and meet Mother. They'll get along like gangbusters when they do meet." Jan's voice trailed off. "Whenever that is."

Clint sat up on the side of the bed and stretched.

"Yeah. It doesn't sound like your mother's coming back, does it? I mean, not to that wonderful husband of hers anyway."

"No. And she shouldn't, God knows! She should have split years ago. Maybe she would have, if it hadn't been for Chris and me. It makes me feel terrible to think she might have gone through all she did just to keep a house together for us. We'd all have been better off if she'd had the guts years ago to tell him to get lost. You heard her on the phone when she and John called last night. She sounded so carefree. I haven't heard her sound that way ever." Janice sat up and let out another moan. "Oh, lord, that was a mistake." She slid down under the covers again. "I think I won't move for several days. It could be hazardous to my health."

"You're a nut." Clint looked at her soberly. "Jan, you mustn't think you were to blame for your mother's staying with Spencer. Some women do that kind of thing out of fear. Fear that they can't take care of themselves. Or they do it out of an irrational feeling of worthlessness. A need to be punished for imagined inadequacy. That was the case with Alice. We know that now. She had such terrible guilts about John. And now they're gone and she's free. Free of the inferiority. And free of that bastard, your father."

"Yes. I know. I'm so glad for her, Clint. She's a nice lady. I only hope it isn't too late for her."

"How so?"

"Well, what's she going to do now? You know my father won't meekly give her a divorce. He's much too vicious for that." Jan frowned. "Is it sick to hate your father?"

"No, love. Not when he's a miserable sonofabitch. You're too intelligent to think you have to love him just because he's your father. Look at Chris. Chris openly hates him. And why not? Your brother may lead an 'unconventional' life, but his instincts are good all the way. Look how he took the news about John Peck. No 'disappointment' in his mother. Nothing but joy that she has another child to love. He's okay. He and John will like each other when they meet. My God, it's all too much happiness around here suddenly! Good thing I'm not a diabetic. I'd go into a coma from all this sweetness!"

"I'm still worried about Mother. I don't think Dad will give her a divorce. And if he does, what then? Will she stay in Denver and live with my grandparents? She won't have enough money to come back here and live."

"She has three kids who would gladly support her, Jan. Four, if you count me."

Janice looked at him lovingly. "That's dear. But I don't think she'd let us take care of her. She wouldn't live with Chris and David when they offered a long while ago. She certainly wouldn't move in with John and Carol. Or you and me. I don't know. I don't think she could be happy going back to her parents' home after all the years of running her own establishment. She's really displaced, isn't she? She's seen her dream come true, but where does she go from here?"

"Maybe she'll move in with Richards. Even if good old Spencer won't divorce her, she could live with John's father. He's alone too."

Despite the seriousness of it, Jan began to giggle. "It's almost too much. My quiet, proper little mother. I wouldn't have believed she wasn't a virgin when she married. Or that years later she'd tell her husband to go to hell. Or that we'd be discussing her 'living in sin' with the father of her child! I'm having a hard time adjusting to this new view of her. To me, she's a wife and mother. Period."

"Are they such awful things to be?" Clint took her hand and kissed the palm. "Lately I've been thinking of you in those roles. Maybe about time I made an honest, pregnant woman of you. What do you think?"

Janice stared. "Get married? Have a baby? Us?"

"Well, you don't have to say it as though I suggested we go out and rip off a bank! Is it such an awful idea? You don't have to stop working. I mean, just long enough to have the kid. Look at Carol. She's not planning to shrivel up and die because she and John are going to have a baby. Hell, we don't even have to rush into that part. Let's get married and see what happens."

"I didn't think you wanted . . ."

"And I didn't think *you* wanted. So we're even. But I want. Do you?"

Jan looked at him searchingly. "I don't think I knew until this moment how much I do. I thought marriage was superfluous. Kids, too. But in the last few days, seeing everything around me . . ."

"Sorry. That won't do. There's only one reason to get married."

"What's that?"

"It's called 'advertised love,' baby. It's wanting everybody in the world to know that we respect each other enough to share more than two names on the mailbox. It's old-fashioned, sentimental, corny, terrific, unchanging pride in announcing that the one person you think is perfect thinks the same of you." His handsome face was very serious. "We have a commitment, you and I. We don't need a paper to make it stick. But we need that piece of paper for our egos, believe it or not. Not for kids. Not for respectability, Jan. For us. For what we still believe in. Miss Winters, here in the sanctity of our premarital bed, will you do me the honor of becoming my wife?"

She sat up and kissed him gently. "Mr. Darby, I'd be delighted." A look of amazement crossed her face. "Hey, my hangover's gone! Can a proposal of marriage cure the morning-after blahs?"

"If so," Clint said solemnly, "we'll bottle it and make a fortune."

Midway in the process of throwing a clean shirt and his shaving equipment into an attaché case, Spencer Winters suddenly stopped. He had his first-class ticket to Denver and his hotel reservation efficiently dispatched the evening before by that sniveling secretary of his. But he hadn't been thinking clearly when he ordered them. What in hell was he rushing back to that hick town for? To bodily drag Alice home? To punch out that arrogant John Peck, who'd simply taken matters into his own hands and gone to find the woman he claimed was his mother? It was a stupid waste of time to fly thousands of miles to accomplish what was going to happen anyway. That screaming match on the phone with Alice, added to the nonappearance of her alleged son in Spencer's office and the final break with Janice had thrown his usually orderly mind into emotional chaos. This morning, things were clearer. It was beneath him to rush across the country like some hysterical, rejected husband. He was about to respond exactly as Alice wanted. It would please her to see him make a spectacle of himself in front of other people. As for that Peck person, Spencer would deal with him when he came back to Boston. He'd deal with Alice too. Because she'd come back. She had to. Where else would she go? It was easy enough, safely removed from him, to say the extraordinary things she'd screamed at him the day before. It was no trick to declare independence when a couple of thousand miles of telephone wire protected her. She wouldn't be so sure of herself when she walked back into his house. She was going to pay for this rebellion. And she was going to keep her mouth shut about the whole messy incident. "Long-lost child" indeed! Spencer grimaced. Somehow, he'd prove Peck was a phony, a clever opportunist trying to take advantage of a stupid woman like Alice.

No, there was no need to go charging out there to waste time on a silly woman who talked about "starting a new life for herself." He didn't love her. Privately, he'd be just as glad if she followed through with her nonsense about a divorce. But losing anything he possessed was foreign to Spencer's image of himself. And that included the approval of J. B. Thompson and the other partners in the firm. Alice was necessary to that image, which revolved around a steady, conservative home life with no hint of scandal. That's what the world thought he had. That's what he would keep. All he had to do was sit back and wait for his idiot wife to come to her senses. Bolstered by that trashy family of hers, she probably thought she *could* start over, as she'd said. But when she found herself without funds, and removed from the comforts she was used to, she'd see there was no answer except to come home. And if nothing else, she'd never be able to live away from those obnoxious children of theirs. If nothing else would bring her back to Boston, Janice and Christopher would. She was too fatuous to lose her daily contact with them.

He felt better. He'd been about to do something rash and oddly disorganized for a man who prided himself on his analytical powers. Damn these undisciplined people like Alice who could throw even the most rational man temporarily off base! No matter. All he had to do now was let nature take its inevitable course.

He called his office and told Martha Perrone to cancel his flight and his Denver hotel. He'd be in the office later.

"You've changed your plans, Mr. Winters?" Why did the woman sound relieved?

"No," Spencer said sarcastically. "I'm flying out on my Superman cape and staying at the Governor's mansion. Obviously, I've changed my plans, Miss Perrone! I don't telephone you for the sheer pleasure of hearing your refined voice!"

He banged the receiver back into its cradle. Women! He was surrounded by foolish women—his wife, his daughter, even his secretary. What was that thing Hitler had once said? Oh, yes, "The greater the man, the more insignificant the woman." That was the damned truth. Old Adolf had had the right idea about that. Spencer had believed it all his life.

Chapter 28

As he slowly dressed in a dark suit and knotted his black four-in-hand tie, Buzz still couldn't believe it was true. He forced himself to say the words silently. "Dorothy is dead. Dorothy killed herself. She didn't want to live." For the tenth time, he reread the almost childish scrawl that had been her last message to him, the brief note Larry had considerately kept from everyone else's eyes.

> I don't have to explain this to you, Buzz. Life is over for me. You were a good husband, but you never loved me. I loved you, though. So much that I don't want to be around to see you belong to someone else. This is better for everybody. Kiss the children for me. And don't be sorry. Dorothy.

It crossed his mind, almost irrelevantly, that even in her final words she would not mention Fran's name. She'd been jealous of Frances since they were all teen-agers, never able to compete with her in any way, not in her whole life. She could compete only in death. And she'd won that last battle. She hadn't killed only herself. She'd destroyed Buzz's ceaseless obsession with her rival. It was finally over for him and Fran. No passion, no insane infatuation was stronger than the memory of despair. They'd killed a desperately weak woman who couldn't face the loneliness and rejection her husband and his mistress selfishly demanded she accept.

Standing there, waiting to go to the funeral, his body shook with sobs. He wept for Dorothy. Poor, inadequate Dorothy, who tried so hard, in her own way, to take another woman's place in his heart. She'd been irrational in the past, foolish and irritating and sometimes hostile. But yesterday morning she was none of those things. She knew exactly what she was doing when she made that noose and stood on a wooden chair and kicked it . . . Buzz stopped. He couldn't think about it. He refused to remember the way she looked when he went to identify the body. But he'd never forget it, much as he wanted to. She'd made that impossible. If only he could hate her for what she'd done to all of them. If only he could stop hating himself.

He was grateful that the boys, with a maturity of understanding beyond their years, had suggested that the final, awful business be completed quickly. The terrible night before, Larry had taken charge, his brothers and their young wives backing him up.

"Dad, I don't think we should make this a long, drawn-out thing." His son's voice had been firm but gentle. "Mother wanted to be cremated. We feel it should be tomorrow, if you agree."

Buzz had simply nodded, wondering how much they knew and whether they felt shame for what Dorothy had done or hatred for the father who'd caused it. As though Larry read his mind, the young man said, "She hadn't been herself for years. You know that better than anyone. Don't feel guilty, Dad. You were good to her always. It's rotten it had to end this way, but maybe . . . maybe it was inevitable."

Buzz had pressed his son's hand, unable to speak. If the children knew anything, they'd never say so. They wouldn't compound the sense of failure they recognized in him. They'd be kind and thoughtful as they were now. Larry's wife put her hand on his arm. "It's hard, Dad. We can only imagine how hard. But you'll be all right. Give it time."

He'd tried to smile. She was so sweet. So amazingly wise for a little thing in her early twenties. What would she think if she knew the truth? What would any of them think if they knew where he'd spent the night before Dorothy's death? He shuddered. He wasn't so foolish, even in this moment of shock, to think he'd never pick up his life again. He would. But not with

Fran. Never with Fran. That, at least, would give some meaning to what Dorothy had done.

"Barbara, do you think it would be out of place for me to call on Buzz in the next few days?"

"Out of place? No, I don't think so, dear." Barb looked affectionately at her troubled mother. "You were always fond of him and you liked Dorothy. It's better to do what you'd ordinarily do under such circumstances."

"Yes, but . . . well, that business with Frances. Your father thinks it would be shameful for any of us to go near the Paiges. He's not taking this well. Not since we heard she . . . she died by her own hand."

"I think it would be worse if we acted as if we didn't care."

Laura sighed. "That's the way I feel. But Sam . . ." She hesitated. "Barbara, how do you think this will affect Frances? Her plans with Buzz, I mean, I don't mean to sound awful. That poor girl isn't even buried yet. But do you think the two of them . . . ?"

"No, Mother, I don't. Not now. Not because of Fran. Because of Buzz. I'm afraid he's going to blame himself."

Laura was silent. Nothing seemed to go right these days. She felt constantly fearful. Why was that? Last night she'd dreamed an awful dream. A nightmare. She'd been running around in a chicken yard, chasing three fluttering, frightened hens. She wanted to catch them, to put them back in their nests where they'd be warm and safe, but they kept slipping away from her. She went round and round the place for a long while, calling to them, reaching out to pick them up, but they wriggled out of her grasp. And then finally a man—she didn't know who he was—came out with a big axe and grabbed one of the hens, and Laura screamed that he mustn't kill her. The scream had been real, apparently. She'd been awakened to find Sam shaking her and commanding her to wake up, that she was having a nightmare. She'd been happy to. It had been so terrifying, and it made no sense. She'd been afraid to go back to sleep, fearful she'd have the same dream, but she hadn't. She'd merely slept fitfully the rest of the night.

"Mother?"

Laura came back to the moment. Barbara was looking at her quizzically. "You were a million miles away. We were talking about making a condolence call on Buzz. Do you want me to go with you? Not today, of course. Today's the funeral. Private, Fran says. But maybe tomorrow or the day after."

"I don't know. I mean, I don't know whether any of us should go. But if I do, I'd like you to go with me. How long will you be here, Barbara? I'm not trying to rush you. You know that, but I wondered about your job . . . and about Charles."

"I haven't made up my mind about the job, or Washington. I wrote and told them I needed some time at home." Barb paused. "I also wrote and broke it off with Charles."

"I see." The sadness of the world was in those two words. "You had to, of course. You're so strong, Barbara. So sensible. If only your sisters . . ."

Barbara tried to keep her temper. "If only they *what?* Had my common sense? My discipline? All those phony virtues everybody's constantly endowing me with?" She sounded weary. "I'm so tired of doing 'the right thing.' It's not the way I want to act at all. I want to throw myself on the floor and beat my fists and kick my feet! Does that surprise you, Mother? Of course it does. I'm so self-reliant, so pulled-together. Don't believe it. I'm as selfish as Fran and as frightened as Allie. Or I would be, if I ever allowed myself to show all of you the real Barbara. I'm bloody tired of hearing everybody worry about Fran and Alice. What about me, dammit?" Her voice had risen slightly and there was resentment in it. "Even Charles. Even the man I love expects me to understand that his needs come before mine." She laughed harshly. "And what's even worse, I almost make myself believe it. I'm not strong, Mother. I'm not sensible and forbearing. I'm scared and lonely and fed up with being the pillar of strength around here while Fran drives a woman to suicide and Allie wallows in absolution! It's not fair. It's never been fair!"

Laura didn't look at her. Staring at the floor, she said, quietly, "Nobody asked you to take that role, Barbara. Seems you chose it. Just as the other girls chose theirs."

It was more deflating than any surprise or protest her mother could have registered. Laura was right, of course. You made your own destiny, shaped your own character. And, Barb thought ruefully, took your own licks.

"I'm sorry, Mother. You're right. We're all masochists, your children. Seems as though we each punish ourselves in our own way. What a sorry lot we are! What a trio of messed-up lives. And what heartaches we must give you." Barb smiled. "Never mind, dear. Fran will get over Buzz and I'll recover from Charles. As for Allie, who knows? I suppose she'll marry Jack and live more or less happily ever after. One out of three isn't such a terrific average, but it's better than none at all." She tried to change the subject. "John Peck's a nice young man, isn't he? I'm glad about that. Imagine what it would have been like if he'd turned out to be some terrible, crude, unscrupulous man! That's the danger of letting children find their real parents, I suppose. It could be an invitation to blackmail in the wrong hands. It's not fair to deprive a person of the right to know his origins, but it's not fair to deprive the natural mother or father of his anonymity either."

She realized she was babbling, trying to make Laura forget the earlier outburst. Her mother was only half-listening, though. Her mind was somewhere else. Had been, most of the time. "What's wrong, Mother? You don't seem like yourself today."

Laura was tempted to tell her about the dream. It must have meant something. It was like a fearsome omen. She didn't believe in such things, but this was so vivid. Even awake, she couldn't shake it, couldn't stop thinking that her unconscious was trying to tell her something, trying to warn her. Nonsense. Next she'd begin to think she had some sixth sense or other. It must have been that cheese she had at dinner. She never slept well after she ate cheese at night. You'd think after seventy years, she'd have sense enough to know that.

"Nothing's wrong," she said. "That is, nothing you don't already know about. Heavens, that's enough to make me distracted, don't you think?" Laura got up briskly. "Time to get on with my work. Do you know it's nearly eleven o'clock? Your father will be wanting lunch soon. Will you be in? I suppose Fran will stay in her room. What about Allie?"

"She's getting dressed. I think she and Jack are taking John to lunch and then to the airport this afternoon. He has to get back to Boston." She paused before she said softly, "Mother, do you wish we'd all go away? We're an awful lot of work and worry for you, aren't we?"

"Don't talk foolish, Barbara. You know your father and I love having all of you here. Even if it's not been quite the quiet reunion any of us expected."

Barb couldn't help smiling. That, surely, was the understatement of the week. Of the century. They'd come home to celebrate an anniversary and everybody's life had changed in a matter of days. We have to leave, she realized suddenly. They love us, but our problems are too much for them. Sometimes separation is less distressing than having your loved ones' problems right under your nose. Even devoted parents can reach their limit. Laura had certainly reached hers. Sam probably had too, though most of the time he kept his thoughts to himself. I'll talk to Fran and Allie, Barb thought. Fran knows she's lost Buzz. She must know that. As for Allie, let her make up her mind about Jack. Stay here with him or find some other answer. But we've all got to get out of here and get on with our crazy destinies, whatever they are.

The phone rang again. It had been ringing all morning. First with Jack arranging to pick up Allie. Then Buzz with the terrible message Fran curtly reported before she went up to her room. Probably she's in there drinking, Barb thought. That didn't go well in this house either.

"I'll get it," Barb said.

"This is Western Union," the caller said when she answered. "I have a telegram for Miss Barbara Dalton."

She felt her knees begin to shake. "This is she."

"The message is from Washington, D.C. Shall I read it to you?"

Agony. Why didn't the disembodied voice get on with it? "Yes, please."

In the emotionless tones of a robot the operator began to recite. "Have your letter. Unacceptable due to changes in congressman who has come to his senses. Understand everything. Repeat everything. You are the world's loveliest liar. Come home. I need you and love you as never before. Charles." There was a pause and the voice said, "Shall I repeat that?"

"No. No, thank you."

"Would you like a copy mailed to you?"

Barbara was impassive. "That won't be necessary. I remember every word."

Her sisters stared at her as though she'd taken leave of her senses. In the late afternoon when Alice returned from the airport, still red-eyed from her emotional parting scene with Johnny, Barbara dragged her into Fran's room and firmly closed the door. Then she told them she thought it was about time they all got out from underfoot.

"We're overstaying our welcome," Barb said. "The folks aren't up to all the chaos we've created. I realized it today. I'm going to get going and leave them in peace, and I think it would be a good idea if you two did the same."

"Leave?" Alice asked incredulously. "Why? Why would they want us to?"

"Because they're no longer used to a houseful of people. They can't handle all this, Allie. It isn't just the extra work for Mother, though that can't be easy. It's that we upset their routine, give them things to worry about that they don't know about when we're not here. They're not ancient, but they're not young. I think they'd like nothing better than to be alone again."

"But we're their children!" Alice said. "I don't understand your thinking. If my children wanted to spend time with me, I'd be overjoyed! I don't think you know what you're talking about, Barbara. I think Mother and Dad are delighted to have us here. And it isn't as though we plan to stay forever. My lord, it's the first time they've had us all together in thirty years! I don't see what the rush is."

Barbara sighed. Why didn't Allie come out and say what she really was thinking? It wasn't that she was so anxious to stay in this house. It was that she hadn't made up her mind where she was going to go when she left it. Probably the same was true of Fran, who hadn't said a word so far. Barb turned to her older sister.

"What do you think, Fran? Don't you think it's time we moved on?"

"I don't know about you two, but I'm not leaving Denver. Not just yet. Maybe you're right about not staying in the house. I'll probably go to a hotel. Fact is, I'd rather. I always hated this place. But I'm sticking around town awhile."

The words were spoken very slowly, very deliberately. She's half-sloshed, Barb realized. She's probably been drinking all afternoon, sitting up here trying to figure out what to do about Buzz. Fran hadn't reported much about her phone call. Only that Dorothy's death was suicide and the services private, but Barbara knew there was more. It didn't take a genius to understand the remorse Buzz Paige must be feeling. Or the fact that he probably never wanted to see the woman who'd pushed him to Dorothy's breaking point. She isn't going to accept that, Barb thought sadly. She still thinks she's going to get Buzz if she stays around and waits for the shock to wear off. Both she and Allie are trying to buy time, just as I was. It was no good playing games with these women. Somehow they had to be made to face their situations. Barbara took a deep breath and plunged in.

"Listen," she said almost desperately, "we've all got to come to a decision. Allie, I know you're confused about the future. None of us wants to see you go back to Spencer, but if you don't, then you've got to make up your mind what you *are* going to do. Jack will marry you, if that's what you want. Hell, you can even go live with him until you get a divorce. And Fran, darling, you must be realistic about Buzz. He's probably going to take a long time to recover from this. Your staying around will only be agonizing for both of you. Why don't you go back to Europe? He'll come for you when he's ready." It was a kind lie. Barb hadn't the heart to say that Buzz undoubtedly wanted nothing more than to put Frances out of his life. Let her think that she was giving him breathing space; that when he'd gotten over this they'd be reunited.

But Frances wasn't buying it. "No way, kiddo. I'm camping right here in town for the so-called 'decent interval of mourning.' Buzz Paige wants me and now he's free to have me. The fact is, he can't wait! Oh, he may not know it right now, but he will. And soon. Do you think I'd be such a damned fool as to go off and let some of these local vultures get to him when he's at his most vul . . . vulnerable?" Her words were a little slurred. "Forget it. Butt out, babe. Allie and I are big girls. We can handle our own lives without a lot of unasked-for advice from you." She smiled unpleasantly. "Doesn't seem to me you've done so well with your own troubles. At least Allie and I haven't been kicked out by some quote wonderful, faithful lover unquote. What are you going to do, Sister dear, when you so nobly leave the nest again? Moon around Washington, hoping for a glimpse of the great man? Go into faith-healing? Maybe you can get a job on the *Post* writing a lovelorn column, since you think you're so damned good at it!"

Barbara's anger was greater than her compassion for this blind, self-indulgent woman. Her words came hotly, heedlessly as she struck back. "*I'm* not the one who's been kicked out, Fran. *You* are. Buzz will never want to set eyes on you again. If it hadn't been for you, Dorothy Paige would be alive today! You're a fool. A dangerous, blind fool! Don't you know Buzz must hate you as much as he hates himself?"

Fran smiled, a superior, condescending smile. "Darling little Barbara. Taking out her own disappointment on someone sensible enough not to play the martyr. A fool, am I? Well, we'll see. When I'm in a warm bed with Buzz Paige and you're at the movies with your girlfriends, we'll see who's a fool. You'll never understand men, dear girl. You never have. No doubt that's why you've never really had one of your own."

There was a moment of silence while Fran continued to smile and Barbara drew back, aghast at her sister's words and ashamed of her own. At last she said, "Fran, this is silly. We don't mean the things we've said. We're all upset. That's why we're carrying on like this. Come on. Let's talk about the situation calmly. We should leave here. Even you and I agree on that. You're probably right. I shouldn't presume to advise you two on what to do after that, but I'm sure Mother and Dad should have their nice, peaceful life back again. She turned to Alice, who'd been listening in horrified silence to the other two. "Allie? Don't you think we should all go?"

Alice looked at her helplessly. "I don't know. It's safe here and I don't know what would happen to me if I left. I'm afraid of Spencer. Of what he might do if I moved in with Jack. He might kill me, Barb."

"Oh, for God's sake!" Fran's impatience was now directed at Alice. "He hasn't killed you in twenty-five years. He's a bluff, can't you see that? A damned, egomaniacal bully! And you're as crazy as he is! What the hell's the matter with you, Allie? Jack

Richards is willing to take you in. Where do think you'll get a better offer? Or do you want to go back to Boston and let Spencer treat you like the dirt you think you are? You make me sick. You're so bloody pious and timid. You're afraid of life, afraid to slug it out because somebody might harm you."

Alice didn't fight back. She simply said, "I can't argue with what you're saying, Fran. But there's something else. I don't know whether I love Jack. Or even whether he really loves me. I wouldn't want him to take me in out of pity or guilt. I wouldn't want to go that way either."

"Stop it, Fran!" Barbara's voice was strong. "We're not solving anything by hurling accusations at one another."

Fran poured herself another drink. "I don't know. I think it's all rather refreshing. Healthy to say what we've always thought of each other. You think I'm a selfish fool. I think you're a spineless idiot. And Allie, well, poor little Allie doesn't think at all, do you, dear?"

Alice stood up. Suddenly there was a dignity about her that was in contrast to the frightened, confused woman who hadn't defended herself against Fran's ugly words. "I think a great deal," she said. "Perhaps that's been my trouble. I've thought too much of the past. I wanted so to come home, to be with my family. I thought I could find the comfort and help I needed. But it isn't here. It isn't anywhere except within myself. Yes, I'm afraid. Yes, I'm uncertain about many things. But I'm also at peace, Fran. At peace with my conscience. And that's more than you'll ever be."

Barb looked at Fran as Alice left the room. "You bitch," she said. "You utter, consummate bitch."

Chapter 29

Flying back to Boston, John Peck couldn't concentrate on the paperback he'd picked up at the airport. He put the book aside and sat back, letting his thoughts go, almost minute by minute, over the past forty-eight hours and allowing himself the luxury of self-congratulation. It had been worth it, the long search for his mother. To know, after all these years, what his heritage was gave him a sense of grateful contentment. He was a lucky man. Alice was the prototype of everything a mother is supposed to be: pretty, refined, gentle and loving.

It also was an enormous relief to know he'd pass on to his own child a healthy genetic background. He thought lovingly of Carol and the baby she carried. The secure, wanted baby whom Alice would also love. He'd done her a kindness with his persistence. She seemed to look ten years younger in two days, happy even while she cried at the airport when he boarded his plane. Only her last words to him as he was about to go through the gate hinted at the insecurity she still felt.

"I'll see you soon again, won't I, Johnny? We won't lose touch now that we've found each other?"

He'd put his arms around her and gently kissed her cheek. "Of course we'll see each other. You have to meet Carol. And the baby's coming, remember? You don't think I'm going to let you get away after I spent so much time looking for you?"

She'd nodded, smiling through her tears. "Give Carol my love. And Janice, when you see her. And, Johnny, please get to know

Christopher. He's not like you, but in his own way he's just as sweet and sensitive."

He'd promised he'd do all those things. He wanted to ask about her own plans, but it seemed awkward to do so with Jack Richards standing silently by. He hadn't quite known what to do about his father. Though they'd spent two nights under the same roof, he didn't feel as close to Jack as he did to Allie, and he couldn't put his arms around him for a goodbye hug. He settled for a handshake and an exchange of smiles.

"Goodbye, Son," Jack said. "Take care of yourself."

"I will. You too."

Take care of *her*, Johnny wanted to say. Look after this nice woman you used to love. Even at that moment, the realization that he was thinking in the past tense surprised him. But it was true. A young Jack Richards had, perhaps, loved Alice. A grown-up one did not. He cared about her, felt responsible for the trouble he'd caused, but he didn't love her. I'm not sure my father can deeply love anyone, Johnny thought. There's nothing wrong with the man. He's kind and decent, but he doesn't love his childhood sweetheart. And she no longer loves him. They were like two reconciled friends with an important shared experience. She won't marry him, Johnny knew in that instant. And he doesn't want her to.

The recognition of that fact troubled him as the plane droned eastward. What would happen to his mother? Now that she'd left Spencer Winters, where would she go? He couldn't imagine her staying in the South Carona Street house with her parents, or going to live with one of those dissimilar sisters. Perhaps she'd come to live with Carol and him. It would make more sense than going to Jan and Clint Darby or moving in with Christopher and his "roommate." He'd discuss it with Carol when he got home. Realistically, he wasn't sure Carol would be too thrilled about having her mother-in-law in residence, but she'd do it gracefully if it seemed the only answer. He was even less sure that Alice would take to the idea. She'd know it wasn't right for two generations of women to share the same house, especially when they didn't know each other.

It still seemed strange to have a whole family. Grandparents and aunts, as well as parents. Strange and splendidly solid. Everything would work out, now that they'd gotten this far. Peacefully, Johnny put his head back on the seat and fell into a light, happy sleep.

Almost at the moment her son dozed off, thousands of feet in the air, Alice was having the terrible confrontation with Fran. After she spoke her little piece about a clear conscience, she left her sisters and, fighting back the tears, half-ran out of the house she wasn't ready to leave for good. I must decide, she told herself. They're right. I must make up my mind where I'm going from here. Unthinkingly, she turned and headed for Washington Park. It was a beautiful evening and dusk was just beginning to fall. How many nights, long ago, she had walked through this park with Fran or Barb or the friends of her youth. How many times she and Jack had strolled here, stopping to kiss discreetly. It was all different now, of course. More "organized" with its tennis courts and recreation areas, but it was still beautiful and peaceful, and at this hour there were few people to interrupt her thoughts.

As she walked across the nearly deserted park, she was sure of only two things: She would never go back to Spencer and she did not want to live with Jack Richards. The Jack she remembered was no more. He had become a pleasant alien, no more to her than an old friend. Though she shared the joy of Johnny's return with him, she did not feel that Jack really was part of their child. He'd fathered him, but she'd carried him for nine months, seen him briefly as an infant, despaired when they took him away. Her life had been motivated by her guilt about the baby. Jack had thought of him rarely, had considered looking for him only because his wife had thought it might make him happy. And even then he'd refused. No, Jack was only a biological father. Just as he'd been only a hot-blooded, passionate young man without sensitivity in the beginning and without courage in the end. She'd been right all those years ago when she'd said she'd never marry such a man. She was still right thirty-one years later.

It was a long walk across the park, but Allie was unaware of the distance until she came to the other side and saw the little cottage she remembered. It was a designated landmark now, Laura had told her recently, carefully preserved in honor of the poet Eugene Field, who had lived there. It was the house in which he'd written the poem she'd often read to Janice and Christopher when they were children. A sweet little poem. What was it? Oh, yes. "Little Boy Blue." Alice stood pensively in front of the cottage, trying to remember it. How did it go?

> The little toy dog is covered with dust,
> But sturdy and staunch he stands;
> And the little toy soldier is red with rust,
> And his musket moulds in his hands.

She wrinkled her brow, concentrating, trying to remember the rest of it. Something about when the dog was new and the soldier was fair and Little Boy Blue kissed them and put them there.

Why had she read such a sad poem to her children? It was about death. About a little boy dying. She knew why. She didn't want to think about that. It was part of the nightmare years when she was afraid Johhny was dead.

The evening was warm but a chill came over her. It had become quite dark. She could hardly make out the details of the house so painstakingly cared for by people who wished to preserve the memory of one of their famous citizens. She turned quickly. It was a long way back across the park and it was getting late. The family would be worried about her.

She'd gone only a few steps when she felt a presence behind her. Another evening stroller, she told herself. Nothing to be alarmed about. She quickened her pace and the stranger did the same. It was a man. She could hear his heavy tread. She began to be frightened, remembering her father's remarks about the park, no different from any park in any city these days, a place for perverts and muggers. People didn't go walking in lonely areas after sundown any more. Not in Boston or New York or any town. Not even in Denver. She felt panic rising. The man was following her, closing the distance between them. Frantically, Alice looked around, hoping to see someone, anyone. There was no one in sight. No one heard her gasp as the gloved hand came from behind and covered her mouth. No one saw her forced to the ground, her clothes roughly torn off her body. No one heard her pleading as she begged him not to do this. And no one heard her single terrified scream as the man finally raised a heavy stone and brought it crashing down onto her head.

When Laura knocked on Fran's door shortly before six o'clock, there was no answer. She quietly opened it and saw her eldest daughter lying on the bed. Laura went over and shook her gently.

"Frances, dear, dinner's almost ready."

The woman stirred. Laura could smell the liquor even from a distance. She's drunk, Laura thought, dismayed.

"Frances, I'm about to put dinner on the table," she repeated. "You'd better get ready to come down."

Fran turned over. "Don't want any dinner."

"You must eat. You didn't have any lunch."

"No. Going to sleep. Leave me alone, Mother."

Laura sighed. It was useless. She went next door and rapped lightly. Barbara's voice told her to come in.

"You and Alice ready for dinner?"

"Alice isn't here, Mother. I heard her go out about an hour ago."

"Out? Out where?"

"I don't know."

Laura was annoyed. "Really, I do think that's inconsiderate. She could have let me know. It's not like her. She always tells me when she's not going to eat here. I don't know what's gotten into you girls, I really don't. Fran's in bed and refuses to get up and . . . and I'm sorry to say I think she's been drinking. And now Allie disappears without a word. She's never done that. Do you think she's all right, Barbara?"

"Of course. She'll probably call in a little while. Maybe she met Jack and decided to have dinner with him."

"Well, I guess it's just the three of us, then. You're coming down, aren't you?"

"Yes, I'll be right with you."

Barbara was not so unconcerned as she seemed. Laura was right. It wasn't like Allie not to say where she was going or when she'd be back. It was nothing to worry about, of course, but she'd been upset, and rightly so, by Fran's cruelty. Even I upset her, Barb thought, with that sudden business of all of us leaving. I still think we must, but it's harder for Allie than for Fran or me. At least we have somewhere to go.

She thought again of Charles's telegram. She'd told no one about it, not sure of what it meant. Had he figured out a way to continue his love affair with her, even though he'd accepted the new position? What did he mean that he understood "everything"? Somehow he must have found out about Andrea's letter. Obviously he recognized that Barb's dismissal of him was a pack of lies. He'd probably pieced it all together and wanted her to come home so they could talk. But what was this about "coming to his senses"? Did he mean the job or his marriage or the two of them? She'd been so happy when the telegram came. He loved her and wanted her. More than ever. But on what terms? At what sacrifice to himself and, yes, at what sacrifice to her?

I must go back, Barbara thought. Tomorrow. They'll all just have to cope here. Fran can do what she wants, and so can Allie. They're not my responsibility. I hope they'll leave, for Mother and Dad's sake, but I'm not saying one more word about it.

Her mind went back to Allie. Laura's concern was based on more than the anxiety of an aging woman. Where had Allie run to? Because she *had* run. Barb heard her dash down the stairs and out the front door as though she was being pursued. If she took a walk to clear her head, she should be back by now. It was getting dark.

Don't be silly, Barbara told herself. Nothing's happened to her. She probably called Jack from a phone booth and met him. They're together right now, feeling sad about their son's departure. Still, if they didn't hear anything from Allie in another hour it might not be a bad idea to call Jack's apartment. That was the only place she was likely to go.

When Barb called at seven o'clock, Jack answered. "No, Allie's not here. That last time I saw her was this afternoon. I brought her home after we took John to the airport. What's wrong, Barb?"

"Nothing, probably. I saw her after that, but then she went out after five and didn't say where she was going. We haven't heard from her and Mother's a little upset. I mean, it isn't like Allie to disappear without a word." She laughed. "You probably think we're crazy. Worrying about a grown woman who's only been gone less than two hours." Barbara lowered her voice. "But, to tell you the truth, Jack, I am worried. I keep having the nutty idea that

Spencer Winters might have shown up. He's really a maniac and Allie's so frightened of him. You don't think . . ."

"No. Of course not. Think about it, Barb. If Spencer were in town he'd have called her, wouldn't he? And she didn't get a phone call before she left the house, did she?"

"No. We were all together, Allie and Fran and I. Then Allie left." No point telling him about the ugly argument.

"Well, then, she didn't go to meet Spencer. And I'm sure he's not the type who'd be lurking in the bushes, waiting to kidnap her. She's all right, Barb. I'm sure of it. She'll probably be home soon. Maybe she went to a movie."

"How? She didn't take any money."

Jack was quiet. "Could she have gone to visit anybody?"

"I can't think of anybody except you. Oh, look, this is silly. She's somewhere. Maybe she's just taking a long walk to think things through. She has a lot on her mind these days."

"Yes. We all do. I agree with you that she's okay, but she shouldn't be walking around alone after dark. I don't like that idea very much. Listen, will you call me when she comes in? I'll sleep a lot better when I know she's home."

"Certainly. I'll call the minute she returns. And you'll call me if she shows up there, won't you?"

"Naturally. Don't worry, Barb. She's all right."

"Yes, I'm sure she is."

But by ten o'clock when there'd been no word from Alice, Barbara was as frantic as Laura. Sam, oblivious of the problem, had gone to bed and Fran presumably was still sleeping it off in her room.

"Barbara, I'm worried sick. Where could she be?"

"I honestly don't know, Mother."

"It's been five hours. Maybe we should call the police."

Barb hesitated. It seemed so drastic. Almost melodramatic. But in Alice's state of mind anything was possible. Not wanting to, Barb thought of poor Dorothy Paige buried only that afternoon. No. Allie would never kill herself. She was too considerate to inflict such punishment on those who loved her. Still, it was strange for her to be gone so long, and impossible to think where she'd been. Accidents did happen. She might have been walking and been hit by a car. She had no identification with her. Barb had quietly checked. Allie hadn't even taken a purse when she left the house. With no money, she couldn't even have made a phone call. She must have been in an accident. Even now she might be lying, unidentified, in some hospital. Laura was right. It was time to call the police.

On the phone, the desk sergeant was briskly impersonal. "How long has your sister been missing, Miss Dalton?"

"About five hours."

Barbara could hear the policeman's small, exasperated sigh. "We can't classify her as a 'missing person.' Not for at least twenty-four hours." His voice became reassuring. "I wouldn't worry, if I were you. She probably went to visit friends, or to a movie. She'll show up. She's not a child, after all."

Yes she is, Barbara wanted to say. She is like a defenseless, trusting child. In spite of Spencer's mistreatment, she's lived a sheltered life for a quarter of a century in that safe and privileged Boston where nothing violent happened to "nice people." She doesn't know about terror in the streets. To her, Denver is the "small town" of her early life, a place where we went anywhere, anytime. It's changed, like the rest of the world. I don't go out alone after dark in Washington. Even Frances wouldn't roam around by herself in Rome or Paris. Miserably certain of it, Barb knew something had happened to her sister. A lost, lonely, confused Allie was out there somewhere and in trouble. Barbara tried to be reasonable.

"I know you have rules, Sergeant, but Mrs. Winters hasn't been in Denver for a long while. She hardly knows her way around any more. She might have been in an accident and she has no identification with her. Couldn't you put out a call to try and find her?"

"Sorry, Miss Dalton. Not yet."

"Then what should we do?"

"If you're really worried, why don't you check with some of her friends?"

"I've done that."

"Well," the man said reluctantly, "you could call the hospitals. See if she's been taken sick on the street or . . . Wait a minute." She could hear him shuffling papers. When he spoke again, he sounded a little less certain. "I'm looking through the reports just in. Is your sister a female Caucasian between forty-five and fifty, wearing a navy-blue and white dress and blue shoes?"

Barbara couldn't breathe. "Yes. Yes, she is."

"Squad car found a woman answering that description in Washington Park at 7:22 P.M. They took her to Denver General Hospital at Sixth and Bannock." He read aloud. "Victim unconscious, suffering from head wounds. Presumed to have been sexually assaulted. No identification."

"Oh, my God!"

"Now hold on, Miss Dalton. Could be a lot of women answering that description. Doesn't have to be your sister."

"Is she . . ." Barb couldn't finish the question.

"She was alive when they found her. I guess she's being treated there right now, but I still say . . ."

"It's my sister," Barbara said. Suddenly she was angry. "Why haven't you tried to find out who she is? It's been more than two hours since she was picked up! Why weren't the police trying to locate her family? My God, what kind of inhumanity is this?"

"Take it easy, Miss Dalton. These routine things take time."

"Routine!"

"I mean, the report just reached me. Of course we're trying to locate her people, but the first thing is to take care of the victim. I'm sorry. You have no idea how many calls I get every night from people worrying because somebody's out for a few hours. Nine times out of ten . . ."

"I don't give a damn about nine times out of ten! My sister may be dying and you don't even care!"

Even as she screamed at the police officer, Barbara wondered why she was wasting time berating this man who saw Allie as only another anonymous casualty. She clutched at the hope that perhaps he was right. Maybe the injured woman wasn't Allie at all, but in any case she was losing precious minutes for no reason.

"I'm sorry," she managed to say civilly. "I know the details of every single incident can't be at your fingertips. Thank you."

"Good luck, Miss Dalton. I hope it's a false alarm. Your sister probably will walk in, just fine, in a little while."

Barbara was frantic as she hung up. She had to get to Denver General and she didn't want to go alone. Couldn't face it alone. Why was she so certain it was Alice lying there? She just was. It had to be, and yet there was always the slim hope that the sergeant might be right. It would be cruel to frighten Laura now, if it turned out to be a hoped-for "false alarm." But who else could go with her? Not her father. Sam was not even aware that Alice was missing. And not Fran, probably still drunk or totally passed out. Jack. Of course. Jack would go with her.

She called him and told him what she knew. There was alarm in his voice, but he tried to hide it. "It might not be Alice."

"I know. I pray not. But I'm sure it is. Will you meet me there as soon as you can?"

"Of course. Shall I come and get you?"

"No. I don't want Mother to know anything yet. I'll have to make up some excuse for going out at this hour. Please hurry, Jack. I need you."

"I'll leave right away."

Barb took a moment to compose herself and then walked into the living room where Laura sat staring at Allie's photograph.

"It's all right," Barb said. "I was just on the phone with Jack Richards. Allie's there now. In fact, I have to go and pick her up. His car won't start."

Laura shook her head. "Don't try to spare me, Barbara. I heard you on the phone. You were talking to the police first. Something's happened to Alice. Something terrible. Where is she?"

No use pretending. It wasn't fair. If, God forbid, Allie was dead or dying, her mother had to know. And if the unidentified woman in the hospital was someone else, there was nothing to lose but this momentary anxiety, even though it would be replaced, unfortunately, by continuing worry about Allie's disappearance.

Once again, Barbara repeated what she knew, but this time she echoed the words of Jack and the policeman. "It's a long shot, Mother. It may not be Allie. Probably isn't. But Jack and I are going to see."

"I'm going with you."

"No, darling, please don't. I'll call you the minute I get to the hospital."

"I'm going," Laura repeated. "Don't you see, Barbara? I have to know. That could be my child. I can't just sit here and wait to find out." It was she who was reassuring now. "I'll be all right, dear. No matter what. Don't be concerned about me. I'm stronger than you think. I may not seem so, but I really am."

Yes, Barbara thought, you are. You've lived through so much. Taken so many hours of sadness without whimpering. We think of you as a helpless, provincial woman who must be protected. But you're not. You're as strong as any of us. Stronger, maybe. You come from a generation of women who didn't scream about their "rightful place in the world" or blame everybody else for their hardships and disappointments. You've just gone on, patiently, quietly understanding that life isn't going to give us anything more than that to which we're entitled. And that we have to take the loneliness with the laughter.

Laura interrupted her thoughts. "Get your coat, Barbara. It's chilly out there."

The hospital was quiet, the visitors' hours over and the patients bedded down for the night by the time Laura and Barb arrived. Jack came in a few seconds after they entered the front door. He must have driven like a maniac, Barb thought idly. She took his hand gratefully and he pressed hers in reassurance before he went to the desk to make inquiries.

"Whoever it is is in intensive care," he said quietly when he returned. "But they'll let us go in for a minute to . . . to make an identification." He looked anxiously at Laura. "Mrs. Dalton, wouldn't you rather wait here while Barbara and I . . ."

"No. Thank you, Jack, but I'll go with you."

Mutely, they took the elevator to the area where busy doctors and nurses monitored the conditions of the critically ill. After a few whispered words from Jack, a nurse at the desk pointed toward a bed where a still figure lay, its head wrapped in bandages and its body sprouting tubes to overhanging bottles. Barb took her mother's arm as they walked silently to the bedside and looked down at what could be seen of the white, still face of Allie.

Barbara let out an involuntary gasp and tightened her hold on Laura, but the older woman did not flinch. She simply looked sadly at her injured daughter, stood waiting as though she expected Alice to open her eyes and speak. She didn't expect that, of course. She knew Alice was near death, that she'd never open her eyes again, never speak. Yet Laura stood patiently, silently, as though she would will strength and life into her child, as though she refused to accept what she knew.

I can't bear it, Barb thought. This can't have happened to Allie! I can't stand Mother's heart breaking without a sound. I can't look at Jack's face. She saw him move away from the bed in response to a silent signal from the nurse. She saw him speaking with the woman, nodding his head, giving answers which she wrote on some kind of chart. He came back at last and said in a low voice, "They think we should leave now, Mrs. Dalton."

Laura seemed to come out of her trance. "Leave? How can we leave? I have to be here when she wakes up."

Jack looked at Barbara. "We'll just go to a reception room, dear," Barb said. "We'll stay close by. I'll call home and tell Dad where we are."

"I want to stay right here."

"You can't, Mother. They don't allow it. We'll sit and wait until she's conscious. Come on, darling. Please. They'll let us know the minute we can talk to Allie."

It was three in the morning before a young doctor came into the Visitors Lounge with the last of the bulletins they'd been getting every half hour. Sam was there, his face gray, his arm protectively around Laura as they sat and waited for news. Frances, looking destroyed, paced the room, drinking endless cups of black coffee from plastic containers. There had been almost no words spoken in hours, only the anxious questioning of the doctor when he appeared occasionally to say there was no change. They did not even have the heart to ask yet for details, though Jack disappeared at one point to talk to the police, who'd been notified of Allie's identity by the hospital and who had arrived to tell the whole ghastly story. He looked sick when he returned, but all he said was, "It was a rapist. In the park. They have no leads."

It was as though they were numb when the doctor finally said to Laura, "I'm sorry, Mrs. Dalton. We couldn't save your daughter. We did everything we could." And then, in unprofessional anger, he burst out, "Goddamn these savages on our streets!" He seemed surprised, embarrassed, by his own emotion. "I'm sorry," he said again. "We had her in surgery for over an hour, but we couldn't help. She . . . she never knew what hit her," he added lamely. "I hope that's some small consolation."

Jack and Barbara turned their heads away, and Sam broke into great, racking sobs. Only Laura and Frances moved. Fran ran from the room, but Laura rose and took the young doctor's hand. "Thank you," she said. "Thank you for caring."

Chapter 30

Guilt.

Like a creeping, poisonous vine, guilt took root in the Dalton household and its tendrils reached out across Denver and stretched as far as Boston, threatening to strangle those who, reasonably or not, felt themselves unwitting contributors to Alice Winters' death.

Whether the truly guilty party, the man who had raped and murdered, felt remorse, only he would ever know. The homicide men who pursued the case "came up empty," in their words. They were not surprised. Where did one start to look for a pervert sick enough to skulk around a park at nightfall, waiting to attack and kill an unsuspecting female with no "known enemies"? The next day, they routinely questioned the family and the woman's "boyfriend," looking for any detail that might provide a clue to the identity of this maniac. Considerate as they tried to be, it was agony for those who loved Allie, for it forced them to relive the event, regret the past and realize the depth of self-reproach each of them felt in varying degrees.

Frances, selfish, cynical Frances, was, of them all, most devastated by the tragedy. As the doctor gave his final, terrible news to the family, Fran had run blindly from the room. She hardly remembered getting into her car and driving downtown. She knew only that over and over in her head she heard the words, "I killed Allie. If it hadn't been for the fight with me, she'd never have left the house. I killed her as surely as if I'd been the monster who did the deed." At half-past three in the morning she found herself pounding on the door of Cary Venzetti's seedy little apartment.

The young waiter from LaFitte's finally opened the door a crack and peered out. He was astonished to see Frances. Astonished and shocked. She looked old, haggard, far from the elegant "older woman" he'd once been to bed with.

"Let me in." It was a command.

He hesitated. Was she drunk? Crazy? He'd not seen her since that one and only night.

"I said, let me in!" Fran's voice was harsh and angry. "Or do you already have company?"

"No. I'm alone." He opened the door and she came into the disorderly room. She barely looked at him, but Cary, completely naked, reached for a pair of trousers slung on a nearby chair.

"Don't bother," Fran said. "I've seen it all before."

"Okay." Cary leaned against the door. "Mind if I ask what you're doing here?"

"What do you think I'm doing?" She was pulling off her clothes, dropping them on the floor. "You have any objections? You didn't before. And I paid you well enough, didn't I?" She was nude now, facing him, the trim, beautiful body somehow in terrible contrast with the wild-eyes, grim-lipped face. "Well? What the hell's the matter with you? Last time you couldn't wait. You were drooling, begging me to come back. So I'm here. What's the problem, sonny?"

He wondered why he wasn't excited. "I . . . I don't understand. I mean, all of a sudden, at this hour, you just appear."

"For God's sake, what are you? A dentist? Must I have an appointment? I want sex. Remember the word? S-E-X. It's good for the soul and the complexion."

She'd gotten into his rumpled bed and lay waiting for him. Cary didn't move. She was here, this poised, worldy creature, asking, no, *demanding* he make love to her, and he felt nothing but confusion and a slight sense of fear.

"Frances, what's wrong? You're not yourself."

"How would *you* know? How would you know what's myself? *I* don't even know that. All I know is I don't want to think about anything for a while. Is that too much to ask?"

"What happened?"

"My God, will you stop with the questions! Are you or are you not ready, willing and able?"

He came and sat on the edge of the bed. "None of them, I guess," he said slowly. "That other time was wonderful. I didn't even want your money. I wanted you. And I knew you wanted me. But tonight it could be anybody, couldn't it? There's something you're running from. Something terrible you have to forget, even for a little while. I don't amount to much, Frances, but I'm not a machine that you can turn on like you're pressing a switch. I don't think I can make it with you tonight. I'm sorry."

She was too surprised to answer for a moment, and then she began to laugh. It was a terrible sound, hollow and desperate, half laughter and half tears. "That's funny," Fran gasped. "I mean that's really, really funny! I've reached rock bottom. Begging a lousy little creep like you to take me! And being turned down at that!" She was hysterical. "What's the matter? Am I suddenly too old and too ugly?" Don't give me that crap about being a machine! That's exactly what you are: a machine in good condition, still new enough to turn out efficient work. And that's all I want from you. I didn't come here for some cocktail-party analysis of my motives! Don't go cerebral on me, baby. It's not your style!" Suddenly she shrugged, deflated. She pushed Cary aside, got up and began to put on her clothes. "That really ties it. Rejected twice in a week, once by a man and now by a dumb kid."

Cary looked up at her. "So that's it. Somebody you really want doesn't want you. You came here to forget him with me."

Fran shook her head. "No. I wasn't even thinking about him tonight. I was just running toward anything as far removed as possible from reality." She stood at the door, her hand on the knob. "You were right, Cary. It wasn't like the other time. That was fun and games. Tonight I wanted oblivion, and that other man couldn't give it to me, even if he were around. He was too close to the real thing." She gave a sad little smile. "Would you like to know why I really came here tonight?"

"Yes, if you want to tell me."

"Tonight I killed my sister."

"What? What in Christ's name are you saying?"

"I killed her. I said terrible things to her this afternoon. I called her pious and stupid and told her she made me sick. I drove her from the house. Into the park. And some fiend attacked her and she's dead."

He came toward her. "Frances, stop! *You* didn't kill her. It's horrible. Unbelievable. But *you* didn't do it!"

"Oh, yes, I did. I sent her out to be murdered. It's as though I did it myself." She began to cry. "Poor Allie. Poor, good, sweet, helpless Allie. Why is she dead and I'm alive? There's no sense to it. No sense at all."

Cary put his strong young arms around her, cradling her. "Frances, no. You're not responsible. Come back to bed. Let me hold you. You need comfort more than sex. You need to be with someone understanding. Someone who thinks you're wonderful."

She shook her head. "I have to go home. I shouldn't have come here. I don't know why I did, except it's the kind of thing I always do: look for some way to keep from facing myself. I have to go back and be with my family. They're probably already frantic, wondering where I've gone." She gently removed his arms. "There's so much about me you don't know, Cary." She thought of Dorothy Paige. "So much I don't ever want you to know because you're a nice young man. And I'm not a very nice lady." She kissed him lightly on the cheek. "Goodbye, little one. Thanks for turning me down. How did you know it was for all the right reasons?"

Before he could answer she was out the door and down the stairs. He heard the entry door close. She's gone forever this time, Cary thought. And tomorrow when I read the papers I'll finally know who she was.

The lights were burning when Frances let herself into the house a little past four. They were all there in the shabby living room, her parents and Barb and Jack Richards, and they looked up when she walked in.

"I hope I didn't worry you," Fran apologized. "I've been driving around, thinking of her, remembering all the good things."

"Yes," Laura said. "We've all been doing that. Thinking of our Alice. Wondering why God chose this for her." Her mother began to weep silently. "She was a good girl. She was always a good girl, even though your father and I made her feel she was bad. We'll never forgive ourselves for that."

"Don't, Mother," Barbara said. "That was all so long ago. Don't think about that. Think about how happy she was the last two days of her life when she was reunited with Johnny. She blossomed. The thing that haunted her all those years, her own guilt, was removed. Remember that, not the other." Barb brushed at the tears in her own eyes. "If anyone should feel guilty, I should. I told her we should all leave here and give you and Dad some peace. Poor Allie. She didn't know where to go. She didn't want to leave. If only I hadn't said it! She wouldn't have gone rushing out of the house all upset. This never would have happened."

"I was worse," Fran said, almost inaudibly. "I was the one who really sent her out. I was cruel and terrible to her."

Jack said nothing, but there was guilt in his heart too. Guilt he was sure Allie's sisters recognized. Why didn't I insist she marry me? I could have saved her. She'd have known where she belonged. He remembered what the police had told him: the rape, the brutal crushing of her skull, probably with a heavy rock. God! He couldn't stand to think about it. Allie alone and frightened and maybe begging for her life. Jack buried his head in his hands.

It was Sam Dalton, the one who had seemed most out of control at the hospital, who now spoke sadly but firmly. "Blaming ourselves won't bring Alice back. Every one of us in this room wishes he could take back something, as though it would have changed anything. It wouldn't have. We don't understand why God moves as He does. We'll never understand. We just have to live with our faith and believe that it was His way of sparing that child from something worse to come. We have to hang onto that while we grieve for that innocent girl." His voice broke. "I loved her so much. I never was able to show her. I'll regret that to my dying day."

"She knew, Daddy," Barbara said. "She knew you loved her, just as Fran and I know you love us and forgive us anything."

Sam looked at his daughters. "I do love you and I want you to be happy. Whatever you do, be happy."

There was a long moment of silence as they thought of all that had been and might have been, remembering, regretting, trying to find some meaning in all this, searching for some shred of consolation in this senseless taking of a life. At last, Barbara spoke.

"Mother, I think you and Dad should get some rest. Lie down, even if you can't sleep. We're facing some hard days. You need your strength. It's almost five o'clock. In a couple of hours, things will begin to happen. There'll be the newspapers, I'm afraid. And . . . and we have to make arrangements."

The others looked at her, knowing what was in her mind. Spencer would have to be notified. And Allie's children, including John Peck, who'd left her, happy, only a little more than twelve hours before.

Fran voiced their thoughts. "I'll call Spencer. I don't know how to reach Janice and Chris, but I'll find out. Jack, will you call Johnny?"

He nodded, mutely.

"Charlotte," Laura said. "Somebody has to tell Aunt Charlotte. I don't want her to hear it from Spencer."

"I'll call her, Mother," Barbara said. "And, Fran, I think I should call Spencer. You dislike him even more than the rest of us."

"That's exactly why I should call. I hate his guts. If anyone is to blame for Allie's death, it's that beast she married." She hesitated. "I'm afraid he's going to want to take her back to Boston. I'm sure Mother and Dad don't want that, and I'm the only one tough enough to tell him he can't."

"But he can," Sam said. "He is her husband. We can't stop him, even though we'd like to keep her here, near us."

Laura's soft voice interrupted this painful conversation. "I'm not sure Allie would want that, Sam. I think she'd want to be close to her children, and I think they'd like to know their mother was nearby. We lost her once, my dear, but wherever she rests she'll never be lost to us again. She came home and spent her last days here. To me, she'll always be here."

Again, that strength, Barbara thought. She's remarkable. What I would give for the special kind of wisdom Mother has! Even at this terrible time, when she must be dying inside, she's thinking of what Allie and her children might want, not what she and Dad would prefer.

Fran recognized the same unselfishness Barb saw. Allie was like Mother, she thought. She cared about people more than she cared about herself. She wouldn't want us to be petty and spiteful. Not even with Spencer. But I'm not sure I can please either of them. Not in this case.

"All right, Mother," Fran said. "I'll call Spencer and I'll try not to be rotten to him. Maybe I don't have to be. Let's hope he has enough of a conscience to be punished by it."

It was a half-truth. She would try to be civil to the man who'd made life a living hell for Allie, but she would not give in easily if he insisted on bringing his wife to Boston for burial. Her mother was wrong about that. Alice would want to be in Denver. She'd been a happy child here, and it was here she'd found her last moments of joy with Jack and Johnny. As for her children, there was no reason to think they'd want their mother nearby, as Laura believed. Janice sounded like a selfish little witch who didn't care enough to come to her grandparents' anniversary party. Christopher had his own, estranged life. Even the new-found son could not have formed such an attachment that he'd spend time at Allie's grave. But Sam and Laura would. It would comfort them. Fran didn't go along with the idea that it was meaningful to visit a cemetery. There was no one there under that smooth, grassy covering. But her parents didn't feel that way. They made regular trips to the family plots where their own parents were buried. They were of a generation that "paid their respects" to the dead. And if she could manage it, she'd see that they'd find the same solace in "visiting" the daughter they'd lost.

I don't know whether I can convince Spencer of that, Fran thought as she picked up the phone. But I'm damned well going to try, even if I have to blackmail him.

The shrill, persistent ringing of the telephone awakened two men in Boston almost at the same moment. And with almost the same foggy reaction, Spencer Winters and John Peck glanced at their bedside clocks as they reached for the jangling instruments. It was seven-thirty in the morning.

Spencer grunted with annoyance as he picked up the receiver. Who'd call at this ungodly hour?

"Yes?"

"Spencer? It's Frances."

For a moment it didn't register. "Frances? Frances who?"

"Déspres. Dalton. Your sister-in-law, remember?"

He came wide-awake. "Of course. Sorry."

"I have some bad news. It's about Allie."

He listened, incredulous, to the story. Alice dead? It wasn't possible. Raped and murdered? Unthinkable! For a moment he wondered if this was some sick joke. It was five-thirty in the morning in Denver. Frances, who so obviously hated him, must be drunk and looking for a way to torture him. But the tone of her voice, controlled but heavy with grief, told him otherwise. She was sober and telling the truth. As the realization hit him, he was stunned. There was no wrenching feeling of sorrow or loss. Only amazement and a terrible sense of distaste for the sordid details.

"I imagine you and your children will want to come out right away." Fran tried to choose her words carefully. If she could get him to agree while he was still in shock, one problem would be solved. "We'll make the arrangements here. There's room in the family plot for Allie and Barbara and me. The services will be day after tomorrow. I assume Janice and Christopher will come too. I'm sorry, Spencer. I know this must be a terrible shock for you. It's been a nightmare for all of us since ten o'clock last night."

Pettishly, he seized on her last words. "Ten o'clock? You've known since ten o'clock last night and you're only calling me now?"

Fool! Fran thought. Arrogant ass! She forced herself to sound repentent. "I'm sorry, Spencer. I suppose you should have been called, but we didn't know she . . . wasn't going to make it. We kept hoping all night that she'd pull through. She died at three this morning. It's been terrible for Mother and Dad, these past few hours. We've had our hands full, and there didn't seem to be much point in calling you at five o'clock in the morning. Forgive us. I guess we were wrong not to have let you know immediately. We really weren't thinking straight. We still aren't." Fran paused. "But Barbara and I are managing everything." The words were now genuinely reluctant. "We'll pick out the . . . the casket. And find the right thing for her to wear. You won't have to do anything but be here. You and your children. Will you let us know when you're arriving?"

Her overlong speech was a mistake. It gave Spencer time to collect himself and formulate his own intentions.

"That won't be necessary. I'll fly out this morning and bring her back. This was Alice's home. She'll be buried here, quietly and fittingly."

Here it comes, Fran thought. The showdown.

"We'd like the interment to be here, Spencer. It would mean a great deal to Mother and Dad. I hope you agree to that. It would be a kindness to a pair of elderly people. I'm sure you understand that generation's view of such things."

"No, I can't agree. Alice was my wife. She lived in Boston society. People would think it very strange if she died mysteriously and was quickly buried in Denver. I'm sorry, Frances, but I must insist. It's the only proper thing to do."

For whom? Frances wanted to ask. Proper for Allie? Allie didn't know. Proper for her children? Unlikely. Their generation certainly didn't hold with the macabre formality of drawn-out mourning and funerals. No, it's proper for you, Spencer, she thought. It's your chance to play the bereaved husband, to show off with a five-thousand-dollar casket and a fleet of limousines.

"I fail to see where it's any less proper for Allie to be buried here. And I seriously doubt anyone would find it strange." Fran's voice was cool and level, but she was revolted by this cat-and-mouse game she and Spencer were playing. God, it was like a tug-of-war over her sister's body!

"There's really no need to discuss it. I've made up my mind. I'll fly out today and bring the remains back to Boston. Alice had many friends here. It's only considerate that I allow them to pay their respects. Please give my sympathy to your parents and tell them I've decided to do what's right for Allie."

All right, you bastard, Fran thought. You've driven me to it. "Just as you always did what was right when you were married to her?"

"What?"

"You're very considerate of Alice and her friends now that she's dead. Too bad you couldn't have been as kind when she was alive. Listen to me, Spencer. You may be legally able to do this, but you'll pay for it. I know every damn gossip columnist in the world and I won't hesitate to tell them what you really are—a wife-beater, among other sadistic things. And I think they'd like to know about the illegitimate child Alice had before you were married. I gather you haven't been too anxious to advertise that piece of scandal to your very proper Boston friends."

Even over the miles she could feel his anger. "You'd do that? You'd sully your sister's reputation? What kind of woman are you?"

"Yes, I'd do that," Fran said grimly. "It can't hurt her now. In fact, it would be justice, even though she wouldn't know you were finally paying for all the unspeakable things you did to her. I think you and your children had better come out here, Spencer. Or do you want me to tell my newspaper friends you didn't even have the decency to attend your own wife's funeral?"

"Bitch!" Spencer slammed down the receiver.

Fran closed her eyes for a moment. She felt sick, but she'd done the right thing. It's for you, Allie, she thought. I couldn't let you spend eternity next to that creature.

When his telephone rang, John Peck couldn't remember for a moment where he was. So much had happened since he got home last night. He'd told Carol everything and shared her happy tears. He'd called Jan, who was delighted and who told him, almost shyly, that she and Clint had decided to "make it legal." They were coming over tonight and bringing Chris, who was eager to meet him. The phone continued to demand his attention. Sleepily, he reached for it.

"John? It's . . . it's your father."

"Dad? What in the world? It's five-thirty in Denver! Are you all right?"

"Yes. No. It's your mother."

Once again the horror story was told, this time to an incredulous and heartbroken listener. Jack was trying not to break down, but Johnny began to sob unashamedly. When, at last, he could speak, he said, "Why? Why her? She was the dearest, finest . . ."

"I know. We can't comprehend these things, Johnny. I blame myself. I should have protected her, should have sheltered her. If I had, she might be alive now." Johnny knew his father was also crying. He felt sorry for the man and suddenly angry as well. Yes, you should have, John thought. You should have looked after her.

But he said merely, "We both should have. We were too selfish to realize how troubled she was, but we couldn't anticipate this. No one could."

Jack was breathing hard, taking in air in great gulps. "No, no one could imagine a thing like this. It's like a bad dream, Son."

"What . . . what are the plans?"

"I don't know yet. Frances is calling Spencer Winters now. I suppose he'll call Allie's other children. Maybe you'll want to reach them too. I'll get back to you later. When I know more."

"Yes. How are my . . . How are her parents?"

"Remarkable. They're unusual people, John. They're crushed, but they have faith to sustain them. I wish I had. I hope you have. We all need it now."

Johnny put the receiver gently back into its cradle. Faith? He had none of the kind his father meant. He was angry at God. Angry that a lovely woman was so savagely destroyed. Angry that he'd had so few hours of his life with her. But I did have that much, he thought. It was destiny that I found her in time. Almost as though God was good enough to give me a face and a voice and a touch to remember. And as though He knew Alice could rest in peace because she'd found her firstborn.

He threw himself back on the bed and wept bitterly.

The boys and their wives stayed overnight after the simple ceremony that preceded Dorothy Paige's cremation. It made Buzz feel a little better to see them that morning, all gathered around his breakfast table. Everyone was trying very hard to act normally. Larry, browsing through the morning paper as he drank his coffee, suddenly looked up.

"Dad, don't you know some people named Dalton?"

Buzz almost jumped. "Yes, of course. They're friends of your mother's and mine. Why?"

"Terrible thing. One of the Daltons' daughters was murdered while she was walking in Washington Park last night."

Buzz felt the color drain from his face. Fran. It must be Fran. Barbara and Alice weren't the type to go rambling around at any hour by themselves.

"Who . . . who was it?"

"Alice Dalton Winters. Somebody raped and killed her. Jesus, what is this world coming to?"

Alice. Sweet, soft, timid Alice. What was she doing there? How could such a thing happen? "May I see the paper, please?"

"Sure." Larry handed it over. "Say, was she the woman who called here?"

"No. That was another sister. Frances." Buzz read the second-page article. It was quite short. Violence was so rampant everywhere these days that muggings, rapes and murders didn't even make big headlines any more. It was just another unsolved crime.

BOSTON WOMAN KILLED IN PARK

At seven twenty-two last night, police discovered the unconscious body of Alice Dalton Winters, aged 48, in the bushes in Washington Park. The victim had been criminally assaulted a short time before. Police rushed her to Denver General Hospital, where she died of her injuries a few hours later. Identification was made by her parents, Mr. and Mrs. Samuel Dalton of Denver. Mrs. Winters had been visiting the city to celebrate the fiftieth wedding anniversary of Mr. and Mrs. Dalton, long-time residents. Police said they had no clues to the identity of the assailant who sexually attacked Mrs. Winters before crushing her skull with a heavy object.

Buzz lowered the paper. Those poor people. What was worse—the death of a woman so unhappy she willed it, or that of one who became its unsuspecting prey? No difference, he decided. The survivors were burdened with the same terrible cloak of sadness and guilt. The Daltons probably blamed themselves as much for whatever took Allie alone to the park as he blamed himself for the events that drove Dorothy down the cellar stairs. He sighed heavily. There was nothing but futility and gloom everywhere. Nothing seemed to matter any more.

Chapter 31

Charles Tallent swiveled his big leather chair around and stared out the window of his office. Washington had never looked more beautiful than it did this October day, clear, with a bright blue sky and the first nip of autumn in the air. The kind of day Barbara loved, all fresh and invigorating and alive. Over the years they'd sometimes played "hookey" on days like this, driving down into Virginia to see the turning of the leaves, stopping at some little inn for lunch, returning, refreshed and happy to see their haven in Georgetown to make love in the afternoon. Before, Charles reminisced in bitter afterthought, he had to go home to Andrea and his "obligations."

Well, no more. He was through cheating himself and Barbara. Her letter had opened his eyes to a lot of things, including the realization of his own selfishness. How could he ever have considered giving her up? It would be like cutting out his heart. And he had no obligations to anyone but her. His children were grown, no longer babies to be "traumatized" by a broken home. Andrea was capable of making her own way without him, much as she'd dislike giving up her "official" prerogatives. The Candidate had responded in a gentlemanly fashion to Charles's telegram of regret that "for personal reasons" he could not accept the Cabinet membership so flatteringly offered. The Senator was an ambitious man, but a compassionate one. He understood. And Charles would work hard to get him elected, just as Charles would put even more effort into the committees he served on. In the long run, he probably could be more useful in the House than lost in the obscurity of a Cabinet post which changed with every administration. He had no worries about his own constituency. Even as a divorced man, the voters in his state would send him back to Congress term after term to do the good job he'd always done for them. With Barbara at his side, encouraging and loving him, he'd serve his country better. As a congressman he'd be remembered long after some frustrated Secretary of Agriculture was forgotten. As for the possible chance at the presidency one day, he'd been kidding himself. It had been momentarily tempting, but it was a long shot, a vague come-on, certainly not worth the destruction of his happiness and Barbara's.

All in all, he felt more at peace than he had in days. He hadn't told Andrea of his decision, neither the political nor the personal one. He'd not even mentioned Barbara's letter nor the part he suspected his wife had played in its writing. It hadn't been easy not to lash out at Andrea, to tell her she'd outsmarted herself. But he'd held his tongue, sent the telegram to Barbara and waited.

Only the waiting made him uneasy. It had been more than twenty-four hours since he'd sent his message and there'd been no reply from the woman he loved. For a moment, he was filled with terrible doubt. What if the letter was true? What if she had met someone she could care for? Suppose she really didn't intend to come back? No. His first reaction had been right. She was letting him out of his involvement easily and humanely. But why hadn't she answered his wire? It wasn't like her.

"Damn it!" He spoke the words aloud. This uncertainty was driving him mad. Ridiculous of him to sit here brooding. He fished in his desk drawer for the Daltons' phone number in Denver and dialed it on his private wire. It was eleven o'clock. Nine in the morning out there. They'd certainly be up.

Barbara wearily answered the phone. It had been ringing all morning, just as she'd predicted, with the press calling for information, asking for interviews and photographs of Allie. It was ghoulish. It was their job, but it was heartless. She'd protected Laura and Sam from this invasion so far, just as she'd spared them the shocked and sympathetic calls from friends and family. When

Buzz Paige called, she hadn't known what to do. After accepting his condolences and offering her own for his loss, she hesitantly asked, "Do you want to speak to Fran?"

There'd been a pause before he said, "No. Don't disturb her. Just tell her and your parents how terribly sorry I am." There was another moment of silence before Buzz said, "Will the services be in Boston?"

"No. Here." Fran had reported the conversation with Spencer. "You're welcome, of course, Buzz. You're like family to us." She hadn't meant it as a reproach that he hadn't wanted any of them at Dorothy's funeral, but Buzz took it that way.

"I hope you understand why I couldn't . . . I mean, we thought under the circumstances it would be better if we kept yesterday private."

"Of course. And we'll understand if you're not here day after tomorrow. You've been through so much yourself."

"It isn't that. Not exactly. The fact is, I'm going away tomorrow, for a few weeks. I've got to get out of this house for a while. I'm going to visit my brother in San Diego."

"I see. That sounds like a good idea."

"Tell Fran for me, will you? And, Barbara, once again I can't tell you how shocked and grieved I am about Allie. It's a monstrous thing. Monstrous. God, it makes you wonder what life's all about. It's so crazy. Everything can change in a minute."

What about Fran? Barbara thought, it's certainly changed for her too. At that moment she hated Buzz Paige. He's blaming Fran for what happened to Dorothy. All right, she was partially responsible. But no more than he. Why won't he even speak to her? Hasn't he the guts to tell her there can't be anything between them ever again?

The thought brought her back, momentarily, to her own situation with Charles. She'd spent yesterday wondering what his telegram meant, debating what to do about it, and then this blow fell and for more than twelve hours her thoughts had been only with her family. It will have to wait, Barb thought. The whole thing will have to wait until this is over and I can try to sort my own problems. Death made even life unimportant. For a little while. She couldn't set Allie aside while she selfishly tried to interpret

Charles's message. He'd understand when he finally heard why she hadn't answered.

It was almost eerie that the next voice on the phone should be his.

"Darling, is that you? I've been going crazy waiting to hear from you! Didn't you get my wire? Is something wrong?" He didn't wait for an answer. "Your lettter was beautiful. Almost as beautiful as you. But I don't believe it, love. It isn't true, is it? There isn't anyone else. Tell me you still love me, Barbara. I adore you. I need you so much."

The warm rush of words, the outpouring of devotion, destroyed the control she'd been able to manage through the whole nightmare. Helplessly, she began to sob and no words could pass the aching lump in her throat. Just hearing him brought back all the yearning for him, all the hopelessness she felt without him.

"Sweetheart, what is it?" The alarm in his voice was somehow comforting. He cared, and she desperately needed someone to care.

Stammering, crying, she told him what had happened.

"Oh, my God! Barbara, darling! What can I say?"

She managed to calm down. "Nothing. There's nothing anyone can say. Or do. Just bear with me, Charles. Let me get through this and then we'll talk about . . . the rest."

"I'm getting the next plane out there."

"No! You can't! The idea's insane! What would people say if you suddenly showed up here?"

"I don't give a damn what people would say! I'm not going to let you struggle through this by yourself. I want to be right there beside you. That's where I ought to be. That's where I'm going to be, for the rest of our lives."

She protested feebly, but he brushed aside her words about Andrea and his place in the public eye.

"None of that matters. That's what my telegram meant. I've come to my senses. We won't talk about it now, but there's no way in the world you could keep me from coming to Denver, not unless there really is someone else. Someone you'd rather have with you."

"There's no one, dearest. No one in the world but you."

She heard his sigh of relief. "That's all you had to say. I'll leave here in a couple of hours. Be a brave girl. I'll be with you soon. I love you, Barbara. You'll never know how much."

Janice and Clint were asleep when Spencer called Darby's apartment. Clint answered and handed the phone to the young woman beside him, covering the mouthpiece with his hand.

"Guess who's calling. Your old man."

Jan shook herself awake. "My father? What does he want?"

"How should I know? He just barked for you."

She took the phone. "Yes, Father?"

"Your mother's dead."

Jan stared stupidly at the phone. "Dead? What do you mean, dead? What are you talking about?"

"Your mother died in Denver last night, Janice. She'll be buried there day after tomorrow. As soon as my office opens in half an hour I'll have Miss Perrone get three tickets on the one P.M. United flight. Please be good enough to call your brother and say we expect him to go with us. Tell him to be at the airport at twelve-fifteen. I'd do it myself, but I don't have his telephone number."

She couldn't believe it. Not the fact nor the cold way in which he was making plans, as though they were off on a family holiday. "Father, what happened to her? She was always in perfect health."

"She was murdered. Her sister called half an hour ago. Someone attacked her in a park and killed her." Spencer gave a mirthless little laugh. "It's a good thing I was in Boston, wasn't it? Otherwise, I'm sure I'd be the prime suspect."

Jan felt her whole body turn to ice. "My God, have you no feelings? How can you be so cold-blooded?"

"I am not a hypocrite, Janice, whatever else I may be. There's been no love between your mother and me for years. I'm sorry she died, especially in this cruel way, but you wouldn't expect me to make a spectacle of myself, would you?"

"No," Janice said bitterly, "I wouldn't even expect you to give a damn. And you obviously don't." She paused. "What about John Peck?"

"Who?"

"Your stepson. My half-brother. Mother's first child." Jan's voice was now as hard as her father's. "Has he been notified? Are you getting a plane ticket for him too?"

"Don't be absurd, Janice. John Peck is just some blackmailer who tried to frighten your Aunt Charlotte." Spencer dismissed him. "Which reminds me. I suppose I'd better call your great-aunt, though I have no intention of dragging her out to Denver."

The last words sparked something in Jan's mind. "Why is Mother being buried there? I'd have thought you would have insisted on bringing her here."

Spencer didn't skip a beat. "It seems more convenient this way. I'll see you at the airport."

"Are you going back to Denver, darling?" Carol Peck put her arms around her husband. "Shall I go with you?"

John shook his head. "No. I'm not going back. It would be an embarrassment for her family. And I don't want to be within striking distance of Spencer Winters. I might kill him. Jan and Christopher are going. They're the 'real' children."

"I think to her you were the most real of all."

John kissed her gently. "Yes, dear, I think I was, at that."

Barbara had a terrible time making Aunt Charlotte understand who she was. When she finally got through, she gently told her that Alice had passed away suddenly. No need to go into the sordid story with this old woman who seemed to grasp very little.

"Alice has passed away?" Charlotte did not seem sad, only a little puzzled. "That's strange. I certainly thought she'd outlive me. The young generation just doesn't seem to have the stamina we had. Poor little Alice. Thank you for telling me, young lady. I must hang up now. It's time for me to lie down before lunch. I always have a little rest between meals."

When Spencer called, the housekeeper told him that Mrs. Rudolph was resting.

"Wake her up," Spencer commanded. "This is important."

"Excuse me, sir, but is it about her niece?"

"Yes. Yes, it is."

"I believe Mrs. Rudolph already knows. She had a telephone call from Miss Barbara Dalton in Denver about an hour ago. Mrs.

Rudolph told me her niece had passed away. I'm very sorry, Mr. Winters."

Spencer didn't acknowledge the sympathy. "She knows? Good. Then don't disturb her. If she asks, tell her I've gone away and will be back in a couple of days. Is she all right?"

"Oh, yes, sir. I don't think she quite comprehends things any more. The seriousness of them, I mean."

Lucky Charlotte, Spencer thought.

On the Boston-to-Denver flight, Janice and Christopher sat side by side in first class. Their father, across the aisle, was apparently absorbed in the current issue of *Fortune*.

"Look at him," Christopher said. "The sonofabitch has ice water in his veins."

Jan nodded. Spencer was unbelievable. He'd not spoken to Chris at the airport and had barely said half a dozen words to Jan since their telephone conversation. He seemed coldly angry, not just "normally angry" as he always was with his children, but inwardly furious about something. It has to do with Mother being buried in Denver, Jan thought. He didn't want that, and somebody forced him into it. Somebody was able to make Spencer Winters do what he didn't want to, and he is enraged about it. His was not the silence of grief but of fury. It was in his eyes. It had even been in his voice when he told her that interment in Denver was more "convenient." Jan didn't believe that for a moment. Not that he'd give a damn where Alice was buried, but Jan knew her father well. It was not like him to give up the spotlight he'd hold during a period of mourning and funeral in his own town. Janice reached for her brother's hand.

"We'll miss her, Chris. God knows she and I didn't always see eye to eye, but I liked her."

She saw him swallow hard and felt his grip tighten on her fingers.

"I still can't accept it, Jan. It doesn't seem real."

"I know."

"I'm sorry for Grandmother and Grandfather. We hardly know them, but they must be going through hell. Her sisters too. We don't know them at all. Funny to have aunts you've never seen. For that matter, it's a damned funny family."

"Worse," Jan said. "It's no family at all, now that Mother's gone." She hesitated. "I wish I could have told her something that would have made her happy. I haven't told anybody except John Peck, but Clint and I are going to be married. Mother would have been pleased. She never made a fuss about my living with Clint, but I know she didn't like it." Janice reached for a tissue in her bag and dabbed at her eyes. "Damn it to hell! Why couldn't she have lived to see me become an honest woman?"

Christopher gently patted her cheek. "Let me be glad in her place. I'm happy for you, Jan. That's a nice guy you've got." He indicated Spencer. "You going to tell *him?*"

"Not now, certainly. Maybe not until after the ceremony. He's not going to force me into a big public wedding as a publicity gimmick. Clint and I will go quietly to City Hall one day soon, and I'll tell dear Father when the deed is done."

She realized what was in her mind even as she spoke. Spencer wasn't going to substitute an elaborate engagement and wedding for the vulgar funeral he'd have arranged if he could. It was a gruesome thought, but it was true. A terrible trade-off. She didn't want a big wedding, but even if she had, she'd have rejected it just to deprive him of the chance to show off. She shuddered.

"Are you all right?"

"Yes. I'm just thinking what a strange couple of days it's going to be. Strange and sad."

"I wish we'd come for the Golden Anniversary," Chris said slowly.

"Yes. I wish so too."

On another western flight, Charles Tallent gazed out of the window, seeing only the whipped-cream clouds below, thinking regretfully of the ugly scene he'd just left. Andrea had been like a madwoman when he'd told her what he planned to do. He'd never seen her so out of control. All the veneer was stripped away as she called him everything from a middle-aged fool to an incompetent politician who'd never be anything more than "a lousy little public servant from the sticks." He hadn't answered until his bag was packed and he was on the way to the front door. Even then he didn't raise his voice, didn't point out that in a way she'd brought this on herself with the ill-advised letter to Barbara. He didn't care enough to get into that. All he wanted was to leave and never come back to this vicious woman or this unhappy house.

"I thought you'd be more civilized about this," he'd said. "We don't love each other, Andrea. You'll be well provided for. The children are grown. They have their own lives. Before it's too late, I'd like to find some real happiness in the rest of my life. I wish the same for you."

"Happiness!" She spat out the word. "You don't know the meaning of it! You're so juvenile you think you'll find 'happiness' in bed. My God! You'd give up position, recognition, maybe a place in history for that damned little tart? You must be crazy. You must be going through male menopause."

He'd allowed himself one little flicker of nastiness as his parting shot. "If menopause means 'change of life,'" Charles said, "I'm not only going through it, I'm going to love every second of it."

He smiled now, remembering. A change of life. Long overdue for him and the woman who waited for him in Denver.

Barbara and Frances drove in silence toward the funeral home. Theirs was a dreadful task: to see that Alice was properly dressed and arranged in her coffin before her parents and sorrowing friends and family came during the usual seven-to-nine o'clock "viewing hours" for the next two nights. The thought of it made both of them sick. Barb could not put her dread into words, but as they neared their destination Fran couldn't contain herself.

"It's barbaric! If you're around when I die, for God's sake don't let people come and look at me. Promise me, Barb. I want them to remember me alive and kicking. That's the way I want to remember Allie. I don't want to look at her all painted up like some doll in a box." She lit a cigarette nervously. "Must I look at her, Barb?"

"No. Not if you don't want to. I'll see that everything's in order."

Perversely, Fran shook her head. "No, dammit, I will do it. We promised Mother we'd do it together. It's not fair to shove it off on you. It's just that I can't stand this kind of thing!"

Barbara couldn't help herself. "Then, for God's sake, why didn't you let Spencer take her back to Boston? Mother thought that was the right thing to do and I rather agreed with her. But no, you had to make sure Spencer wouldn't get his way. If the services had been back East you wouldn't even have had to go. I don't understand you, Fran."

Her sister gave a joyless laugh. "Funny. That's more or less what somebody else said to me very early this morning. I told him he couldn't know me because I don't know myself."

"Who is 'he'?"

"The Venzetti kid. I went there from the hospital."

Barbara was genuinely shocked. "You went to that waiter? Last night? Right after we heard . . ."

"We all have our ways of trying to block out grief, Barb. That was mine. Only it didn't work. He turned me down. There was only one person I wanted to run to for comfort, and he didn't want me either. Buzz. I haven't heard a word from him today. Wouldn't you think he'd have the decency to telephone? He must know about Allie."

"He knows," Barbara said slowly. "He phoned this morning."

"And didn't want to speak to me." Fran's voice was flat.

"He's pretty badly broken up about Dorothy. You know that."

"Sure. But not so broken up he couldn't speak to *you*. Oh, I know I've lost this battle. I thought, 'Give him a little time. He'll come back when the guilt and shock wear off.' But I guess I've known since the minute I heard about Dorothy that he'd never be able to look at me again."

"He's going away tomorrow," Barb said. "To visit his brother in California. He told me to tell you. But he will come back. And maybe you're right. He loves you, Fran. Given enough time . . ."

"No. No way. He'll marry some nice woman. Somebody he deserves." She paused. "Hell, Barb, maybe he'll marry you. You'd be good for each other. You're both decent people."

"Me? Don't be crazy! Buzz Paige and I don't belong together! That would be a wild thought even if Charles . . ."

"Even if Charles what?"

"He's coming this afternoon. I haven't told anyone. He wants to be here with me. I told him not to, but he wouldn't listen. I . . . I think he means to divorce Andrea. I don't know what's happening. Good God, this isn't the time to be thinking about ourselves, Fran! How can we even be discussing our own lives at this moment? It's dreadful! Allie's dead, and you and I are chewing over romances! We should be ashamed!"

Frances suddenly looked composed and wise. "There's no reason to be ashamed. It doesn't change things for Allie. I'm not heartless, Barb. I'm realistic. Life goes on. I'm glad it's going to go on well for you, at least. I'd be a rotten sister to begrudge you joy because I don't see much for myself. Allie would feel the same. I'm happy for you."

"I told you, I don't even know what's happening. Only that Charles is coming."

"You know what's happening, my dear. He's coming for you. He wouldn't show up here at this time if he weren't. You know that's true, Barb. Your Charles has finally come to his senses."

A tear rolled down Barbara's face. "I've lived so long not daring to hope . . . I suppose I can't get used to the idea that the waiting might be over. What right have I, of the three of us, to be the only one things turn out right for? Allie's dead. You've lost the only man you ever really loved. How can I believe . . ."

"You can believe, little one. Allie saw her dream come true when she found Johnny. And who knows? My soulmate may be waiting in the wings. Don't ever feel unworthy of happiness, Barb. Don't be an Alice, God rest her soul, who thought she didn't deserve any better than she got. You've given Charles Tallent everything through the years. It's about time he paid some of it back. And, for God's sake, don't feel guilty because things are working out for you as they didn't for Allie and me! Just be damned glad one of us got lucky."

Barbara managed to smile. It was good to hear her sister talking like the "old Frances." She was the true survivor among them. She and Laura. Strong women in different ways—the mother long on forbearance and faith; the daughter tough enough to take disappointments and romantic enough not to abandon the girlish ideals she hid under the cloak of cynicism.

"I love you," Barb said. "I'm sorry for some of the nasty things I said. I didn't mean them. They just came out because I was upset."

"Forget it. I've heard a lot worse and deserved it all. 'Sticks and stones . . .' You know." Fran closed her eyes for a moment. "There's one good thing about me. I've discovered over the years that, as the old saying goes, 'I bruise easy but I heal quick.' " She opened her eyes and stared straight ahead. "Subject closed, at least for now. We have to take care of Allie."

Sam Dalton came into the kitchen and stopped short in amazement. His wife was on her hands and knees, scrubbing the kitchen floor.

"Laura! What in the name of heaven are you doing?"

She looked up at him, a wisp of gray hair falling down over her eyes. "I couldn't just sit any more. I was going out of my mind." She stood up, slowly, painfully. "Funny. I remember my mother doing the same thing. Whenever she had a terrible problem she scrubbed a floor or ran the carpet sweeper or rearranged the furniture. Sometimes it's the only thing that can get you through: hard, physical work that keeps you from thinking about what's happened." She sighed heavily. "I never thought about it before, but I suppose that's why you put in those long hours in the garden, isn't it? To keep you from thinking about how unhappy you are away from the job and how much you miss the people you worked with."

"It's not exactly the same," Sam said gently. "That's a different kind of unhappiness. A very minor one compared to this." He looked as though he were about to weep again. Please don't, Laura silently begged. Seeing a man cry, watching him being ashamed of his "unmanly" tears, was heartbreaking. And Sam had cried often in the past twelve hours or so. He tried hard to contain his tears, but they had to come. He's lucky, Laura thought. I haven't been able to cry. Not once. I wish I could. It would be such a relief from this awful numbness, this dreadful, strangling feeling of loss. Why can't I weep? she wondered almost angrily. When will the blessed, healing tears come? Later, I pray. Lord, give me the luxury of letting go. I've lost a child, a baby I pushed out of me, sweating and crying with pain, almost fifty years ago. Let me weep for her and the life she had. Let me weep for her father and sisters. For her children. And, Lord, let me weep for myself.

But she stayed dry-eyed, moving robot-like to empty the pail of sudsy water and put away the scrub brush. Automatically, she tidied her hair and straightened her dress.

"We'd better get cleaned up, Sam. Spencer and the children will be arriving soon. We don't want them to see us looking like this."

He made an effort to pull himself together. "Where are they staying?"

"I don't know. Frances just said they'd be coming today. They'll be at one of the hotels. I suppose they'll call when they get in."

"I don't want that man in my house." Sam's voice was suddenly strong. "I don't even think he should be allowed to receive people who come to pay their respects. Allie hated him. She wouldn't want him around, pretending to grieve."

"Dear, you said yourself he was her husband. He has his rights. He's a bad man, but I'm grateful to him now for letting us keep Allie nearby as long as we live. I thought at first it wouldn't be right, but I know it is. He wouldn't go to visit her grave. We will." Laura took a deep breath. "Besides, there are the children. We scarcely know them. I want them to feel we love them. No matter what we feel, Sam, we must be civil to Spencer for Janice and Christopher's sake."

He didn't answer, but he turned to go upstairs and "make himself presentable," as she'd suggested. Laura looked after him pityingly. She dreaded the sight of Spencer Winters as much as Sam did, but there was no way around it. She'd tell Frances and Barbara to keep the man away from their father. And from Jack Richards, too, she thought suddenly. What would Jack feel when he came face to face with Allie's husband? She was relieved that John Peck had sent a telegram of condolence and the news that he would not return. He was a sensitive young man. Laura knew he must want to be at the funeral of the mother he'd known so briefly. But obviously he realized how awkward that would be. She liked Alice's firstborn. In time she could have come to love him deeply, if things had not taken this tragic turn. Poor Johnny, she thought. The rest of them had had some part of Alice for years, but that child had seen his mother for only forty-eight hours. It was cruel. Cruel to have found her after all the years, only to lose her again, this time forever.

Laura stood in the middle of her kitchen thinking of John Peck. And the realization of his loss did what nothing else had been able to do. It brought the warm, gushing tears that streamed down her face and untied the horrible knot of agony in her breast. Sobs wracked her slender frame while she stood rooted, hands clenched at her sides, able at last to weep for them all.

Chapter 32

It's like some eerie ballet, Christopher thought as he stood alone, almost unnoticed, in a corner of the room. It's as though it's all been choreographed, our moves, our responses. An almost soundless ebb and flow of people following some unseen impresario's direction.

He'd never even been in a funeral home before, much less been a participant in the strange, prolonged ritual that preceded his mother's funeral. His eyes took in the room assigned to Alice Dalton Winters. What did they call it? A "slumber room." God! It was terrible beyond belief. The open-lidded container at the far end in which she lay; the cloying smell of flowers; the stream of curious callers who came and went, murmuring their hushed words of condolence which Laura acknowledged before she passed the visitor along to his grandfather and aunts and, in some few cases, to Christopher's father and sister and even to Chris himself.

He didn't know what to say to these people who pressed his hand and expressed their sympathy. He had no idea who they were. They usually identified themselves as an "old friend of your mother's," but they were nameless strangers. The sight and touch of them sickened him. The whole primitive process was endless torture and he felt alone and frightened. Even Janice seemed to manage as he couldn't. She was polite and subdued, gracefully composed. Occasionally, though, she glanced over at Chris, who was trying to lose himself in the far corner. He couldn't tell whether she understood his revulsion or whether she was annoyed that he did not play the game by the mysterious rules everyone else seemed to know.

What am I doing here? Chris wondered. I don't fit in among the conventions of death any more than I do among those of life. I loved my mother. She understood and accepted me for what I am. She'd know how I hate this. She'd hate it too. He hadn't been able to look at Alice. Had refused to, even though Spencer Winters ordered him roughly to. It was one of the few times Spencer had spoken directly to his son since they'd been together.

"Go pay your respects to your mother," Spencer commanded. "It's the last time you'll ever see her."

"No." Chris was surprised by his calm voice. "I'll see her forever. She'll always be alive to me." He was relieved that a roomful of people had prevented his father from shouting at him or dragging him bodily to the other end of the room. Spencer would have been capable of both if they'd been alone. Instead, the man stared at him scornfully and said, almost under his breath, "Damned little sissy. Not even enough guts to do that."

Chris didn't answer, and Spencer stalked away, ignoring Frances, who stood nearby, taking in the whole incident. As Spencer left, Chris's aunt approached her nephew. They'd been only briefly introduced. He'd had no more than a fleeting impression of a tall, handsome, quietly dressed woman who kindly but almost impersonally acknowledged her sister's child. Now she said, gently, "Let's take a little walk, Chris. I could use a breath of air. How about you?"

He nodded gratefully and they slipped quietly out. On the street they walked a few yards from the entrance before Frances stopped and leaned against a tree.

"I'm out of cigarettes. Do you have one?"

"Sure." He offered her the pack, took one himself and flicked his gold lighter. The small flame briefly illuminated Fran's big sad eyes, which stayed on him as she took the light and inhaled deeply. Chris nervously lit his own cigarette and waited.

"You loved your mother and you hate all this, don't you?"

"Yes to both questions. It's indecent. Everyone staring at her, and she unable to tell them she doesn't want them to." He took a long drag. "Does that sound crazy?"

"No. I share your feelings about this archaic business. That is, I did share them until now. Ever since I was introduced to this kind of thing I've thought it morbid and uncivilized. Outdated, at least. And cruel to the survivors. But, Chris, I've realized something in the past two days." Frances paused to make sure her words would have the impact she intended. "I've realized that for many people, perhaps for most people, this period which you and I find so excruciating is necessary. They need to look at death to accept it. They need this little time to recognize the truth—that someone they loved is dead. It is comfort rather than cruelty to most people. It occupies them and lets them adjust to the grief. Can you understand that?"

"No. I wish I could." His voice was sad in the darkness. "I think it's like cutting someone away piece by piece instead of making a clean amputation. I know Mother's dead. I don't have to see her that way or stand around making small talk like I'm at some ghastly cocktail party. I'm sorry, but to me it's bizarre."

Frances nodded, though he couldn't see her. "Yes, you'd feel that way because you're intelligent and aware and sensitive. But most people have to have time to understand that someone is gone forever. If everything's too quick, they can never really grasp it. Never make peace with themselves. It's . . . it's as though someone you love dies in a faraway country and you only hear that they've died. You never see them that way. You have to take someone else's word for it. Then, I imagine, it would never be real to you. You'd always feel that the person was just away on a trip, and that you'd be hearing from them or that they'd be coming back. That must be worse agony than this. If your mother had died and been buried here without your coming, perhaps you'd have had that sense of unreality, Chris. If we hadn't gone through this wake, your grandparents would be less able to adjust to the horror. I know," Frances said, "that's hard for you to believe. I never believed it myself before. But I do now. I promise you, it's true."

He was silent for a long moment. "I suppose I see what you mean," he said at last. "I don't know. I find it a difficult theory to buy, but I've never lived through anything like that, so I can't be sure how I'd feel. It's incredible to me that people have to mourn in public. That they have to be so organized about it."

"I know. It seems macabre. Masochistic, even. But have you watched the people here? They're drawing comfort from each other. And strength. Minute by minute, Allie's death becomes more real and thus less frightening. We only fear what we don't know, Chris. We can only accept what we can see. I see that sad but peaceful resignation on one face in particular: Jack Richards'. He loved your mother once. He felt he let her down years ago, and again during her last visit. I've seen the agony begin to disappear from his face. Oh, he still grieves. He will, for a long while. But he's coming out of the nightmare stage, the shock we all suffered. He may not know it, but he's beginning to accept. That's the purpose of all this, Chris. That's what you must accept emotionally, even if you reject it intellectually."

"Jack Richards." Chris repeated the name slowly. "Was he . . . ?"

"He was your mother's childhood sweetheart. He's the father of your half-brother. Haven't you met him?"

"I . . . I don't know. So many people have come up to me. Most of them don't even say their names. I'd like to meet him." There was pain in the young man's voice. "I'd like to meet a man Mother loved, and one who loved her. Will you point him out to me when we go back? I'd honestly like to tell him I'm glad he made her happy, even for a little while."

Frances stretched out her hand and found her nephew's. "I wish you were my child," she said.

Like her sister, Barbara deplored what Christopher called "a ghastly cocktail party." But, also like Frances, she knew it was necessary, particularly to people of her parents' generation—a time of confirmation and occupation. The let-down would come later when Allie was laid to rest; when the neighbors stopped coming by with vast quantities of food so the bereaved family would not have to trouble themselves with cooking; when there were no longer people to be polite to at the funeral home; when Barbara and Frances had left and Sam and Laura were alone. That's when they'd feel the full, hideous awareness of their loss. Until now, devastated as they were, the enormity of what happened hadn't really sunk in. It wouldn't until they had nothing but time on their hands. The dreadful days were still to come for

Allie's mother and father, and there was nothing anyone could do about it. There was no way their grown daughters could come home to live with them. Frances would resume her pointless journey to nowhere. And I, Barbara thought, will be back in Washington, starting a new life with Charles.

She still felt selfish and irrationally guilty about her own good fortune. If only it had come sooner, or even later, she wouldn't have this apologetic feeling about the wonderful turn her own life had taken. It made no sense to feel that way, but the joy of her reunion with Charles had been overshadowed by the circumstances which surrounded it. She'd been torn between wanting him to come to Denver, bringing a strong shoulder to lean on, and wishing he'd stay away. It was almost indecent that at this moment of utter misery she should be introducing her long-time lover to her family. Not that Charles hadn't handled it with the utmost tact and understanding. He'd called from the Brown Palace when he checked in and said simply, "I'm here, darling. Whenever you're ready to see me, I'll come to you."

Bone-weary, just back from seeing that Allie was "properly arranged," her poor little head softly swathed in pale tulle to hide the ugly evidence, Barbara was tempted to tell him to go back to Washington. He didn't belong here. She couldn't handle this jarring note in the most intimate of family gatherings. He had no place in their sorrow, and for a moment Barbara didn't know what to say. She'd had no sleep since the night before last. None of them had. And they still had to face the awful days ahead. She yearned to be with him, to be held and comforted like a child, and yet, ambivalently, he seemed an added burden. Charles instinctively understood her silence.

"I don't want to make things harder for you, sweetheart. You must be going through hell. It's enough for me to be in the same city with you. At least you know I'm near if you need me. Would you rather I call you tomorrow? Would that be better?"

Her heart melted. He'd flown thousands of miles simply to be there if she wanted him. He asked nothing. He was willing to wait in the hotel for days, if she preferred. He sensed her distress, her divided feelings, and she loved him for it.

"I'll come down and pick you up," Barb said. "The family will be glad you're here. They'll be grateful." She broke down. "Oh, dearest, I'm so glad you're here. I love you so much. I need you terribly."

"Stay put," he said. "I'll be there as quickly as I can get a cab."

He arrived at the house within minutes and she ran into his arms. He held her close, looking over her shoulder at the three other adults in the hallway, nodding at them silently while Barbara tried to get herself under control. At last she separated herself from him and dried her eyes. Then she turned and said, "Mother. Dad. Fran. This is Charles. Charles Tallent."

Frances, the only one who knew he was coming, stepped forward and kissed his cheek. "How wonderful you're here," she said.

Laura looked stunned for an instant. Charles Tallent, the man Barbara loved, the one she thought she'd lost, was here in Laura's own house. What did it mean? What had happened? Never mind. What did it matter now? There'd be time for explanations later.

"We're glad to see you, Charles," she said, "Sam, dear, this is Barbara's friend, the congressman from Washington."

"Yes. Yes, of course." Sam extended his hand. "Good of you to come."

Charles returned the handshake. "Mrs. Dalton. Mr. Dalton. I can't begin to tell you how sorry I am. When Barbara told me what happened to your daughter, I just had to come. I hope it doesn't . . . embarrass you, my being here. I won't intrude. I simply wanted to be around in case there's anything I can do."

"You're welcome," Laura said simply.

Now, standing in the funeral home with Charles beside her, Barbara wondered what she'd have done if he'd not come. He'd been a tower of strength these past two days, running errands, keeping track of who sent what flowers, behaving like a family friend willing to take on any chore that needed doing. Their only concession to the awkwardness of his presence had been to agree among themselves that he'd be introduced as "Charles Tallent" or "Mr. Tallent." In Colorado, most people did not know he was a congressman and they accepted him as a friend of Barbara's from Washington. There'd be no publicity about a public figure. Only Spencer Winters sparked when he and Charles were introduced at the funeral home.

"Tallent? Charles Tallent? Are you by chance the congressman?"

Charles shot Barbara a baleful look as she left them. "Yes. I'm on The Hill."

"Well, well!" Spencer was visibly impressed. "Read a lot about you. You're a big man on the Foreign Relations Committee. Didn't know you knew my wife."

"Unfortunately, I never had the pleasure. I'm a friend of Barbara's. And, I hope, of the whole family now."

Spencer raised an eyebrow. "Oh. I see. Like to talk to you, Tallent, about some projects my firm is handling overseas. Get your advice about opening a few doors in Washington."

Charles did not try to disguise his distaste. "I'm amazed you can put your mind to such things at this moment, Mr. Winters."

Spencer was unsnubbable. "Naturally, I didn't mean *here*. I could run down and see you in your office one day."

"I'm sure we can schedule it sometime. Have your secretary call mine."

"Good." Spencer did not seem to even notice the rudeness. "We can probably do a little mutual back-scratching."

Charles walked away, not answering. "My God," he said when he reached Barbara's side, "what kind of a man was your sister married to? He was actually trying to talk business to me!"

"He's a terrible man," Barb said. "It was a terrible marriage."

"Ours won't be, darling. I promise you that." He put his hand gently on her arm. "No, don't turn away. I know this isn't the time or place to propose. I just want you to know I'm going to be free and I intend to make you happy."

She looked up at him with adoration. They hadn't been alone since he arrived. They knew without discussion, this was not the time for that. Charles had not even hinted at it, and Barb respected the delicacy that made him know physical lovemaking was not what she needed. He unselfishly gave her what she did need—undemanding comfort and strength through his presence. He represented security and reality, a promise of a sane future in a world gone mad. Sex was good with them and would be again, but it would have been almost agony for Barbara in this atmosphere of pain for the living and respect for the dead.

From his place on the other side of the room, Jack Richards watched Barbara and Charles Tallent in that brief but unmistakably loving communication. He'd been introduced to Charles by Frances, who whispered later, "Isn't it wonderful? They're so in love."

Jack was startled to feel a terrible sense of disappointment at those words. Startled and ashamed. Standing there, only a few feet from the body of the woman he should have loved, he admitted to himself that from the moment Barbara had brought Alice to his apartment he'd wanted her, not the sister. She'd been in his mind ever since. Even in his agony over Allie, he'd selfishly thought that perhaps, after a decent interval, he could begin to "court" Barb. He'd even dared hope she was attracted to him too. He fantasized that she might stay on in Denver with her parents, that they'd begin to see each other, that, in time, they would marry. She'd be the right woman for him—witty and bright and strong, capable of being wife and playmate. What an animal he was, allowing himself such dreams when Alice was not even in her grave! And, as it now turned out, what a stupid animal as well. He should have known someone as magnetic as Barbara would have a man in her life. How could he have deluded himself that she'd want him for a husband as much as he desired her for a wife?

He looked at Charles Tallent and hated him. Hated him for his good looks, his easy manner. Hated him most of all because he was the man Barbara loved and went to bed with.

It's all a big zero, Jack thought. Nothing works out the way it's supposed to. I've lost everyone. I'll probably never even see Johnny again. The boy didn't fool him. He'd been glad to find his father, but it was his mother who mattered to him. John Peck tolerated Jack. Perhaps he even felt some slight affection for him. But it was Allie their son cared about. Allie who'd borne the agony and frustration while Jack made a life of his own with little thought of the child he'd fathered. John Peck knew that. Deep down, Jack thought, he must resent me for not having taken care of his mother either in the early or late years of life. I meant well. I did. I'm just a selfish man. That's the way I'm made.

It was over. The brief eulogy delivered by the minister had been simple and moving, a good job since the man had never met Alice and had to rely on her sisters and her daughter for the bits of personal tribute, the references to her parents and sisters and husband and children, the citing of her charitable work in Boston and her goodness as a mother, wife and child. The clergyman had quietly but firmly denounced the violence that pervaded the world, the insanity that had caused the death of an innocent woman. But he urged those at the funeral to find mercy and forgiveness in their hearts, to see Allie's death as the work of a sick mind and to believe that God had taken her to a peaceful and happy place.

"We know that to forgive is divine," the young minister said earnestly. "We know too that it is the most difficult, as well as the most Christian, assignment a shocked and bereaved family can be asked to accept. But those who deeply and truly loved Alice remember her generosity of spirit, her lovely childlike belief in the basic goodness of people, her capacity for understanding and faith and compassion. May they find it with themselves to pray not only for her but also for the deranged soul who perpetrated this tragic act."

Damned young bleeding heart! Sam Dalton thought angrily. How would he know what it was like to have your daughter violated and murdered? How could he brazenly stand there and ask them to pray for some animal who was still loose and probably never would be brought to justice? It was insufferable. Sam considered himself a religious, God-fearing man. Not as good a church-goer as Laura, but as good as most. It would take a saint not to wish for vengeance. Pray for my daughter's killer? I pray for only one thing: that he's caught and made to pay for his crime.

That's what's wrong with the world, Sam thought. All this permissiveness, all this psychological mumbo-jumbo about rehabilitating criminals and finding something in their upbringing or their environment to explain the lawless things they do. Even the ministers are spouting it from the pulpit, as concerned with the redemption of evil men as they are with the eternal life of the good people who try to live by the Commandments. Whatever happened to "Thou Shalt Not Kill"? Do these young wearers of the cloth really believe rape and murder are understandable? Forgivable? Never in a million years!

He clenched his teeth in rage, and it was as though this fury brought him back to life. In the three days since Allie's death he'd been like a dead man himself, walking, talking, trying to eat and sleep, consumed with a grief so deep he could feel the physical pain of it. Now, even as he left the church with Laura, even as he climbed slowly into the limousine that would follow the hearse, his sorrow did not diminish, but he prayed that the beast-at-large would suffer in some monstrous way for his sins. Sam would never forget. How dare anyone ask him to forgive?

Late that afternoon, Laura answered the front-door bell and was surprised to find Janice Winters there. The young woman looked so utterly drained that, involuntarily, Laura held out her arms. Jan fell into them, her tears mingling with her grandmother's.

"Come in, Janice dear," Laura said at last. "I thought you'd gone back to Boston."

"We have a flight later this evening." She glanced around. "You aren't all alone, are you?"

"No. Your grandfather and aunts are upstairs trying to rest. I couldn't be still, so I came down to make myself a cup of tea. Would you like one?"

"Yes, thank you. I would."

"Let's have it in the kitchen. We always seemed to end up talking in there, Frances and Barbara and . . . and your mother. We had many a conversation around that table when the girls were young, and even in these past days when they were home for the anniversary." Laura was trying hard to act normally. "Just sit yourself down there. The kettle's already boiling."

Janice looked around the cheerful, old-fashioned kitchen. It was thoroughly out of date, with its four-burner gas range and refrigerator, its porcelain sink and plastic rack for draining dishes. It was a far cry from the one in Boston that Spencer had insisted be "modernized" with dishwasher and freezer and wall oven and miles of butcher blocks and stainless steel. The Boston kitchen did not invite sitting. It was cold and efficient. Like Spencer. This one was warm and cozy, welcoming, as though it had received fifty years of confidences and seen more than its share of tragedies and triumphs. Bright curtains hung at the windows and Laura's precious African violets bloomed on the ledge. There was a big round table and plenty of room for the once-reunited family of five.

"I love this room," Jan said. "It makes me feel safe."

Laura, returning with the tea things, nodded. "Yes. It's always made me feel that way too." She poured the tea, waiting, but Janice seemed reluctant to say why she'd come. She sipped her tea, took out a package of cigarettes and asked if Laura minded her smoking.

"No. Help yourself. I just hope you're not a fiend, like your Aunt Frances. I do worry about how much she smokes."

What does this child want? Laura wondered. They'd all said goodbye at the cemetery. Sam had barely looked at Spencer, had not even shaken hands with the man, but she and Fran and Barbara had tried to be composed. Horror that Spencer was, he had been Allie's husband for twenty-five years and one had to acknowledge that. Besides, Allie's children were sweet, even if they'd been rather reserved. Only Fran had seemed to get close to young Christopher. She'd said he was sensitive, a nice boy. None of them knew much about Janice. Only that she was pretty and well-mannered. Why has she come here now? Laura thought again. There must be something she wants to say to me or to all of us.

As though she picked up Laura's thoughts, Janice suddenly spoke. "I wanted to see you, Grandmother, before I left. I . . . I want you to know how much I regret never having been close to you. Any of you. Mother wanted me to come with her to your anniversary party and I didn't want to. It didn't seem to mean anything to me, coming all this way to see grandparents I barely remembered. She was disappointed. I guess I disappointed her in many ways. I loved her, and I think she knew that. But I'm sure she also knew that I didn't have much respect for her. Because she stayed with my father, I mean. Because she let him be so cruel to her . . . and to me and Chris."

Laura said nothing. She was listening to a confession, a cleansing of the soul. Jan took a deep breath and went on.

"I didn't know, until John Peck turned up, how little respect Mother had for herself. And how wrong she was to feel she had to pay for that early mistake. I see now why she did what she did. Why she stayed with my father. She *was* punishing herself, but she was also making sure her other two children had a home, no matter how troubled a one. We, that is Chris and I, had no idea of her feelings. Chris was much closer to her than I was, even though he couldn't stay in that house, not even for her sake. He didn't understand why she didn't leave, any more than I did. But she wouldn't leave. Maybe she was afraid to. Maybe she didn't know where to go. I don't know. I only know I didn't try to help."

Laura reached across the table and touched Jan's arm. "Don't blame yourself, Janice. You didn't know. None of us knew how she felt. We were all to blame in one way or another. We more than you, dear. Much more."

"I was glad when she didn't come back to Boston after your anniversary. Glad for her sake, I mean. And when John told me about their reunion, I was so happy. I thought maybe she'd marry his father and finally have some kind of life worth living. I helped get Mother and John together, you know." There was a little trace of pride in her voice. "It was a crazy coincidence, but I was the one who finally helped him sort out the clues and find her."

"Thank the Lord you did," Laura said. "It meant more to her than anything in the world."

"Yes. I know. And then to have it all blow up so suddenly, so terribly. All the good years she might have had at last." Jan began to cry again. "Maybe we'd have finally understood each other." She wiped her eyes. "I've been a smart-aleck most of my life, Grandmother. Very sophisticated. Very liberated. Very stupid. I wanted Mother to know that I'd finally grown up, that I'm going to marry Clint Darby, the man I've been living with. I want the conventional life I've always sneered at. I want it all. The wedding ring and his name and all that goes with it. I never had a chance to tell her any of that. Or to tell her how I finally realize what she sacrificed for Chris and me, and how grateful we are."

"I like to believe she knows," Laura said softly. She was crying now too. Crying for Alice and for this dear child who never gave herself a chance to know her mother. "I'm glad you have someone you love, Janice. Someone who loves you and wants you to marry him. He must be very proud of you. I think that's what it means when a man wants you to take his name—that he's proud of you and respects you, as he should. And as you should respect him. That's the way your mother would want it."

Jan looked lost. "I feel that I can almost speak to her through you. She was your baby. That's why I came today. To tell you these things and to ask you . . ."

"What? Ask anything you like, dear."

"I've been thinking. Clint and I decided to have a City Hall wedding. I won't let my father turn it into a circus, a chance to show how rich and successful he is. But since I've been here, I wondered, well, could we be married out here, from your house, Grandmother? I won't let Dad come. Just Chris and John and his wife. I want to be married in front of my family, and you and Grandfather and my two brothers are all I have. Doing it that way would make it seem as though Mother was here. May I, please? May I plan that?"

It seemed an eternity before Laura answered. "No one could pay your grandfather and me a bigger compliment, Janice. We'd be proud to have you married from our house. But it wouldn't be right, dear. I'm not your mother. I'm her mother. I'm too old to be a substitute mother for my daughter. Maybe you're too young to understand that. I can't replace her, dear. No one can. And just being married in the place your mother once lived doesn't mean you'll have your mother back. This house is part of her past, not yours. Your place is in Boston, Janice. Where your friends are, where your roots are. Even where your father is. I know you have no love for him, nor have I. He was cruel to my child and that's hard to forgive. But he's still your father, and a father is entitled to give his only daughter in marriage. You can have your wedding any way you want it, but my advice is to have it there and let your father be part of it. He may not be what you deserve or want, but I suspect if there's anyone in the world he cares for, it probably is you. Men feel that way about their girl-children. No," she said as Janice started to protest, "don't tell me I'm wrong. Think about it. Try to understand that, wicked as he is, underneath he's a pathetic man, driven and insecure. He's been hateful, horrible, and none of us can forget what he did to Alice. But take pity on him, because no one else ever will."

"I can't. I can't be that magnanimous."

"At least consider it. And if you decide you want to be married here, we'll welcome you with open arms. But don't take revenge, Janice. And don't mistake the emotions of this moment for something more than they are. Just think it over, all of it. And let us know your decision. We'll abide by it, whatever it is." She kissed her granddaughter's cheek. "I love you. We all do. That takes no thinking over at all."

Chapter 33

It was raining lightly. A quiet, thin but steady rain that blew red, yellow and orange leaves against the library window and reminded Charles that another brutal Washington winter was all too close. He looked up from his desk and took pleasure in the sight of Barbara curled up in a chair next to the small, crackling, wood-burning fireplace. A year ago he'd never hoped for this idyllic life. Last October he'd had a different wife, one for whom he felt nothing, and a mistress he loved who was now his wife. He felt a rush of affection for the woman he'd nearly lost in the temporary headiness of a political plum dangled before his greedy eyes. Thank you, God, he said silently. You do, indeed, work in wondrous ways.

"Anything interesting?"

Barbara looked up from her letter. "Everything's fine at home, Mother says. They're both all right and sorry we won't be there next week to celebrate their fifty-first."

"Do you want to go?"

"No. They've promised to come here for Christmas. I want them to see our new house. Do you realize they've never been to Washington? Dad will have a wonderful time grousing about the Administration, and Mother will love the sightseeing." Barbara smiled. "About as much as I'll hate showing another visitor the White House and the Jefferson Memorial for the nine-hundredth time. It ain't easy being a congressman's wife, old buddy. Sometimes I feel like a tour guide for the constituents."

For a moment he was troubled. "You don't regret it, darling, do you? All the extra work? This big house instead of your little apartment? Being a Washington hostess instead of a business-woman? You're not bored, are you?"

"I hate every minute of it." Seeing the dismay on his face, she laughed. "You really are mad, Congressman. Regret it? It's like a dream, every second of it. Do you know, sometimes I wake up in the morning and watch you while you sleep? You're a lovely sleeper. Quiet, with a little smile on your face. It's still a new feeling to me, knowing where I belong, being part of you, helping a little." She became quiet. "I'm always afraid you're the one who might have regrets," she said softly. "You gave up so much to marry me. I never want you to be sorry."

Charles left the desk to come over and kiss her. "Now who's the mad one? Oh, I suppose I should regret it," he teased. "What's so terrific about being married to the most beautiful, brightest, kindest, sexiest lady who ever lived? What's so great about a stepmother who's totally captivated my children and loves them in return? How could I possibly be happy in a warm, loving house? Or content to know I have a stronger voice in the future of the world than I ever could have had if I'd sat like a stick in Cabinet meetings worrying about government subsidics for hog growers? Regret? Lady, that word is missing from my vocabulary."

In her Paris apartment, Frances pushed aside the remnants of her croissant and café-au-lait and propped herself higher on the frilly white pillows in the king-sized bed. Funny how she could read this letter and feel nothing. Buzz had written to say he was being married next month. Some friend of Dorothy's. He wanted her to know she'd always have a special place in his heart and he hoped she wished him happiness.

"I suppose it was never to be for us, Fran," he wrote. "For a little while I thought I could be what you wanted. That we had a second chance. But I know, as I suspect you do, that even if circumstances had not pulled us apart again, we'd not have been happy together for very long. You're a free spirit, my dear, eternally young and curious. I'm a quite dull, middle-aged homebody who enjoyed a brief moment of rapture and believed I could sustain it with you. I'd have disappointed you very soon. I wouldn't have fit in with your exotic life or your friends. It was a lovely dream, like something we used to see in movies before they became real and ugly. But I couldn't have supported that dream in any way. With a year to analyze it, I'm sure you know that too."

She tossed the letter aside. He was right, of course. It had all been make-believe. She'd tried to recapture something that had intrigued a girl thirty years ago. She'd been swept up in nostalgia and foolish memories. And she'd been afraid of the future, fearful of the loneliness ahead, convinced she could buy back her youth. She was glad he was going to marry a replica of Dorothy, hopefully a saner and more predictable one, but with the same housewifely instincts, the same utter dependence he needed above all else.

There were two other letters from Denver in the morning mail. She opened Laura's first. They were both well, her mother wrote, and planning to be in Washington with Barbara and Charles for Christmas. Was there any hope she might be there too? It would be wonderful if she and Sam were with their two dear daughters.

No mention of Allie, who'd been dead almost a year. No need to mention her. She was never long out of their thoughts. She had, in a terrible way, brought them all closer together. At least they were all in touch now, a family reunited by a tragedy that nearly destroyed them all. Christmas in Washington sounded good. The Concorde could take her there in a few hours. She'd write to Barb and invite herself.

Idly, she opened the third letter, surprised to see it was from Jack Richards, a surprise he anticipated in the first sentence.

"You'll be startled to hear from me, I suspect, but I've thought of you often in the past year, Fran. A great deal has happened. Johnny and Carol have a beautiful little girl whom they named Alice. They're very happy, and I've visited them twice since Allie died. For the first time I feel like a father and, good God, a grandfather!

"I hope this doesn't sound terrible, but I want to be utterly selfish and travel a lot. I can afford it, and, like you, I have no obligations. I guess I was never made for obligations, the way most people are. I don't think you were made for them either, Fran. Maybe together we can enjoy the practical joke we know life really is. It's a helluva lot better to take a pratfall with a friend than to be safe and bored alone. Not that I think you're alone! You're probably so besieged with invitations and plans you won't want to bother with me. But I hope not. I'd like to see Paris and you. Could you spare some time to show a country boy what Europe is all about?"

She was smiling as she put the letter down. He was incredibly naïve. Like a kid planning a holiday. But he was attractive, and he might be fun. She'd never let him know how few invitations she received. Even the young waiters and bartenders and lifeguards had begun to pall. At least Jack Richards was grown-up and willing to learn cosmopolitan ways, unlike Buzz, who never could. Why not? Why not enjoy the company of an honest-to-God intelligent male who thought she was glamorous? Who cared where it led or how long it lasted?

She wrote out a cable and reread it. "Adored your letter and applaud your attitude. Come ahead. Love and laughter. Fran."

Yes, that was the right, light touch. She was still smiling, but now with a touch of wistfulness. She raised her eyes upward and said aloud, "Is it okay with you, Allie? We no-good bastards probably deserve each other, don't you think?"

She felt foolish but better, somehow.

Martha Perrone carefully noted three dinner parties in her employer's engagement book and saw, penciled in his own hand, a weekend invitation at one of the great houses of Newport. "Cottages," she remembered they were called. Some "cottages"! Great mansions is what they were. She'd seen pictures of them. Spencer Winters spent a lot of weekends in Newport last summer. This was probably the offbeat idea of one of those crazy society women he ran around with, having an "out of season" weekend party. Funny he hadn't given her the invitation to note, as he usually did. She was turning into a social secretary. Ever since his wife's death, Mr. Winters had been so in demand he could hardly keep up with the whirl. Martha sniffed. Widowers had it made. An eligible, available man could be out every night in the week. Men were always in short supply, even if they were old and dull. Not like single women or divorcees or widows. They could rot on the shelf after the age of thirty.

Not that Mr. Winters was so old, but he was dull. Snobbish.

Pompous. Even more so now that his wife's aunt had died and left him all that money. Funny she didn't leave anything to any of her relatives, Mrs. Winters' family. Funny, that is, until she remembered that Mr. Winters himself had drawn up her new will last November.

Martha shrugged. She wasn't sure why she kept on working for him. His social and financial life had improved, but his disposition certainly hadn't. He'd been furious about the way his daughter got married. In one of his rare, unguarded moments, he'd said to Martha, "Damn, headstrong young people! Janice won't have a wedding suitable to her social standing. No. She has to be married in some crumby little chapel in Lexington. Someplace 'picturesque.' No big wedding. No reception. Nobody there. I'm surprised she's letting *me* come!" He'd stopped abruptly, annoyed that he'd shown such emotion in front of "the hired help." Martha hadn't said anything. She'd been too surprised. She simply stood there until Spencer said, "Never mind, Miss Perrone. Forget it. It doesn't matter."

"Certainly, Mr. Winters." But she hadn't forgotten it. It gave her a kind of satisfaction to know that in some things even the great Spencer Winters could be thwarted. Not many. He had everything now. Money, power, position. She wondered if he'd marry again. Maybe that strange October weekend in Newport was some kind of assignation. Well, it was none of her business. He was free to live any way he chose. Even the job wasn't so important to him now that he was independently rich. Probably Mrs. Winters would have inherited if she'd lived, poor thing. Not that she'd have seen the money anyway.

It was terrible the way Mrs. Winters died. All so strange. Martha had never found out what that whole business was about, a year ago when Mrs. Winters was in Denver. She remembered the phone calls she'd eavesdropped on. She'd never heard another word about the mysterious John Peck or figured out what Janice meant about being "her brother's keeper." Most of all, she'd never know what Alice Winters meant about "A new life" and "long-lost child." It would remain forever a mystery, just as, sadly, it would always be a mystery about who killed that nice lady. They'd never solved the crime. At least she never read that they had. When it happened it was in the Boston papers, but since then, nothing.

Mr. Winters hadn't spent much time grieving. That was for sure. What an awful man he was. No heart. Not a trace of one. He never even mentioned his wife after he came back from her funeral. It was as though she never existed. Martha wished her mother would stop harping on the "nice, secure job" Martha had, and pointedly asking all about Mr. Winters' life as a widower. She probably thought if Martha stayed there Spencer would one day "discover her," rip off her glasses and say, "My God, Martha, you're beautiful! I love you! Marry me!"

The idea made her snicker. If anything was far-fetched, that was. But she almost wished it would happen, like it used to in old Doris Day films. Plain girl becomes raving beauty. She knew just how she'd handle it. She'd look at him scornfully and say, "Yes, Mr. Winters, I *am* beautiful, but *you* are a pig!" And she'd walk out, leaving him heartbroken, his hopes dashed. He'd drink himself to death.

Martha giggled again.

"What's so funny?" Wallingford's secretary asked.

Martha's comic fantasy faded and she resumed her usual scowl. "Nothing's funny," she said. "Not a damned thing."

"Clint?"

"Um?"

"I've been thinking."

Darby put down his book and regarded his wife with amused interest. "That's pretty heavy. Cerebral activity, I mean. What's the topic?"

Jan was very serious. "Babies. Or, more correctly, the lack of them. Would you mind very much if we didn't have any?"

"You mean right away or never?"

"Never. We haven't actually talked about it lately, but I don't want children. Is that awful?"

"No. Not if you don't want them for the right reason. It's like wanting them for the wrong reason, if you follow me." He smiled. "That sounds pretty convoluted, doesn't it? What I mean is, I don't think there's anything worse than people having kids because they think it is expected of them. That's a wrong reason. Peer pressure. Family pressure. A parent who wants to be a grandparent. Wrong. Like having a baby in the hope it will hold a bad marriage together, or replace the love you're not getting from a husband. Also wrong. Now, there must be equally wrong reasons for *not* wanting a baby. And equally *right* ones. So if you don't want children, let's examine your reasons and find out if they're wrong or right. Am I making any sense to you?"

Janice returned his smile. "In your verbose way, yes. You're asking me why I don't want children. Period."

"Astonishing. You should have been an editor. Press on."

"I have several reasons. First, I don't really come on all-over dewy-eyed at the sight of babies. Somebody omitted the maternal instinct when they put the pieces of Janice Winters together. Second, I like our marriage the way it is, the free-to-be-you-and-me part, without the distractions, worries and expense of kids. Third, I think the world is sufficiently overpopulated without people like us—at least like me who doesn't care—adding to future problems. Right reasons?"

Clint considered her arguments for a minute. "Sure. All the right reasons. Or are they *all?*"

"Meaning?"

"Meaning, Janice darling, are you leaving out one? Are you afraid of having a family because your own home life was so unhappy? I know you don't think I'll beat you, but are you being influenced by your mother's life? Do you still feel guilty because you think she stayed with her husband to keep a home together for you and Chris? Hell, I'm not trying to be a road-company Freud, but are you worried that kids might somehow suffer if they belonged to you? The way you suffered belonging to your parents? The way your mother suffered at the hands of her parents? All I'm saying is, If you don't want babies because you just plain don't want them, like you don't want canaries or goldfish, then I respect that. I'm not that hung up on the subject either, to tell you the truth. But I don't want you to be pressured into *not* having kids any more than I'd want you to be pressured into *having* them. Oh, hell, this is getting awfully complicated! I just mean this kind of decision should be based on us, our relationship, our feelings. Not on anything you've seen or lived through in the past."

Janice looked thoughtful. "I don't think any of that enters into it. I really don't. For some people, like Carol, babies are the fulfillment of a lifetime desire. For John too, who spent years searching for his real parents. But children aren't necessary to my life. I'd have them if you really wanted them, Clint. And I wouldn't mind. I'd love them and be good to them and try to understand them. I'd probably make a damned good mother, believe it or not. But I truly have no urge in that direction."

"Nor have I. So that's settled. I guess it was about time we talked about it. I hadn't really given it much thought. Which is a pretty good indication that I'm no more the papa-bear type than you're the den-mother variety."

She sighed with relief. "It's not an irrevocable decision, of course. We have plenty of time in case either of us changes his mind. I still have what is known as a lot of 'child-bearing years' ahead. Or we could even adopt later on if we felt we didn't want to add to the world's numbers."

"Right." Clint grinned. "But promise me that if we do adopt it will be some little ghetto kid. Some child who needs a good home."

"That's nice. That's as it should be. Unselfish and generous."

"Well, not entirely. It would also give me pleasure to introduce your stuffy old man to his only 'grandchild.' Think how thrilled he'd be."

"Sadist!" Jan gave him a playful shove. "*Now* who's talking about wrong reasons?"

Clint became very serious. "All kidding aside, babe, it's a different world than your mother's was. There's no stigma to having a childless marriage, just as it's no disgrace for women not to marry at all. Or for men to choose their own lifestyles, as Chris has. Don't feel you're failing anybody by preferring not to have babies. Not me, not your grandparents, and certainly not yourself. I married a woman, not a brood mare. Kids are for those who want them and all that goes with them, and plenty of people do. But that's their thing. I respect freedom of choice, as long as it's an honest choice."

For a moment, Christopher was tempted to accept Barbara's invitation to go to Washington for Christmas. His grandparents were coming from Denver, and Frances from Paris, or wherever she happened to be at the moment.

"I've also written to Janice and Clint," his aunt wrote, "and

I'm going to invite John and Carol and little Allie. It will be quite a houseful, but we can manage. Foxhall Road is big enough for ten adults and a baby, though it may feel more like a sardine can than a house! Anyway, Christopher, please try to come. None of us had the heart for celebrations last year, but it would be lovely to have the family together. I know your mother would like it if she knew."

Yes, Mother would like it, Chris thought. She was a frustrated traditionalist, if ever there was one. God knows she never had a chance to enjoy those storybook gatherings of family one reads about. Not in that hostile house with a constantly angry husband, a rebellious daughter and an unhappy son. A house to which her parents and sisters never came. A house which was open only to "important people" who could be useful to Spencer Winters. He hadn't stepped foot in that house in years, not since the day he'd left it and begged Alice to go with him. He hadn't seen or heard of his father since the funeral almost a year ago, and he had no wish to. He did regret not going to Jan's wedding, but he declined when she told him Spencer would be there to give her away.

"Why?" Chris asked. "You loathe him as much as I do! Why would you want him there?"

"I don't. I don't really want him within ten miles of me, and I'll probably never see him after this. But, well, I guess this is going to sound silly, but Grandmother asked me to do it. She asked me to be kind to him because no one else ever would."

He'd been aghast. "Kind to him! After what he's done? After what he did to Mother?"

"Chris, I can't destroy myself with anger. It's over. It wasn't something of our making, and like it or not, he's our father. That's why I'm going to have him at the wedding. I don't forgive him, but I'm trying to understand what made him the way he is. There must be a great deal of self-loathing in him."

"Damned well hidden, if there is." Chris shook his head. "I love you, Jan. I'd like to be at your wedding, but I can't. Not with him there." He wanted to say it seemed like a betrayal of Alice, but he couldn't hurt Janice that way. She'd obviously made a promise to Laura Dalton, an irrational one in a moment of emotion, he supposed, and she was going to keep it despite the reluctance she must feel. Good for her, but he couldn't be that hypocritical, or maybe that big.

Jan accepted his decision. "I understand, Chris. John feels the same way. He and Carol won't come either. I'm not even going to ask anyone else of Mother's family. Not Frances or Barbara or even the grandparents, though I think they'd come out of deference to Mother." She paused. "I'll be honest with you. I hoped Father would refuse to take part in any wedding he couldn't mastermind. Then Clint and I could go to City Hall, the way we wanted. But he didn't decline, so I'm stuck with it. Look, it's no big deal. A couple of our friends from the office will stand up for us, and a few days later we'll have a party at the apartment to celebrate. You'll come to that, won't you? And bring Peter?"

"Sure. Of course we'll come." He felt terribly selfish. "I'm sorry, Jan. I know I'm letting you down. I just can't bring myself to . . ."

"No need to be sorry. It's a silly commitment on my part, but I made it and it's something I have to do for a nice, elderly, sentimental lady."

His grandmother had been pleased. Jan had shown him her letter and a check for fifty dollars, which was probably more than Sam and Laura could afford. For all her toughness, Clint thought, my sister is more sensitive than I. He wondered whether she and Clint would go to Washington for Christmas. Probably. Barbara had made it clear by omission that she had no intention of including Spencer. They'd probably all go and have the kind of gathering his aunt hoped for, full of gifts and love and nonsense.

But that's not the place for me, Chris thought. My family is Peter, and there's no way I could include him. It would only make things tense and awkward, spotlight the very situation I know Mother wanted to play down. She understood, but she knew my grandparents wouldn't. That's why I didn't go to their golden anniversary, though I wanted to. She never said why she didn't want me to go, but I knew. She didn't want to embarrass them or me by presenting a son who was gay. Ironic. They didn't know when I went out for the funeral. No one suspected. Not even Frances, who surely would have been the first to recognize what I am.

But they'd all know if I showed up in Washington with Peter, and I wouldn't go without him. He's made my life happy. Aside from Mother, he's the only one who ever cared.

God, how it must gall Father to know that the precious Winters name ends with me! This is the end of the line. Even if Jan has children they'll be Darbys. Well, good riddance is all I can say. It's appropriate in a way. Everyone waits for the end of Boston's cold, cruel winters.

Christopher smiled humorlessly at his own pathetic little play on words. In a way, it was terribly unfunny.

"Shall we accept Barbara's invitation for Christmas?"

"I wouldn't mind," John Peck said. "How about you?"

"I think it would be nice. They haven't seen Alice, any of them." Carol hugged her daughter. "Would you like to meet your great-grandparents, Allie? Want to let your great-aunts and -uncles make a fuss over you?"

If only the woman she was named for could see her, John thought. What high hopes we had when we said goodbye in Denver. She was looking forward to meeting Carol and so happy about the baby coming. I think she must have sensed Carol and I were her only hope for grandchildren. She knew Chris would never marry. And she probably suspected Jan wouldn't either. Or that she wouldn't want children if she did.

The old anger returned. Why? He'd asked himself that a thousand times in the past year. Why did my mother have to die? Why, after all the bad times, were she and I deprived of the good ones?

He hoped, childishly, that she forgave him for not being at her funeral. It would have stirred up too much talk, opened old wounds for her parents, maybe precipitated a confrontation with Spencer Winters. But, most of all, John knew he couldn't have borne it. He could live better with the memory of those two golden days.

He brought himself back to the present. "You haven't met my grandparents either," he said. "You'll like them, Carol. They're salt-of-the-earth people. And Frances will fascinate you. Not every family has its own Auntie Mame."

"If she's as nice as Barbara, I won't complain. They were lovely to come up when Allie was born."

John tickled his daughter. "Well, how about it, sweetheart? Want to spend your first Christmas in the bosom of your old dad's family?"

The baby gurgled.

"See?" Carol said. "Of course she does. She knows someday she's going back to Washington as the first female President."

"Wouldn't surprise me. Wouldn't surprise me a bit."

Chapter 34

On the morning of her fifty-first wedding anniversary, Laura Dalton opened her eyes and lay staring at the ceiling above the bed. Almost reluctantly, she allowed her mind to retrace the events of the past year, something she seldom did, not only because much of it was painful or incomprehensible, but because she was determined not to be one of those aging women who wallow in the past. She preferred to think of the tranquillity of the present and optimistically contemplate the future.

And there was something more. She was almost superstitious about the good and the bad of the months since last October. Funny how different the years were in one's life. Some of them passed swiftly, uneventfully, lulling one into a false sense of security. Others were like a newsreel, full of drama, with brief moments of joy and lingering periods of despair, disrupting the normal flow of things with unexpected twists and turns. Unconsciously, she crossed her fingers. Let Barbara's life go smoothly now. Give Frances some sense of peace. Let Sam stay well.

She'd been so terrified in January when he'd had his heart attack. Terrified and guilt-ridden that she'd allowed him to ignore those early-warning signs back in October. Thank God the attack had been mild, but there'd been a few terrible hours when she'd felt so alone, when she thought she was going to lose him. It all happened so swiftly in the middle of that bitter cold night. She remembered his waking her, almost apologetically, saying he had chest pains and felt nauseous. She'd phoned Dr. Jacoby, who'd sent an ambulance and was waiting at Presbyterian Hospital when they arrived. She remembered how helpless she felt sitting in the waiting room while Sam was rushed into intensive care. There was no one close. No one to call. Her daughters were thousands of miles away, and though she knew they'd come to her, it would take many hours. It might even, she'd thought, be too late.

Recalling it now, she shuddered. Even then she'd been superstitiously glad they hadn't taken Sam to Denver General, where they'd lost Allie. She'd concentrated on the doctors' quick opinion that the attack was "slight," willing it true, wondering how she'd go on without him if it was not.

How selfish people are, Laura thought. I was frantic with worry about Sam, yet part of my mind was consumed with what would happen to me if he died. I was thinking as much of my loss as of his life. That's the way it works, I suppose, though it's a shameful thing to admit. In times of trouble, we're subconsciously absorbed with ourselves and the effect sickness and death have on us. Even Allie's tragedy was that way. The hateful truth is that, much as we grieved for the end of her life, we were pitying ourselves for our pain, desolate that such misery had been inflicted on us who loved her. Why are we like that? Is it because "every man's death diminishes us a little?" Do we see in it the inevitable reflection of our own?

She turned her thoughts away from this morbid introspection, remembering the relief she'd felt when Dr. Jacoby finally came and said Sam would be okay. She'd burst into tears, realizing how much she loved this man she'd lived with for more than fifty years, and how fortunate she was to have him for a while longer. Only then had she called Barbara, assuring her there was no need to come, grateful for the offer to cable Frances.

"You're sure you don't need me, Mother?"

I need you terribly, Laura had thought. But I have no right to disrupt your life when there's nothing you can do but hold my hand.

"No, everything's fine, dear. Your father is out of danger. There's nothing to worry about now."

"You should have called me hours ago." Barbara was reproachful. "I could have been there by now. I hate your having gone through this all alone."

"I'm fine," Laura repeated. "And so is your father. He'll just need time to recuperate. I'll take good care of him."

"You always have," Barbara said gently. "He's a lucky man."

"I'm pretty lucky myself."

I really am, Laura thought now, looking at Sam sleeping peacefully beside her. He was well now, better than he'd been in years, looking forward to going to Washington for Christmas. He'd been pleased, even enthusiastic, about Barbara and Charles's invitation. A quite different Sam. He'd begun to change when the girls were home last year. His daughters' tragedies had humbled him, and his own brush with death made him thankful for every new day.

That's another thing about us mere mortals, Laura mused. Sadness and regret can take one of two routes—either embittering the sufferer, or making him more gentle, more compassionate and considerate. Trouble had mellowed Sam Dalton. The self-righteousness and stubbornness that had been his only real flaws had given way to a new tolerance. He rejoiced with Laura when Barbara and Charles were married. In years past he'd have been the disapproving patriarch, frowning on Charles's divorce, perhaps even thinking of his youngest child as a "home wrecker." Not now. He was happy for her happiness, as though he savored every piece of good fortune even when it happened to others.

They didn't often speak of Frances, but when they did, Laura knew he was as troubled about her as her mother was, though, manlike, he could not grasp the roots of her restlessness. Only another woman could understand how much Fran hated growing old, losing her beauty and her desirability. She'll never be truly serene, Laura thought regretfully. She's the eternally lost soul, always seeking something or someone, in quest of the magic answer. Fran didn't know what she wanted. Not really. So it sadly followed that she'd not recognize happiness if she ever found it. She'd be an angry, hostile old lady. Lucky she has enough money that people will put up with her when she reaches that stage. Only the rich can afford to be impossible. Her unusually cynical analysis made Laura smile. I'm glad I won't be around when

Frances reaches that stage. My pity might show. And pity is one thing Frances can't abide. She'd be outraged.

On Sam's side of the big old bed, Karat stirred and stretched. She saw the golden dog rise and nuzzle his master's hand. These days it was Karat who acted as Sam's alarm clock. Since the heart attack, Karat had attached himself firmly to Sam, as though he would protect him from whatever happened that January night when all "his humans" had rushed frantically from the house, leaving Karat to whine at the window, puzzled by the unusual desertion. They'd had to restrain him from leaping on Sam and covering him with kisses when he finally came home from the hospital. And since that day, Karat had been the man's constant companion. It was the only thing that dampened Sam's enthusiasm about going away for Christmas: leaving Karat. But Buzz Paige had kindly volunteered to look after him while they were gone.

The thought of Buzz made Laura wonder how Frances would take the news of his impending marriage. No one would ever know. Fran had her pride. She'd been vulnerable during her visit last October, more honest about her emotions than her mother had ever known her to be. But she was not a woman who easily exposed her hurt or, probably, forgave the one who hurt her.

Janice, Allie's child, was different. Laura was proud of her, knowing what a sacrifice it must have been for her to have Spencer Winters at her wedding. But she'd done it to please Laura. Bless that child, her grandmother thought. I can't wait to see her and meet her husband. Just as I can't wait to see John's wife and the baby who's been named for Alice. I want to hold her and tell her to grow up sweet and pretty and kind, like the grandmother she never knew. But she must be stronger. Not frightened of life. Not full of guilt. Not sad and lost as Allie was.

Sam mumbled and reached out to stroke Karat's shining head. He turned over and opened one eye.

"You been awake long?"

"A few minutes," Laura said. "I've just been lying here thinking."

"'Bout what?"

"Oh, I don't know. A little of everything. The children. The grandchildren. Even the great-grandchild we're going to meet."

"Oh." Sam sounded disappointed. "I thought you'd be thinking about us."

She pretended innocence. "Us? Any special reason?"

"Don't try to fool me. You know as well as I do that it's our fifty-first anniversary."

She went on with the game. "Why, so it is! Imagine my forgetting!"

"You're a fraud, Laura Dalton. Happy anniversary, dear." Sam leaned over and kissed her. "Happy gold-plus-one. Thanks for putting up with me all these years."

She patted his stubby cheek. "I hope we have another twenty-four. I'm already planning our diamond jubilee."

Sam sat up and scratched his head, stood, stretched and hitched up his pajamas. Laura smiled, remembering a year ago when she'd asked him what habits of hers got on his nerves. He'd been puzzled then. He'd be puzzled today. Men. They were basically uncomplex. And indispensable.

He addressed himself to Karat. "She's really crazy, you know, boy. Wants to be married for seventy-five years! Good Lord!"

Sam winked at her on his way out of the room.

Laura relaxed, content. Things would never be the same. Not after Allie. Not even after Dorothy Paige. She mourned for both those unhappy women. She'd never forget the past year, but a new one had begun. There'd be no party for this anniversary. The house would be quiet, peaceful. Maybe she and Sam would go out for dinner, but the day would be routine, unremarkable, the way they really liked it. You could love your children with all your heart, rejoice for them, grieve for them, try to help. But in the end, with luck, you were alone with the man you'd chosen to live with. And in the end, there was something to be said for the undemanding life that was a compensation for growing old. You had your regrets and disappointments, even a kind of haunting depression, knowing that any day it could all end. But mostly you gave thanks for what you had in the past and what you hoped for in the future, for health and serenity for yourself and the ones you loved. Life was more kind than cruel.

At least for Mrs. Samuel Dalton of Denver.